THE FOURTH TREASURE

Todd Shimoda is the author of *365 Views of Mt. Fuji*. A third generation Japanese American, he received his Ph.D. in science and mathematics from the University of California, Berkeley, and now works as a cognitive scientist doing research in artificial intelligence applications at Colorado State University.

L.J.C. Shimoda, Todd Shimoda's wife and the illustrator of this book and *365 Views of Mt. Fuji*, is an artist who studied Japanese art and calligraphy in Japan.

ALSO BY TODD SHIMODA

365 Views of Mt. Fuji
Mono no aware: the Japanese aesthetic of oh!

Todd Shimoda

THE FOURTH TREASURE

VINTAGE

Published by Vintage 2003
First published in the USA by Nan A. Talese,
an imprint of Doubleday, New York

2 4 6 8 10 9 7 5 3 1

First published in Great Britain in 2003 by Vintage

Vintage
Random House, 20 Vauxhall Bridge Road,
London SW1V 2SA

Random House Australia (Pty) Limited
20 Alfred Street, Milsons Point, Sydney,
New South Wales 2061, Australia

Random House New Zealand Limited
18 Poland Road, Glenfield,
Auckland 10, New Zealand

Random House (Pty) Limited
Endulini, 5A Jubilee Road, Parktown 2193, South Africa

The Random House Group Limited Reg. No. 954009
www.randomhouse.co.uk

A CIP catalogue record for this book
is available from the British Library

ISBN 0 099 445077

Printed and bound in Great Britain by
Bookmarque Ltd, Croydon, Surrey

For Adrielle and Karen

第四の二十五

the fourth treasure **A NOVEL**

shodô calligraphy. The method of writing with a Japanese brush and *sumi* or
dark Japanese-style India ink. It is re-
garded as an art as well as writing as a
means of communication.

From *A Cultural Dictionary of Japan,* Momoo
Yamaguchi and Setsuko Kojima, editors
[Japan Times, 1979]

Riding backwards this wooden horse,
I'm about to gallop through the void.
Would you seek to trace me?
Ha! Try catching the tempest in a net.

—KUKOKU [1328–1407]

From *Zen Poetry: Let the Spring Breeze Enter,*
Lucien Stryk and Takashi Ikemoto,
translators and editors
[Grove Press, 1995]

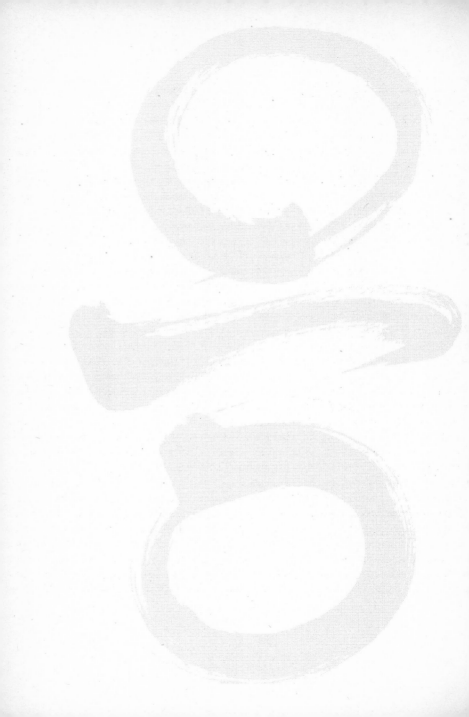

theories of consciousness **PART ONE**

Kiichi Shimano, founder and sensei of the Zenzen School of Japanese Calligraphy, dipped a brush into the well of black *sumi* ink. He gently pressed the brush against the inkstone until a precise droplet of excess ink had oozed back into the well. Then, with a fluid motion of brush on paper, he drew a simple horizontal stroke. "You see," he said to Gozen, his number-one student, "when the angle is too flat, the brush-stroke lacks life. Try again." Gozen nodded and wet his brush with ink.

While Gozen was practicing the horizontal radical, Zenzen sensei wished he had returned home, to Kyoto, twenty-three years ago, when he finally grasped that she would have nothing more to do with him. She never told him why, but without her, he had no reason to stay in America. Of course, he had nothing left in Japan either: no school to teach in, no students to teach, no family—none that would have anything to do with him. But at least in Japan he would have been home.

Yet, even after he knew it was **futile to** pursue her, he wandered the neighborhoods of San Francisco, eventually passing her apartment building at the corner of Bush and Taylor, on the steep slope of Nob Hill. Not stopping, he would walk past the Tempura House restaurant on Powell Street, where she worked. Still, though, he was without hope that meeting her would change her mind. Or her feelings.

Always, after a day of meandering, he would find an inexpensive restaurant where he would dine alone.

Back then, he taught calligraphy at the East Bay Center for Japanese Arts, a loosely organized school in Berkeley. The center was in an old house in the south campus area, half a block from the craziness of Telegraph Avenue, the last

The horizontal stroke is one of the basic twenty-four radicals (*gakunen-betsu kanji haitôhyô*) approved by the Japanese Cultural Affairs Agency. Each kanji—Japanese characters adopted from Chinese—is composed of combinations of radicals. Other classifications of these radicals range from eight (*eiji happô*) to as many as seventy-two. The horizontal radical looks easy, yet it is one of the most difficult to perfect. It must not be too horizontal or symmetrical, nor too angled or unsymmetrical.

bastion of the sixties' hippie culture. The first time he walked into the center was still a sharp memory of ratty chairs around a wood table scarred with thin burns from incense sticks. On the table was an unruly pile of magazines—from the *Economist* to *Mad*. A bulletin board was deluged with handwritten flyers for Japanese-language tutoring, karate and *aikidô* martial art instruction, and a Zen pet-sitting service.

Surprisingly, many of his calligraphy students became good, despite their enthusiastically undisciplined approach, compared with students in Japan. Perhaps the rigid, focused practices had held back his Japanese students. Or, maybe, his American students lacked a fear of making mistakes, allowing them to progress more rapidly.

Away from Japan, his own calligraphy style began to evolve into a more personal, nontraditional style. More inward. His nights spent alone, most likely, had contributed to the change. During his time alone, he discovered a sadness within him. Not depressing, the feeling was comfortable, and it became his companion. He no longer had to dine alone.

Within two years, he was teaching a core of excellent and dedicated students, while the center began to undergo many changes—instructors left, new ones were hired, students left, fewer replaced them. Getting paid had become a problem, keeping a regular schedule became impossible. When the disruption was too much to bear, he decided to strike out on his own, to start his own school of *shodô*—the "way of calligraphy."

He would have preferred to locate his school in San Francisco, perhaps in the Japantown area, but the number of potential students was greater in Berkeley, where there were several Zen centers and other Asian religious and art groups. He found a house where he could both live and teach in a quiet neighborhood west of campus several blocks. With commitments from several of his calligraphy students to continue lessons, and with the money he had saved teaching, he was able to buy the house.

A name for the school was required for the business registration forms. He could think of absolutely nothing—*zenzen,* in Japanese. Nothing, nothing. So that's what he named his school. And he became Zenzen sensei.

"You see"—he pointed to the brushstroke Gozen had just completed—"even modest pressure fattens the stroke unacceptably."

"Yes, sensei."

Zenzen sensei had given Gozen that dictum many times, yet mastering the concept was not simply a matter of hearing, but practicing it countless times until the stroke became pure feeling and no thought.

"Try again," he said to Gozen. "Try not to think."

Gozen applied ink to his brush and stared intently at the paper.

Pure feeling and no thought . . . and better yet, no feeling and no thought. What artist could create something as beautiful as autumn leaves? Or as moving as an old, dying tree putting out one last spring blossom?

Thoughts and emotions only get in the way of creating art. That's what he would have told her, if she would have let him. He would have told her to throw away the brushes, the ink, the paper, and the inkstone. Especially, the inkstone. Throw them away and find art in herself.

The inkstone . . . discovering who she was . . . he finally understood why she would have nothing more to do with him—

A burst of pain behind the sensei's left eye was so intense he gulped and clapped his hand to his head. He grabbed at the air, blindly groping, finally upending the low table they were working on, spilling ink, sending brushes flying. The brush stand skittered across the *tatami* mat flooring. Rice paper glided through the air and floated near the sensei who had collapsed, moaning, then nothing.

If I stop talking
will she listen

Crimson leaves,
Falling

NOVEMBER 1975
KYOTO, JAPAN

Kiichi Shimano, the head sensei of the Daizen School of Calligraphy, gazed out of his studio into the garden. An autumn breeze had plucked crimson leaves from the maple tree and scattered them on the moss-covered grounds in a pattern that was random yet had strong balance and lively rhythm. So easy for nature, so difficult for the artist. The difference must be that the artist creates art by thinking and feeling. Nature creates its art with neither; it is merely obeying a few simple rules—gravity, the force of the wind, the change of seasons—combined in infinite ways.

Daizen sensei picked up his calligraphy brush as he focused on the Japanese kanji characters for "crimson." The word was the part of a poem he had started:

> *Crimson leaves,*
> *Falling*

Not much of a poem, he would have admitted.

There was not enough time to write better poetry, not since he had been named the twenty-ninth head sensei of the Daizen school a few months earlier. Scheduling practice sessions, assigning students to the school's instructors, judging competitions, dealing with the school's finances: these were a few of the many duties he had inherited as Daizen sensei. And there were the interviews, the latest was just that morning, a live broadcast for an Osaka television station's morn-

Together, the characters for "crimson"—*makka*—literally mean "true red" or "blood red." Fall colors, especially crimson, represent the true essence of life: an intrinsic sadness. Therefore, the brushstrokes for *makka* should reflect this feeling with a subtle downward, slightly heavy, emphasis.

The first character of
"crimson"—ma—is "true"
or "quintessence." Ma
evolved from the charac-
ters meaning "fallen per-
son." Why a fallen person
would represent "true" is
not known. Perhaps a per-
son's spirit represents his
true essence.

Instructor's Journal,
Zenzen School of
Japanese Calligraphy

ing show. The interviewer, though enthusiastic (overly at times), seemed interested only in superficial aspects of *shodō*: "What kind of brush do you use? Where do you get your ink? How often do you practice? For how long?" Exhausting her repertoire, she had asked his age and, when he answered, she christened him the "Young Sensei." Only thirty-four years old—fifteen to twenty years younger than the usual age of a new head sensei—he was the second-youngest Daizen sensei. The youngest had been the samurai Sakata, the fifteenth head sensei, and known as the father of the current era of competitive Japanese calligraphy.

The reporter asked one final question: How well did the Young Sensei think he would do in the next Daizen-Kurokawa competition?

The reporter referred to the competition between his school and the Kurokawa School of Calligraphy. Daizen sensei had anticipated that question, and had prepared a brief history of the competition in case she asked: In 1659, Sakata and the founder of the Kurokawa school initiated the Daizen-Kurokawa Calligraphy Competition, still the most prestigious in Japan. Held every three years since, the competition helped assure that the two schools maintained their eminence.

Daizen sensei answered that he didn't know how he would do, but he would try hard to do his best.

He hoped the reporter would have asked him why calligraphy done correctly is imbued with spiritual power. He wanted her to ask him why calligraphy takes so much dedicated practice to achieve even a mediocre level of accomplishment. He wished she had asked why one should study such an old art form in these days of the popular mass media.

She had asked none of those questions.

Exhaling slowly, steadily, the sensei settled his weight onto his center of gravity. In the proper posture, he dipped his brush into the well of his inkstone, the Daizen Inkstone. If the reporter had asked him about the inkstone, he would have explained that the first Daizen sensei—the poet Jinmai, who founded the school in the year 1409—had carved the stone. When he retired, he gave it to his successor. That benefaction became a tradition until the inaugural Daizen-Kurokawa competition, when the inkstone was awarded to the winner as a traveling trophy. Recently, the inkstone had been recaptured by the Daizen school after three losses. The horrible run of defeats finally ended with a victory by the previous Daizen sensei, the twenty-eighth, who had died of pancreatic cancer only a few months later.

Winning the competition was the Daizen sensei's most important duty. Everything else could be put aside, if that was necessary to win. Not only were calligraphy enthusiasts enthralled with the arcane competition, but it mysteriously excited much of Japan as well. Television coverage was broadcast not only during the competition itself, but also before, with expert predictions and interviews with the contestants, and after, with detailed analyses of the results and more interviews. Each competition stimulated a rush of new students at both schools. Of course, the winning school always attracted the better prospects.

To win the head-to-head competition against the rival school's head sensei, Daizen sensei knew he had to commit time and energy, much more than he had as a student or even as an instructor. He had, of course, been in hundreds of competitions, major and minor, but the pressure of even the most important would be like a summer evening stroll along Kyoto's tranquil Path of Philosophy compared with the Daizen-Kurokawa competition.

Six months before each of those competitions, the senior instructors competed to determine their relative ranking. Before the last competition, Daizen sensei had defeated Ara-

Good posture is essential when practicing *shodō*; it allows the calligrapher to harness the power of the mind-body connection. The correct posture is natural and relaxed. The shoulders, for example, should not be tensed so they lift up; they should be settled into their naturally relaxed position. Likewise, the spine should not be forced rigid nor allowed to slouch; it should maintain its natural, flexible curve. Kanji drawn by calligraphers with poor posture will appear forced and unnatural, as if the strokes also had poor posture.

Ei means "eternal" as well as "long," and was likely derived from the pictograms for a river and its tributaries. This kanji is well known to calligraphers, because it incorporates the eight basic stroke patterns, or radicals, that are found in all kanji. These eight radicals are collectively called the *eiji happô*.

Instructor's Journal,
Zenzen School of
Japanese Calligraphy

gaki in a close battle. The victory gave him the rank of number-one instructor, which assured him of becoming the current head sensei. He was surprised, thinking back on that competition, that he had defeated Aragaki. For one thing, Aragaki had wanted to win much more than he had. His rival had closeted himself in his studio for two months before the competition, practicing for hours at a time. Daizen sensei had not added a minute to his normal practice schedule of three mornings a week.

During the competition, Daizen sensei had glanced up to see the intense concentration pinching Aragaki's face and beads of sweat dotting his temples. Perhaps Aragaki had sensed that the school's head sensei would be dead before the end of that year, and the current number-one senior instructor would become the new Daizen sensei.

Aragaki was not the most senior instructor in the Daizen school; still young, he had been in the school ten years longer than Shimano. The other two senior instructors (both proficient in technique but, in Daizen sensei's judgment, lacking a creative flair) had been in the school for eleven and eighteen years longer than Aragaki. In nearly all Japanese art schools, whether calligraphy or tea ceremony or the *biwa* flute, the successor to the leadership was usually the oldest son of the school's head sensei.

In the Daizen school, the head sensei was selected in a competition of senior instructors. Although that determination was subjective—a degree of favoritism by the head sensei who remained the final judge was hard to avoid—the system had worked well over the centuries. The school had stayed strong, winning more than half of the Daizen-Kurokawa competitions.

Unable to concentrate, Daizen sensei gave up his practice session. He cleaned his brush, then emptied and cleaned the Daizen Inkstone. He had yet to appreciate using it. Bulkier than the inkstones he used for the first twenty years of his calligraphy practice, the Daizen Inkstone had a different feel, one that frequently distracted him. Of most concern was the difficulty of mixing ink to the proper shade of black. Carved from a slab of natural slate, the Daizen Inkstone was uneven, lined with tiny crevices that made tricky business of rubbing a precise amount of inkstick onto the surface.

It was odd, disconcertingly so, that he should have so much trouble with the Daizen Inkstone. According to legend, using it should have instantly improved his calligraphy, as well as evoked an enlightenment.

He had experienced neither.

Before leaving his studio, the sensei quickly bowed toward a wall scroll, a work of calligraphy completed by the first Daizen sensei on the day he founded the school. The poem—"Live Life as Art"—had become the Daizen school's motto. Standing up, the sensei went out of his studio into the brisk air and walked through the garden to his personal residence. Inside, Yuriko, his wife, was putting on her coat.

"Finished practice already?" she asked. "I'm going to the department store, then to see Mother and bring her groceries. I'll take her to the hospital to see Father. Do you need anything while I'm out?"

"No, nothing." Her father had had an appendectomy several days earlier. After the operation, a blood clot floated through his body and nearly killed him. "Wish him well for me."

"All right." She slipped her feet into her shoes, picked up her bag, and started to walk out the door. She stopped and said, "Oh, there's a phone message for you. It's someone who would like to be a student. I told her that she could contact the school directly to talk with one of the instructors, but she wanted to discuss it only with you." With a quick nod, as if telling herself that was all she needed to relay, she was out the door, walking down the street to the bus stop.

Daizen sensei slipped off his wooden *geta* sandals. He walked through the pleasantly quiet house to the main room, where he sat on the *tatami* mat flooring, next to the phone on a low table. On a square of paper, the caller's name—Hanako Suzuki—was written above a phone number.

He should have crumpled the message and thrown it away. To contact the head of a major school in such a manner was a severe breach of etiquette. It was too direct, too presumptuous.

Despite that, he was intrigued that a woman would call him to express interest in studying *shodô*. Only two of the Daizen students were women—*shodô* was still a traditionally male art—and more women would benefit the art in general, and the school in particular.

It was also good she had called him, rather than the other senior instructors, because she would have been dissuaded from joining the school. His colleagues had never admitted a woman student, and likely never would, though he had never discussed the matter directly with them.

Daizen sensei stared at the phone number. He really shouldn't be considering working with a new student, his sole focus should be the next Daizen-Kurokawa competition.

He picked up the phone and dialed the number. A woman answered after two rings.

"Yes, is this Suzuki-*san*?" the sensei asked.

"Yes."

"This is Daizen, of the Daizen school."

"Thank you for calling, sensei. I'm sorry to bother you like this. But I saw your interview on television and had to talk with you."

Daizen sensei could have guessed. "I understand you are interested in taking lessons. Have you taken them before?"

"No, never. I was in my high school calligraphy club, but I wouldn't call that taking lessons."

The sensei nodded. Many prospective students said they had studied calligraphy before, but to become a Daizen student required much more than a few casual lessons. "We have limited space for only the most serious students." He hoped that would be enough to discourage her if she wasn't serious.

After a long moment, she said, "I'm serious, sensei." Her voice was soft yet insistent.

"Of course," he said. Most who called were serious, at least at first. But there was calm focus to her words that gave them strength. "Perhaps we should meet to discuss the matter. I do have some time this afternoon before my evening lessons. Where would you be coming from?"

"Kobe."

"By train?"

"Yes."

"Perhaps we could meet at the Kyoto train station. At three o'clock. I have to stop at a supply store not too far away. There's a coffee shop just inside the station, past the ticket booths to the right."

"Thank you very much, sensei."

THREE O'CLOCK—that would work just fine. Hanako guessed her meeting with the sensei would last no more than an hour. Adding an hour for travel back to Kobe from Kyoto, she would still be home in plenty of time to prepare dinner. Still, in case the outing took longer, she wanted to prepare some of the meal before leaving.

Of course, she ran almost no risk in being late with dinner. Only a handful of times in the two years since their wedding had her husband, Tetsuo, made it home at a normal dinner hour. He often had meetings that spilled over into night. And he traveled at least once a week, sometimes on a minute's notice: to Nagoya, to Tokyo, to any of the cities where the Suzuki empire ranged. Yet she wanted dinner to be ready, not only in case he did show up, but simply because she wanted to have dinner ready. Besides, what else would she do with her day?

She peeled and seeded a cucumber, then sliced it into slivers, each precisely one half the width of the nail on her little finger. As she sliced, she thought about the television interview she had watched that morning. The sensei had spoken so softly, yet confidently, as if he knew great secrets from a different world. His world would be unlike her world.

For one thing, she lived in a new house, in a new subdivision developed by her husband's company. The developers had bought up and razed an area of rickety homes, not without some difficulty convincing the previous homeowners they should be part of the modernization of Japan. Her house had been the show model, furnished and even stocked with food when she walked in for the first time. Tetsuo's company couldn't sell the show home—no one would buy it. If customers were going to buy new homes, they were going to buy new homes, not one trampled by hundreds of feet, pawed over, every corner intimately inspected.

Hanako didn't mind; the house had been thoroughly cleaned.

No, the sensei's world would be one of traditional beauty, one of introspection, one of treasures. That's what he called the Daizen Inkstone he had shown during the interview— one of the four treasures. "Four treasures?" the interviewer quizzed. "Yes," the sensei answered, "the four implements necessary to practice *shodô*: *fude* brush, *sumi* ink, *kami* paper, and *suzuri* inkstone."

She too had four treasures: automatic rice cooker, electric knife sharpener, defrosting refrigerator, and the newest model microwave oven, one with a rotating carousel.

WHEN DAIZEN SENSEI opened the door to the coffee shop, a woman acknowledged him with a deep bow. The sensei returned her bow with one that barely lowered his head. When she had straightened up, he said, "Suzuki-*san*?"

"Yes, sensei. Thank you very much for meeting with me."

They sat at a table near the door. He ordered a cup of coffee, she the same. She had a slightly narrow face and rounded forehead that gave her a vaguely European appearance. Although he knew nothing about designer fashion, the woman's dress seemed expensive—not something he would see his wife buying; Yuriko preferred functional, everyday clothes. Hanako's hairstyle also struck him as contemporary, cut to a modern length with a hint of curl. Yuriko still wore hers in the long, traditional length.

"If I might ask," the sensei said, "why are you interested in studying *shodô* at the Daizen school?"

"Well," Hanako began, then paused. She nodded once, to herself, as if she had made up her mind about something. "I've been married for two years. I was young and somewhat naive when I got married, but now I feel as if I know who I am."

At first, the sensei thought her statement too direct, even self-centered. Certainly an uncharacteristic statement from a Japanese housewife. Then he started to grin; he stopped the corners of his mouth from turning up.

She must have caught the slight movement because she smiled, almost mischievously. "I know that sounds silly. What difference could two years possibly make?"

He smiled fully now.

They watched the waitress place their coffee cups and a plate of small sweets on the table. When she left, he said, "It depends on the two years, I suppose."

Her head tilted away as if to hide another smile. "Exactly.

You are very perceptive. I married the son of a well-known real estate developer."

That Suzuki, thought the sensei.

"Not that I mention it to impress you," she said. Her gaze was cast down to the table. "But it might help explain why I said that."

The sensei took a sip of coffee. "I see," he said, at a loss for words. "What did you mean, exactly? About knowing who you are?"

She thought for a moment. "I don't know if this will help me become one of your students, sensei."

"No, likely not. I'm sorry if I was prying."

"Of course not. After all, I was the one who brought it up."

The sensei nodded. "Perhaps if you just explained why you want to practice *shodô*."

She took a sip of coffee before speaking. "I found that I need something else to define me."

The sensei blinked twice while tracing the curve of his coffee cup. That was a reason he'd never heard before. Potential students usually said they wanted to be proficient at one of the traditional arts, or that they wanted to do something "calming." Most admitted they didn't know why exactly. He asked, "You said that you need something to define you, but you also said that you know who you are?"

Hanako closed her eyes softly, then opened them. "That does sound contradictory."

"I didn't mean to suggest . . ."

"You're right, of course. Let me see if I can explain."

She thought for a moment; long enough for the silence to grow uncomfortable.

"I know—and please forgive me for talking so much— that I am a person who needs something to define me, to give me something solid in my life. I believe I can find it through *shodô*." Her head was still tilted down and to the side, yet she had spoken confidently, as if confessing her feelings was the real reason for their meeting.

"When I was practicing calligraphy in the school club, I had a feeling that I was me. A strange thing to say, I know. Not that I understood the feeling then. I don't know what I was thinking, actually. Maybe it's what I feel now, thinking back on the experience."

The sensei nodded, then took another sip of coffee. "I don't know if *shodô* will help you with your search. In the end, calligraphy is only an art. But it's true that you can increase self-realization through any disciplined practice. Discipline is the key—you can put as much of yourself into a practice as you want. The more you do so, the more you live your life as art."

Her eyes were watching him with softly focused attention, as if she were contemplating a deeper meaning of the words.

Suddenly, his own words sounded vacuous, as if he had mindlessly chanted an advertising slogan. "So," he said quickly as if to get the thought out of his head, "when did you wish to begin your lessons?"

Her face brightened. "Would tomorrow be too soon, sensei?"

"Tomorrow would be a perfect day."

BERKELEY

Gozen watched Zenzen sensei twitch once, then again, but not another sound came out of his sensei's clenched-jaw mouth. He kneeled down and put his ear close to the sensei's mouth—his breathing was shallow. Reaching around the sensei, he started to pick up the mess: No, not now. He got up and hurried out of the studio to the front of the house, into the main meeting room of the school where there was a phone.

During the four minutes he waited for the ambulance, Gozen could only stand in the studio's doorway and stare at the sensei, at his white hair, which had contributed to his air of authority but now just made him look old and feeble, close to death. When the ambulance arrived, its siren echoing off the homes in the neighborhood, Gozen opened the front door and let the crew into the house. The paramedics banged their equipment—orange, hard plastic boxes, carried with hands in latex gloves—against the walls of the narrow corridor as they followed Gozen to the studio.

One of the paramedics asked him questions while the other began to work on the sensei. Patting his own forehead, Gozen said, "He grabbed here."

"Okay," the paramedic said. He dropped to his knees close to his partner and said to her, "Could be a stroke." She nodded. Using a handheld radio, he called into the hospital and talked with an emergency room doctor. When he finished, he said to his partner, "We need to take him in now."

Gozen drove to the hospital closely following the ambulance until he dropped back because of their high speed. He arrived as they were wheeling the sensei through double doors. When the doors closed, he could see a sign: "No Admittance—Emergency Crews Only."

Driving away from the doors, he found a place to park. Before getting out of the car, its engine making a *tck-png* sound as it cooled off, he thought about the sensei's tortured expression. As if all the world's pain had struck him like a bolt of lightning.

Gozen walked around to the front of the hospital. At the entrance, he stopped and crossed his arms. Should he call someone? Did the sensei have a family? No one had ever talked about the sensei's family, not even the sensei. He lived alone in the house but, of course, that didn't mean he didn't have family somewhere.

Why couldn't someone else have been there when the sensei had his stroke? Someone who would know what to do, whom to call.

Gozen stood outside the hospital for fifteen minutes before he took a step toward the building. One slow step at a time and, after another minute, he reached the door and stopped. A woman dressed in a business suit, an ID photo held around her neck with a slender, beaded cord, stopped next to him and reached for the door handle. She pulled on the polished steel handle and held the door open for him. He took a couple of steps into the hospital, then stopped again as the woman breezed past him.

The information desk was another few steps and, when he finally reached it, he held onto the edge tightly. "May I help you?" the receptionist asked. She wore a phone headset that framed her profile.

"Yes, please, my sensei. Zenzen sensei came here."

"He's a patient?" the receptionist asked. "Name?"

"My name?"

The receptionist shook her head. "No, the patient's."

"Zenzen sensei."

"That's his name?"

"Well, that's what we call him. I'm his student."

"Zenzen?" The receptionist started typing. "How do you spell that?"

"Um . . . z-e-n-z-e-n."

"That's what I put in. Let's try this, when was he admitted?"

"Just now, in the ambulance."

"He's in the ER? Why didn't you say so in the first

place?" The receptionist held up her index finger, as if directing traffic, and punched buttons with her other hand. She spoke into the headset, waited a few moments, then said to Gozen, "Someone will be out to speak to you in a few minutes. Please have a seat." With the same finger, she pointed to the waiting area.

Gozen said, "May I wait outside?"

"Outside? You can't smoke anywhere on the hospital grounds. Not even outside."

"Smoke?" He tightened his grip on the desk. "Oh, no, just outside."

"Stay close to the front door so we don't have to look all over for you."

"Thank you very much." He bowed deeply, as if she were the empress of Japan, then ran out of the waiting room. He took a deep breath of air and slouched against the wall.

A few minutes later, a woman in a doctor's coat came out of the hospital. "You're here with the Asian male admitted into emergency?" she asked Gozen.

"Zenzen sensei?"

"Yes, him," she said matter-of-factly. "He had a stroke, probably a hemorrhagic stroke. A burst blood vessel. We're treating him and running tests to find out the extent of possible damage. He's breathing fine, his heartbeat is fine, so there's no immediate danger of death. However, he is in a coma. But that is good for him, for now anyway."

Gozen struggled to make sense of the flurry of words.

"I'm Dr. Raman. Here's my card. We need someone in his immediate family to fill out some forms. Are you related, or do you know whom we can call?"

Gozen wanted to run away. "I don't know of anyone."

"No one? What's his name? Zenzen?"

Gozen squeezed his eyes shut. "He is Zenzen sensei," he said, as if that were sufficient.

The doctor frowned at him. "He's Japanese? From Japan?"

"Yes."

"Could you try to find a family member, and have them call me, if they speak English? Or you can translate. We need his insurance information."

He nodded, hoping that would satisfy the doctor.

She pointed to the card. "Have them call this number as soon as possible."

"Yes, Doctor." He bowed after her as she hurried back into the hospital.

He drove back to the school, gripping the steering wheel to keep his hands from trembling. He had no idea what the sensei's real name was, everyone called him Zenzen sensei, as was common practice in any traditional Japanese art school. To call him by his real name would have been rude.

"Gozen" wasn't his real name either; it was Shinichi Takagawa. As a student and instructor of the highest rank in the Zenzen school, Zenzen sensei had awarded him with the nom de plume. Gozen hardly ever thought of himself as Shinichi Takagawa any longer. He was Gozen. Just as Zenzen sensei was just Zenzen sensei.

Back at the school, he parked his car and went inside. He took a deep breath and went into the studio to clean up the mess.

He quickly restored the room to its tidy functionality, except for the ghostly outline of the ink stains on the *tatami*. He had scrubbed them until the mats had begun to fray. He stopped cleaning and searched the studio for any personal information about the sensei.

Sheets of practice paper, which had wrinkled as the ink had dried, were stacked against the walls. Rolls of high-

quality rice paper, used for final works, filled a cabinet. Boxes of inksticks and brushes were organized in a short stack of drawers. A row of shelving held brush stands—as intricate as carved works of art. Scrolls of calligraphy hung from the walls.

Finding nothing—he doubted there would be, the studio was strictly for practicing *shodô*—he searched the main room at the front of the house, where they gave talks or group lessons. In the room, there were hanging scrolls, framed pieces, a few plants, and cushions scattered around. There was a tea set with several cups, a table with a flower arrangement that was a gift from one of the students who was also studying *ikebana*.

Wanting to get the task over with, Gozen went quickly through the kitchen, finding nothing unusual. He glanced around the bathroom, then went into the sensei's study and the school's business office. He checked through a filing cabinet filled with utility and other bills, all with the school's name on them but not the sensei's. There were also student records, reference materials, and catalogs. Nothing of a more personal nature. Even the address book listed no one that he didn't recognize as being affiliated with the school, directly or indirectly.

Finally, he found the school's nonprofit status tax forms—signed by the sensei in his full name: Kiichi Shimano. At least that was a start.

The sensei's bedroom was the room in the back of the house. Gozen peeked in the doorway. The room was sparsely furnished: two floor lamps, a dresser, and a futon rolled up and placed in a long, open cabinet. A simple framed work of calligraphy was hanging on the wall—the characters for "deep," "self," and "discovery." Gozen slowly walked over to it. He checked the red signature mark composed of stylized characters for the name "Suzuki." Below

Fukai, meaning "deep," is a combination of the characters "water" and "hole." The strokes should be fluid and profound, as if meaning can be found at the bottom of a well. Be careful not to make the "water" strokes too light and lively, otherwise the effect will be spoiled. The second character is *I,* making the word the adjective form.

that was a second seal, a countersignature. He peered at the mark: it was the seal of the twenty-ninth Daizen sensei.

Gozen, who had lived in Japan until several years ago, when he came to Berkeley for graduate school, had heard of the famous Daizen School of Calligraphy. Curiously, though, Daizen, or any of the other Japanese schools, had never been mentioned in the Zenzen school. Perhaps the sensei did not want to be aligned with any of them, wanting his school to be independent, even to the point of isolation. But why would the sensei have a Daizen student's work?

Gozen kept digging. In a closet, he found clothes on hangers, shoes, and a stack of books—mostly English and English-Japanese dictionaries. He closed the closet and looked around the room; the last place to search was the three-drawer dresser. He opened the top drawer—it held nothing but socks and underwear. He quickly shut it and looked in the second, in which were odds and ends—a watch that wasn't running, coins, a map of San Francisco.

He opened the bottom drawer. It held two items: a dusty wooden box about the size of one of the large reference books in the closet, and an envelope. It was unaddressed, but in the corner was a faded business name—"Kando Investigative Services"—and a Kyoto address. He turned the envelope over; it had been sealed shut with cellophane tape that was now brittle and yellow.

He put the envelope and the box on top of the dresser. The lid of the box was held closed with a simple latch. He undid it and the box opened. Resting inside on thick velvet lining was an inkstone. It was beautiful, carved from natural stone, with flecks of dried ink in its deeper crevices.

The scroll's seal . . . the inkstone . . . the story he had heard as a boy, about a missing sensei and a school's valuable inkstone. "Oh!" he said out loud. The inkstone must be the Daizen Inkstone. He closed the box and put it and the enve-

Jibun, meaning "self," is derived from "nose" and "divide." In Japan, you point to your nose to signify self, not to your chest. The second character, "divide" or "understand" (as in breaking something down), is a sword cut. The reasoning behind the use of these two characters to mean "self" has been lost, although it likely refers to the true being of a person. This meaning might refer to the subconscious level rather than the conscious level, although that is mere speculation. These characters should be drawn with introspection, not retrospection.

The last two characters—*hakken*—meaning "discovery," come from the characters for "start" (from the position of an archer shooting an arrow) and "look" (from a person kneeling to inspect something). As with the characters for "deep" and "self," the characters for

lope back in the drawer. Hurrying through the house to the studio, he found a scrap sheet of paper and wrote, "Lessons canceled, sensei is ill." He tacked it to the front door and ran away from the house.

K Y O T O

Reading the newspaper in his office on a slow morning of a slow week, Kando, owner and sole employee of Kando Investigative Services, found that he appreciated the lulls in his business more than the busy times, which had become busier but less profitable. In the deepening recession of the nineties that had no sign of improving, most of his clients didn't have the money to pay him for investigations. He took most of the cases anyway, on the chance that they might eventually find a way to compensate him.

He took a last gulp of tea and set the old, chipped cup on his desk next to the shiny stiletto knife he had taken away from a scrawny eight- or nine-year-old boy who was using it to threaten a stray cat. He had come across the two when he was looking for a back entrance to a yakitori restaurant that had gone bankrupt and been abandoned.

He had almost finished reading the newspaper when he noticed a brief item reporting the results of the latest ranking competition at the Daizen School of Calligraphy. The article listed the instructors and their ranks, and the change from the previous ranks. The article also speculated that the head of the school—the thirtieth Daizen sensei, Aragaki—was going to retire after the next Daizen-Kurokawa competition.

The article, and any mention of the Daizen school, reminded Kando of the case of the missing student. Twenty-three years ago, he had been hired by the twenty-ninth Daizen sensei, Kiichi Shimano, Aragaki's predecessor, to find one of his students who had stopped coming to lessons and disappeared. He had found the student, Hanako Suzuki, and though he never met her, he rarely went for long without thinking of her.

IN HIS PRACTICE STUDIO, the thirtieth Daizen sensei—Hideo Aragaki—inspected the tip of his favorite brush. It had begun to fray, just slightly, not enough to make a difference in his calligraphy, but it would last only one more Daizen-Kurokawa competition. As would he.

Retiring would be a relief from the dissatisfaction that had crept up on him during his reign as the Daizen sensei. His desire to practice calligraphy, especially to compete at the highest levels, had not died, but it was no longer a bright flame either. His desire to achieve greatness was at its peak more than twenty years ago, while his predecessor, Shimano, was still at the Daizen school. His desire to defeat Shimano and become the Daizen sensei had driven him much more than any of the great rivals he faced during the competitions.

At least initially, Aragaki was glad that Shimano was gone, even if he had taken the Daizen Inkstone with him. He had strong doubts that Shimano could have won a single Daizen-Kurokawa competition. His predecessor's style, while in some cases spectacular, was not solid. If one studied his work closely (as Aragaki had countless times), many weaknesses that were hidden under his brash fluidity came to light. Not only in balance and execution, but in personal character, as if each of his strokes revealed a flaw in his personality. Aragaki had never understood why most of the instructors, especially the head sensei, preferred Shimano's work to his.

A breeze flowing through the open window ruffled the rice paper on his practice table. The distraction was enough

Paper, especially high-quality paper, was once very precious in Japan. It was prepared by hand, and only those who had mastered the craft could produce the best-quality paper. Because the glue used in paper production tended to go bad in warm weather, paper could only be made from November to March.

Today, very little paper is made in the old way, yet manufactured paper provides a much more consistent surface to work on. As with all of the treasures, use the highest-quality paper. Inexpensive rag paper is best for practice; use the rough side as it makes control more dif-

ficult. When using high-
quality Japanese paper
(*washi*), the brush will be
much easier to control and
the calligrapher can work
faster (although it is easier
to make mistakes).

Instructor's Journal,
Zenzen School of
Japanese Calligraphy

for him to put up his calligraphy supplies and leave his studio. He walked along the narrow street that fronted his
home and studio in the Arashiyama area of Kyoto. He
headed for his favorite walking path that passed by the Ten-
ryuji Temple before leading him to the bamboo forest of the
Okochi Sanso Villa. The Arashiyama area was known for its
bamboo forests, but this was the best. The quiet and the
cool, deep shadows never failed to revive his spirits. If only
the forest could purge his increasing obsession with Shimano
and the Daizen Inkstone.

BERKELEY

Tina Suzuki exited the downtown Berkeley BART on Shattuck Avenue. While she waited for the light to cross the
street, she checked her watch: just over half an hour—precisely thirty-two minutes—before her class would start.
Enough time for a coffee, she calculated. Not wanting to be
late for her first class as a graduate student, she had taken the
10:13 Richmond train from San Francisco instead of the
10:33, just in case there was a delay, as had been happening
frequently on the rail system that was brittle with age.

When the light changed, she started across the street with
the rest of the crowd, most of them students—their backpacks
giving them away. Many of them were Asian American; nearly
every other undergraduate student at Cal, she heard, was Chinese American. Many were from San Francisco's Chinatown,
which was only three blocks from where she grew up.

With a few quick steps, she broke away from the crowd,
turned onto a side street, then another, and found the Half
Note Coffee House. She bought a large coffee—the house

blend, "for here"—and took the heavy mug to a tiny round table, not much bigger than a large ashtray. The size of the tables seemed designed to discourage students from spreading out texts and notebooks to study for hours, nursing a single cup of coffee. Only a few tables, about a third, were occupied, mostly by professors, or older graduate students, reading or chatting with colleagues. A foursome was listening intently to the classical music playing over the Half Note's sound system, nodding appreciatively or wincing in response to the peculiarities of a passage.

Looking out of the coffee shop window that was opened to the warm day—warm for the Bay Area—and across the expanse of grass of People's Park, she could see the Berkeley Institute for Brain and Behavior Studies. Two large homes clad in stained cedar shingles had been connected with a glass-and-aluminum wing of offices and classrooms. It vaguely reminded her of the two hemispheres of the brain connected by the corpus callosum.

She took a sip of coffee and noted with satisfaction that the caffeine was already dutifully blocking her brain's neuronal receptors for adenosine, allowing the excitatory glutamate to flow more freely. With her attention-focusing mechanism sharpened and her basal ganglia–frontal lobe pathway wide open, she glanced at the clock on the wall, downed the rest of her house blend, and reached for her backpack.

She walked across the park and into the institute. At the T intersection of the two corridors, she looked left, then right. The rooms weren't numbered, and she didn't see a sign for the conference room. She glanced back, checking to see if she had missed it.

A woman with a healthy-looking tan and a mop of rusty-blond dreadlocks, toting an overloaded backpack slung over one shoulder, turned the corner. She was holding a paper

Corpus callosum: the white matter tissue (neuronal axons) connecting the brain's two hemispheres, and relatively larger in women's brains than men's, although not sure what that would mean, functionally speaking. Perhaps women are more able to coordinate emotions and language. Interestingly, people with autism tend to have smaller corpora callosa. The main symptoms of autism are social and language difficulties.

Neuroscience Notebook,
Christina Hana Suzuki

cup topped with a plastic lid and wrapped with a puffy, insu-
lated sleeve. The aroma was latte-ish from steamed milk.

She smiled and asked Tina, "Looking for Hebb?"

"That's the conference room? Yes."

"Thought so. That's where I'm headed." With a toss of
her hip to adjust her backpack, she took off. When Tina
caught up, she said, "I'm Gillian Rock, by the way. You must
be a first-year? I mean, I haven't seen you around."

"Tina Suzuki. Nice to meet you," she said. "Yeah, I'm
first-year. And you?"

"Third year, sort of. I switched from IGB last year."
Gillian took a sip of the drink without slowing her pace.
After swallowing, she added, "Integrative Biology."

"Oh. Right. IGB."

They turned down another corridor, then into a room—
the sign on the door said, "Donald O. Hebb Conference
Room." Tina and Gillian took the last chairs at the far end
of the long conference table. Tina fished out a notebook and
pen from her backpack.

Except for the seminar professor—obviously so, as he was
the oldest and the only one wearing a button shirt, and he
was staring intently at a legal pad of handwritten notes—the
other students were mostly under twenty-five, as was Tina,
although a couple were older, mid-thirties, perhaps. Most of
the students had a plastic bottle of water—Calistoga, Napa,
Arrowhead—in front of them. Other students hurried into
the room and, seeing there were no seats, dropped their
backpacks and leaned against the walls.

Gillian asked Tina, "Are you one of Professor Alamo's
students?"

Tina shook her head. "No. Professor Porter's. How
about you?"

"Greenwald's. What's Porter into? Something to do with
language, right?"

"Yes." Tina noticed the professor had looked up from his notes. He checked his watch, then spoke sharply. Even though Tina was looking at him, his voice startled her.

"We will start on time. Today as every day." He paused very briefly, waiting for the room to quiet as the students shifted their attention. "I am Alonzo Alamo. As you can tell, we have more people than seats. That situation will be remedied by our next meeting in a week as there will be twelve students allowed in the course."

One of the older-looking male students, seated on the other side of Gillian, leaned toward her and whispered something that Tina couldn't hear. Gillian grinned. After a moment, Gillian leaned toward Tina and whispered, "Like Christ and the twelve apostles."

Tina gave her a wry smile and glanced at the student next to Gillian. He was a good-looking guy, dark hair, Latino. He smiled at her.

The professor was reading from his legal pad: "This seminar is the 'Neural Theory of Consciousness.' That means, in other words, what is it about our bodies, in particular, the neurons, that provide us with our consciousness? Our awareness, our phenomenological feelings. In other words, why a red object appears red to us, or salt tastes salty, or fear feels like fear."

He looked up from his notes, glanced around the room, and turned back to his notes. "First, some ground rules. The most important is that this is a neuroscience seminar, not a philosophy seminar."

Gillian whispered to the Latino guy next to her, just loud enough for Tina to hear, "In other words . . ."

"In other words," the professor continued reading, "we will be studying this topic from a purely scientific point of view, in particular, from a neuroscience perspective, although we will include some neuropsychology in the mix—

reluctantly. One thing we will *not* include is philosophy. We will not be debating Descartes's dualism, or the merits of functionalism over, say, extreme materialism, or any other 'ism,' no matter how well thought out or how deeply applicable. So, if there are any philosophers in the room who do not have a strong grounding in neuroscience or at least functional neuroanatomy, or who are here to engage in philosophical debates, then I am telling you now that you will not be in the final group of twelve. You may as well leave and not waste any more of your time."

He looked up and down the rows of students. One, with a thin goatee and wearing a black knit cap, stuffed his notepad into his backpack and shoved his chair backward. He gave the professor a glare as he swung his backpack to his shoulder and left the room. One of the standing students immediately took his chair.

After sniffing nonchalantly, as if testing the atmosphere of the room after the philosophy student left, the professor said, "Anyone else?" He waited a moment, then returned to his notes. "Another rule is that we won't discuss consciousness through metaphor. In other words, we won't be saying, 'The brain is like a computer,' or, 'Consciousness is like a theater production, with front stage and back stage,' or 'The mind is like a cloud, coalescing from drops of neuronal activity.' " He paused, glanced up, then returned to his notes.

"This is an intense, one-semester course. Those who will be attending are required to attend every session, no exceptions. I will be here for every session, so why shouldn't you? You are the reason I am here. If you know now that you cannot make even a single session, then I will have to ask you to join our philosopher friend."

No one moved.

"All right. The first three weeks we will be doing a lot of reading, from a variety of sources, some more related to a theory of human consciousness than others, at least at first blush. Those who survive and prosper during this first barrage of information will be able to integrate the material at a deep level. In other words, they will be the ones who get it."

He turned the page of his notes. "Of course, there is no general theory of consciousness. None that is widely accepted, very few accepted by anyone at all. The objective of this class is to move toward such a theory. If you cannot contribute to the building of this theory, then your time, my time, and the time of your fellow students will be wasted. By contribution, I primarily mean being prepared for each class.

"The main portion of your course evaluation will be leading one of the seminars. Each of you, the twelve selected, that is, will take a turn facilitating the discussion after giving a presentation that integrates scientific evidence from the readings into a coherent aspect of a theory. In other words, you will need to provide a claim, a warrant, and a backing."

He looked up. "And if you don't know what those words mean, then I suggest you acquaint yourselves with them."

One of the students raised his hand and asked, "Sorry to interrupt, but what were the second two again? After claim?" The student had his pen poised above his notepad.

"Warrant and backing."

"Thank you," the student said as he hurriedly wrote down the words.

Professor Alamo returned to reading his notes. "Today, I want you to take out two or three sheets of paper. You will write down your name, e-mail address, and the answers to two questions, which I will give to you shortly. I will read your responses today and select the twelve students. You will be informed either way by e-mail by ten P.M. this evening. For those of you who are the successful candidates, you may pick up the semester reader at the copy center of the institute. Please have the first week's papers read and most importantly comprehended by the next class meeting."

He looked up and asked, "Need I clarify anything before I give you the questions? . . . No? Good. Question number one is: What can you contribute to this course, and in particular to the development of a theory of consciousness?" He waited until they had jotted it down. "Question number two: Santiago Ramón y Cajal and Camillo Golgi shared the Nobel prize in 1906 for their pioneering work on neurons. They violently disagreed, however, on a fundamental aspect of neurons. What was that aspect, and what were their differing opinions?" When no one asked for clarification, Alamo turned to a blank page in his notepad and began writing.

Tina stared at her page, blank except for her name and e-mail address. She listened to the others with their pens already scratching across paper, the sound of crawling insects.

SAN FRANCISCO

Tina climbed the staircase to her mother's fifth-floor, one-bedroom apartment, the same apartment where Tina had grown up. The elevator maintenance company had dismantled the building's only elevator for a complete overhaul that was going to take a week but had already stretched to two. Reaching the fifth floor, Tina turned toward Apartment 504. The door was open a crack; Tina went inside and closed the door behind her. "Ma?"

"Ha-*chan*," her mother, Hanako, called out from the sitting room. She had always called Tina by her middle name, shortened, and with the Japanese suffix connoting affection.

She walked down the hallway; on her left was the door

to her mother's bedroom, on the right were large, side-by-side walk-in closets. The door to the first was open; Tina stopped and peered inside. Years ago, the wall between the two closets had been removed, expanding them into a small room. The closets had been Tina's bedroom until she moved out when she went to college in San Diego.

Until she was eight, Tina slept on a rollaway bed in her mother's room. On her eighth birthday, she said she was too big to sleep in the same room with her mother and wanted her own room. She didn't tell her mother that she was also tired of the dank, greasy smell of the oil in which they fried tempura at the Tempura House restaurant where her mother worked. The odor impregnated her mother's work kimono and clung to her hair and skin.

Several weeks before her eighth birthday, they had visited her Aunt Kiyomi's house out in the Avenues near Golden Gate Park. Aunt Kiyomi's two kids had their own rooms. On the way home, Tina asked her mother why they didn't move to a bigger place. Hanako said, "You know. Your college education, *neh*? You need money to go to college." Instead of moving to a new apartment, Hanako offered the sole bedroom to her daughter, and she would sleep on the sofa. But Tina already had her eye on the cozy closets. She played in them anyway; lately she had been making a tent with a blanket. Inside she would read books with a flashlight.

Hanako balked for a few days, then one morning the carpenter brother of one of the cooks at the Tempura House showed up at their apartment with a tool chest. Tina never heard if her mother had gotten permission to turn the walk-in closets into a bedroom, but supposed it could be restored as easily as it had been built.

After Tina went away to college, her mother had gradually returned the closets to their original purpose. Hanako's clothes, which had been hanging in a small armoire in the bedroom, were again in the closet. Tina's bed and furnish-ings—a doll-sized dresser and school desk—were still there in the closet, but were stacked with boxes and piles of mail and newspapers. Her mother was becoming a pack rat.

Tina walked into the sitting room and put her backpack on the floor. Hanako was stretched out on the sofa. A pillow supported her back and a woman's magazine from Japan was open on her lap. While her mother closed the magazine and sat up, Tina said, "Ma, you shouldn't leave your door open."

"But I knew you were coming up," Hanako said. "Re-member you called me—"

"Even if you know I'm coming up."

"Okay, Ha-*chan*." She placed the magazine on the coffee table and put the pillow on a stack near the sofa.

Tina sat on the floor in the middle of the room. "How are you feeling today?" Her mother had been diagnosed with multiple sclerosis, just over a year ago.

"*Genki.*" Fine. "I was just reading before work. How was your school?"

"It was okay, just the one class today. Just a test."

"A test? First day?"

"Sort of a test." Tina had been the last one to turn in her answers. Gillian and the male student she had been joking with were the first two to finish. They left together.

Professor Alamo had barely glanced at Tina when she handed the pages to him. She had written that she was sure that others in the class knew more about neuroscience than she did. Her undergraduate degree was in psychology, but she had taken a course in the neuroscience aspects of psy-chology, and had found it to be her most interesting class. She added that she knew that there was so much more to learn, but that she was a hardworking student and always prepared. Her most valuable contribution to the development of a neural theory of consciousness would be an "open mind."

For the second question, she wrote that she had heard of both Santiago Ramón y Cajal and Camillo Golgi, particularly Golgi, whose name was attached to a staining method that allowed individual neurons to become visible under microscopes. There were also some cells in the brain—the cerebellum—named after him. About Cajal, she knew less, except that he had used Golgi's staining method to do much of the original work of identifying the different kinds of neurons, and that he was generally credited with being the founder of modern neuroanatomy. That the two had shared a Nobel prize, or what their disagreement might have been, she had admitted she didn't know. She speculated (and so noted on her essay) that, perhaps, they disagreed on how the neurons worked, how they passed activation from one to the other, maybe. One may have thought that the neurons were connected directly—hardwired—rather than passing activation across the synapses through neurotransmitting chemicals. Which of the scientists might have proposed which theory, she didn't know.

"Are you sure you'll be okay going to work, Ma?"

"Robert-*san* is giving me *reiki*."

Hanako had developed an attachment to Robert, Tina's boyfriend. Everyone except her mother called him "Mr. Robert," which was the name his students called him when he was teaching English in Japan. He spoke fluent Japanese, much more fluently than Tina, and he could write both kana—the two forms of Japanese syllables—and kanji—the more elaborate and complex characters derived from Chinese. Tina could only recognize kana and a few kanji, and could write only a couple of dozen. Besides *shodô,* Mr. Robert was an expert in *reiki* pressure massage, *aikidô, taiko*

Cerebellum: the "little brain," a mass of tightly folded brain tissue below the cerebral hemispheres that coordinates the planning and fine-tuning of movement.

Golgi cells: inhibitory interneurons (cells that pass activation between other neurons) found in the cerebellum.

Neuroscience Notebook, Christina Hana Suzuki

drumming, *chadô* tea ceremony, *kendô* sword fighting, and Zen meditation. He could make professional sushi, cook tempura as well as the chefs at the Tempura House, knew the many grades of *sake* by taste, and could recite at least a hundred Japanese poems. In school, he had studied Japanese literature and philosophy, and had lived in Japan for five years. He and Tina met when he was finishing an M.A. in Japanese studies at the University of California, San Diego.

"Does the *reiki* help?"

Hanako nodded, as she winced and reached down to her legs.

"What is it?"

"Nothing," Hanako said, giving her daughter a reassuring smile. "I'm fine."

"Have you been to the doctor lately?"

Hanako nodded. "Yes. Last week. He said I was okay."

Tina doubted she had seen her doctor; they cost money. And if she had, he probably wouldn't have said she was "okay." Her mother had been suffering more lately, not complaining, but she wasn't her usual lively self. "Ma, you don't have to worry about my education expenses anymore. I've got a fellowship, remember I told you? I've got a research assistantship. I don't need any money." Tina had never needed any of her mother's money to go to school. A scholarship covered most of her tuition at UC–San Diego, and with the monthly salary she made in the work–study program, she had been self-supporting.

A buzzer rang at the door to the apartment. Tina walked back down the hallway and pushed the button that would open the building's entry door. She went back into the sitting room; her mother was up, straightening the room that was already neat.

Tina picked up her backpack and brought it to the front

of the apartment. When she got there, there was a knock on the door and she opened it.

Mr. Robert looked surprised when he saw her. "Tina. I thought you were at school."

"I went to class this morning. There's a reception for new students tonight. So I thought I'd come over and see Ma instead of sitting around Berkeley all afternoon."

She said her mother was waiting for him in the sitting room, then followed him down the hallway. His hair was just long enough to tie back into the ponytail Tina disliked, though not enough to mention.

"How was school?" he asked.

"Great," Tina said. "It'll be fun." She didn't feel like going into the entry quiz to Professor Alamo's class, Mr. Robert would have some comment about it.

"That's good," he said. When they entered the sitting room, Mr. Robert said to Hanako, *"Konnichiwa, ogenki desu ka?"*

Hanako was sitting on the couch. *"Genki, Robert-san,"* she answered.

Tina said, "She says she's doing much better. But I don't know if she should go to work. She's on her feet all night. It's got to be torture."

"I'm fine, Ha-*chan*," Hanako said. "I like to go to work. What would I do here? Nothing."

"Okay, okay," Tina said. "You're probably right."

Mr. Robert squatted next to her. "A *reiki* treatment would help, wouldn't it?"

Hanako glanced at Tina before replying, "Yes, please."

Mr. Robert spread a blanket on the floor. Hanako lay on the blanket facedown. Kneeling over her legs, Mr. Robert slowly pressed a point just below her knee with one of his blunt thumbs, its nail trimmed back to nothing.

When Hanako winced, Tina said, "Ma, are you sure this is good for you?"

Mr. Robert said, "Of course it is. I'm replenishing her *ki*. How could that be bad?"

"I'm okay," Hanako said.

"Focus on accepting my *ki*," Mr. Robert said to Hanako. Hanako took a deep breath and let it out slowly.

"All I'm doing," Mr. Robert said quietly to Tina, "is helping her body use *ki* to heal itself."

Tina wanted to argue with Mr. Robert that there was no evidence, scientific or otherwise, of a mysterious life force called *ki*. Not only that, but there was no cure for MS, Eastern or Western medicine. But she didn't want to argue in front of her mother. "I've got to go back to Berkeley for the reception. Can I get you anything before I go, Ma?"

"No, thank you. I'm fine," her mother said, her voice muffled by the blanket to almost nothing.

First Lesson

NOVEMBER 1975
KYOTO, JAPAN

The taxi dropped Hanako at Daizen sensei's studio at twenty-five minutes after one. Traffic had been light. The hour-and-a-half lesson would end at three, in time to take a taxi to Kyoto station and catch the train home before Tetsuo might possibly get there.

From the outside, the sensei's studio seemed smaller than it had looked on television. A grouping of three large, flat stones formed a short walkway through a front garden. She admired the well-placed dwarf bamboo plants, the gently flowing water in the stone basin, and a camellia, its leaves beaded with moisture.

She walked up to the door and rapped lightly. The sensei opened it immediately. "Suzuki-*san*," he said. *"Yoku irasshaimashita."* Welcome, I'm glad you could come.

"*Onegaishimasu*, sensei," she replied with a deep bow. Please help me learn.

In a small room with a view of the side garden between the studio and the main house, he began teaching. "First, a proper mind is important. Your conscious thoughts can both interfere and help when you are doing your art. You must be able to coordinate the conscious and the subconscious. This, however, is very difficult as one or the other tends to dominate."

Hanako sat perfectly still, barely breathing.

"Second, proper posture is important. Sitting in *seiza* style, as if meditating, is best, if you can maintain that position for long periods of time. The position keeps your body in the correct alignment. Of course, many people now sit on a chair at a table to practice. That is all right."

With a quick shift, Hanako corrected her posture.

"Good," the sensei said. "Third, holding the brush is important." The sensei picked up a brush. "Notice that my fingers are pointing downward, my thumb is parallel to the paper. Notice also that my wrist is slightly bent. Do you see?"

"Yes, I see," she said as she stared intently at the brush in his hand.

"Good. Applying the proper pressure with your thumb holds the brush against your fingers. You must be able to move the brush freely but with control. Please try."

Hanako tried to hold the brush as the sensei had demon-

The *soku* radical is one of
the *eiji happô*. Begin the
stroke with the brush tip
nearly horizontal, pointed
toward the upper left corner of the paper. Pull the
brush off the paper in the
direction of the lower left.
The radical may also end
slightly in the direction of
the next stroke.

Soku means "side," per-
haps because the radical is
made with a movement
from side to side. The inside angle of the corner
should be fairly sharp, not
too rounded. It requires
strong mind-body unifica-
tion to change the direc-
tion of the brush with
such fluid precision.

Instructor's Journal,
Zenzen School of
Japanese Calligraphy

strated, but her fingers gripped either too tightly or too loosely.

The sensei lightly touched her fingers. "Your *ki*—your life energy—is on top of your fingers, hand, and arm, making them unbalanced, difficult to control. In this case, your conscious mind is dominating your subconscious. Relax and let the subconscious take over. The weight will naturally settle toward the bottom of your hand and arm." The sensei touched the underside of her arm, just above her elbow. "Here. That's right. Feel the difference?"

The touch gave her a shiver. "Yes. I can feel the difference."

"Now, send your *ki* through the tip of the brush, don't let it stop at the end of the brush. I will try to pull the brush out of your hand."

The sensei grasped the end and pulled on it steadily. It remained poised over the paper.

"Good," he said. "Yes, that's good."

"It's difficult."

"You'll get it," the sensei said. "One day it will just come to you without thinking."

"I don't know."

BERKELEY

Tina was the first one at the reception, except for the caterers, even though she purposely arrived nearly five minutes after its scheduled start. The reception was in a large conference room at the institute. A conference table that was long enough to land a small plane had been moved against one wall. The caterers were finishing setting up the food and drinks on the table. Plates of raw vegetables were artfully arranged around bowls of dip. Cold cuts and cheese were rolled and placed in neat rows. An overflowing basket of sliced rolls was placed next to the meats and cheese. Ice buckets held beer, soft drinks, and bottled water. Bottles of wine were surrounded by Burgundy and Chablis glasses.

Standing there in the room, it all seemed wrong—coming here, home, to get a Ph.D. What was she going to do with the degree? She couldn't see herself as a hotshot researcher or professor, like Professor Alamo. What else would she do, though? In the interview for acceptance into the program, they had asked what she wanted to do with her degree. She had replied that she wanted to learn as much as possible and then see where her interests took her. Pretty vague, but the truth, for the most part.

Tina started backing out of the room, to hide out until someone else showed up, when Professor Karyn Porter came up behind her. "Looks like we're the first ones here."

"Hello, Professor Porter."

"Please, call me Karyn." Her smile was broad, revealing very white teeth and pink gums.

"All right, Karyn." Tina followed her to the drinks, where the professor picked up a glass of red wine. Tina chose a glass of white.

"How is your first week?" The professor held the glass cupped in her palm, the stem of the glass descending between her fingers.

"Just fine. Although I've only had Professor Alamo's class so far."

"Don't worry, not all of us here are such . . . well . . . like him." The professor smirked. "Let's leave it at that."

"Actually, I don't know if I'm in the class. He has a screening process."

Porter nodded as she drank; the motion caused a wave of red wine to splash and stain the skin above her lip. Tina wanted to dab it away with her napkin. "Don't worry, I'll have a word with him."

"Really?" Tina said, not sure if that would be a good idea.

Porter nodded vaguely as the tip of her tongue ran across her upper lip. She spied a pile of napkins. "Excuse me," she said and ducked away.

Tina wandered over to the other end of the table and inspected the food. The room was starting to fill up when Gillian walked over to her. She was holding a bottle of beer.

"This looks kind of boring," Gillian said, taking a sip of beer while she looked around the room.

"So far I'd say you're right."

"What did you think of Alamo?"

Tina wondered if Professor Porter could really get her in the class just by talking to him. She hesitated, then said, "He's different."

"Kind of a different asshole."

"The philosophy student who walked out probably called him worse."

"No doubt. Hey, there's Wijjie." Gillian waved toward the door. Tina turned and recognized the Latino student who had been sitting next to Gillian. He waved at them, grabbed a beer, and walked over.

Gillian introduced them. "This is Tina Suzuki. Tina, Wijjie."

"Tina, pleasure," he said, shaking hands after he transferred the beer bottle to his left.

"Nice to meet you too . . . Wijjie?" His hand was cool from the bottle, but he had a pleasant grip.

"Wasn't my idea," he said, looking at Gillian.

She laughed. "I'll take credit."

"Don't know if I like it."

"It'll grow on you, I promise."

"So why Wijjie?" Tina asked.

"My real name is William James. William James Cruz."

"I think Wijjie is perfect," Gillian said. "Don't you, Tina?"

"William James. Wijjie. I like it. Wait, is that William James as in William James the psychologist?"

"Very astute. Psychologist and, heaven forbid, *philosopher*. It was my mother's idea. She's a psychologist and philosopher, with a joint appointment at the University of Colorado."

Tina said, "I hope Professor Alamo doesn't find out."

"No kidding," Wijjie said, pointing his beer at her. "What's your story?"

"Not much to tell. Just graduated from UC–San Diego in psychology. Interested in the brain, the mind, all that. How about you?"

Gillian punched Wijjie's arm. "He's a fucking M.D., can you believe it?"

Wijjie shrugged and nodded at the same time. "So, you're asking, why am I in this program, back for another long four to six years of school?" He took a big swallow of beer. "I have absolutely no idea."

A voice boomed from across the room. Tina turned and recognized the rotund, bearded director of the institute as he said, "Greetings everyone, let's get the formalities out of the way so we can go back to imbibing."

Wijjie whispered to Tina and Gillian, "Imbibing?"

Gillian snickered. Tina smiled at Gillian's laugh.

After the director gave his welcoming speech and introductions, Tina noticed professors Porter and Alamo talking in a corner. He was taller than she was by almost a foot, and he was bending slightly to the side toward her, as if trying to hear above the din of conversations. Tina turned away, so he wouldn't see her staring. She wished she had told Professor Porter not to talk to him about his class.

When Gillian announced she could no longer stand the reception, she and Tina and Wijjie went to a pub across from the downtown Berkeley BART station, where they found a table upstairs near the front windows that overlooked Shattuck Avenue.

Wijjie brought them a pitcher of beer, and as he filled their glasses, Tina felt a little wave of guilt about staying out and not going home to Mr. Robert. She asked Wijjie, "How long did you work as an M.D.?"

"Not long. Finished my residency and decided it wasn't for me."

"How come?" Gillian asked. "The hardest part was over, wasn't it?"

Wijjie shrugged. "Just realized it was a mistake. I don't know."

"I have a question for Dr. Cruz," Tina said. "Did you ever treat a patient with MS?"

"Multiple sclerosis . . . let's see." Wijjie thought for a moment. "A loss of the myelin sheath around nerve fibers, resulting in decreased muscle and cognitive functions. Symptoms can include numbness, tingling, spasticity, fatigue, pain of varying intensity, paralysis, vision problems. Psychological problems? Depression, for one. There's no cure, but some interferon drugs like Avonex or Betaseron, or Copaxone can reduce the frequency of symptoms and slow progression. There are other drugs prescribed for the muscle rigidity or spasms, or other symptoms. Some patients respond to biofeedback or self-hypnosis to control pain." He took a drink of beer. "Why do you ask?"

"My mother's got it."

"Sorry, Tina."

"That sucks," Gillian said. "Really sucks."

Wijjie picked up his beer, then put it down without taking a drink. "How advanced is it?"

"I'm not sure. She doesn't talk to me about it." Tina paused. "It seems to be getting worse."

Wijjie shook his head. "Stem-cell therapy might be a possible cure. But not likely for many years. Especially if they keep cutting off research funding or access to stem cells."

Gillian spoke up: "I saw a guy on TV with MS who said the best thing you can do is smoke a joint."

"I heard that too," Tina said.

"Yep, medicinal cannabis," Gillian said. "Legal in California."

Tina looked at Wijjie. "What have you heard about it?"

"Obviously there's not a lot of hard scientific evidence right now. And there won't be until it's legal and pharmaceutical companies sell it for a thousand percent markup. But there is anecdotal evidence that it can give relief from symptoms like the spasticity and loss of appetite."

"I can't see my mom smoking a joint. It really helps?"

Gillian slapped the table with her palm. "Yes. That guy swore by it."

"But you need a doctor's prescription, or something, to get it, right?"

"A prescription?" Gillian laughed. "Hell, I've got some ganja now if you want it."

"How come I could have guessed that," Wijjie said.

"Thanks, anyway," Tina said. "I don't think I could even approach my mother about smoking pot."

"Hey, Wijjie, you should talk to Tina's mom about it. Since you're the fucking M.D."

"I wish you'd stop calling me that," Wijjie said. "Sure, I'd be happy to talk to her."

"Thanks. I'll let you know."

When Gillian reached for the pitcher of beer, Tina noticed a tattoo on the back of her shoulder. The tattoo was of the Japanese character for "moon"—*getsu*. It was inked in deep blue and surrounded by a red circle. "Interesting tattoo," Tina said.

"Can you read it?"

"It's the Japanese kanji for 'moon.' Is the red circle the Zen *enso*?"

"Let me see it," Wijjie said.

Gillian turned and pulled her top off her shoulder. "Yep, that's it. *Enso.*"

"What's it mean?" Wijjie said as he traced the circle.

"It symbolizes infinity," Tina said. "I think."

" 'Eternal moon,' " Gillian said. "That's what it's all about. The universal cycles of life."

"The *enso* thing looks like a big zero to me," Wijjie said. "Not to step on any cultural toes, but wouldn't that mean 'nothing,' not 'everything'?"

"It's Zen, Wij," Gillian said. "Everything in nothing. Right, Tina? Help me out here."

"To tell you the truth, I don't know much about Zen." Mr. Robert would know, she thought. "Sounds Zen to me. Do you have any more tattoos?"

"Yeah, but I can't show you them in here."

"Have some more of this," Wijjie said, filling her glass. "We'll get you to show them to the whole bar."

"Take more than that."

"Can you speak Japanese, Tina?" Wijjie asked as he watched Gillian pull her top back over her shoulder.

Tina disliked speaking Japanese to anyone other than her mother. "I understand what my mom says, as long as it's something a Japanese second-grader could understand. I can give her back a few words. What about you? Cruz is Latino, right? Speak any Spanish?"

"About as much as you speak Japanese, sounds like. What about you, Gillian?"

"What about me?"

"Any ethnic undertones to your ancestry?"

"I'm your basic English and Scottish Anglo. And, no, I don't speak the language very well."

"Why the dreads?" Wijjie asked.

"What's the matter, don't you like them?"

"Didn't say that. You into Rastafarianism?"

"In a secular sort of way. I'm not practicing, just dabbling in whatever I think sounds cool. Besides, I'd look damn boring if I didn't do something. Just another Southern California white chick."

Tina touched one of the locks. "How did you do it?"

"It was a pain in the ass. First—"

Wijjie stood up. "I'll get another pitcher while you two talk hair."

"—I made a bunch of tiny braids and permed them. Then I went to a stylist who twisted four or five together using a styling cream. After that, she backcombed it. It was pure torture. I couldn't wash it for three weeks, so the mattings would set right."

"They're great on you," Tina said.

"Thanks. You could do it."

Tina pulled at the ends of her shoulder-length hair. "I don't know. Seen any Asians with dreads?"

Gillian frowned. "Can't say as I have."

When Wijjie returned, he topped off their glasses with beer. "Done talking hair?"

"What I want to know," Tina said, "is the answer to that question about Cajal and Golgi?"

Gillian said, "God, talk about trivia. What's up with that jerk, anyway?"

Wijjie said, "I looked it up after the class. Golgi thought the brain was a network of nerve tissue. The reticular theory. Cajal thought the brain was composed of individual cells. The neuron theory."

"No shit," Gillian said. "That's what I guessed."

"Tina?" Wijjie said.

"I guessed something like that. Not exactly."

"That'll probably be good enough," Wijjie said. "Personally, I had no idea. But then I'm one of Alamo's grad students. He's got to let me in his class. But I don't think getting it right matters, it was how you answered the question that makes the difference."

"Oh?" Tina said.

"What are you talking about, Doc?" Gillian said.

"We'll see." He drained his beer. "I'm starving. Let's go to my place for something to eat. We can check our e-mail there to see if we got the news."

ALAMO FINISHED SENDING the last e-mail to the students in his class. He had let in his new graduate research assistant, Cruz, and a couple of others who had given outstanding answers, sizzling with a sharp focus on what they could contribute, what the rest of the class might gain from their presence. The others he let in were more vague on what they might contribute. The question about Golgi and Cajal was merely a tiebreaker, if needed, and not only if they got the right answer, but if they demonstrated critical thinking. The last two spots had been toss-ups, and he had given one of them to Suzuki—one of Porter's students—but he wouldn't hold that against her.

Porter, and her theory about the role of language and consciousness (that higher levels of consciousness arose from the higher levels of language abilities, indeed, were so intertwined as to be one and the same), irritated him. Why Porter

But a far greater complexity appears if the impulse continues to be transmitted and reaches the centers of consciousness. The impulse progresses along nerve tracts which follow complex pathways until it reaches the surface of the brain, i.e., the cerebral cortex. For consciousness—in man at least—is exclusively located in this area. Until it reaches this area, the transmission of the impulse must remain isolated, otherwise, if other pathways corresponding to other parts of the skin become involved, the site of the injury may

prized language so highly was a mystery. Human speech was nothing more interesting than dogs barking.

The seed of irritation was planted at a faculty research seminar at the institute when he was presenting a summary of the evidence supporting his predictions of what a neural theory of consciousness might be like. His focus was in the prefrontal lobe of the brain, not that consciousness was necessarily localized to that region, but it showed the most activity during consciousness. He showed slides of brain scans from patients with prefrontal damage, and speculated why studying such damage might be useful in developing a theory.

After his presentation, Porter asked long, rambling questions. It was obvious she was grandstanding, rather than offering constructive dialogue. Her brow furrowed—puckering like cortical tissue—with every research result he offered in evidence. Then she would start again: "But . . ." She would offer counterexplanations for the evidence, and then point to her own research as an example.

Porter or not, Suzuki had been a tough choice: she was particularly vague on what her contribution might be. Worse, she may have been trying to be witty—bringing an "open mind" to the study of consciousness. She wasn't sure about the second question, although her guess was correct. Still, it was a guess, as she admitted. At least she had been honest and thoughtful. If he couldn't have a student with razor-sharp intellect and a superior knowledge base, then he would take honesty and thoughtfulness over bombastic fakery. Indeed, it was the honest students, the slow starters, who often became his favorites, who did the best in the end.

be incorrectly located. If a painful sensation is eventually perceived, limited to the irritated area of skin, this sensation may in its turn give rise to a number of different activities within the central nervous system. It can give rise to thought and action.

From the presentation speech by Professor the Count K. A. H. Mörner, Rector of the Royal Caroline Institute, for the Nobel Prize in Physiology or Medicine, 1906, awarded to Santiago Ramón y Cajal and Camillo Golgi

Neuroscience Notebook, Christina Hana Suzuki

Tina caught the last BART train into the city: the 12:32 A.M. from Oakland's Rockridge station. Wijjie lived in an apartment in a three-story house that was two blocks from the station. He and Gillian had walked her to the station. Wijjie gave her a hug.

"This is for your mom," Gillian had said, putting a joint in Tina's hand. Tina put it in a pocket of her backpack.

"Congratulations again," Wijjie said to Tina. She had gotten into Alamo's class, as had Wijjie and Gillian.

The BART car was empty, except for a couple of sleeping homeless-looking men, their heads bobbing loosely in time with the swaying of the train. The floors of the car were littered with newspapers, fast food wrappers, and soft drink cups—even though eating and drinking weren't allowed on the trains.

It was a thirty-seven-minute trip to the Sixteenth Street station in San Francisco, the closest station to the condominium she and Mr. Robert rented.

When Wijjie had asked her if she spoke Japanese, it reminded her of a rare rainy day in San Diego, the day Tina first met Mr. Robert. She was sitting in the student union food court; everyone had to eat indoors because of the rain and the tables were nearly full. Mr. Robert had asked politely if he could sit in the vacant chair across from her. "Of course."

"Excuse me for asking," he said, after eyeing her over his sandwich. "Are you of Japanese ancestry?"

Oddly put, Tina thought. "Yes. My mother's from Osaka. My name's Suzuki."

"Ah," he said, as if confirming a theory. "Suzuki. What a coincidence. My name's Smith. Robert Smith."

"Coincidence?"

"You know . . . Suzuki's the most common family name in Japan, just as Smith is here."

"I have to confess, I didn't know that. It is a coincidence, isn't it?" She gave him a smile.

He looked at her blankly for a moment, then smiled too. "Sorry, I guess that was kind of obtuse. Do you speak Japanese? If you don't mind my asking."

"Well, a little," Tina said.

"Your parents speak it at home."

"It's just my mother and me. She tries to get me to speak in Japanese every now and then. But since I've been in school, I only see her a couple of weeks out of the year. So I'm sure I've forgotten most of it."

Mr. Robert told her that he had lived in Japan for five years, in Nishinomiya, a city near Osaka. Tina had never been to Japan; Mr. Robert was surprised to hear that. Even her mother hadn't been back to Japan since she moved to San Francisco before Tina was born.

Eventually, he got around to asking her if she wanted to go out for dinner. He wanted to take her to a great sushi bar, a little hole-in-the-wall place that few people knew about. Tina said that would be fine. She didn't tell him that she'd been to that sushi bar before and knew of three or four better places downtown.

The rain had stopped by the time he came to pick her up, the air refreshed with the moisture, reminding Tina of perpetually damp San Francisco. Mr. Robert talked to the sushi chef in Japanese. Tina could understand some of his Japanese, he sounded fluent—at least to her relatively tin ear. Mr. Robert would ask her something in Japanese, but she would always answer in English, if she understood the question. After a while, he gave up trying to impress her with his lan-

49

guage skills—if that was what he was doing—and spoke in English the rest of the date.

They slept together that night. Tina thought that he was nice enough, perhaps a little one-track-minded. Japan this, Japan that. Within a few weeks, they were living together. She liked his knowledge and respect of Japan; he made her feel good to be "of Japanese ancestry." He appreciated her in ways other boyfriends—all two of them, both short-lived relationships—hadn't. Maybe it was because her mother never talked about Japan, never taught her the customs, the history, the traditions. Though Tina would have admitted she had never been too curious; other things were more interesting.

Her BART train shot into the Sixteenth Street station and stopped. She got out and hurried out of the station, past the Mission District late-nighters who hung around the station—the drunks, those hopped-up on speed, those looking to score a hit of the Mexican heroin flooding the area. Tina made it safely to her and Mr. Robert's rented condo, four blocks from the station, without being hassled.

Mr. Robert was already in bed, but woke up when she came into the bedroom and sleepily asked how the reception had been. "Oh, fine," she said with a twinge of guilt for not telling him she had had an excellent time. He mumbled something, then was asleep.

She undressed, except for a T-shirt, and got into bed.

TINA WOKE BEFORE DAWN to the sound of a siren blaring past the building. She couldn't go back to sleep, and eased out of bed and went into the kitchen. She sat in the dim light, yawning, yet wide awake. The quiet and darkness were enveloping. Like a big *enso* tattoo encircling her, cocooning her.

She had been shaken by the first class with Professor Alamo. The feeling was like the residue of a vague fear after a nightmare. As if an invisible force were pushing her toward something or someone unfamiliar. Take another step, it's good for you.

Talking with Gillian and Wijjie after the reception had been enjoyable, more so than she had experienced in a long time. And they had taken the edge off the first day, given her confidence.

She wrote a note to Mr. Robert telling him that she was going to Berkeley to get an early start on her day. The only thing she wanted to do was start reading for Professor Alamo's class.

HANAKO GOT UP and started water for her morning cup of green tea. While it heated, she put away the dishes she had used to make a quick bowl of noodles when she got home from work. When she opened a drawer to put away a pair of chopsticks, three bottles of pills rolled toward the front. They were the prescriptions she was supposed to take for pain, muscle spasms, and depression. In the very back of the drawer was the syringe kit with the doses of Betaseron she was supposed to inject under her skin every other day. She had tried doing it for two weeks, then decided to stop taking them until she felt an attack coming on. The injections were painful, and they made her feel chilled and achy, and worse, a kind of tired sadness would crawl through her.

The doctor told her that might happen. He had longish hair and a bushy mustache that covered his mouth. He was nice to her, patient, making sure she understood him. Depression was a side effect of the drug, he explained. He said that he wouldn't prescribe it to patients if they'd been diagnosed with depression or with suicidal tendencies because it would likely make the depression return, or worsen. He asked her if she had ever been diagnosed with depression.

No, she said.

Good, he said. He prescribed an antidepressant, just in case. Avoid stress, he told her. Absolutely, avoid stress.

Last night had been a good night at work. No stress. All of her customers were cheerful and complimentary. She had experienced no symptoms, none of the pain or tingling. Or the loss of feeling, which was just as bad as the pain.

She put a pinch of tea leaves, then another, into the teapot. Her left leg went a little numb, then began to tingle, as if she were being shocked with a weak electrical current. She tried to ignore it.

Her medicine also made her feel nauseated. It was hard to work in a restaurant feeling nauseated, watching people eat, smelling all the smells in the kitchen, wiping up the tables of bits of food, the rings the water glasses left, and the drips of soy sauce splashed out of their little dipping dishes. All the grains of rice scattered about that hadn't made it into the mouths of the diners.

She didn't like feeling weak, not being able to carry the trays of plates full of tempura, or the big wooden trays of sushi, or the trays of bottles of beer. She didn't like feeling that she couldn't pull her weight, having to ask the dishwasher to bring in the full tubs of dirty dishes, or having to go to the manager's room to sit down while she caught her breath as if she had just tried to catch a Muni bus by running up Taylor to the top of Nob Hill.

She didn't mind the pain so much—the tingling, pins and needles pain, or the gripping, twisting, deep pain of the spasms—as much as the weakness. At least the pain was her pain, her body's pain. It wasn't caused by the medicine.

A touch of her palm on the kettle told her the water had reached the right temperature. She poured the hot, not-quite-boiling water onto the leaves in the teapot.

After drinking her tea at the kitchen table, she spent the

morning doing laundry and cleaning the apartment. Just before noon, the door buzzer rang. It would be Robert-*san*. She pushed the button for the entry door to let him in. While she waited for him to climb the stairs, she set out two teacups on the small kitchen table pushed against the wall between the stove and the window.

In a minute or two, he came through the apartment door and into the kitchen. "*O-genki desu ka,* Hanako-*san*?"

"*Arigatô, genki desu.*"

Hanako poured tea into the cups and motioned for him to sit. Both sat down and sipped their tea. After a quiet moment, Hanako said, "Have you heard about your *shodô* sensei?"

"No, nothing. I'm going to Berkeley today, to see if I can find out anything. The sign saying he is ill was still up the last time I went there. No one answers the phone."

Hanako nodded. When he and Hana moved to San Francisco several months ago, she told him about an excellent instructor in Berkeley—at the Zenzen School of Japanese Calligraphy. She had quickly added, "Please don't even mention my name."

Robert-*san* finished his tea and said, "Are you ready for *reiki*?"

"*Hai, onegaishimasu.*"

Mountain Retreat

FEBRUARY 1976
KYOTO, JAPAN

"Sensei," Hanako said. A light snow was falling, sticking to the limbs of the tree and the plants, in Daizen sensei's garden. The snow that had fallen on the rocks had melted.

"Yes?"

"I feel I am ready to learn more."

"More?"

She looked away as she spoke: "I feel I have reached a certain level of proficiency, but something is missing."

The Daizen sensei didn't say anything.

She continued: "I don't know how to describe what I am feeling. There must be something that will bridge my calligraphy to who I am."

Shodô must become a way of existence beyond the drawing of kanji. It is difficult to become completely focused within the moment that is required for true, spiritual *sho*. To become so focused merely for a few minutes while practicing is impossible, one must become so focused continually. Only then will *shodô* reach into the true depths of one's existence.

The sensei put his brush onto the stand that was carved from jade in the shape of a sleeping dragon. "You haven't found yourself in *shodô* as you thought you would?"

"No, not yet. So far, I feel like I'm a housewife taking calligraphy lessons to amuse myself on winter afternoons."

"But you've progressed so well. You have already passed some students who have been here for much longer."

Bowing her head slightly, she said, "Perhaps that's because I work harder. I do not have much else to do, after all."

"No, you have a genuine talent. Perhaps you would like to enter competitions?"

"No, I don't want that. I do this for private reasons."

The sensei nodded.

"What about you?" Hanako said. "You must have made the connection between self and calligraphy."

Not wanting to admit it, the sensei wasn't sure what she meant. Not exactly. He lived the way of calligraphy; he was a teacher and now Daizen sensei, the latest in the long line. That was it. "Well, I believe that's a difficult thing to say. Yes, I have become one with my calligraphy in one sense. It defines my existence."

"Your existence, yes. But doesn't it also define your being?"

"My being . . . no, I can't say for sure. What might you describe your being as, um, being?"

Hanako twisted her body slightly, adjusting her legs in their sheer stockings to the opposite side. "We put a lot of wrappings around it. The way others see us. We need to unwrap those layers to find our true essence, what we are really like." Her head tilted slightly as she quickly glanced at him.

Daizen sensei was seized by a flood of emotions, a realization that he had no idea who he was, and that person who was hidden was crying to be released. It was as if she had seen through those layers and touched that person that he was, but had never known or experienced.

He gathered his composure. "Well, yes, well . . ."

Hanako said, "I don't know if there is such a life deep inside, but I want to see if I can find mine."

The sensei could say nothing.

Her voice was soft as the snow when she asked, "Would you like to see if you can find yours?"

HANAKO FOLDED HER HUSBAND'S TIE exactly in half and hung it alongside the others on the expandable rack in the closet. She took his coat from him, slipped the wooden hanger through the shoulders, and returned it to the closet.

"Thank you," Tetsuo said.

The words surprised her; Hanako felt her cheeks blush. Her husband's words had almost sounded tender. Maybe he was just tired.

The *do* radical is one of the *eiji happō*. The radical is drawn using the wrist, rather than moving the hand. Gradually reduce the pressure of the brush on the paper beginning from the top to the bottom. The end of the stroke should be upward, rather than to the left or right. If the character demands that the stroke be drawn thin, draw it quickly to reduce the chance that the brush will waver.

Do means "endeavor" or "try." Perhaps because one has to try hard to keep the brush steady? Or keeping on a straight line is the path to accomplishment?

Instructor's Journal,
Zenzen School of
Japanese Calligraphy

"I'm going to take a bath," he said.

"May I scrub your back?"

Tetsuo raised an eyebrow. "You haven't done that for a while."

"I'm sorry."

"If you'd like."

Although their house was mostly Western-style, the bath was Japanese: the floor was tiled with a drain so the bather could scrub and rinse off before getting in the soaking tub. Hanako slipped off her hose while Tetsuo took off the rest of his clothes. They walked into the bathroom, he in a *yukata* robe, she in her dress and barefoot.

She started filling the tub with scalding water. He took off his *yukata* and hung it on the hook. In front of a water faucet, he sat on the wooden stool that was only a few inches tall. Water flowed strongly out of the faucet as he turned the knobs. When the temperature was right, he filled a plastic bowl with the water, then dumped the water over his head. He started soaping himself.

Hanako squatted on her heels. She took the soap from him and ran the slick bar over his shoulders and back until covered in lather. She put the soap down and massaged his neck and shoulders. She continued down his back, rubbing hard with her palms, fingers pushing on his muscles.

"You're getting your dress wet," he said.

She scrubbed for a while longer, then said, "That's all right."

He turned and pulled her to him his mouth on her face, on her neck, on her mouth. She kissed him too, as he leaned into her. On her back, on the slippery wet tiles, he pushed up her dress, fumbled with her panties until they were off. He pushed into her, and she pulled him tightly against her with her hands on his back as it rose and fell, her hands working up the lather, still rubbing his muscles as they relaxed and knotted, relaxed and knotted.

After his bath, they ate dinner in silence. She cleared away the dishes; he sipped brandy. "I'll be in Tokyo all next week," he said. "Meetings."

"All right," she said.

"I'M GOING TO THE RETREAT in Jûzu-mura for a few days," Daizen sensei said to Yuriko.

She looked up from her embroidery. "Oh? This time of year? Isn't the next retreat in the summer?"

"That's the retreat for the instructors. This is more of a personal retreat."

She went back to her embroidery for a moment before she said, "Sorry to ask you, but is something wrong?"

"No, nothing. I need some time to practice in solitude. Since I became the chief instructor I have had almost no time to practice. My skills have deteriorated. As chief instructor, my skills are the most important part of my existence."

"Of course, you must go."

FROM KYOTO, it took four hours on three different train lines to reach Jûzu-mura, the mountain village where the Daizen Inkstone had been found, according to the *History of the Daizen Inkstone*. The history had been written by Ihara, the founder of the Kurokawa School of Calligraphy. Over a hundred years ago, the Daizen school had purchased and set up a retreat in an old house. It was a typical mountain home, made from hand-planed, heavy beams, and capped with a steeply pitched roof. An open hearth was at the center of the house and the focal point of all activities. There were large areas of *tatami* on which the instructors practiced *shodô*.

Daizen sensei trudged from the station through the cold

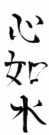

air and hard-packed snow to the retreat. He opened the solid wood door; a draft of pleasantly warm air greeted him. Alerted by the sensei that he was coming, the caretaker had turned on the gas-burning heat. Daizen sensei placed his bags in the sleeping room, and then took a long bath in the room that looked out to the mountain forest.

When he finished, he found the food left by the caretaker and had a light lunch of rice balls and instant soup. The second train to the mountain village wouldn't arrive for a few more hours, so he went for a walk in the brisk air. When he returned, he set up his calligraphy supplies.

But he couldn't focus on his practice, so he walked through the aromatic pine and cedar forest to the village, where he found a tiny tavern of only four tables; he was the only customer. He slowly sipped *sake* and munched on boiled soybeans that the owner brought to his table. The old man gave him a friendly smile but didn't say more than two words to him, for which the sensei was grateful. When he finished the flask of *sake,* he thanked the tavern owner, who smiled and nodded, and then he walked to the village station. The train of only one car—reminding him of a toy train or one at a children's amusement park—arrived on time. Six or seven passengers disembarked, Hanako Suzuki one of them.

AT THE RETREAT, he showed her around the old home. "Wonderful. It's so peaceful here."

"Are you hungry?" he asked.

"Yes."

"Would you like to have dinner here or in town?"

"Do we have food here?"

"Yes, it's been stocked. Enough for a few days."

"Then let's eat here."

She insisted on cooking, making a country stew of mountain potatoes, slivered onions, chunks of cabbage, and sliced beef in a soy sauce and *sake* broth. He started a fire in the old-style open hearth. They ate near it, drinking beer.

"Delicious," he said.

"Thank you."

She cleaned up the dishes while he got some more wood from the stack outside. She made them tea in an iron kettle placed in the hearth. They stared at the kettle and the fire, waiting for the water to warm. She touched her hand lightly against the kettle. It was ready, just before the boiling point. She poured the water into the teapot over the leaves.

They drank the tea as the fire died.

"Shall we go for a walk?" she asked.

"In the dark?"

"I would like to see the stars."

They carefully picked their way along the path that followed the river, its banks rimmed with ice. In the openings of the forest canopy, they admired the multitude of stars. When they were cold to the bone, they hurried back to the house, spread out the futons near the embers of the fire, and crawled under the quilts.

"Hanako," the sensei said, "the stars were beautiful."

"Beautiful," she repeated.

He moved over to her, she reached up to him and drew him to her.

THEY SPENT THREE DAYS at the retreat. During the afternoons, they walked in the air that was laced with the bite of snow and ice, along the river path, up to the mountain where the Daizen Inkstone began its life, according to the *History*. When they felt like it, they practiced calligraphy. They spent the rest of the time on the futon.

On the last evening, in the yellow light of an old lantern, they worked side by side on an old poem by Bunchô Mei: "The Spirit Is Like Water."

The second character—*jo*—means "similar" and comes from two characters, one for "woman" and one for "mouth," possibly connoting "doing as one is told," although this interpretation has its doubters. The square radical in *jo* is drawn in three strokes, not four. The left side is drawn first, then the top and right side in one stroke, and finally the bottom is drawn.

The third character—*sui* or *mizu*—representing "water," is derived from a river being squeezed. The center stroke (always drawn first) should always be vertical, that is, not sloping, and should have a powerful, flowing look.

Instructor's Journal,
Zenzen School of
Japanese Calligraphy

The best *sumi* ink is prepared with inksticks
(*kokeiboku*), which are
made from soot and glue.
The inksticks age like a
good wine. A few very
rare Chinese inksticks
worth thousands of dol-
lars remain from the Ming
dynasty.

Most beginning students
should use liquid *sumi*
(*ekitaiboku*). After learning
the basics, all students
should begin using ink-
sticks. Making ink by
grinding it against the inkstone and mixing it with
water is part of the ritual
that is essential to spiritual
shodô. The calligrapher
also can better control the
thickness and darkness of
the ink, as well as become
more intimate with all of
the treasures.

Instructor's Journal,
Zenzen School of
Japanese Calligraphy

The Daizen sensei watched Hanako add liquid ink to the
well of her inkstone. "Would you like to use the Daizen Inkstone?"

Her hand froze. "Me? I couldn't. Only the Daizen sensei
may use it."

"You've given me so much though, shown me so much
about myself. I only want to share everything."

"Perhaps not everything should be shared."

"Perhaps not, but . . ."

Hanako moved over to him. He placed a fresh piece of
paper on the table. She studied the inkstone for several moments, then dipped her brush into the inkwell.

She placed the brush on the paper and drew the character for "spirit." A sudden swell of power, of feeling, filled her.
As if the inkstone had infused her brush and the ink with life.

She placed her brush down. "Thank you," she said, as she
slipped off her sweater and out of her skirt. She pressed her
warm skin against the sensei and helped him take off his clothes.

"DON'T EVER GIVE UP the Daizen Inkstone," she said to the
sensei, as they waited for the train to leave Jûzu-mura station.

"I have to do my best work to keep it."

"You must never give it up," she repeated.

BERKELEY

Gozen unlocked the door to the Zenzen school. He picked
up the mail that littered the floor underneath the slot in the
door. He glanced through the stack, separating the bills and
other important-looking mail from the junk. He dropped
the two stacks onto the desk, and checked around the office

and studio. Nothing had been disturbed, although a layer of dust had settled on everything.

From the closet of cleaning supplies, he got out the feather duster, and began making his way through the house, dusting as he went. In the sensei's bedroom, after he brushed the top of the dresser, he pulled open the bottom drawer. He opened the box and picked up the inkstone. In the light, he inspected it carefully.

Two days ago, he located a copy of the *History of the Daizen Inkstone* in the Asian studies library at the university. Sitting at a table for more than three hours, he read as much of the one-hundred-page document as he could understand. It was written in old Japanese, difficult to read except by scholars of the classics. But he could comprehend enough to confirm he was holding the Daizen Inkstone.

INTERLUDE

History of the Daizen Inkstone
Part 1

SUMMER 1655
KYOTO, JAPAN

Smelling mildly of fresh tea leaves, being a tea merchant's son, Ihara bowed until he was prostrate on the *tatami* mat. Next to him, the samurai, Sakata, son of a distant cousin of the shogunate, bowed equally low. The old sensei—the fourteenth Daizen sensei—gave his two students an impatient cluck and they straightened up. They shuffled on their knees over to the low table where they would begin to prepare their teacher's ink. Both were reaching for the inkstick when the sensei said, "No."

Sakata was already shuffling back from the table, but Ihara hesitated. The old sensei tilted his head at Ihara and the student backed away to join Sakata. He waited until the students were side by side. Ihara looked down to the *tatami,* unable to meet his teacher's gaze. The sensei said, "You will do what I say."

"Yes, sensei," the students answered. Ihara's voice wavered slightly; Sakata's was cool and steady.

"I am very old. If I never picked up the brush again I would be happy. The fire has burned out." The sensei coughed quietly. "If I wished to die, would I?"

Ihara glanced up, wondering if he was supposed to answer the question. Or was it even a question? His sensei's words sounded like a death poem.

The old sensei was staring out into the courtyard. Ihara lowered his eyes when the sensei turned his gaze back into the room. Sakata remained still, barely breathing.

Daizen sensei said softly, "You must go now."

Frozen by the finality of those words, Ihara could only blink.

"Go and make your own way. You are my best students. I have taught my last lesson. I no longer have anything to teach, I no longer know the way."

Ihara still didn't move. Sakata bowed, then started to rise.

The old sensei picked up the Daizen Inkstone. The dark gray, almost black rock was stained with ink that had dried in its crevices over the two hundred years it had served as inkstone. "My sensei gave me this, as his sensei had before him, and his sensei before him, for fourteen generations. But I cannot decide who should become head of the Daizen school. Sakata, your style is so precise, so clean. You have practiced long hours to achieve perfect brushstrokes."

Sakata bowed until his entire face was smashed against the *tatami*.

"Ihara, your style is so full of life, bursting with energy, each stroke has its soul. I do not know . . ." The sensei's voice trailed off to nothing as Ihara bowed low.

"You each should find your own way," the sensei said after a long silence. "Find your own life."

The sensei grunted once as he unfolded his legs and stood up. He wobbled over to the open *shoji* screen. With the ink-stone grasped in both hands, he raised his arms and threw the inkstone out into the courtyard. The inkstone seemed to float too lightly for its weight. It landed near the stone shaped like a dogtooth near the middle of the garden.

LATER, AS A HALF-MOON hung above the portico of the sensei's studio and residence, Ihara slipped into the courtyard illuminated by dull, silvery moonlight.

Stepping lightly as a ghost, Ihara crossed the mossy path to the dogtooth stone. He dropped to his knees and felt for the inkstone. He touched it, and his fingers curled around it. As he started to stand up, he heard a breath of air behind him and the whisper of steel.

Sakata stood with his short sword drawn and held out from his body. He said, "Like a thief in the night, eh, Ihara? The inkstone, please. Sensei mentioned me first."

Ihara said, "Yes, that is true, but he could not have spoken both our names in the same breath."

"He was being kind to you." Sakata took a step forward with a hand outstretched. Ihara handed the inkstone to him.

Sakata walked backward a few steps, sheathed his sword, then turned and left. Ihara waited a moment, then walked out of the garden.

The sensei watched the two leave. The elements for a poem were there: the moon, the garden at midnight, his two best students, the sword, and the inkstone. But a poem never came.

In his garden, the old sensei died, curled around the dog-tooth stone. His last sight was the moon.

IHARA DIPPED THE TIP of his brush into the inkstone and poised it above the paper. Ten thousand strokes a day for ten thousand days, his sensei had exhorted. And then you might become good. But, until then, you cannot know the way of calligraphy.

"Son." His mother's voice broke his concentration.

"Yes?" He placed his brush on the holder. He turned to the side and looked at her.

Her vacant expression rarely changed; the only time she had shown emotion was when he had told her that he had been accepted to the Daizen school. It had softened a little then, around the eyes. "I am sorry to interrupt," she said, "but it is your father. I received a message sent from Edo. He is very ill. Please, you must go to him."

"Will he recover?"

She thought for a moment, "It is unlikely."

"I see. I am sorry to hear that."

"Please."

A long moment of breathless quiet was finally interrupted by Ihara: "Mother, may I speak honestly?"

"Yes, if you will go."

"Yes, I will go, but I would like to not become my father's heir. I will happily let my younger brother become heir."

His mother stood silently, in the quiet room that muffled against the cicadas screeching and crows jeering in the nearby forest. After a long time, she said, "Our family business is also ill."

"Oh?"

"I do not know what to do. Your brother has many good traits . . ."

Ihara knew the meaning of his mother's unspoken words: his brother preferred the floating world of drinking, gambling, and illicit teahouses.

"I will go to Edo. But would I be wrong to sell our family business? We could make some profit, enough for us to start over."

Ihara's mother tilted her head. "Forgive me for saying this, but I believe the debts of the business would take away much of the sale. Of course, if the business were more stable, it might be sold for a profit."

"I understand."

His mother bowed low. "I am sorry to interrupt your work."

"I am sorry about my father."

IHARA FOUND HIS FATHER in a boarding inn near the Yoshiwara area of Edo. The room stank of body odor, rancid food, and cheap *sake*. His father glanced up from his thin mat, his eyes opaque with a sticky film.

His father was not ill; he was a drunk.

Ihara turned away as his father reached out for him. He hurried away down the narrow, winding corridors to the outside. Stepping into the sunlight and fresh air, he nearly ran into a woman carrying a package wrapped in a tattered cloth.

"Excuse me," she said. "I am sorry."

"No matter," Ihara said and took a step past her.

"Wait," she said, then touched his sleeve.

Ihara stopped, as much because of her imploring voice as the unexpected, brazen touch. The woman was dressed in a kimono that was at one time elegant but now frayed. She looked several years younger than his mother and yet older at the same time. She gazed at his face for a moment, then said, "Ihara-*san*?"

"Yes?"

"You resemble your father. If only I had known him when he was your age."

Ihara knew immediately the role of the woman in his father's life. His stomach flipped; he wished he had Sakata's sword. He would have killed the woman, his father, then himself.

"Have you seen him? In here," she said, gesturing to the run-down inn.

Ihara followed her, unable to tell her that he had just seen him, what was left of him. They wound through the corridors to the room that Ihara had no desire to enter, but he could not stop. She stopped at the door to his father's room, waited for him to catch up, then burst in. "Father," she called out, likely in deference to Ihara being there. He hoped she did not call him Father all the time.

Ihara's father was on his side with his back to the door and he rolled over to face them. "Noguchi-*san*," he said in his hoarse voice.

Noguchi dropped to the ratty *tatami* and bowed toward the older man, then to Ihara. "Your son has arrived."

The two men stared at opposite walls. Noguchi glanced at both of them, then untied the knot of the cloth-wrapped package. "Look. Grilled fish and rice cakes."

His father grimaced as he sat up. Noguchi said to Ihara, "Join us."

The three of them ate, she the most. Ihara and his father both picked over the food. His father insisted on pouring *sake* all around to celebrate his son's arrival.

"I am happy," Noguchi said, belching. "Like we are a family."

Ihara squirmed.

HIS FATHER WAS ILL, yes—consumed by alcohol and Noguchi. The elder Ihara would be remarkably lucid one day, passed out cold the next. On his father's lucid days, Ihara tried to find out as much about the business as he could; he updated the accounts in the ledger his father had given to him. He used his small brush in the accounting, tallying the numbers in the book until his hand felt dead.

"You have beautiful handwriting," Noguchi said one night. "You must have studied calligraphy?"

Ihara ignored her, as he had come to do as a matter of course.

"I used to have nice handwriting," Noguchi said. "I wrote a poem or two."

Shoving himself up from the *tatami*, he ran out into the night. Walking quickly, he found a small shrine, where he entered through the *torii* gate and stood in front of the altar.

Noguchi came up next to him. "I am sorry. I do not know what to do about your father."

Ihara let out a long breath of air. "It no longer matters."

"Will you teach me calligraphy?"

"No."

"You can teach me. Your father just told me you are a Daizen student."

"I cannot teach," Ihara said. "I'm here for other reasons."

Noguchi stood with him staring at the altar.

THE CREDITOR—a tall though slim man—brought his two hulking sons to the boarding inn. "Pay me what you promised," he said.

Ihara watched his father bow until he was prostrate on the *tatami*, his exposed neck thin as a reed. Ihara bowed next to his father and said, "I am the oldest son. I am setting the business right, and will pay what is owed. I only ask a little more time."

"More time? No, there is no more time."

The two sons moved quickly through the room, overturning their meager possessions, splintering the bamboo travel boxes, crushing lacquer cases, ripping apart books and bags and clothing. When they were through with those, the two sons pounced on Ihara and his father, beating them, kicking them, ripping at their clothes until they found every thin coin that Ihara had managed to collect.

WHEN THE BLACK FOG that enveloped his mind burned away to reveal a rainbow of pain, Ihara's first sight was Noguchi. A damp cloth was in her hand, held above his face. She twisted her head to look at him closely.

"Ihara-*san*," she said softly.

Ihara groaned. "Father?"

"Ihara-*san*," she said again, even more quietly.

A WEEK PASSED before Ihara could stand by himself; the bruises would last a month.

Noguchi had managed to scrape together a little money to send his father's body home—a few of his father's sympathetic clients had donated. Ihara sent his mother a message and told her that he would stay in Edo until the business was closed.

With his father dead, the Ihara tea business was worth even less. Ihara struggled around Edo, trying to salvage as much as he could, trying to hold out for a good offer. He took a job with one of his father's distributors. The job consisted of weighing and packaging tea. At the end of the day, his hands were like stones.

Noguchi was still there, in the room. Ihara didn't know what to do about her. He thought about giving her some money to leave, but that was not what she seemed to want.

"Noguchi-*san*," he said one night. "Why do you stay?"

She looked at the wall as if she could see through it. "Do you wish me to go?"

"No," he managed to say.

After work the next day, after he received his first salary, he didn't go home, instead he wandered the alleys of the *shitamachi*—the lower area of Edo, in elevation and reputation. Hungry, he stopped at a grilled tofu stand and ate a couple of skewers. Now comfortable, and thirsty, a *sake* stall beckoned. With only a quick thought of his father's demise, he drank a flask, then another.

Feeling happier than he had since his sensei died, he started to walk home, when he came to a small teahouse, its roofline drooping like a stray dog's tail. After admiring its lines, so much like good calligraphy, he stepped inside.

The teahouse was clean, with a patina of age, but empty of customers. The elderly woman proprietor stepped from the back room and welcomed him. Ihara sat on a thin cushion in front of a low table.

The woman—with soft eyes that reminded him of his mother's—served him a warm, moist cloth to wash with, then poured him a bowl of tea. Ihara admired the bowl's rustic shape, took a sip, and bowed to her. She bowed in return and left him alone. Ihara looked around the sparsely furnished tearoom. A well-executed calligraphy scroll hung on one wall. He was going to get up to examine it when the proprietor returned with a small dish of intricately designed rice crackers.

Ihara admired them for the correct length of time, then picked up one and took a bite. "Delicious," he said.

She bowed, then said, "Excuse me for asking, but where are you from?"

"Near Fuji-*san*," he said, then asked her "That scroll . . . the calligraphy is excellent."

The woman turned to look at it. "No, it is a poor piece.

The character for
"quiet"—*shizuka*—is
thought to come from the
abstraction of calm com-
ing from "beautiful green
color," "clear of conflict,"
"staying pure," or "desirable lack of movement."
The brushstrokes must re-
flect this mood. Indeed,
they are difficult to draw
in this manner without a
calm mind.

But it is not a relaxed
calmness that the calligrapher must attain, rather
an energized calmness. It
is a complete union of
mental and physical en-
ergy. Indeed, a *shodô* student's consciousness is
fundamentally changed
through diligent practice,
although it does not come
through conscious effort,

The *kasure* is too loose, the stroke endings too abrupt, the balance off."

Ihara went over to it and looked closer. The calligraphy still struck Ihara as excellent. The proprietor's complaints about it were mostly unfounded, although upon a detailed inspection, she did have a refined eye: the *kasure*—the open, white space that distinguished a brushstroke—was minutely too loose for the thickness of the strokes, the end of the strokes might have been a little longer, and the balance was perhaps a bit too top-heavy. Still, the work was excellent. Ihara did not recognize the stamp of the artist.

Ihara returned to his tea. The woman said, "See, I told you."

"Who was the artist?"

"No one important. My grandfather. Excuse me for asking, but do you practice *shodô*?"

Ihara almost instantly said "No"—he hadn't practiced for many weeks. He said, "I was a student in the Daizen school."

"Daizen! Excellent. You must be a master."

Ihara bowed. "Not at all. I am a tea trader's son."

"But Daizen . . . I cannot believe you are in my run-down shop."

"Daizen sensei has died, you know."

"No, really? Who will succeed him?"

"He appointed no successor." Sakata had the inkstone, was running the school, and had the title of Daizen sensei.

The woman watched Ihara eat the food and she kept his tea bowl full. When he finished, she said to him, "Please, come with me."

Ihara followed the woman through the teahouse to the back, where the walls were cracked and the ceiling sagged, the floors warped, the *tatami* mats insect-ravaged. But all the rooms were as clean as the front. They stopped at a room with an entrance so low that Ihara had to stoop to enter.

The room contained a low table, on top of which was an inkstone, waxed inksticks, paper, a brush holder, a paperweight, and a bundle of brushes. Around the room were stacks of practice sheets, works of calligraphy had been pinned on the walls. A narrow window let in two or three rays of light.

"Wonderful," Ihara said.

"This room is where my grandfather practiced. As you can see, I have left it as he left it."

Ihara longed to pick up the brushes.

"Please," she said. "I would be happy if you could show me a bit of Daizen calligraphy."

"I have not practiced for many months. And this is your grandfather's room. I would not want to spoil it."

"You could not spoil it, you could only honor it."

"I would be happy to repay your kindness." Ihara sat at the table, and unwrapped the brushes, as she fetched him water. Ihara examined the brushes—they were in good condition for being so old. Ihara rubbed the inkstick on the inkstone, mixed it with water, and placed a piece of paper in front of him. He cleared his mind, focused on the paper, and sent his energy through the brush.

The strokes were on the paper, the characters for "quiet" and "worn" and "comfort." The way he felt in the teahouse.

The proprietor smiled. "It is exquisite. I may now die happy."

"Please, it is not as good as your grandfather's. I would have to practice many more years."

"You may practice here, if you have no place in Edo."

"Thank you. I would be very happy practicing here."

She bowed and said, "Would you enjoy some *sake* now?"

"Yes. I would."

but rather a slow upward seeping from the subconscious.

The character for "worn"—*yaburete*—was derived from the characters "rock" and "skin," likely meaning "small piece," which implies the idea of "pulling apart." (The last two characters complete the adjective form of the verb.) The strokes forming the character for "rock" were created from characters that mean "stone hewn from a mountain." Note the sharp angles on the strokes. Sharp strokes are obtained with a slightly drier brush and a lighter, quicker touch.

気
も
ち
の
い
い

The characters—*kimochii
no ii*—literally mean
"pleasant feeling." *Ki,*
meaning "spirit," was ab-
stracted from the vapor
rising above cooked rice.
Mochi, the next two characters, are derived from
the meaning of "hold
with the hands," which
metaphorically means to
"endure." The last characters, *no ii,* mean "good,"
"right," "nice," and the
like. Note the soft angles
of the strokes as com-
pared with the sharpness

NOGUCHI ASKED WHERE he had been. Ihara said, "Wandering.
Seeing the sights of Edo."

"I could show you the sights of Edo."

"I think I have seen all I need to see."

"Your father liked to see the sights of Edo."

"Too much of them, I think."

Noguchi, her face drooping tiredly, thought for a moment, then said, "I am sorry about your father. He was a
good, cheerful man."

Ihara got up and opened the paper *shoji* screen door, trying to get some fresh air into the room.

KYOTO

Tetsuo Suzuki's office was still lavish, despite the economic
ravage his company had suffered during the recession. At least
it was more lavish than Kando's plain office. He watched the
real estate developer read his report on the yakitori restaurant
and its bankrupt owners. Suzuki had aged dramatically in the
last few years—his skin turned sallow, his eyes bloodshot, his
hair streaked with gray. When the Japanese bubble economy
burst, as banks dissolved and corporations were forced to
make unheard-of layoffs, the Suzuki empire had fallen hard.
The developer had leveraged his dramatic expansion in the
late seventies and eighties with inflated real estate values.
When the collapse came in the late eighties and the nineties,
real estate values had plunged, rendering his collateral nearly
worthless. Banks tried to collect on delinquent and bad loans
by foreclosing on properties, but it was too late. Eventually,
they gave up on the foreclosures, deciding they might as well
wait it out for better times instead of collecting a yen or two
on each hundred they had loaned.

Suzuki's Maui resort project had gone first, his pride, the flagship of the Suzuki resort branch. When the economy tanked, tourists stopped going to the islands, especially to up-scale resorts. In the bubble days, ordinary salarymen, with their fat bonuses, could afford to vacation at his resort. Now it was only those newly techno-rich who could. And they were few and far between. Hanako's father's bank took back the resort, then promptly went under. Hanako's father died shortly after of a heart attack, no doubt brought on by severe depression. Hanako's mother swallowed a bottle of sleeping pills the day after his funeral.

Kando felt sorry for Suzuki. Sorry for him despite the humiliation, the psychological torture, that the developer had inflicted on him. The pain had stayed with him for all those years.

"Not much to recover, is there?" Suzuki said when he finished reading the report.

"Not much. The equipment."

"Used. Worthless."

"Practically."

Suzuki sighed. "No cash assets?"

"No. Not a yen." Kando was glad the owners didn't have any cash; Suzuki would have ordered Kando to take it from them.

"I'm tired of this shit," Suzuki said. His voice seemed directed at himself, not at Kando. Not at the world. "Chasing after some fucking yakitori-stand mom and pop who default on their lease."

"Anything you want me to do?" Kando asked.

Suzuki flashed the investigator a grin. "You know how to cook yakitori?"

of *yaburete*. Soft strokes are obtained with a slightly wetter brush, and a heavier touch.

Instructor's Journal, Zenzen School of Japanese Calligraphy

Certain that he was holding the Daizen Inkstone, Gozen weighed the heavy stone in his hands as he tried to decide what to do next. Leaving it there, in the drawer, as if he hadn't found it at all, was what he would have preferred. On the other hand, if Zenzen sensei never recovered, a family member would collect his belongings and the inkstone would be discovered. There would be deep embarrassment then, with the Zenzen school disgraced for associating with the wayward sensei. And he had to consider the tradition and long history of the Daizen-Kurokawa competition; the inkstone as trophy was as much a part of that as the calligraphy itself.

With his discovery, Gozen's place in the world of *shodô* had changed dramatically. He was the number-one student of the twenty-ninth Daizen sensei, and the number-one student at the Daizen school eventually became the Daizen sensei.

The thought made him weak in the knees. Of course, he wasn't at the Daizen school. If he were, would he still be number one?

Deciding that he should wait to see what happened with Zenzen sensei, he put the inkstone back in its box. Zenzen sensei might quickly return to normal, and Gozen could just forget what he had found.

A voice called out from the front of the house. Gozen sensei slammed the drawer shut, picked up the duster, and ran to the front.

"*Konnichiwa,* Gozen sensei," Mr. Robert said with a bow when Gozen walked into the front room.

"*Konnichiwa,* Smith-*san.*"

"I'm sorry for just walking in, but the door was open."

"No problem. I was cleaning." He held up the duster.

"How is sensei? Is he here?"

"He's in the hospital."

"What happened?"

"He had a stroke." Gozen touched his forehead. "He was in a coma, but he has started to come out of it. The doctors think there is some brain damage. They don't know how bad yet, not until they run some tests."

"I'm sorry to hear that."

"Perhaps you could go to the hospital and find out some more?"

"I'd be happy to do that. Which hospital?"

Gozen felt a flood of relief.

"I'M A STUDENT of Zenzen sensei, one of your patients," Mr. Robert said to the receptionist.

"Zenzen?" the receptionist said. She stared at her computer monitor.

"Sorry," Mr. Robert said. He recalled what Gozen sensei had told him. "His name is Shimano."

The receptionist gave him a long, bored gaze, then typed in the name on her keyboard. "He's being moved some time today, so he's either in room two-forty-five or in the rehabilitation wing. Check there first. It's down the hall, turn right at the end, then left. See the RN there to find out if he can have visitors."

"Thank you," he said, but she was already taking a call. He followed her directions, found a nurse, and asked about the sensei.

"He's just getting into his new room. Probably not a good idea to see him just now."

"What's his condition?"

"You are?"

"One of his students."

"That's right. He teaches Japanese writing."

"*Shodô,*" Mr. Robert said. Much more than Japanese writing.

"We usually only give information to family members."

"He doesn't have any family here."

"I suppose I can tell you that he had a burst blood vessel due to an aneurysm. We don't know the full extent of the damage, but he does have some loss of verbal abilities."

"You mean he can't speak?"

The nurse nodded. "He can't speak, or write. It happens with strokes in certain areas of the brain. He's only been out of his coma for a couple of days."

"He can't write?" he asked.

"He just makes these weird scribbles."

"Scribbles?"

"Here." She opened a file and showed him a piece of notepaper. On it were some marks made with a felt-tip pen.

The nurse asked, "Can you make any sense out of it?"

"No," he said after turning it around and looking at it that way. "Some of the marks look like kanji radicals, but most of it looks like abstract doodling."

The nurse gave him a shrug.

In deep sleep
no escape
for me
from me

WALKING ACROSS THE CAMPUS on her way to meet Mr.
Robert for lunch, as they had agreed to earlier that day,
Tina's face was warmed by the sun as it peeked out from the
wispy fog. She had just gotten out of the first meeting of
Professor Porter's class on the brain and language. The professor had given them the syllabus, told them to read the first
three chapters of her book *Wet Language: How the Brain
Talks.* Then she gave an introductory lecture on the still
largely mysterious process of how humans produce language.
One of the few things we do know, she explained, was that
specific areas in the brain had well-defined roles in language:
Broca's area for speech production, Wernicke's area for understanding.

Tina found the Nefeli Café near the intersection of Hearst and Euclid, just across the northern boundary of the campus. The northside café was a tiny place with tables crammed together only a few inches apart. Mr. Robert was waiting for her just inside the door.

As they stood in line, they could smell espresso, foamed milk, and Greek cheeses coming from the coffee bar and kitchen. The crowd was speaking a polyglot of languages: Spanish, Chinese, French, and others Tina couldn't identify. The line moved quickly, and at the counter they ordered sandwiches. Tina ordered a cappuccino, Mr. Robert an iced tea. Carrying their drinks, they squeezed between tables until they found one that was open.

They had taken a couple of sips when one of the employees brought their sandwiches to the table—crusty bread overflowing with smoked red peppers, olives, feta and mozzarella cheese, and tomatoes. They took a bite of the messy sandwiches. Mr. Robert chewed in his thoughtful manner, as if he were trying to taste every molecule. It was the way he did everything, with the intense focus required in his martial arts. Finally, he swallowed. "What class did you have today?"

"Brain and language. Professor Porter's class."

"What's that about?"

"That pretty much describes it. How the brain makes language." Tina started cutting her sandwich into bite-sized pieces.

"That's timely. I just found out my *shodô* sensei had a stroke. He just came out of his coma, and he can't speak or write, at least anything that makes sense. He draws these strange scribbles. They look like abstract art, some of them are like kanji radicals, but they don't make sense. Does that mean anything?"

Tina thought back to her psychology classes. "It sounds like aphasia."

"Aphasia," Mr. Robert repeated. "Is it permanent?"

"I don't know the medical aspects of it. I'll see if I can find out anything more from Professor Porter. Maybe Wijjie knows something, too."

"Wijjie?" He watched her put one of her bite-sized pieces in her mouth.

"One of the other grad students. He's an M.D."

"What kind of name is Wijjie?"

"A nickname, short for William James."

"Oh." He gazed intently at his tea glass, then picked it up and took a thoughtful sip. "I saw your mother today."

"How is she?"

"She seemed pretty good, at first, but then she had some pain."

"Spasticity?"

"Yeah, that. Seemed really painful."

Tina remembered the joint Gillian had given her was still in her backpack. "Was she going to work?"

"Yes."

"That's Ma. She's never missed a day of work that I can remember."

SAN FRANCISCO

"How's your husband?" Hanako asked Kiyomi, the manager of the Tempura House. Kiyomi was filling out the week's schedule while Hanako folded napkins.

"Not too bad," Kiyomi said. "Better, actually. Last week he had lots of pain, said he felt like he was drowning." He had a mild case of emphysema even though, as Kiyomi told everyone, he never smoked a cigarette in his life. But he had worked in smoke-filled restaurants and bars since he was fifteen.

Hanako's legs tingled, making her frown.

"Are you okay?" Kiyomi asked.

"I'm fine."

Kiyomi gave her a look over her reading glasses. "Sure?"

"Sure."

Kiyomi went back to her chart. "I love filling out the schedule."

Hanako smiled at her. "You love everything."

Kiyomi thought for a moment. "Not everything."

"What don't you love?"

She laughed. "I don't know. Something."

Hanako folded another napkin in the twisting knot that looked like a flower. Kiyomi had taught her the fold more than twenty years ago. After only a couple of weeks, Hanako became the fastest napkin folder at the Tempura House.

Kiyomi asked her, "What is Hana studying? I know you told me before."

"Neuroscience. The brain."

"I got that part. There was something else, though."

Hanako looked up from the napkin she was folding. "Language. How we use our brain to speak and understand what people are saying."

"Language."

"And the brain."

"Language and the brain. I think I understand. Hana's smart, isn't she?" Kiyomi pointed with her pencil to the schedule. "Do you want some time off?"

"Time off? Why would I want time off?"

"Take a break. Spend some time with Hana, now that she's back in town."

Hanako shook her head. "She's in school now, she won't have time for me."

"I don't think you've had a vacation in a couple of years."

"I went to Hana's graduation in San Diego."

"For two days. That's not a vacation."

"I don't want a vacation—" She grimaced when a spasm gripped her legs.

"There, see, you did it again."

"Did what?"

"That look on your face. You know like this." She screwed up her face as if in pain.

"I'm okay, don't worry." Hanako grabbed the pile of folded napkins and started placing them on the tables.

Up Powell

MAY 1977

SAN FRANCISCO, CALIFORNIA

Crowded with grinning tourists, a cable car rolled up the steep hill on Powell Street, passing Hanako as she walked to the Tempura House restaurant. She opened the door and peered inside. The staff was cleaning up after the lunch rush, attending to the few remaining customers, and setting up for the dinner crowd. One of the kimono-clad waitresses asked her, "One for lunch?"

"No, sorry," Hanako said. "I'm here to apply for the waitress job."

"Okay. Follow me."

Hanako had to almost run after the woman, who picked up a few empty dishes along the way without breaking stride. They went behind a *noren*—a split half-curtain—and into a small office. The waitress handed her a form to fill out and told her to wait for the manager. She hurried away, taking a half-filled ashtray with her off the desk.

Hanako filled out the employment form, just finishing it when a Japanese woman entered the room. Speaking in Japanese, she introduced herself and picked up Hanako's application.

The manager glanced through it. "You live on Bush and Taylor, just around the corner. That's good. You won't have to take Muni to get here. It takes forever." The woman smiled, briefly. A few lines appeared at the corners of her eyes, then disappeared when she ended her quick smile. In English, she asked, "How long have you lived in San Francisco?"

It took a moment for Hanako to switch to English. "Two weeks."

"When can you start?"

"I have the job?"

"Yes."

"But this is my first time to be a waitress."

"That's no problem. You'll catch on quick."

Hanako wasn't sure what the manager's last phrase meant.

The manager pointed to Hanako's employment form. "You graduated from Kansai Girls' High School. That's a good school. You speak English well enough. We can show you the ropes, and in a few hours you'll be flying around here like you've been flying all your life."

Hanako nodded once, again not sure what she meant.

The manager fiddled with a pack of cigarettes on the desk but didn't take one out. "There's something else, I suppose?" She asked this in Japanese.

"Something else?"

"What's the story you want to tell me?"

"I suppose I should tell you." Hanako took a long breath.

"Are you going to have a baby?" the manager said before Hanako could say another word.

Hanako was stunned. Someone must have told her.

The manager gave her a sympathetic smile. "It's okay. It's happened before."

Hanako stared down at her hands.

"How many months?"

"Two and a half."

"Okay, we can get three, maybe four, months out of you. A little more meat on your bones would look good, anyway. Of course, you can come back as soon as you want after the baby's born. I know a couple of grannies that baby-sit."

"Thank you."

"Can you train now, this afternoon, and work tonight? We've got a couple of Japanese tour groups coming in. They'll be hungry after riding around in their buses all day gawking at the scenery."

"AND HERE'S THE ICE MACHINE," said Kiyomi, the waitress who had shown her to the office. "Don't leave the scoop thing in the ice. The health department doesn't like that."

"Yes," Hanako said.

"Sometimes it gets stuck, the ice does, so you'll have to bang on it . . . up there." Kiyomi bent over and twisted her head to look into the ice bin. She reached inside and banged on the roof of the machine. A cascade of ice fell into the bin. "See? I love this machine."

Hanako bent over and looked up into the bin. "Okay."

Kiyomi was already standing at the drinks machine when Hanako stood up. "See"—she was holding a glass under a spout—"just push here and it comes out. Just like that. I love this machine too. I wish I had one at home."

"Yes, I see."

"If it's running out of Coke, or whatever, when it starts making this sound—*spttt, spttt*—then go into the kitchen and yell at the dishwasher to change out the Coke, or whatever one is going *spttt*."

"Okay."

"Well, that's about it. Any questions? . . . No? Good. Now I've got to go. It's my night off." She lingered at the door momentarily. "I love my night off."

"We've got a lot to do, so let's get started," Professor Porter called out. In one of the conference rooms at the institute, Porter's graduate students gradually ended their conversations and turned toward her. "I'd like to welcome Tina to her first research group meeting. I know you've all met her, so we won't do any more than that. Let's get right to your reports. First, Howard."

Howard Clear was in his late twenties, though the dark circles under his eyes made him look much older. He said, "I'm analyzing all the data I collected over the summer on the aphasic patients. Getting some interesting results about the possible role of the sublenticular fibers in generative grammar." His report went on for several minutes. Tina was taking notes, but got lost in all of the terminology and different studies that Howard talked about. They seemed to involve patients who had suffered some sort of brain trauma—tumors, strokes, swelling caused by disease or accident—and had language impairments. He mentioned "aphasia" often.

When the others had finished, they looked expectantly at Tina. She said, "Thanks for the welcome. I'm not sure what to say, though. I did hear an interesting story today. My boyfriend's Japanese calligraphy teacher just had a stroke of some kind—I don't know the details—but he can't speak, and what he writes doesn't make sense."

"Doesn't make sense?" Howard asked, his brow furrowing. "Can you be more precise?"

"According to my boyfriend, he writes pieces of Japanese characters, but they don't form words."

"Sounds like agraphia," Professor Porter said. "That would make a very interesting clinical case. Let's follow up on that, shall we, Tina?"

"Sure," she said, writing "agraphia" and "follow up?" in her notebook. "Exactly what do I need to do to follow up on it?"

Professor Porter said, "I'm sure Howard and the others will be glad to fill you in on the details. One thing to keep in mind, however, my number-one rule of all rules: never divulge our ongoing research without my approval to anyone outside this room."

Tina nodded. "Of course."

THE MEETING WENT ON for another hour, largely taken up by Professor Porter going through two pages of things-to-do. Tina was assigned to work with Howard, to observe his data collection process and to learn the protocol for dealing with the research subjects. Her immediate task that week was to learn the procedures for using the magnetic resonance imaging machine, the MRI system, located in the basement of the institute.

After the meeting, Tina followed Howard's directions to the basement. Opening the heavy doors at the end of the stairwell, she could smell damp concrete and new carpet. She walked down a ramp to a set of metal doors. She pulled one open.

Inside a room that looked like a doctor's office waiting room, a man was sitting at a desk with several chairs in front of it. He was maybe in his late thirties, dressed in a white coat, with his hair clipped very close. He wore tiny oval

Aphasia: total or partial loss of the ability to use or understand written or spoken language.

Agraphia: total or partial loss of the ability to produce meaningful written language.

Neuroscience Notebook,
Christina Hana Suzuki

glasses that were slightly askew. He said, "Name?" in a heavy Germanic accent.

"Christina Suzuki."

He checked a list in front of him. "Christina Suzuki." He made a mark on the list. "I am Florian. We will wait for the others before we start, so sit over there."

Tina sat in one of the chairs. There was a noise from outside the room; Wijjie and Gillian came in, shortly followed by a couple of other first-year students. "Hey, Tina," Wijjie said.

Florian said, "All right, people. Give me your names."

Wijjie looked at Florian, then gave Tina a questioning look, as the others started reciting their names. Tina touched the bridge of her nose, as if pushing up a pair of glasses. Wijjie adjusted his own pair of invisible glasses with his thumb and forefingers.

"Name?" Florian said to Wijjie.

"William Cruz."

"That's everybody." Florian checked off Wijjie's name. He stood up and said, "I am Florian, the MRI lab technician. In the rooms behind this one is a Hitachi Fifty-one-hundred magnetic resonance imaging device and the data capture system. The H-Five-one-O-O cost this institute three and a half million dollars. We do not have three and a half million dollars to buy another one, or to pay damages to someone who is injured in the machine goofing around. So pay attention." He handed out copies of an instructional packet. On the first page were several rules. Tina glanced at the first two:

No loose metal objects in the machine or near the machine! They will fly around and injure the subject.

Keep all credit cards, ATM cards, library copy cards, BART passes out of the MRI room. They will be erased or scrambled.

Florian said, "Before we go into the MRI suite, I must ask you these questions. Your responses will be individual and they must be 'Yes' or 'No.' Do not nod or shake your head. Do not say 'Uh-huh,' or any other vocalization. Understand?"

"Yes," they said.

"Okay, first question, do you have a pacemaker?"

All answered "No."

"Do you have any surgical clips on blood vessels, or any metal fragments in your brain, eye, or spine?"

All answered "No," except for Gillian, who asked, "What about body piercings?"

"Have to be removed if you're going in the machine. If you're going in the MRI room as a researcher, I'd take them out if they're exposed and not very secure."

Gillian nodded.

"Lastly, and this one is just for the women, are you pregnant?"

All three answered "No."

"Okay," Florian said. "Those are the questions you will have to ask and get unambiguous answers from your research subjects before you allow them in the MRI suite. Leave your backpacks in here, and make sure you leave credit cards, ATM cards, BART passes, anything like that. Rule number two. Follow me."

Standing up to follow Florian, Wijjie whispered to Gillian, "Body piercings, huh?"

"I suppose you're going to lecture me on the danger of blood poisoning, Doc."

Florian opened a thick glass door and shepherded them into a narrow corridor with several doors. He first showed them the observation room, with its glass-paneled window that looked onto the H-5100: it took up half the room, and looked like a round, airport security X-ray machine. He let them look into the power supply room, and the room that contained the magnetic field generator ("Ten thousand times stronger than the earth's magnetic field," Florian announced). He showed them the computer control room, where he pointed out the data collection system.

Then they went into the room where the H-5100 sat. Florian demonstrated the patient table, where the subject was slid into the bore of the magnet. He showed them the head immobilizer, and the stimulus display panel. He explained how the machine's magnetic fields aligned the cells, each type differently, and allowed the image system to capture their positions, showing different types of tissue, or, in the case of functional MRIs, brain activity. Back in the control room, he showed them how to set the controls for precise calibration, and how the computer data collection system worked. "Now I need a volunteer," he said.

Gillian said, "Wijjie will."

"Thanks, Gillian."

Florian cocked his head at Wijjie, further twisting his glasses askew. "Well?"

"All right," Wijjie said. "Scan me."

"Up on the table," Florian said to Wijjie. He helped him position his head in the immobilizer. Florian explained while he worked: "We primarily conduct brain fMRIs in this lab. If you want good results, the subject's head has to be absolutely immobile. The best way to do this is to first make sure they are comfortable on the patient table." He asked Wijjie, "Are you comfortable?"

"I could fall asleep."

"Excellent." Florian adjusted the immobilizer around his head. "Still comfortable?"

"Feels a little odd, but I'm comfortable."

"Okay, now you will go in." He slid Wijjie into the H-5100.

The rest of the group followed Florian into the control room and watched as he operated the machine. It took a couple of minutes before an imaged slice of Wijjie's brain was displayed on the screen.

Florian asked Tina to release Wijjie. Tina went into the MRI room and slid the patient table out of the machine. Wijjie grinned at her. "Am I alive?"

"Sorry," Tina said. "There was nothing in there."

"Not surprising," Wijjie said.

WIJJIE WALKED TINA to the BART station after the training session. Gillian had taken off right after the training, saying she wanted to catch a reggae group playing in a Berkeley club. Wijjie and Tina declined the invitation to join her.

"You don't have to walk with me," Tina said to Wijjie as they started across campus.

"Not to be an alarmist, but you shouldn't be walking on campus alone at night."

"Yeah, you're right." Tina pulled her backpack higher on her shoulder.

"By the way, did you ask your mom about the marijuana?"

"Not yet. I'm going to see her tomorrow."

"Let me know what happens."

They walked in silence for a while, then Tina said, "You and Gillian seem to have hit it off."

"What?"

"Gillian. You know."

Wijjie laughed. "She's not . . ." His voice trailed off.

Tina waited for a moment, then said, "Your type?"

"She's fun, a little too hard for me. 'Hard' as in prickly."

They reached the entrance to the BART station. "Well, I better run," Tina said. She almost said something about getting home to Mr. Robert, but didn't. She hugged Wijjie.

Tina was awake at dawn, sitting on the floor of the former guest bedroom she'd claimed as her office. She was drinking coffee and reading the assigned articles and chapters for her classes. Morning was her best time to study. At night, the day's events had piled up like one of the hundred-car wrecks on the foggy stretches of Interstate 5.

Mr. Robert was up early too, though he was still in their bedroom—stretching, meditating, and doing his deep-breathing exercises. After that, he would be practicing one of his Japanese arts. He spent an hour and a half every morning on his routine; Tina found that she could get a lot of her schoolwork done in that time.

Her coffee had gone cold and there was still half a cup left. She went into the kitchen with the article she was reading and put the mug in the microwave. The article—on human memory and its possible effects on conscious experience—was written by Alamo. It was dry and dense with neuroscience jargon. It could have been interesting, Tina thought, with some personal experience, some good examples. A good metaphor or two would have helped the article immensely. She took her mug out of the microwave when it dinged.

Mr. Robert came out of the bedroom and into the kitchen. "Good morning."

"Morning," Tina said cheerfully, glad for the interruption.

He started hot water for his morning cup of green tea. He filled a saucepan with water and plopped an egg into it. "What are you up to today?"

"Studying for a while. Then I thought I'd stop by Ma's, before I go to school. I've got to do some work for Professor Porter."

"Busy, huh? Another late night?"

"Don't know yet. I'm getting an introduction to our group's research projects, find out what I'm supposed to be doing to earn my living."

Mr. Robert scooped some cold rice from the rice cooker into a bowl, sprinkled a little water on it and put it into the microwave.

"How about you?" Tina asked.

"The usual. Lessons to teach. I'll probably stop by your mom's too. Later this afternoon."

"Okay." She took a sip of coffee. "Do you remember telling me about your *shodō* sensei?"

"Sure." He pulled two sheets of dried seaweed from a cellophane package. "What about him?"

"Well, I mentioned him in my research group. His problem is the kind that we study. People with brain damage and how it relates to language."

Mr. Robert poked at the egg, rolling it onto its other side, as the water began to boil. "What about him?"

"I'm wondering if he might agree to be part of our research."

"You mean like a guinea pig?"

"Well, I wouldn't say 'guinea pig.' Actually, I don't know if they even use guinea pigs in research anymore. Our research might help the sensei, and other people with his condition."

Mr. Robert took out the bowl of steaming rice from the microwave. "I suppose you could ask . . . if, as you say, it might help him. But how's he going to consent if he can't talk?"

"I suppose we can communicate in some other way."

"I don't know," Mr. Robert said. "You should probably talk to Gozen sensei, he's the senior instructor. He's taking care of the sensei."

Mr. Robert turned off the burner and carried the pan to the sink. He plucked the egg out of the pan, and cracked it open with a knife. He let the runny yolk and white flow over the rice, then used the knife to scrape out the cooked egg white. He drizzled soy sauce over the egg and rice. He sat down at the table with the bowl and a pile of seaweed squares. With chopsticks, he placed some of the rice onto a square, then dipped it into the egg yolk and soy sauce, and put it in his mouth.

Tina said, "Gozen sensei is his name?"

"I'll give you his phone number."

"Thanks."

If I stop asking someone suddenly will help me

TINA USED HER KEY to open the entry door to her mother's apartment building. She walked through the lobby with its two potted plants and two stuffed chairs, past the still-broken elevator, and up the five flights of stairs. She wondered if the stairs were good or bad for her mother.

"Hi, Ma," she called out when she walked in the apartment.

Hanako was in the kitchen, cleaning. The stove's burner grates were stacked on the counter near the sink, and the stovetop was sprinkled with cleanser. Hanako's hair was up in a rather fashionable ponytail; it made her look a few years younger, despite the gray.

"How are you feeling?"

"Not bad today, Ha-*chan*."

"Today? Was yesterday bad?"

"No. It was fine too. I'll make tea in a minute."

Her mother finished cleaning the stove and put on the water to boil. Tina sat and watched her mother, moving her well-practiced way about the kitchen. She could have made tea in her sleep.

Hanako dropped green tea leaves in the teapot. "How is school?"

"Fine. We learned how to use the MRI machine, you know, the one they use to get images of your insides."

"You going to look at insides, Ha-*chan*?" She touched the kettle with the palm of her hand, then poured the water into the teapot. She brought it to the table and sat down.

"Someday. Ma, have you been taking your medicine?"

Hanako nodded after a moment.

Tina didn't believe her. "Ma, I don't want to see you suffering."

Hanako got up, and said to the sink, "I'm okay."

"Then why do you have Mr. Robert do that *reiki* on you? Why do you have this look on your face like someone's stabbing you?"

Her mother didn't say anything. Tina turned her head and saw her mother shaking, her hands gripping the sink. Tina sprang to her side. "Are you okay?"

Tina put her arm around her mother's shoulders. She

could feel her trembling, as if her body were being shocked. "Ma? Do you want me to call the doctor?"

Hanako shook her head—two quick, robotlike jerks. Then her body let her go and she collapsed against her daughter. *"Gomen nasai,"* Hanako said. I'm sorry.

THROUGH THE OPEN WINDOW floated street noise of cars driving past the building and the distant wail of a fading siren. The pain that her body had shot through her legs, that had gripped her muscles in spasms, was also fading. Tina was sitting on the floor, gazing at her mother stretched out on the sofa. "You haven't been taking your medicine."

Hanako would never have spoken to her parents that way, as if they were the children. She never disagreed with her parents, never questioned their decisions. But Tina's persistent questioning didn't make her angry; instead, it deepened her sadness, her pain. She shook her head. "I don't like the medicines. They make me feel worse. What good is that, *neh*?"

"How do they make you feel?"

Hanako adjusted the pillow behind her. "They make me feel like I'm not me. *Wakarimasu ka*?" Understand?

"I think I do. But they're supposed to help you, Ma. Tell your doctor if they aren't working."

"He already told me. Side effects." She counted them off with her fingers: "Chills, aches, sweating, dry mouth, dizziness."

"Sure, there will be side effects," Tina said. "But the drugs help your body fight the disease. They reduce the symptoms. Look, why don't I get you to talk to Wijjie. He's a doctor and a student at the institute. He said he'd be glad to talk with you."

"I have a doctor."

"But . . . Look, Ma, I've got something that might help you."

"*Nani?*" What is it?

"It's a different kind of medicine." Tina opened the pocket of her backpack and found the joint. It had gotten slightly crumpled.

Hanako watched Tina straighten the joint. "I know what that is. The dishwashers smoke it, in the alley. I can smell it when I walk by the back door. Kiyomi calls them potheads." Hanako looked at Tina. "Are you a pothead?"

Tina laughed. "No, Ma, I'm not a pothead." She had smoked it a few times, maybe a dozen. One of her boyfriends had smoked it three or four times a week, but she'd never found the dazed feeling to be worth the effort. A good cup of coffee was all she needed. "It's for you." Tina put the joint on the coffee table.

"For me?"

"I was talking with Wijjie and some friends about MS, and one of them heard about an MS sufferer who smoked pot to help reduce the pain and the spasticity. With no side effects."

Hanako glanced at the joint, then out the window. "It's illegal."

"Don't you remember they had that vote a couple of years ago? You can buy it at a clinic."

Hanako looked at Tina. "Where did you get it?"

"I don't know if I should tell you that. Don't worry, though, I won't get into trouble."

"You better not."

"I won't."

They sat for a while, drinking tea. Tina checked her watch, she was already late for her meeting, but wanted to wait until Mr. Robert got there. "Ma, are you going to work today?"

"Of course." She had to work, she didn't like being alone with her thoughts. At work she could forget.

"You still haven't told Aunt Kiyomi?"

"No," Hanako whispered.

Just then, the buzzer rang, and Tina got up from the floor and walked to the front of the apartment. She pushed the entry buzzer, then went back to the sitting room with her mother. "Are you sure you're feeling better?"

"I'm much better," she said.

"Okay, well, I'll leave you with Mr. Robert. I need to go to school."

Hanako nodded. "Go. I'm fine."

"*Konnichiwa,*" Mr. Robert said as he came into the sitting room.

"*Konnichiwa,*" Hanako answered.

Tina said, "She's had a major attack."

"Are you okay?" he asked Hanako.

Hanako said, "It was just a little pain. I'll be fine. A little *reiki* and I'll be good as new."

"That's why I'm here," Mr. Robert said. He asked Tina, "Is that why you're still here? I thought you were going to be in Berkeley by now."

"I was just waiting for you. She really was in pain."

"All right. Just relax, Hanako-*san.*" He moved toward the coffee table to move it out of the way. "What's this?" He pointed to the joint.

"Oops," Tina said. "I forgot about it."

"A joint?"

Tina glanced at her mother, who was staring out the window. Tina said, "Wijjie—I told you about him—the doctor, said it works great for MS patients. Reduces pain and the spasticity."

"You were going to have your mother smoke a joint?"

Hanako said, "I wouldn't."

"But, Ma, how do you know unless you try it?" Tina said.

Mr. Robert said, "Giving your own mother a joint?"

"That's right," Tina said.

Mr. Robert closed his hand around it and left the room. A few seconds later, there was the sound of the toilet flushing.

BERKELEY

Zenzen sensei's darkness gradually lightened, a dawn that took ages in coming. The darkness had been a ghost, wrapping his mind in its essence, obliterating all light. A ghost who embraced his thoughts, oddly unfamiliar and familiar at the same time, and squeezed them until entangled, one on top of another, like a crowd that had been crushed in a stampede.

The ghost dragged him through a world he had no conception of, it was neither real nor unreal. Before . . . there was a before, he had a feeling about a before . . . a feeling that something had happened before the darkness. A feeling of something that was different from now, better. He tried to find his way back from wherever he was to wherever he had been, though he could not remember what that was.

If he could only get to the before, at least he might know what had happened, why all was darkness, why the phantoms had appeared. He tried to guide his thoughts to the before, to the place in his mind where the before existed. He did feel that it was a place, a physical place where the before would be found. A place where he could live, where the darkness didn't exist. A feeling that it would be that way when he found it.

Thoughts, like single photons of light, flickered: a woman's face, a mushy sweetness, a smile seen in close-up. Those thoughts were so elusive, quickly gone, evaporating in the embrace. The more he tried to focus on those thoughts, those comforting thoughts, the more quickly they dissipated in the inky darkness.

*Emerging
to
drowning*

TINA WAS LATE for her meeting with Howard. When she apologized, he said, "No problem," though he had an impatient scowl on his face.

She explained that her mother was ill.

"Nothing serious?"

"No," Tina said, not wanting to talk about it.

"Good." He began the tour by showing her the research filing system: data obtained from research subjects, binders full of brain scans, folders stuffed with statistical analyses, and reports in progress. He showed her the psychological testing labs where subjects could be videotaped as they performed experimental tasks. The lab room was wired for sound and video recording. A large computer monitor, for presenting visual stimuli, hung from the ceiling.

He showed her the computer lab and the printers, the supply cabinet, how to run the copy machine, and, lastly, the office that they would share with a couple other of Professor Porter's research assistants. Tina had a desk, a phone, a computer, two drawers of a four-drawer filing cabinet, and three shelves of a six-shelf bookcase.

Howard had to run to another meeting. Tina apologized again for being late. He waved it off and left her alone in the office.

Tina unzipped her backpack, putting her three books on one of the shelves and her class notes stacked up next to them. Sitting at her desk, she looked through the desk drawers and found bits of some former graduate student's life: paper clips, old bus and BART schedules, Bic pens, and an expired coupon for two dollars off a Panhandler's Pizza.

Tina cleaned out the rubbish, and wiped down the desktop with a paper towel moistened with some water from a bottle left on one of the book shelves. She wiped off the computer keyboard, then turned the computer on, and checked her e-mail. Nothing important.

She picked up the phone and listened to the dial tone. In her notebook, now comfortably placed on her desk, she found the number for Gozen and dialed it. "Hello, Gozen sensei?"

"Yes?"

"This is Tina Suzuki, a friend of Robert Smith. He said I could call to talk with you about Zenzen sensei."

There was a long pause before he said, "Yes?"

"I'm really sorry to hear about what happened. Anyway, I'm a Ph.D. student at Cal, studying the brain. Neuroscience. My professor and I are interested in talking with him about his illness."

Another, longer pause. "I'm not sure . . ."

Tina wanted to say, Okay. Never mind. "It's for research, we are interested in how the brain works, how the mind can form language. I understand the sensei is having trouble speaking and writing?"

"Yes, that is what I hear. You want to do research? I don't know."

"Maybe we could meet somewhere to talk?"

"Talk?"

"About Zenzen sensei."

Another pause. "Okay."

"Shall we meet somewhere easy for you?"

"Easy? Is the Zenzen school easy? It's near the campus."

"Perfect."

TINA RAPPED ON THE DOOR of the Zenzen School of Japanese Calligraphy. A small scroll of calligraphy that Tina couldn't read hung on the door. The Japanese man who opened the door was about Tina's height. He had a full, fleshy face, and was dressed in baggy jeans, loose sweater, and house slippers with white socks. "Gozen sensei?" she asked.

"Yes. Suzuki-*san*?"

"Please call me Tina." She took off her shoes and put on a pair of the slippers near the door. They walked into the first room on the left, where a few chairs were scattered around a couple of small tables. He gestured to one of the chairs where a tea service was already set.

"Tea," Tina said. "That's nice of you."

"It's nothing."

Tina sat down as he poured tea into the cups.

"How long have you been in the Zenzen school?"

His head cocked one way, then another. "About ten years now. I was a doctoral student in international economics. I started studying *shodô* with Zenzen sensei my first year here."

"Mr. . . . I mean Robert told me you are the senior instructor."

Gozen bowed his head a little and said, "I try my best."

Tina gave him a friendly smile for his traditional Japanese modesty. She gazed around the room. "What a friendly looking school."

"Thank you."

She turned her gaze to him. "I'm sorry about your sensei. He's still in the hospital?"

"Yes. He's in rehabilitation."

"I hope he recovers quickly," Tina said, though from what she remembered from her courses, severe stroke damage was always permanent. "Robert said that the sensei can't write? He can no longer do *shodô*?"

Gozen stared into his teacup. "That is the most painful news."

"Robert said the sensei makes drawings that might use some of the kanji radicals? Sorry, I don't know much about *shodô*."

Gozen turned and pointed to a framed work of calligraphy. "That kanji represents the *eiji happô*, the eight radicals."

Gozen got up and stood by the calligraphy. He pointed out the eight radicals.

"You're a good teacher," Tina said when he returned to his chair.

The *yaku* radical is one of the *eiji happô*. At the end of the vertical stroke, apply pressure to the brush. Quickly use the wrist to take the brush off the paper in the direction of the upper left corner. *Yaku* means "leap" or "dance." The last movement of the brush is indeed like the leap of a dancer.

Instructor's Journal,
Zenzen School of
Japanese Calligraphy

"Thank you."

Tina took a sip of her tea. She gave him another friendly smile. "Do you think the sensei would mind if we worked with him in our research?"

Gozen's eyes darted back and forth as if looking for an answer somewhere. "That is difficult. I cannot say. You could ask him, but I don't think he understands."

"I could try."

"I suppose you could try. Would your research help him?"

"I don't know that," she said. "I'm just starting to study."

Gozen turned his teacup several times. "I'll go to the hospital with you."

He drove them to the hospital. It took fifteen minutes from the campus, toward the Berkeley Hills and the Oakland-Berkeley city limits. He found a parking spot and they walked up to the hospital door. "I'll wait here, okay?" Gozen said.

"Okay."

"His name is Shimano. That's the name the hospital uses now."

Tina repeated the name, then walked into the hospital. She found a directory map that showed the location of the rehabilitation wing.

As she walked down the corridors, she wondered if Gozen didn't want to see his sensei in the hospital. He wouldn't be the same sensei who taught him *shodô*. Maybe he just didn't like hospitals.

In the rehabilitation wing, Tina asked the nurse at a workstation, "Could I see a patient named Shimano?"

"The sensei. You can visit, but he can't communicate."

"I heard that."

"And you are?"

"Tina Suzuki."

The nurse entered her name in the computer. "Room five-seventy-seven, down that hall to your right."

"Thanks." Tina walked down the corridor and found the room. She knocked lightly, then pushed open the door. The room was a typical hospital room: two beds, bedside tables, movable curtains, a TV on the other side of the room from the bed.

Only one of the beds was occupied; Tina walked quietly over to it. The Japanese man, lying on his left side, was covered with a blanket. His eyes were closed, his breathing regular. His face looked peaceful, his matted hair was almost completely white.

"Hello?" she said after a minute, her voice just above a whisper.

His forehead—broad and strong—wrinkled slightly before his eyes fluttered open for a moment, then closed again. His head moved slightly.

Tina watched him as his brow furrowed deeply, his eyes fluttering again, as if he were having a bad dream. His eyelids opened slowly, his eyes unfocused, dull, as if he were still asleep—or unconscious—and his eyes open but unseeing, as if his vision were focused backward, into his mind.

"Hello?" Tina said again.

The sensei's eyes seemed to turn to her, at least to the sound of her voice, but only for half a second. His eyes closed again, then opened, and he looked at Tina.

"Sensei?"

His mouth opened a little, and a breath of stagnant air came out but no sound. His mouth closed again, then opened. His eyes rolled down, as if he were looking at his own mouth. A small drop of saliva appeared from the corner of his mouth. Tina took one of the tissues from a box on the bedside table and wiped it away. His eyes blinked at the touch, then closed.

The door opened and a doctor came into the room. He had to stoop a bit to fit through the doorway. The top of his head was bald, as if he had scraped off his hair on countless doorframes.

"Relative?" the doctor said, as he studied the sensei's file.

"Friend of a friend." She glanced at the sensei, his eyes were still closed. "Actually, I'm a graduate student, at Cal. In neuroscience."

"Neuroscience, eh? Ph.D.?"

"Yes."

He stepped forward. "Dr. Geoffry," he said, extending his hand of long, bony fingers.

"Tina Suzuki." She shook his hand.

"Any particular emphasis?" he asked.

"Pardon?"

"In neuro," he said. "Studying anything in particular?"

"I'm working with Dr. Porter. Language."

One of his eyebrows raised. "Really. Aphasia?"

"Yes. Our research group is looking into functional language areas of the brain."

The doctor pulled a piece of paper from the folder and showed it to her. "Make any sense of that?"

On the piece of paper were several markings in black ink, made with a marking pen. The marks looked something like kanji, similar kinds of strokes, but she recognized none of them. "I don't know. I can see some elements that might belong to Japanese characters, but I'm no expert. I can only read a few. If I can borrow the paper, I could ask someone who knows."

The doctor handed it to her. "Sure." He leaned over the sensei. "Hello."

Zenzen's eyes opened. The doctor took out a penlight and shined it into Zenzen sensei's eyes, back and forth. The sensei's eyes blinked, but didn't follow the light.

"What's his condition?" Tina asked.

"He had a hemorrhagic stroke in the left lobe, with some damage to the prefrontal area as well. He was stabilized well in the emergency room, the brain swelling reduced. He was lucky that he got here when he did, just minutes after the hemorrhage. They were able to reduce the ischemic cascade, limit the area of the infarct, using drugs and cooling."

He glanced at Tina to see if she was following. She nodded at him to go on.

He flipped through the pages in the file and said, "However, the damage was extensive." His fingers dipped into the file and extracted a film image. "Yes, extensive damage." He handed it to her.

Tina studied the image. With its black-and-white blobs, she recognized a coronal section of the brain. Where the normal tissue would have shown as light gray, large portions of the left hemisphere were black.

Tina looked from the image to the sensei, his eyes focused on her now, though his face was expressionless. She kneeled near him; his eyes followed her. "Sensei?"

His focus dissolved, and his eyes closed.

There were no words, only feelings. There was a sharp pain, a whizzing feeling that ached. The pain became a dark hole that he would sink into and be devoured, as if all had abandoned him.

For a brief moment that extended forever, there was a stronger feeling, a feeling of longing. A face appeared, so familiar, so tortuously unfamiliar. The face was there in front of him, and he could only stare at it. He could not move toward it, or express the feelings that were of so many kinds he could no longer separate them. The feeling was now of knowing that he knew, and that he had to express the feelings or his life would end.

Then the face was gone, the darkness overtook everything, except a humming. The sound of distant feelings.

Speak to me
kindly
lovely
no hiding
of feeling

TINA FOUND GOZEN in the front of the hospital, sitting on a bench. He stood when she approached. "Sorry that took so long."

He shook his head. "There's no need to apologize."

"The doctor came into the sensei's room and we talked for a long time."

"What did he say?"

"Maybe we should go somewhere to talk. Do you have time?"

"Yes. I have time."

Tina looked around the neighborhood of medical offices and pharmacies. "I don't know where to go around here."

"Would you like to eat something?"

"Actually, I haven't eaten since breakfast."

"I can drive to a place nearby. It's not bad."

"Not bad is fine."

They got in the car and Gozen drove them to a small café only a couple of minutes from the hospital. The café served soup and sandwiches. They sat at one of the tables near the window. Only a few other customers were eating in the late afternoon. The tables were dressed with red-checked cloths. Tina ordered a half veggie sandwich, a cup of cream of mushroom soup, and iced tea to drink. Gozen ordered the same.

After the server had taken their order and brought their tea, Tina said, "The doctor told me that the sensei has suffered extensive damage, particularly to areas of his brain that help produce and understand language. This area." She touched the left side of her head.

"Will he get better?"

"They don't know the full extent of the damage. They want to do some more tests. Some of his condition—his inability to speak or write, or even understand someone talking to him—may be temporary. There's been some swelling in his brain, a natural reaction to the stroke caused by a burst blood vessel. When the swelling goes down, there may be some improvement."

Gozen was gazing at the table, with one ear turned slightly toward her, as if he were listening intently. After a moment, he gave a quick nod, then said, "But he may not improve."

Tina explained she didn't know, but had heard that with rehabilitation, the neural pathways might reestablish themselves, allowing some return of function. Still, she warned him, it was unlikely that he would have a full recovery.

The server brought large plates—one side held the veggie sandwich, bulging with roasted red pepper, red onion, green leaf lettuce, the other side held the sturdy bowl of creamy soup. "Enjoy," the server said. "I'll be back with more tea in a moment."

Tina tried a spoonful of soup. "Delicious," she said. Gozen looked relieved.

Tina put down her spoon and reached into her backpack.

She took out the piece of paper the doctor had given her. "The sensei drew this."

Gozen's gaze moved across the piece of notepaper, his brow furrowing deeply. "That can't be something the sensei did."

"Some of it looks like kanji, maybe kana, but I only learned a little."

Gozen picked up the paper and studied it, briefly turning it upside down. "They are in Zenzen sensei's style, although not very strong. They don't form kanji or kana." He turned the paper around on the table and pointed to a piece of the drawing. "This is part of the kanji for water. Could I borrow a pen?"

Tina took out a pen from her backpack and handed it to him. He drew the kanji for "water" on his napkin. "This is *mizu*, water. The drawing has part of this kanji"—he traced the strokes—"but there is no character that looks like what he drew."

"I see," Tina said. "Do you think he is trying to communicate something, but can't remember the complete characters?"

Gozen sucked a breath of air through his teeth. "I don't know. I can't see any meaning in his drawings. They are all mixed up like . . . scribbles. Is that the word?"

"Doodles?"

"Doodles."

"You said that the strokes looked like they were in the sensei's style, only weaker? In what ways are they weaker?"

Gozen pointed to the stroke he had mentioned. "Here his pen moved around like his mind was unsettled. In *shodô*, we have a word, *byôhitsu*, it means 'sick strokes.' " Gozen drew the kanji on the napkin. "You can tell when a person is ill or his mind is not focused on the task by the quality of the brushstrokes. They can show a person's spiritual and

病
筆

The first character—*byô*—is made of the characters representing a person on a bed, which represents "sickness." The character is derived from the ideogram originally meaning "big altar." This meaning could refer to "big" or "crippling" or "fatal." The feeling of the strokes

mental state. Sensei would say that calligraphy is a picture of a person's mind."

Tina studied the sensei's drawings. "So you would say that these drawings are *byôhitsu*?"

"Very *byôhitsu*."

"Interesting," Tina said. She wrote down the word and copied the kanji in her notebook.

TINA WAS IN Professor Porter's office on the second floor, east wing, of the institute, watching her sign a form that Tina needed for the financial aid office. When she finished, Tina said, "I saw the calligraphy teacher, the one who had the stroke." She showed the professor the sensei's drawings and explained what Gozen sensei had told her.

"Classic signs of agraphia." Professor Porter got up from her desk and went to the white board on the wall. On the board were a few scrawled notes ("ANS Conference, October 30 *deadline*!!" "Rewrite JN article!") and a quick sketch of some neuronal pathway that Tina didn't recognize. Along the pathway a large *X* had been drawn.

Professor Porter uncapped a black marker and drew a few strokes on the board. One looked like part of an *f* without the crossbar, another looked like part of an *a*. "What happens with agraphic patients is that they can no longer write complete letters of the alphabet. Their brain injuries have interrupted the pathways that allow them to remember the ordering of the pieces of the letters. It would be interesting, very interesting, to study this condition in a Japanese calligraphy teacher. We could make some very important findings. Cross-cultural research is all the rage, too. This could be great, great. Did he agree to be a research subject?"

"He can't speak. I don't know if he can even understand what anyone says to him."

should be big, so as to not let the illness overpower the spirit of the afflicted person.

The second character— *hitsu*—combines "bamboo" and "brush in hand." Bamboo brushes were often used for writing, though rarely for calligraphy. Still, the bamboo brush imparts a certain rustic feel, as described by the aesthetic term *wabi-sabi*.

Instructor's Journal, Zenzen School of Japanese Calligraphy

"We have to get permission. Did you talk to his doctor?" Professor Porter capped the marker and returned to her desk.

"He did stop by, but he didn't think the sensei would be able to communicate soon."

"Maybe I should talk with him. We might be able to get permission from a family member."

"Let me try again," Tina said. "The doctor did say that as the swelling goes down, some function might return."

"That's true. All right. Stay on it," the professor said in rapid-fire staccato.

GOZEN SENSEI HELD the Daizen Inkstone under the light. The inkstone glittered when the light hit it at a certain angle. He took the inkstone into the Zenzen sensei's studio and gently placed it on the low table. Opening the supply drawer, he found an unused inkstick. He unwrapped the top of the ink-stick, and put it on the table.

From a small flask, he dribbled several drops of water into the inkstone. Hesitating for a moment, wondering if he should continue, he dipped the end of the inkstick into the water and began to grind it slowly. The black ink came off easily, and the water turned instantly black, as if the inkstone were hungry.

When the ink was the darkest shade of black, Gozen admired the pool. He placed a piece of highest-grade rice paper—its smooth surface would allow the brush to glide effortlessly—onto the table and arranged the paperweight to hold it steady. He selected a brush from an ancient shop in Japan, handmade to Zenzen sensei's exacting specifications.

Gozen dipped the brush into the pool until the bottom third of the tip was moistened. He positioned the brush above the paper and, in a controlled flurry of movement, placed the ink on the paper. He had chosen the characters for *hô* ("treasure"), and when they were complete, his heart was pounding. Never had he performed so well; never had his calligraphy been so alive. Rivaling the best work of his sensei, it was too near perfection for him to contemplate.

He quickly cleaned the inkstone and put it back in its box. Opening the drawer to replace the box, he noticed the old envelope. He set the box in the drawer and took the envelope out. The brittle tape detached easily from the envelope when he slid his finger under it. Inside was a letter dated June 10, 1977, from Kando Investigative Services, in Kyoto, and addressed to the Chief Instructor of the Daizen School of Calligraphy. The report detailed the activities of the investigator in locating a woman named Hanako Suzuki. He found that she lived in San Francisco. Her apartment address was given, as well as her place of employment: the Tempura House restaurant on Powell Street.

Gozen took the report into the studio, where he copied the name and address of the investigator, and the woman's name and address. After he returned the report to the drawer next to the inkstone, he began to compose a letter to the private investigator.

Hô combines the characters for "roof," meaning "building," and "jewel." The combination refers to a "place for precious things," which eventually became "precious things," or "treasure." The strokes should have a solid and humble, not boisterous, quality. Use *nijimi* strokes—wetter strokes that bleed around the edges.

Instructor's Journal, Zenzen School of Japanese Calligraphy

INTERLUDE

Kando Investigative Services

JUNE 1977
KYOTO, JAPAN

Kando thought he was about the same age as the sensei, maybe a couple of years older. In contrast to his crisply pressed white shirt and professionally knotted tie, the sensei was dressed in a rumpled gray shirt and black slacks that had lost any trace of a crease.

Kando knew the sensei's trouble would be a woman. There would have been an affair; no doubt she was married. "How may I be of service?" he asked.

"A student of mine has disappeared."

"Disappeared?"

Kando watched the sensei measure his words. Another sign of an affair: the sensei was deciding how to describe his indiscretion. "She had been coming regularly to lessons, three times a week, for a year and a half. Then she stopped."

The sensei gazed absently at the framed license on the wall behind the investigator. "One day she missed her lesson. It was the first time she had missed. She didn't call. And then she missed the next lesson, too."

"When was this?"

Daizen sensei drew himself up from his slightly slouched posture. His bearing changed immensely when he did; he became sensei-like. "Four weeks ago."

"You tried to contact her, I assume."

"Not at first. Not for a week."

Kando imagined the sensei's long week, jumping whenever the phone rang, his hopes dashed when it wasn't her.

"Then I called her house, but there was no answer." The sensei turned his head slightly, as if listening to the phone ring and ring.

"All right. I will have to know her name, where she lives."

"Her name is Hanako Suzuki. She lives in Kobe, although she was born in Osaka. I don't know her family name—Suzuki is her married name. Her husband is Tetsuo Suzuki." The sensei gave Kando a cold stare.

The investigator couldn't help raising an eyebrow. "*The* Tetsuo Suzuki?"

"Yes."

That would make the job both easy and difficult for

Kando. Tracing the movements of someone that high-profile would be relatively easy. But someone of Tetsuo Suzuki's influence could make life miserable for an investigator caught poking around his private life. People like Suzuki were sensitive about their private lives.

Kando had criteria for accepting or rejecting a job, the likelihood of success being the most critical. In this case, success would be measured as finding the woman without being discovered. A tricky proposition. Challenging. That made the job seem worthwhile.

"Yes, I will try to help you," Kando said.

KANDO SPENT THE FIRST DAY and a half investigating his new client. That was his rule (never expressed to the clients, of course) that he applied whenever a male client wanted information about a woman—especially the woman's whereabouts—who was not related by blood to the client. The investigator did not want a murder-suicide or other crime of passion on his conscience.

Kiichi Shimano was born in the western Japanese city of Fukuoka, to parents who owned a small insurance company. This business was purchased by a larger company in the late 1950s, and the Shimanos were employed to manage their old company as a branch office, which they were still doing. The younger Shimano graduated from one of the public junior high schools in about the middle of his class. He did not excel in math or science, but did well in the visual and language arts. His parents, having the financial resources, sent him to high school in Kyoto to the prestigious Arts High School. Three months after he arrived in Kyoto, he began to study calligraphy at the Daizen school.

Shimano's rise in the school was quick. Two years after he graduated from high school, he became a junior instructor, an unprecedented age for an instructor at the Daizen school. He progressed steadily up Daizen's instructor ranks, until the death of the twenty-eighth Daizen sensei, when Shimano attained the highest rank.

Shimano had married when he was twenty-nine, six years ago, to Yuriko Taniguchi. Her father had been a bureaucrat in the city tax office until his retirement two years ago. Her mother was the daughter of a cousin of the twenty-eighth Daizen sensei. Kando couldn't determine if that marriage had anything to do with Shimano's rise in the school, though it was likely how they met. The Daizen school was different from traditional Japanese arts schools; almost all used the *iemoto* system of passing the school to the oldest son. The Daizen school was held in trust, and was listed as a nonprofit corporation. The school's affairs were managed by the head sensei and a committee of the senior instructors.

By all accounts, Shimano and his wife were happily married—no one Kando managed to talk to could recall an incident of discord. There was no indication of a previous affair. Other than the fact they were childless (no one knew if that was a choice or if there was a problem), they seemed a quietly unremarkable couple. The sensei had no police record, in either Fukuoka or Kyoto; there was not even a hint of past trouble with women. His credit rating was superb and, though not wealthy, he made a comfortable living.

Kando knew that those were the signs of a man very likely to have a destructive affair: a life of early success now settling into a wretchedly numbing existence. Still, Kando saw nothing that would give him any worry. The woman probably had a change of heart about the affair and wanted to end it without the difficulty of telling him. She might still be at home.

IN KOBE, Kando drove slowly past the home of Tetsuo and Hanako Suzuki, then turned around and parked. After watching for several minutes and not seeing any movement, he eased out of his car and walked up to the house. An elegant stone wall surrounded the house, setting it off from its neighbors. To the side of the entrance gate—it was locked—was a button above an intercom speaker. Kando pushed the buzzer once, and again after a few seconds. He peered through a small opening in the gate, but couldn't see anything except a slice of the entry garden.

He got back in his car and drove to the nearby shopping area he had seen on his way up to the house. He parked again and walked into a small grocery store of just two aisles. Up at the counter, he showed the proprietors—a late-middle-aged couple—a picture of his sister, who was about Hanako Suzuki's age: "I'm looking for this woman."

They both leaned forward slightly and stared at the photo. "No, sorry. I've never seen her," the woman said. Her husband shook his head.

"Thanks, anyway," Kando said. He turned to leave, then stopped. "By the way, this is the third woman I've heard of who has gone missing from around here."

"Third?" the woman said. "I haven't heard of any missing women."

"Yeah. Why haven't the police said anything?" her husband demanded.

"They don't want to alarm anyone unnecessarily," Kando said. "You haven't had any regular customers that you haven't seen for a while, have you?"

"There's that Suzuki woman," the man said.

His wife shot him a quick glance. "Not her. Don't you remember, she's on vacation. She told me, the last time I saw her."

"Nothing to worry about then," Kando said. "These disappearances happened months ago. If you saw her just recently . . ." Kando gazed softly at the woman.

"Well, it was over a month ago. Do you think . . . ?"

"A month? No, probably no connection. Still, it's a long vacation. She must have gone abroad?"

The woman said, "I think she did say she was going for a long time. We used to stock special foods for her. Crab from Hokkaido, some imported items. She said we didn't need to worry about ordering those things."

Kando nodded. "A very responsible person." He showed them the picture of his sister again. "I don't think she is the same kind of person."

The two grocers nodded as if they understood what he meant.

KANDO STOPPED TO EAT his lunch at a restaurant in Kobe that his journalist friend had told him about. It served only the best seasonal fish and vegetables, cooked in a new-Kansai style that had adopted French techniques to Japanese tastes. At least that was what his friend—who thought of himself as an amateur food critic—claimed. His friend kept extensive records of his visits to restaurants. He had developed his own ranking system that he said was more accurate than Michelin's.

The food was excellent, a little expensive for lunch— considering he usually downed a quick bowl of ramen noodles at a stand near his office. His friend would be happy when Kando confirmed his assessment of the restaurant.

Going to the Suzukis' neighborhood and up to their home had been only a small risk. It was probable that a neighbor or two had seen him, but Kando doubted that they would tell Tetsuo Suzuki what they had seen. It seemed unlikely that a man of Suzuki's stature and duties would be the type to spend much time chatting with the neighbors. And he definitely wouldn't be going down to the neighborhood grocery store to pick up some fresh fish and vegetables to throw together a dinner.

Actually, it was likely that Tetsuo Suzuki was no longer living in the house. Without his wife to take care of it (and him), he had probably moved somewhere more convenient. Where would Hanako have gone? For a long time, the grocer had said.

HIS FIRST GUESS was that she had moved back to her parents' home. Finding her name before she married would have been a simple matter of checking public records, but with the wife of a man as well known as Tetsuo Suzuki, it was even simpler (and safer) to call his same journalist friend who remembered other people's names better than they could remember their own. Iida—it turned out to be. Kando gave his friend a good report about the Kobe restaurant.

In Osaka, a forty-minute drive from Kyoto, Kando drove past the Iida home, allowing himself a quick glance at the large, well-maintained, traditional home with dark cedar siding and deep blue roof tiles. He wouldn't mind living in a house like that. His house was old, small, and maintained only as well as he had time and money for. He parked a few hundred feet from the house, across from a neighborhood liquor store. Hanako's parents would likely shop there. Kando went inside and selected a modest bottle of *sake*. "It's nice to be back in the old neighborhood," he said.

The proprietor, an elderly woman, squinted at him.

"I lived near here many years ago."

She gave him a good look. "You do look familiar."

"Thank you, but I doubt it. I'm a lot older."

"Not me." She cackled.

"Say, I think I used to know the Iida family up the street. Had a daughter, Hanako."

She handed him his change. "Yes, Hanako. Married now. Married well, too. You're too late."

"She still live around here?"

"No . . . Kobe, I think I heard . . . I haven't seen her since she got married. Except last New Year."

"Really. Not recently, huh? I would like to congratulate her."

"Haven't seen her recently." She handed him his bottle wrapped in purple crepe paper. "You better buy her something better than this *sake.*"

"I will, thank you."

IT TOOK ALMOST a full day of calling to find the Suzukis' travel agent. Claiming to be a representative of Japan Airlines, Kando said a maintenance worker had found some personal items belonging to Hanako Suzuki. He was still trying to contact her, and needed her flight number and day that she flew for the paperwork. "Okay," the agent said after Kando had been on hold for five minutes. "That would be Flight O-one, to San Francisco, one-way, on April 30."

"Thank you."

"You're welcome."

BERKELEY

The institute's branch library was the size of a large dining room and living room combined. At a sturdy old library table, Tina was reading for Professor Alamo's class.

Wijjie came into the library and looked over her shoulder. "Looks like Alamo's class. I'm hungry, how about something to eat."

Tina looked at her watch. "How about a Japanese restaurant in the City? Where my mom works. Maybe you can talk to her. I didn't have much luck on my own."

"Nothing I'd rather do."

They took off for the BART station, through the crowds of students, downtown Berkeley workers, and the panhandlers. Wijjie dropped a few coins in one woman's cup, her "Thank you" barely interrupting her chant of "Spare any change, spare any change."

They found a seat together on the train. The upholstery covering the seat in front of them had been slashed, and the window etched with glass cutters.

Wijjie said, "This'll be fun. I've only been to the City a couple of times since I moved here."

Tina leaned against the wall of the train so she could turn to face him. "Why did you decide to come to graduate school?"

He stared out the window as the train rolled into a station. "Long story. I guess I wasn't cut out to be a doctor."

At the next station, a few people got off, a few got on. A man clutching a briefcase ran down the escalator waving at the operator to hold the train, but the doors closed and the train started rolling. The man cursed and raised his middle finger.

"I guess I couldn't see myself being responsible," Wijjie said.

"Responsible?"

"For someone's life or death." Wijjie sat back in the seat and slumped down, putting one leg on top of the other. "Sooner or later I would screw up. All doctors make mistakes, the odds are too great."

"Medicine isn't an exact science."

Wijjie stared at his foot bouncing in time to the rumbling and screeching as the train turned on a bend. "Sure. I just couldn't live with someone checking out on me because I missed a diagnosis, or prescribed the wrong drug."

THEY ARRIVED in the City a little after seven, and decided to have a drink before dinner. They stopped at the Gold Rush Saloon on Powell, found a table near the window, and ordered Anchor Steam beer.

"It's kind of touristy," Tina said, watching Wijjie look around at the Gold Rush motif: gold pans, miners' axes, assay scales.

When the beer arrived, Wijjie gulped while Tina took a sip.

"What about you?" Wijjie asked. "Why grad school?"

"I couldn't get into med school."

"You tried?"

"Just kidding. I didn't want to go to med school."

"Something wrong with med school?"

Tina pushed a bead of condensation down the beer bottle. "I'm just interested in the brain. The mind. I just want to know how it works."

Wijjie nodded. "Must have been wild growing up in a city like San Francisco."

Tina smirked. "Wouldn't say it was wild."

"But look at all the things you can do here."

"I suppose. But I didn't explore too much, just the few blocks around the neighborhood, really. And Japantown."

"No Japantown in the little town in southern Colorado where I grew up. No Chinatown. No Little Italy. No Mission District. There were mostly white folks, a few of us Latinos. When we got a Seven-Eleven, the town thought we had made the big time. I was about ten, and used to hang there for hours with my friends."

Tina said, "I had the Rats Market."

"Rats Market?"

"It was actually called the Star Market. Just down the block from our building."

"Rats, I get it. 'Star' spelled backward."

Tina took a sip of beer. "They had this bin of potatoes, I guess they didn't sell many because they started sprouting, you know, purple and green shoots growing out of the eyes. I used to stop in every day to see how long they had grown overnight."

"How long did they get?"

"I don't remember, probably down to the floor. Kind of reminds me of neurons, sprouting new dendrites and synapses, now that I think about it."

Wijjie smiled through his beer glass as he took a drink.

"What a glamorous childhood, huh?"

Wijjie shrugged. "I guess it's all relative."

BY THE TIME they got to the Tempura House, about nine, the dinner crowd had already thinned to four or five tables. From the back of the restaurant, Kiyomi saw Tina and Wijjie and hurried over to them.

"Aunt Kiyomi," Tina said. "This is William Cruz, one of the students in school with me."

Kiyomi gave him a smile and shook his hand. "I've known Hana since she was one day old."

"Really . . . I bet she was cute."

"Very cute." Kiyomi patted Tina on her head. "Did you come to see your mother or to eat?"

"Both."

"Then how about that nice table over there." Kiyomi pointed to a corner table on the upper section. "Nice and private."

"Perfect," Tina said.

As she led them to the table, Tina asked, "Busy night?"

"A little slow. But that's okay, I love a slow night every once in a while."

When they sat down, Kiyomi said, "Would you like something to drink?"

Dendrites: the slender, limblike branches of a neuron that receive activation through synapses of other neurons. Dendrites can grow or shrink throughout the life of the neuron, making new connections or abandoning ones that are no longer needed.

Neuroscience Notebook, Christina Hana Suzuki

121

Tina turned to Wijjie. "Should we split a large beer?"

"Okay by me."

"Large Sapporo, please," Tina told Kiyomi.

Kiyomi nodded. "I'll tell Hanako."

When Kiyomi left their table, Wijjie asked Tina, "Why did your aunt call you Hana?"

"That's my middle name. It means 'flower' in Japanese. My mom's name means 'little flower.' She and Aunt Kiyomi have always called me that."

"You prefer Tina, I take it."

"Please. How would you like to be called 'flower'?"

"Better than Wijjie."

"I'm sorry. You don't like Wijjie?"

"Just kidding. I do."

Hanako came from out of the back of the restaurant, carrying a tray with a large bottle and two glasses.

"Ma," Tina said, "this is Dr. William Cruz, Wijjie. Remember I told you about him? This is my mother, Hanako."

Hanako bowed her head. *"Hajimemashite."*

Tina said, "That means she's pleased to meet you."

"Nice to meet you too."

Hanako put the bottle and small beer glasses on the table. "Do you like fish, Dr. Cruz? We have fresh sea bass."

Tina leaned toward him and said, "I usually just leave my order up to the chef."

"Absolutely. Bring on the sea bass."

Hanako nodded. "Okay." She held back the sleeve of her kimono to keep it off their table, and poured their glasses full of beer. She gave Tina a brief, questioning glance. Tina gave her a casual smile meant to convey "He's just a friend."

Watching her walk toward the kitchen, Wijjie said, "She seems to be doing pretty well."

"She does better here than at home."

"The physical and mental activity is good for her." Wijjie took a sip of beer.

Hanako brought them bowls of miso soup and *tsukemono* pickled cabbage. Tina asked her for tea and water. Hanako nodded while she refilled their beer glasses.

"Thanks," Wijjie said. Hanako smiled and left to take an order at another table. Tina drank some of the tea her mother brought in the mugs.

"What about your father?" Wijjie asked as he stirred his soup with the tips of his chopsticks. "Does he work here too?"

"Actually, I never knew him."

"Oops. Sorry."

"No problem." When she was growing up, there were so many kids with single parents, gay parents, divorced and re-married parents, no parents, that no one considered her situation odd. When she realized that her mother might not ever tell her about her father, she stopped caring if she ever knew. Tina had thought her mother was waiting for some opportune time: maybe when she turned a teenager, maybe when she was in high school, maybe when she graduated from high school. All of those milestones had come and gone without a word.

Tina asked Wijjie, "You get along with your parents?"

"Great. Now that I'm far away."

"What's up?"

"The usual parent-child crap. They have no clue about why I'm going to school again. 'Not enough initials behind your name?' That's what Dad said when I told him."

Hanako came by and cleared their soup bowls and plates.

"That was great soup," Wijjie said.

"You like miso soup?" Hanako asked.

"It's delicious."

"It's good for you, too," Hanako said. "Your dinner will be right here." She left with their dishes.

"What's it like being one of Alamo's students?" Tina asked.

"That's hard to say so far. He's a bit reclusive, but when he's there, he's there. If you know what I mean."

"He's focused?"

"Intense. As if everything mattered to the nth degree. He's like a chess master, he can see ahead several moves in the game. You bring up a point, like a proposed research study, and his mind is already way ahead of you and he'll tell you what will likely happen. He's brilliant, but has zero social skills."

"I guess brilliant is all that matters." After a pause, Tina said, "I've got a question for you."

"Shoot."

"I've been working with a *shodô* sensei, a Japanese calligraphy teacher, who had a hemorrhagic stroke. A lot of damage to the temporal lobe. The interesting thing is that he can no longer put together the elements of a Japanese character word, like this would be 'water.'" Tina dipped her finger in the water glass and drew the kanji character on the table. "He seems to be able to draw only one stroke of this character. Or puts them in the wrong order. Professor Porter says it's called agraphia."

Wijjie nodded. "Heard of it, a kind of aphasia. I never had any experience with it, though."

"I'd like to know if he will ever recover his ability to put them back together the right way."

Wijjie shook his head. "With the severe damage you described? Doubt it. There may be some improvement, but he'll never fully regain his prestroke abilities."

Tina sat back as their dinners arrived. Kiyomi helped Hanako with the tray of dishes. Hanako announced, "Sea

Bass Three Ways." Kiyomi pointed to one of the dishes. "I love this one: sea bass with ginger sauce. Of course, the sea bass *sashimi* is excellent too."

Tina asked Wijjie, "Do you like raw fish?"

"As long as it's still wiggling."

Hanako laughed. Then she grimaced just as she was placing the dish in front of Wijjie. It dropped hard on the table, clattered against the bottle of beer and toppled it. Wijjie caught it before it fell over.

"Ma, are you okay?"

Hanako tried to smile, but a grimace of pain overtook it. She took a faltering step back, then seemed to fall so slowly, as if attached to a string that was letting her down gently. Wijjie was quickly out of his seat, holding her with one hand under her arm and one hand around her waist. Tina got up and held her from the other side. *"Gomen nasai,"* Hanako said.

Kiyomi said, "Hanako, what's wrong?"

Tina said, "Let's take her to the office."

While the small crowd of diners watched, they helped Hanako toward the back of the restaurant. In the manager's office, she sat in the chair. Wijjie squatted down and asked her, "Are you having spasms in your legs?"

Her face winced, eyes shut tightly, lips pressed together so tightly they were white.

Kiyomi whispered to Tina, "Do you know what's wrong?"

Tina looked at her mother as Wijjie talked to her. She whispered to Kiyomi, "She has MS, multiple sclerosis. She's known since early this year."

Kiyomi looked surprised, then confused. "She never told me. She just said she was getting old. It's bad?"

Hanako moaned a tiny little noise. Tina squatted next to her.

Wijjie asked Hanako, "Do you have some medicine? Did the doctor give you something for this?"

Hanako nodded. "It's at home."

"Let's take her home," Wijjie said. "Where does she live?"

"Not too far. Just a couple of blocks, but I don't think she can walk."

Wijjie said, "No, I don't think she can."

Hanako said, "I can walk . . . in a minute."

"I didn't know," Kiyomi said. One of her hands was in front of her mouth, the other reaching toward Hanako.

Wijjie said, "I can run and get the medicine."

Tina said, "I'll go." Tina patted her mom's arm. "Where are the pills?"

"Chopstick drawer."

Tina walked quickly through the restaurant and out the door. She turned left, and as she ran up steep Powell Street, she thought of the times as a kid when she would run home from the Tempura House, after seeing her mother before the dinner rush started. She would watch the chef, who wore a white headband, mixing tempura batter. He'd make a small bowl of batter with sugar in it, coat a sliver of cantaloupe or whole strawberry with the batter, and put it in the fryer. After a minute or two, he'd fish it out, blow on it to cool it, then sprinkle it with powdered sugar. "Yummy," she'd say, and the chef would laugh and repeat, "Yummy."

Tina turned left on Bush Street; its gentle slope let her run faster. She sprinted past the Nob Hill Theater, the Sushi Man restaurant, the Rats Market, then into the apartment building.

She bounded up the stairway, slowing at the third floor when her lungs and legs were burning. She had to walk the last two floors. On the fifth floor, she ran into the apartment, into the kitchen, and found the bottles of pills in the kitchen cabinet. They seemed to be full. Tina opened them—it looked as if she hadn't taken any of them.

Tina ran out of the apartment clutching the bottles of pills. At least it was all downhill back to the Tempura House.

HER MOTHER WAS STILL SITTING DOWN, but looking better when Tina came in. "Here." She handed the bottles to Wijjie. "I don't know which ones are which."

Wijjie glanced at the labels. "Zanaflex. This one." He unscrewed the top. Kiyomi brought in a glass of water.

Hanako took the pill and swallowed it with water.

Tina said, "I've never seen her take so much as an aspirin."

Wijjie said, "It will take about twenty minutes to have any effect."

Tina sat in a chair and asked Wijjie, "Would smoking marijuana work faster?"

"I've never seen it used, but I've heard it works almost instantly."

They waited in the manager's office until Hanako was feeling better. She wanted to stay and finish working, but Kiyomi told her to take the rest of the night off. Kiyomi had put Tina and Wijjie's dinners, and an extra serving for Hanako, in "to go" boxes and plastic bags. Tina carried the bags while Wijjie kept his hands free to help Hanako in case she had another attack.

In the apartment building, they took the stairs slowly. "I'm going to complain to the manager about that elevator," Tina said.

"Don't do that," Hanako said.

"Why not?"

"It's not his fault."

On the fifth floor, they entered Hanako's apartment. Tina took the boxed dinners into the kitchen while Wijjie went with Hanako into the sitting room. Tina opened the boxes and arranged the food on plates. She brought them into the sitting room, putting the plates onto the low table. They sat on the floor around the table.

Hanako took a bite. "Sorry, the sea bass is no longer wiggling."

"It's delicious," Wijjie said after taking a bite. "The freshest fish I've ever had."

Hanako stood up. "I'm sorry, I'm not very hungry." She picked up her plate and went into the kitchen.

Tina gave Wijjie an apologetic smile.

TINA SAID GOOD-BYE to Wijjie outside the apartment. "Thanks for helping."

"I almost forgot to tell you in the excitement. I'm having a little party tomorrow night for us first-years. Gillian said she'd make it. A few others."

"Sounds like fun. I'll try to be there."

"Good." He looked toward the stairs. "I better get to BART." He turned back to her and opened his arms. Tina hugged him and started to pull away. He gently pulled her toward him and they kissed quickly. With his hand resting on the small of her back, they kissed again, this time much longer.

"Sorry about that," Wijjie said when he leaned back. "It must be the sea bass. Always affects me that way."

"Have sea bass anytime."

THE PHONE RANG at seven the next morning. Tina opened her eyes and shifted on the sofa in her mother's apartment. She sat up, thinking that she was late for school when she realized it was Friday and she had no classes. The phone was silent after the second ring. Tina got up, straightened her T-shirt, and pulled on her jeans.

The door to her mother's bedroom opened. "Ha-*chan*? Are you still here?"

"Yes." Tina walked to her mother's room.

"It's Robert-*san*."

"Could you tell him I'm on my way home?"

Hanako looked at her daughter, then pointed to the phone in her room. "You tell him."

Tina went into the bedroom and picked up the phone. "Sorry I didn't call."

"I was worried," Mr. Robert said.

"It was late. Ma had a bit of a problem at work. I helped her."

"Problem?"

"With her MS."

"Does she need a *reiki* treatment?"

Tina let his question go unanswered for a long moment. "Hang on." She covered the mouthpiece with her hand and said loudly, "He wants to know if you want a *reiki* treatment."

Hanako came back into the room wearing a robe. "Yes, please. Before work."

Tina held out the phone. "You tell him. If he asks, I'm on my way home."

Hanako frowned and took the phone. "*Hai,* Robert-*san. Ohayo gozaimasu.*"

BACK AT HOME, Tina dropped her backpack onto the floor of her office. Mr. Robert came out of the bedroom, his hair still wet. He was rubbing a hand towel on the back of his head. "I wish you would have called."

"I know."

"She was really bad?"

"She collapsed in the middle of the restaurant."

"Good thing you were there."

Good thing she was there with Wijjie, she thought. "She hadn't told Aunt Kiyomi."

"About her MS?"

"She knows now." Tina walked into the kitchen and started coffee brewing. "I had to run home and get her medicine. She wasn't taking it, you know."

"But she doesn't like what it does to her."

"Why did she tell you? She didn't tell me until I dragged it out of her."

"I don't know . . . she told me." He was drying the top of his head and the towel hid his face.

Mr. Robert turned and went into the bathroom. From there, he said, "I told her *reiki* would do just as much good, without the side effects."

Tina watched the coffee brewer that was taking an eternity. "Why would you tell her that? You don't know that."

"I do know that. Besides, if she believes it, her body will react to her belief and send her *ki* to the spots that need the energy."

Tina appeared in the bathroom doorway. "What are you talking about? She went to a doctor who told her what was wrong and prescribed the medicine that would help her. That's all she needs to believe."

Mr. Robert pulled his hair back into his ponytail. "What's that toxic medicine do for her? It doesn't cure her, does it? All it does is treat symptoms, right?"

"It can reduce the frequency of episodes. Reduce the severity of the symptoms."

"Wouldn't your mother know what works best?" Mr. Robert flipped his ponytail a few times to get it into place. "Shouldn't we let her decide?"

Mr. Robert walked past her and out into the kitchen. "*Reiki* treats the symptoms without any side effects."

Tina didn't move. "She took some of her medicine last night and it worked."

Mr. Robert shrugged. "That's not the point. The toxicity builds up in her system. And sooner or later the drugs stop working. That's a fact, you can ask any doctor." He started cleaning up his dishes.

Tina walked away, into the office, and closed the door. Tina flopped onto the floor, pulled her backpack over to her, and dug through it until she found the reader for Professor Alamo's class. She opened to where she had left off and started reading. After a few minutes of not registering the words as her eyes moved down the page, she heard the front door close. She got up and went into the kitchen.

A note on the counter read: "Sorry. Have a good day."

She wrote on the bottom of the note: "Sorry, too." Then she added: "Going to school to study, then to a party for first-year students. Don't wait up."

BERKELEY

Tina studied in her office at school. None of her officemates showed up; they must have been doing research, or studying at home, where it would be more comfortable than the cramped and dingy office.

By the end of the afternoon, she was only halfway through the reading for Professor Alamo's class. The density of the articles was mind-numbing.

When she finished one of the research articles—the second out of the five assigned—she closed the reader and put it in her backpack. She checked her e-mail. There was nothing but junk—students looking for places to live, announcements for courses and times—except for one from Wijjie reminding her about the party and telling her that he had a nice time last night. Tina sent a quick reply: "Me too! See you at the party."

She slung her backpack over her shoulder and walked out of the office. The halls of the institute were quiet, most of the students and professors gone. Only a few staff people were still working.

She wandered down Telegraph Avenue, the street vendors were selling their wares in the bright afternoon sun: tie-dyed shirts, bumper stickers ("Don't Eat Meat—You'll Be Sweet," "Welcome to the Police State of Berkeley, CA"), handcrafted jewelry, incense. The sidewalks were full, students mostly in their new-old polyester look, some in baggies, some in jeans and T-shirts. A knot of street kids with spikes, multiple piercings, and puppies were sitting in front of Intermezzo—a soup and salad place—waiting for customers to bring them their leftovers or spare change.

Tina turned a corner and went into the nearly empty Half Note Coffee House. Tina got a latte and sat at the same table she used the first day of classes.

She balanced Professor Alamo's reader on her lap. At the rate she was going, she would still be on the first week's assignments when the semester ended. She took a couple of sips, then plunged into the article that hypothesized consciousness was in the brain's synapses, in the transmission of neurochemicals. The author speculated that when a synapse fired, it was a spark of consciousness, the right mix of sparks created a specific type of subjective experience.

After reading a few pages, about a quarter of the article, Tina looked up. She was the only customer left and the employees were busy cleaning up. Tina drained her latte and closed the reader. She still had a couple of hours until Wijjie's party started, but she couldn't read another word. She took her empty glass to the bus tub, put it in, and walked outside.

She wandered around the main campus, following her feet through the student union stores of Cal sweatshirts, T-shirts, and ball caps. She looked at the books in the window displays of the student-run bookstore. She walked on the path that followed Strawberry Creek as it wound through campus before disappearing in an underground culvert.

At the downtown Berkeley BART station, she got on the train to the Ashby station. From there, she walked twenty minutes to the sensei's hospital. In the rehabilitation wing, she asked the nurse on duty if she could see the sensei.

The sensei was on his back, his eyes open. He blinked when Tina stood over him and said, "Sensei."

She couldn't tell if he blinked at her or if he just blinked. His focus was not on her, not even on the ceiling, but far past that point. Tina sat down on the chair next to him. "How are you?" she asked. *"Ogenki desu ka?"*

The sensei didn't move for a long moment; his mouth opened slightly, as if he were going to say something, then it closed. His head turned toward Tina, or at least to the sound of her voice. When his gaze found her, the left side of his mouth pulled upward, as if he were trying to smile.

"Sensei?"

His mouth opened and closed again. The movement was like a fish, caught in a net and hauled aboard a boat, slowly drowning in the air.

What are you seeing that I am not?
a lot
nothing

TINA WATCHED THE SENSEI, occasionally talking to him, until Dr. Geoffry came in. "How are we today?" he asked.

"Still unable to communicate. Do you think he can understand what we're saying?"

"Possibly. At times he seems to understand a word or two. But unless he tells us he understands, we won't know."

The sensei was staring through the ceiling. The doctor leaned over the bed and looked into the sensei's eyes.

"Do you remember those drawings he made?" Tina asked.

"Yes."

"One of his students said they consisted of pieces of Japanese characters—radicals—but together they made no sense. That sounds like agraphia."

The doctor had his penlight out and was shining it in the sensei's eyes. "Agraphia, sure, that makes sense."

"Maybe he's trying to communicate through writing, but he can't get the characters right."

"Possibly." The doctor wrote something in his folder.

Tina reached into her backpack and took out a notebook and felt marker. She asked the doctor, "May I try something?"

Without looking up, the doctor said, "Sure."

Tina put the notebook opened to a blank page near the sensei on the bed. She held the marker out to him.

He focused on her, then at the marker. He took it and rolled onto his side. In the notebook, he slowly made several marks on the page. Then he dropped the marker, rolled onto his back, and closed his eyes.

Tina picked up the notebook. She didn't recognize any of the drawings as Japanese characters. They didn't look like anything. She showed them to the doctor.

"Mean anything to you?" he asked.

"No. It's interesting, though, beautiful in a sad kind of way."

The doctor jotted something else in his notebook. "I've got to see another patient."

Tina took one last look at the sensei—who looked asleep—before walking out with the doctor.

The belly
of regret
is soft
has legs

"DON'T TELL ME I'm the first one here," Tina said, as Wijjie guided her from the front door into the kitchen.

"The very first. You can help me get ready."

Wijjie had a bottle of white wine open and he poured them both a glass. After taking a drink, Tina cut up carrots, celery, and bell peppers—red, green, and yellow—while Wijjie fried corn tortillas wrapped around cheese.

"How's your mother today?"

"She seemed fine this morning."

"That's good." Wijjie started mashing avocados for guacamole. "I think she should go back to her doctor. He or she could adjust her medication if it's not working for her."

"I told her that."

"She doesn't like doctors?" Wijjie tested the guacamole, then added a pinch of salt. "Or just independent?"

"Both. I think it's the money mostly. She never liked spending money."

"No health insurance?"

"She said she has some, but it's probably got a high deductible." Tina pushed the pepper slices off the cutting board onto a plate. "But she could afford it. I'm not sure what her real problem is."

TINA AND WIJJIE had already finished two glasses of wine when the others started arriving. Gillian and Tina were standing on the deck off the living room.

"What's all that crap about a 'spark of consciousness,' anyway?" Gillian said. "You get that?"

"I didn't get very far in that article. But I kind of pictured it as fireworks. You get enough sparks going and an image emerges. The spark of consciousness is what happens when nerves release their neurotransmitter, and this firing is observed, or experienced, by the brain. Get enough sparks and you have conscious awareness."

"Wow. I get what you're saying. That's cool." Gillian reached in the pocket of her batik dress and took out a joint. "Care for a hit?"

"Maybe just one."

Gillian handed the joint to Tina, and took a lighter out of her pocket. Tina put the joint between her lips, and Gillian flicked the lighter and held the flame under the end.

She gave the joint to Gillian quickly so it wouldn't go out. Gillian took a long hit.

Tina took a tiny hit. "I tried to get my mom to take that joint you gave me."

"Did she freak out?"

"Called me a pothead."

Gillian laughed loudly. Tina laughed too.

"Then my boyfriend found it and flushed it down the toilet."

"He did what? Why did he do that?"

Tina shrugged and handed the joint back to Gillian. She took another hit, then offered the joint to Tina, who waved it off.

"I don't know," Tina said. "He's into *reiki*, self-healing and all that."

"What a jerk. Flushing it!" She reached into her pocket and took out two more joints. "Keep these away from him."

Tina put them in the pocket of her sweatshirt.

Gillian said, "Here's a question. But what makes the awareness of the spark? Another spark?"

"It must be a feedback mechanism, part of the association areas of the cortex, perhaps, that senses what other nerves are doing or experiencing."

"Like a metalevel of brain activity." Gillian stepped across the deck and handed the joint to the first person inside the house.

"I guess that's right. Another level, a metalevel."

Gillian said, "I'm hungry. That guacamole sure looks good."

SAN FRANCISCO

Tina woke up at nine-thirty. Mr. Robert had already gotten up to exercise, meditate, practice *shodô*, and eat before leaving for his Saturday classes that he taught: English for Japanese students in a Japantown school. Tina stayed in bed, listening to the birds chattering in the courtyard.

The party had ended after the last BART train, so Wijjie drove her back to the City. Gillian said she wanted to go to a nightclub in the City, so she came along. Gillian had convinced Wijjie to go clubbing with her. Tina declined, saying she had early plans. Besides, it seemed like Wijjie wanted to be with Gillian.

Tina got out of bed and took a short shower, then filled up the bathtub. When it was full, she went into the kitchen and started coffee. She took a cup of coffee into the bath with another article she had to read for Alamo's class. She soaked in the hot water for a while with her eyes closed, floating, without thinking.

But she couldn't stop thinking of the party, the talk about mind and consciousness, of Wijjie proclaiming that consciousness was merely an emergent property, not primary in the functional world. We could get along without consciousness just fine, thank you very much. Gillian had said she agreed, that we try to deaden our consciousness as much as enhance it. Pain, anguish, depression. Who needs them?

Tina took a gulp of coffee and picked up the article for Alamo's class. She read the abstract; the article was about the brain's resonance cycles, how that might be the source of consciousness. She put the article down on the floor, took another gulp of coffee, and turned on the hot water to warm up the bath. She turned it off, then sank into the water.

TINA TOOK THE BART to the Powell Street station and walked up the hill to her mother's apartment. The day was sunny, bright, without a breath of wind. The tourists were out, most wearing shorts—though Tina knew they would regret it later when the summer fog rolled in. A line of them waited for the cable car all the way up to Blondie's Pizza a block away. They looked either bored or anxious, ready to bolt if a panhandler hassled them.

Inside her mother's apartment building, the guts of the elevator were spread on canvas tarps. Tina walked up the staircase and opened the door to her mother's apartment.

"In here, Ha-*chan*." Hanako's voice came from the bedroom. Her mother was slumped in a chair, putting on a sock.

"Are you okay?"

"*Hai,*" she said.

"How was work?"

"Fine. Busy."

"How about if I take you out for brunch?"

"Brunch?"

"You know, between breakfast and lunch."

"I know that. I'm not too hungry."

"Come on, let's go to the Saint Fran."

"So expensive."

"I'm buying. Please."

After convincing her mother to go with her, they walked down the staircase. "When are they going to finish the elevator?" Tina asked.

"The manager said one more week."

"Hasn't it been a week for about three weeks now?"

"They'll get it done."

Tina decided not to mention it again; she had made many such vows. Not to ask if they could move to another place to live where she might have a real bedroom, not to ask her mother to stop working as a waitress, not to ask about her father, not to bring up Japan.

It didn't leave them much to talk about.

Tina and Hanako walked down Bush to Powell, then to the Westin Saint Francis on Union Square. In the restaurant, they were seated right away. Their waiter looked as young as Tina, his hair tastefully streaked with blond highlights. "Hi, I'm Jeremie. I'll be your waiter today."

Tina ordered sparkling water with lemon. Hanako ordered green tea. Tina almost rolled her eyes, wanting her mother to have something other than what she had every day at home and work; besides, they probably didn't even have green tea. Jeremie smiled and said, "Excellent choice, ma'am."

Hanako seemed pleased with the waiter's praise. She glanced around the restaurant with its massive chandeliers and gilt-framed oil paintings. "We haven't been here for a long time. Since your high school graduation."

The word "school" reminded Tina of the articles she had to read. She hadn't even started on her other classes. A knot of anxiety tightened her stomach. She would have to read all day tomorrow. Maybe go to the library, or a coffee shop. The thought made her relax, even look forward to a day by herself and her books.

Hanako studied the menu. "What are you going to order?"

Tina picked up her menu. "Don't know yet."

Jeremie brought them their drinks and asked if they were ready to order. "You first, Ha-*chan*."

Tina selected the salmon poached in sauvignon blanc and herbs. When the waiter said it was an excellent choice, Hanako ordered the same.

When he left, Tina said, "I've got something to show you." She got out Zenzen sensei's drawings. "What do you make of this?"

Hanako took the pieces of paper. *"Nani?"*

"You know Mr. Robert's *shodô* sensei?"

Hanako glanced up at her daughter. "Zenzen sensei?"

Tina pointed to the paper. "He had a brain stroke and can't write. He drew these drawings, though. One of the instructors at the school said they looked like kanji radicals."

Hanako flipped through the pages. "They don't make sense."

"The sensei has something called agraphia. A kind of brain damage that means he can no longer draw kanji. Like if you were writing a *t* and you'd forget to cross it. Or maybe draw only half of the *o*."

"You saw him?"

"The sensei?"

Hanako nodded.

"Yes, a couple of times now at the hospital. A lot of the research I'm going to be doing comes from people who have had a brain injury. Stroke, tumors, surgery." Tina pointed to the drawings. "Can you understand them?"

"What does he look like?"

"Huh? What's he look like?"

"Never mind," Hanako said, her attention returned to the drawings. "No, I can't. But can I keep them?"

"Sure," Tina answered as Jeremie brought their salmon. Hanako put the papers in her lap and held them tightly, as if they might fly away.

Butterfly
is
beautiful
to
be free

"HERE, MOM, what about this?" Tina was holding a set of towels in the linen section of Macy's.

Hanako ran her hand across the fabric.

"Well?"

"I don't need new towels."

"You've had the same ones for ten years. They're starting to wear out."

Hanako squeezed the fabric as if testing a cantaloupe. "I know what you are doing, Ha-*chan*."

"I'm not doing anything, except trying to buy you some towels."

"You think I don't spend enough money. Because I like to save it for you."

"Ma, they're just some towels."

Hanako put the towels back on the shelf. She patted them and said, "They are nice towels. Maybe I'll need them someday."

HANAKO TRACED THE PEN MARKINGS of Zenzen sensei with her finger. The strokes were strong, identifiable as the sensei's, even though they were written with a marker and not a brush. Some were obviously radicals—pieces of kanji characters—but, as Hana had said, together they made no sense. She held the paper to the light, as if perhaps the completion of the strokes into characters was too faint to see.

Nothing. None of it made any sense.

Yet there was a feeling to them. A sense of meaning. She stared at one of the markings, trying to feel the meaning without thinking about it, as she had during her lessons with the sensei. So many years ago.

Nothing came to her. No meaning. No feeling. She closed her eyes, the image was reversed on the back of her eyelids. White on black. But still no meaning.

She held the drawings, not letting them go until she had to put on her kimono for that night's shift.

Balance
by
opposites

In the sensei's diluted mind there was a flash flood of knowing, a firestorm of awareness, a billion synapses exploding into a nova of cognizance. So much to resolve, nearly no time left.

But what was to be resolved? The light couldn't reach that far. It only illuminated the possibility of a destination. Whatever that was to be.

The brief light faded to black.

I'm not sure
of the point
yet
but
I have something
to say

第四の計画

pathways of pain   PART TWO

"I don't know what to do," Gozen said. He had just told Tina that the hospital was releasing Zenzen sensei in a day. He would still have to go back for checkups and rehabilitation, but he had recovered enough function to leave.

Tina asked Gozen, "You can't stay here with him?"

He got up and paced in a tight circle. "I can stay some of the time, not all the time, though. I have a part-time job. Translation."

"The sensei has no family?"

"Not here."

"In Japan?"

"That's a problem." Gozen slowed his pacing. "I don't believe his family would be helpful at this point."

"What about a nurse?"

"A nurse. That's what we need." Gozen stopped pacing. "Do you know how to arrange that?"

"The hospital can help find someone. And his insurance company . . . they should be able to set up the home care."

Gozen started pacing again. "Insurance. That's a problem."

"No insurance?"

Gozen shook his head. "What should I do?" He took a gulp of his tea.

"What about his students? They could take turns staying here."

"That's a good idea. I can contact them."

"I can help. I'll be the first to sign up."

Gozen sensei bowed his head as he said, "Thank you."

THE DATA FILING ROOM was a windowless, closet-sized space at the institute. Tina picked up a brain scan—a functional MRI image. Each image was annotated with a note describ-

Parietal lobe: extends from the central sulcus (the groove separating areas of the cerebral cortex) back to the occipital lobe. This area has the bodily sensation neurons, including the ends of the pain pathways.

What good is consciousness, anyway? Take pain. Ma is conscious of her pain, as the body attacks itself. So why can't her body stop its destructive actions? Consciousness seems only capable of subjective experience, like "that hurts," but can't do anything about it, at least not directly.

Neuroscience Notebook,
Christina Hana Suzuki

ing the scan. Tina had to assign a number to the scan, type in the annotation into a database, then file the scan in the cabinets.

The barely legible scrawl on the image she just picked up read, "Extensive Wernicke area damage. Loss of 70–80% of language understanding. Difficulty producing coherent speech."

Tina yawned and wished she could take a nap in the quiet and dark room. She was looking around to see if there was a place to stretch out, when Professor Porter came in the room. Her hair was piled on top of her head, held with a large plastic clip. "How is the filing going?" she asked.

"Just fine. It's actually interesting, looking at the scans and reading the notes." Tina gestured to the two-foot-high stack. "It gets me familiar with the research, too."

"Exactly. That's why we have the first-year students do it."

Who else would want to do it? Tina thought.

The professor sat in a chair next to the table. "Have you followed up with the calligraphy teacher you were telling me about?"

"He's still in the hospital. Still unable to communicate."

"No family members?"

"None," Tina said. "Not yet."

"I know it might be difficult, but you have to keep trying. A good research subject like this can make a person's career. Like patient H. M., whose fever destroyed his hippocampus and left him with no ability to transform short-term memory into long-term memory. Every minute of his life was as if it were his first. That subject made more than one researcher famous."

"Okay," Tina said. "I'll try again."

It was nearly ten when Tina got to the Tempura House. There were only two tables of customers left. Tina waited inside the door, looking for but not seeing her mother. Kiyomi came over to her; she was holding a sheaf of dinner tickets.

"How's your mother, Hana?"

"I haven't seen her today. Why? What happened?"

Kiyomi frowned and looked around. "I'll tell you in the manager's office. I'll be right there as soon as I close out the cash registers."

Tina went into the manager's office, dropped her backpack to the floor, and sat in a chair. On top of the filing cabinet was a jade plant. On one wall was a calendar from WestCo Imported Oriental Foods, most of which was a photograph of bottles of soy sauce and fish sauce, bags of tempura flour, jumbo-sized cans of bamboo shoots, and cellophane bags of dried shrimp.

Tina shifted in the chair, and was getting ready to get out Professor Alamo's reader from her backpack when Kiyomi came in with a cash register tape rolled up and secured with a rubber band. "Sorry to keep you waiting." She sat in the chair behind the desk. "She had some pain. Too much for her to work."

"You had to send her home?" Tina couldn't remember her mother ever missing her shift.

"She wasn't walking very well, kind of like she was drunk," Kiyomi said, then quickly added, "Of course, she wasn't, it was her MS."

Tina had never heard her mother complain, not about her health, anyway. Sure she complained about the trash in the streets that seemed to get worse every year, or the noisy neighbor they used to have above them, or the graffiti that was all over the city. But there never seemed to be a problem in her own life. Of course, it was a simple life: work and Tina, that was about it. That was how she seemed to want it.

"Her mood is different, too."

"I've noticed, too," Tina said.

"Moody, that's what she is. Moody."

Tina nodded.

"She was never moody before. Always cheerful. Hardworking." Kiyomi thought for a moment, then asked Tina, "Is it the MS problem?"

"Could be. I don't know for sure. Damage to nerve cells in the brain can cause a change in personality."

The two contemplated that for a while. Tina said, "She's never missed work before, has she, Aunt Kiyomi?" Just saying the word "aunt" made Tina relax. She knew that Kiyomi wasn't her real aunt, but it was always comforting to call her that. Kiyomi had been part of her family, along with the "grannies," Tina's baby-sitters until she was old enough to stay alone at home. The grannies seemed ancient when Tina was a child, yet both were still alive, living in one of the elder-care homes in Japantown. Tina didn't really care that they weren't *blood* relatives. She could point to one of the nannies or Kiyomi's kids on the street and say, "That's my granny. That's my cousin James. That's my cousin Annie."

Kiyomi said, "No, I can't remember a day that she's missed. What's going to happen to her?"

Tina had been doing some reading about MS. She knew what the disease did to the nerves, knew that it was irreversible but didn't itself kill a person. "No one can be sure. Doctors can't say. Every person is different."

Kiyomi gazed to the wall, to the calendar, looking at the days as if Hanako's future were there. "She won't get better?"

Tina didn't know what to say. "Most get a recurrent-relapsing form of the disease. They can treat it with drugs,

Multiple sclerosis: For unknown reasons, a person's immune system attacks the myelin sheath surrounding the axon of some nerve cells. The result leaves plaque and stiff scar tissue—"sclerosis"—that drastically reduce nerve function. An MRI can detect brain lesions (the scarring) and brain shrinkage associated with MS. (Questions to follow up: What kind of brain shrinkage? Where does it occur? What effects does it have?)

Axon: the slender, wirelike tissue trailing from the cell

trying to keep it from getting worse. They can treat some of the symptoms. The problem is, it's hard to repair nerve damage."

"Your mother is so beautiful, hardly changed at all since I first met her." Kiyomi made a small sound, a cross between "Oh" and the gulp of air someone takes before swimming under water.

TINA OPENED THE DOOR to her mother's apartment.

"Ha-*chan*? What are you doing here?"

"Sorry it's so late. I just stopped at the Tempura House on my way home."

Hanako was watching TV in the sitting room. Tina dropped her backpack on the floor and sat next to the sofa where her mother was stretched out.

"Aunt Kiyomi said you went home from work."

"It was a slow night."

"She said you were in pain."

"A little."

The Asian cable station was on, a game show from Japan. Ever since the building had gotten wired for cable, the only TV Hanako watched were shows from Japan. Cooking, dramas, talk, travel. Lots of game shows. Tina could only understand about a quarter of their rapid-fire Japanese.

They watched for a while before Tina said, "Did you have any dinner?"

"*Hai*. Did you?"

"Not yet."

Hanako got up. "Leftovers okay?"

"I was going to get something on the way home."

Hanako went into the kitchen. Tina followed. Hanako started heating up some fried rice.

"You're feeling okay now?"

Hanako nodded.

body; electric nerve pulses are sent down the axon to other neurons.

Myelin: a fatty substance of cholesterol, cerebrosides, phospholipids, glycoproteins, and water. Myelin insulates the axon, helping to contain the electrical impulse. The sheath is not continuous; small gaps called nodes of Ranvier act like booster stations, increasing the strength of the signal. Myelin is formed as Schwann cells wrap around the axon forming layers, like rolled sushi.

Neuroscience Notebook, Christina Hana Suzuki

"Did you look some more at the sensei's drawings?"

Hanako stirred the rice. "*Hai*. I don't know what they mean."

After finishing the rice, Hanako served it to Tina in a blue-and-white bowl. She put soy sauce on the table and a pair of chopsticks.

"Thanks, Ma."

After watching Tina eat a few bites, Hanako said, "I'm tired."

"I'll clean up."

"Okay. *Oyasumi nasai*." Good night.

"*Oyasumi nasai.*"

After Tina cleaned the kitchen, she took out the two joints Gillian had given her. She put them on the kitchen counter on top of a note: "Ma, try a couple of puffs of this (hold the smoke in your lungs) when you have pain. Tina. PS: Hide them from Mr. Robert."

TINA OPENED THE DOOR to her condo. The television cast its bluish glare, the volume on low. When she closed the door, Mr. Robert came out of the living room. "Another long day?"

"Yeah. Sorry." He followed her into her office. She unzipped her backpack and took out her reader, books, and notebook and put them on her desk. "How was your day?"

"The usual. Taught my evening classes. Came home. Ate."

Tina draped her empty backpack on the chair. "I stopped by Ma's on the way home."

"How was she?"

"Okay. She seemed okay." She didn't feel like telling him that she came home early from work.

"Good. I can stop by to see her tomorrow."

Tina walked past him and into their bedroom. "I'm tired," she said. She took off her jacket and hung it up.

"Gozen sensei said you've been to see Zenzen sensei."

"Yes, I have a couple of times." Tina took off her black jeans and blouse and hung them up. She took off her bra, put it on a hook in the closet, and pulled off a T-shirt from a hanger and slipped it over her head.

"How is he?" Mr. Robert had followed her into the bathroom.

"He still can't talk or write." Tina got out her toothbrush from the drawer and squeezed a little toothpaste on it.

"Gozen sensei said you volunteered to help when sensei comes home."

"Huh-huh," she mumbled through a lather of toothpaste. She looked at his reflection in the mirror.

"That's nice of you," Mr. Robert said. He watched her scrubbing her teeth before he asked, "Why didn't you mention it?"

Tina spit out the toothpaste. "Mention what?"

"About his condition, that you had seen him, that you had volunteered to help him."

Tina rinsed her mouth. "Sorry, I'm just bushed."

Mr. Robert turned, and leaned against the doorframe. His profile was now reflected in the mirror. Tina suddenly felt a wave of sadness as she put away her toothbrush. When she looked up, he was gone.

BERKELEY

Tina was in the sensei's hospital room with Dr. Geoffry and the sensei's physical therapist, Georgina, a black woman, who squeezed Tina's hand with incredible strength when they were introduced. Zenzen sensei was sitting on the edge of the bed. His gaze was unfocused, as if he was unaware of the others in the room.

"Are you sure he should be leaving the hospital?" Tina asked the doctor.

"Patients recovering from a stroke do much better at home. He should rehabilitate much quicker, improve his cognitive functioning sooner."

Georgina added, "He's had some good progress in the last few days with his mobility. He should be able to handle most tasks, but he will need help with some of the more intricate activities, like cooking. He should not go out alone."

Tina peered closely at the sensei, his eyes focused softly on her. She asked the doctor and therapist, "He still can't talk?"

"That's true," the doctor said. "He may slowly regain that ability to some degree. The brain will try to rewire itself; however, with the extent of damage he suffered, there will always be some impairment."

"What about another stroke?" Tina asked.

"Of course, that's always possible," Dr. Geoffry said. "He needs to take his prescription and follow the diet and exercise program that Georgina has set up. Along with his regular checkups."

They helped the sensei to his feet. The three of them walked with him out of the rehabilitation ward, through the main hospital, then out the front doors.

Gozen was waiting in his car in the patient pickup and drop-off zone. He sprang out of his car and opened the passenger-side door. He avoided looking at the sensei. They eased the sensei into the car. Georgina buckled him in and patted his shoulder. "Good luck. We'll see you again soon."

The sensei stared straight ahead.

When one has achieved the completeness of being in the moment, a firm sense of resolve, relaxation, and focus will follow. Only in this moment can one achieve the most truly spiritual calligraphy.

Instructor's Journal,
Zenzen School of
Japanese Calligraphy

*Why always up
and one step
at a time*

AT THE ZENZEN SCHOOL, Gozen and Tina helped the sensei up the steps and through the doorway. When they were through, Gozen hurried ahead of them and pulled out one of the chairs in the front main room. Tina started to head the sensei in that direction, but he pulled away from Tina, so she let go of his arm. They watched him walk out of the room.

They followed him into his studio. He was standing just inside, staring at his worktable, at the stained *tatami* mat. The sensei took an awkward, lurching step forward. Tina and Gozen reached out to steady him, but he regained his balance and walked to his table. He kneeled down and sat on his heels, facing the table as if readying himself for a session of *shodô.*

Beginning students usually become bored when practicing radicals over and over. They have not been able to grasp the fundamental principle of focus, and of seeing the deep, subtle meaning of their strokes. Students unable

to maintain focus will not
be able to extend their *ki*
through the brush, and
they will not pass this test:
hold your brush a few
inches above the paper.
Have someone try to pull
the brush out of your
hand or bend your arm.
A more difficult test is to
have another person try to
pull the brush out of your
hand while drawing a
character. Students should
always focus as if they
were taking the test, and
then there will be no bore-
dom.

The sensei picked up the brush that was on the table. He held it gingerly, as if he had picked up an injured bird.

Gozen dropped to his knees and slid over to the sensei. While the Zenzen sensei held the brush vertical and still, Gozen pinched the brush halfway between the end of the brush and the sensei's fingers. He pulled up on the brush, but it didn't move. He pulled harder, and still the brush did not move.

Gozen sensei released his grip. Zenzen sensei put the brush back on the table, and propped it on the brush holder. He reached for the inkstick and small flask of water on the table. He poured and stared at it as if he had never seen it before. Gozen helped him prepare the ink. The sensei dipped his brush into the ink and drew several abstract strokes slowly, deliberately.

*If I could only be
tamed and trained and
gathered
if only to be held*

TINA STAYED with Gozen and the sensei until she had to go to class. The sensei never stopped drawing, and she and Gozen couldn't stop watching him.

After class, she found Wijjie in his office at the institute. His reader for Alamo's class was spread out on his desk. Tina looked out his window. "Nice view of the hills."

Wijjie grabbed one of the chairs and moved it closer to his desk.

"You're actually studying?" Tina said. She put her backpack on one of the vacant desks in the office and sat in the chair.

"Hard to believe, I know. What's up?"

"Just got out of neuroanatomy. Neuron classification. Purkinje, stellate, pyramidal."

"Don't forget the anterior horn cell. I'm glad I already took all that in med school." He pulled open a drawer of his desk and took out a brain scan. "Guess what this is."

He handed it to Tina. "Looks like a brain scan from the H-Fifty-one-hundred."

"Exactly. Guess who and what it is."

"You?"

"Gillian. Remember the other night?"

"Don't tell me this is Gillian on dope."

Wijjie grinned and scooted his chair closer to her. "We snuck in after the last research study that night. The top two are before smoking a joint, although she had some a couple of hours before we took the image. The bottom two are five minutes after smoking about half a joint."

"The bottom two show a lot more activation. About fifty percent more."

"Look at this area here," Wijjie pointed out. "The amygdala, the center of emotion. It's less active than the other. Cannabinoids tend to reduce emotional responses."

"That's why they call it dope, I guess."

The *saku* radical is one of the *eiji happô*. Minimal pressure is applied to the brush throughout the stroke, especially at the beginning. The stroke starts with the brush pointed toward the lower left corner of the paper and finishes toward the upper right. The tip of the brush should be pulled along the top edge of the stroke, that is, pointing to the top of the paper, during its execution. *Saku* means "whip," perhaps because the stroke is best made with a whiplike movement of the brush.

Instructor's Journal,
Zenzen School of
Japanese Calligraphy

Wijjie pointed to other light areas on the scan. "These areas are related to hunger and sexual activity."

"Sorry I missed the event," Tina said. She handed the scan back to him. "If Florian only knew."

Wijjie slid his chair back and put the scan print in his desk. "Yeah, we broke eleven of his ten commandments."

"At least." Tina took out a folder from her backpack, and moved over to Wijjie's desk with her chair. "I've got one of those too. What do you think of this?" She opened the folder, on the top was one of the sensei's brain scans that his doctor let her borrow. Porter's warning about divulging research crossed her mind, but the sensei wasn't really part of their research yet. Besides, it was just Wijjie.

Wijjie studied it. "Definitely temporal lobe and prefrontal lobe damage caused by a hemorrhagic stroke. Is this the sensei you told me about?"

"Yes." She pulled out one of the abstract drawings the sensei had completed before Tina left for school.

"What is it?"

"It's something the sensei drew."

"His calligraphy?"

"It's kind of like that, except it makes no sense. It's not anything. Just some pieces of Japanese characters, some not even that. A lot are just random lines. But are they meaningless?"

"Interesting question. Obviously, he's had some major damage to his language areas. I would guess that they mean something to him, like he's trying to communicate in some way. The only way he can."

"That's what I think. But how can we figure out what he's trying to say?"

Wijjie picked up the sensei's brain scan and the drawing. "I have no idea."

Here
I bear promise

SAN FRANCISCO

Hanako placed the tablespoon heaped with thick miso paste into the hot, delicately green broth made with a strip of *kombu* seaweed. With the tips of a pair of chopsticks, she rubbed the top of the miso paste, gradually dissolving it into the broth. When the paste was gone, she dropped diced cubes of tofu into the soup. She poured two bowls full and sprinkled a bit of chopped green onion on top.

She placed them on the kitchen table, one in front of Mr.

Robert, and one in front of her. He said the traditional Japanese grace: *"Itadakimasu."*

Hanako repeated the grace and warmed her hands around the bowl. She raised the bowl to her lips and took a sip. She put down the bowl, and fished out a cube of tofu with her chopsticks.

"How is your teaching?" Hanako asked.

"It's going well." Mr. Robert took another noisy sip, as was considered polite—at least not rude—for men in Japan. "Busy, though. I've got a full load."

Hanako took another sip. "Tina has never liked miso soup."

"She doesn't know what she's missing."

"She likes Campbell's chicken noodle."

"Why would she want that when she could have your delicious miso?" Mr. Robert placed a cube of tofu into his mouth. Hanako watched him let it slowly dissolve before he swallowed.

Hanako took another sip, then put her bowl to the side. Nothing had much taste anymore.

Mr. Robert looked at her half-full bowl. "Tina said you had to leave work?"

"It was a slow night."

Mr. Robert took another slurp of soup.

"Excuse me, Robert-*san*. May I ask you a personal question?"

"Of course."

"You don't like marijuana?"

He frowned. "I think it's a bad idea for you, if that's what you mean."

"Tina's doctor friend said it might help better than the drugs."

"Doctor friend?"

"Dr. Cruz. Wijjie. He's a student, too. They came to the Tempura House the other night."

"Tina and him?"

Hanako looked confused. "Oh, maybe I shouldn't have said."

Mr. Robert finished his soup, then folded his hands on the table in front of him. "She must have told me. I just forgot."

Hanako picked up the bowls and brought them to the sink. She splashed water into Mr. Robert's bowl and rinsed out the remaining grains of miso paste that clung to its sides.

"Robert-*san*," she said quietly. "Could you do me a favor?"

"Of course. A *reiki* treatment?"

"No, thank you." She let out a sigh of resignation. It was a very difficult thing she had to ask him. "I would like you to keep Hana away from Zenzen sensei."

Mr. Robert unfolded his hands and dropped them onto his knees. "Keep her away?"

"Please." Hanako gazed at him.

It looked as if he were about to ask why, but all he said was, "All right, Hanako-*san*."

KYOTO

Kando used the stiletto knife to open the envelope that was postmarked "Oakland, CA." He took out the letter, and placed his reading glasses on the rounded end of his flat nose. The letter was handwritten in elegant Japanese script.

Kando-*san*: You do not know me, we have never met. It is a delicate matter that I approach you with. To refresh your memory, an incident occurred several years ago, concerning the Daizen School of Calligraphy in Kyoto. The incident I refer to happened when the twenty-ninth Daizen sensei abandoned his position as head of the Daizen school. At this time, the Daizen Inkstone was also discovered to be missing. I'm sure I do not need to tell you that the Daizen Inkstone was the trophy for the Daizen-Kurokawa Calligraphy Competition. To get to the point, I believe that I have seen the Daizen Inkstone.

I first came across it when I saw a work of calligraphy drawn by a student and countersigned by the twenty-ninth Daizen sensei. Near this work I discovered a particularly interesting inkstone. Intrigued, I studied it for some length of time. At first I did not believe it could be the Daizen Inkstone. However, I was able to obtain a detailed description of it. Based on my research, I am certain that I have seen the Daizen Inkstone.

As I wrote in the beginning of this letter, I am in a delicate position in regard to the Daizen Inkstone. I do not wish to cause any embarrassment to the person who has possession of the inkstone, who you might have guessed is most likely the twenty-ninth Daizen sensei. This person, known to me by another name, has given me much over the last several years, indeed, I owe him more than I can ever repay.

However, his circumstances have changed. I feel it is my duty to facilitate returning the Daizen Inkstone to the rightful owner. I will help accomplish this if only it can be handled in the most discreet manner possible. I hope that you will be able to act as an intermediary, that is, between me and the Daizen school. I know that you previously provided service to the twenty-ninth Daizen sensei. If you would like to discuss this matter further, please contact me at your convenience.

The letter was signed "Gozen." There was a street address and an apartment number, in Berkeley, California, and a phone number.

Kando Investigative Services

The fact that Hanako Suzuki had flown to San Francisco was a starting point—a clue—but not much of one. She may not have stayed in the city, or the state. And if she was in San Francisco, finding her would be difficult. It was a big city. Too many places to be, too many places to hide, if that was what she wanted to do. It would be a waste of his time, and his client's money, for him to fly there with her picture and start showing it around. He needed more information. Someone knew where she was and how long she was going to be there. Narrow down the possibilities. For instance, was she staying with relatives or friends? Why did she leave in the first place?

This was the tricky part about the case he had anticipated: getting information without Tetsuo Suzuki finding out. He decided to start with her family.

Kando's journalist contact provided some background, including pictures, from the archives of his newspaper. Using that and what Kando gleaned from public records—such as family registries, business records, school yearbooks—he had assembled several facts. Hanako was born February 20, 1952. Her father, Hideyuki Iida, was vice-president of the Central

Kansai Bank, an institution that had a long, if unspectacular past, at least until the mid-1960s. In the five years that followed, Central Kansai emerged as one of the top five regional financial institutions. The rise coincided—according to his source—with an alliance with the development branch of the Suzuki enterprises. Hanako's mother was named Remi, and her family name was Masachika, a lesser noble lineage that extended deep into feudal times.

Hanako had attended the best elementary and junior high schools in Osaka. She was admitted to the prestigious Kansai Girls' High School, from which she graduated in the top ten percent. Her highest scores were in English and Japanese. After high school, she briefly attended Kyoto Women's Junior College. The record of her first and only complete term—information Kando obtained by pretending to be a university registrar inquiring about transfer credits—indicated that she had mediocre scores. The next documented record of her life was in 1974, five years later, when she became engaged to Tetsuo Suzuki. They married in 1975 just before her twenty-third birthday. Her life was rather unremarkable, certainly nothing that might indicate where she might be in America.

Kando drove to Osaka, and slowed as he passed the Iida home. A block away from the home, he parked on a side street. Using the rearview mirror, he flicked at his hair until it was professorially unkempt. He had streaked the hair just above his ears; the gray added ten years to his appearance.

At the door to the Iida home, he walked through the entry gate and rang the bell. A woman came to the door, her face was puffy around the eyes, as if she had recently woken up from an afternoon nap. Kando could see a resemblance between the woman and the picture of Hanako—a high forehead and cheekbones, eyes larger than average.

"I'm very sorry to bother you. This is the Iida residence?"

"Yes."

"I was one of Hanako's instructors at Kyoto Women's Junior College and, as I was in the neighborhood, I thought I would pay her a visit." He smiled a little, not too much.

The woman's expression didn't change, didn't impart suspicion or curiosity. "Hanako no longer lives here," she said.

"Oh, too bad. Well, I had anticipated that might be the case. It's been a long time." He gave the woman a smile. She didn't smile back.

"I was sorry to see her leave the college and never got to tell her that. I've been out of the country, a long sabbatical, and just returned."

When she didn't ask where, he said, "I was in the States, as they say there. America. Specifically, San Francisco."

"San Francisco? She's—" She didn't finish her sentence. "She's in San Francisco?"

When the woman's eyelids dropped, Kando knew he was right. "I wish I had known. It would have been nice to see her." He was about to say "What a coincidence" and ask what Hanako was doing in San Francisco when her mother said, "I'm sorry, I have to go now." She stepped back into the house and closed the door.

KANDO WALKED from his office on the second floor of a three-story office building not far from the Kyoto train station. The ramen shop where he often ate lunch was in a block of small restaurants and other establishments, such as souvenir stores aimed at the many tourists who visit Kyoto.

The shop was nearly empty, as the main lunch crowd had already slurped down their bowls of ramen and gone back to work. He sat at the counter. The owner of the shop, a woman of uncertain age, brought him a glass of water and asked if he wanted his usual. He nodded.

Kando knew that he needed to focus his efforts to find Hanako, even if she was still in San Francisco. But trying to get more information out of her parents, or her husband, seemed too risky. He had already pushed the limit with Hanako's mother.

If she had gone to the U.S., she would have needed a visa to enter. He wasn't especially familiar with their customs and immigration rules, but did know she would have needed to include where she would be staying on the entry form. Getting that information wouldn't be easy.

His bowl of ramen with pork cutlet and pickled greens was placed in front of him, a cloud of steam rising from the broth and filling his nostrils.

IT TURNED OUT to be easier than he thought. He called the U.S. visa office in Tokyo and claimed to be Dr. So-and-so. Hanako's parents, he explained in an authoritative voice, had been in a car accident and were in comas due to head injuries. He needed immediate authorization to operate. Their daughter, Hanako, being the only child, was the only one who could give permission. Kando said he had found out that she was staying in San Francisco, but had no other contact information. Within five minutes, he had the address Hanako Suzuki had listed on her visa form.

It took another hour and a half to find out the phone number for that address. He called the number and Hanako Suzuki answered. He claimed to be a clerk at the Japanese consulate, verifying her address for their records. Hanako verified that the address was correct. Kando also asked her if she had a place of employment. The Tempura House restaurant on Powell Street, she told him.

Aragaki had just finished his calligraphy practice session, when Kando called. The investigator said he had recently come across information that would be of great interest to him.

"Of great interest?" Aragaki repeated. "I can't imagine what that would be." Probably a sales call, he thought.

"Would the Daizen Inkstone be of interest?"

Conflicting thoughts swirled in Aragaki's mind: it was a ruse to distract him before the next competition; it was some sort of scam. But if it were true . . . "Of course it would be of interest."

They agreed to meet at Kando's office. On his way there, Aragaki continued to be skeptical and tantalized. When his predecessor, Shimano, the twenty-ninth Daizen sensei, disappeared along with the Daizen Inkstone, Aragaki had assumed he had committed suicide, possibly in the mountains near the school's retreat. Aragaki had heard from the caretaker that Shimano had been spending time there. Aragaki speculated that Shimano could not bear the responsibility of being the Daizen sensei at such a young age. He also speculated that he had taken the Daizen Inkstone with him so it would always be with him, even in death. Aragaki, then the top instructor and soon to be crowned the thirtieth Daizen sensei, had led the instructors on a search of the mountains near the retreat. They found no trace of Shimano.

Aragaki still vividly remembered the last time he saw Shimano. That morning, he had met with him and the other instructors at the Daizen school's business office and classrooms that were housed in a Kyoto-style *machiya* town house. The offices took up the front half of the long and narrow building, and the classrooms that looked out onto the garden were in the back.

When he saw the sensei, Aragaki had wanted to greet him with: "Hello, Young Sensei!" But he resisted the affront.

During that meeting of instructors, Aragaki wanted to discuss the procedure of selecting a new head Daizen sensei. The vague selection process was almost entirely the preference of the current Daizen sensei, although the candidate instructors' bodies of work and competition records were factors. The preference of the Daizen sensei would never be completely eliminated from the process, but Aragaki was prepared to argue (and most of his fellow instructors agreed) that it should be weighted a third at most.

While not on the official agenda, Aragaki also was curious about one of Shimano's new students, a woman who had never been officially registered in the school. If any other instructor had taken a student without such notification, he would have been disciplined.

When the meeting began with a discussion of the next retreat, Aragaki noticed Shimano staring off into space. All of the discussion items went by without him saying more than a word or two. Even the discussion of the head sensei selection process didn't cause Shimano to do more than nod two or three times. Aragaki's proposal to establish quantifiable criteria was quietly approved.

All that happened years ago, but it still gave Aragaki a shiver of discomfort. Though no excuse, he realized that ambition had affected his rationality. He always wondered how much he had to do with Shimano's disappearance. Some days, he thought he had nothing to do with it, others he held himself completely to blame. On the latter days, his dissatisfaction grew.

During a recent walk in the bamboo forest near his studio, Aragaki decided this dissatisfaction had come from a desire to leave a legacy. Something that would distinguish his era in the long history of the Daizen School of Calligraphy beyond his success in the competitions. In the cool shade, it came to him that his legacy could only be one thing: finding and returning the Daizen Inkstone. He would write another chapter in the *History of the Daizen Inkstone*.

KANDO HANDED Aragaki sensei a photocopy of Gozen's letter. He had blocked out Gozen's name and address.

The handwriting immediately impressed Aragaki—the strokes were very precise, well executed, yet with an artistic flourish. The writer undoubtedly had studied *shodô*, perhaps with Shimano. Aragaki read the short letter twice.

"What should I do?" he asked Kando.

"The best course would be a personal meeting with the person who wrote the letter. Can you fly to California? That's where he lives."

"And the Daizen Inkstone is there as well?"

"I assume so. He didn't say in the letter."

Aragaki glanced at the letter again. "That's right." He looked at Kando. "I will go. Today if I have to."

"I'll arrange the meeting."

SAN FRANCISCO

As they did every Tuesday—the slowest night at the Tempura House—Hanako and Kiyomi took a booth in the China Seas seafood restaurant deep in Chinatown on Clay Street between Grant and Stockton, a fifteen-minute walk from the Tempura House. Their dinner out had been a regular event since shortly after Hanako started working with Kiyomi. On their first few Tuesday dinner dates, Hanako hadn't much to say, but Kiyomi had made her feel comfortable with the small talk she never seemed to run out of.

Hanako picked up a sliver of lightly sautéed green pepper glazed in the slightly sweet garlic sauce. It had just the right crunch. "Very fresh." They always ordered the same meal: spicy rock shrimp, steamed white fish with light garlic sauce, and seasonal vegetables.

Kiyomi nodded. "The fish is good too."

Hanako flaked away a piece of white fish from translucent bone and tried it. *"Oishii."* Delicious.

After a sip of oolong tea, Kiyomi asked, "Hanako, why didn't you tell me about your illness?"

"Gomen nasai," she said quietly. She *was* sorry, especially that Kiyomi had to find out when she suffered the attack at work. She was going to tell her, if—when—it got really bad. But how much was really bad? At first, she thought her symptoms were minor aches and tiredness that came with age. But she knew something was really wrong one morning when she couldn't get out of bed. Her legs weren't working; she had to stay in bed for two hours until she could stand.

When she finally went to a doctor and heard the diagnosis, she found herself even less able to talk about it. She didn't really understand it, for one thing. How could a person's own body destroy part of itself? The doctor said no one knew why; he told Hanako that the human body was so complex that it didn't take much for something to go wrong. Hanako wanted to know if it was something she had done that caused it. The doctor didn't know. Maybe nothing, he said. Maybe it was going to happen to her sooner or later.

"Didn't you want me to know?" Kiyomi asked.

Hanako pushed a shrimp around her plate, as if it might come back to life. "No. I don't know . . ." Her voice trailed off. She picked up the shrimp with her chopsticks and said, "It's not me." She put the shrimp in her mouth.

Kiyomi tilted her head and looked away, debating with

herself. "You're right, it's not you," she finally said. "The Hanako I know is always cheerful and hardworking. Is that what you mean?"

"It's another person inside me. I want it to go away. I want to work and be Hana's mother." Hanako took a sip of tea.

The stoic waiter, who had served them since the first Tuesday night they visited the China Seas, came to their table. He motioned toward Kiyomi's empty rice bowl. When she nodded, he whisked it away. After only a few seconds, he returned with a fresh bowl heaped with rice.

Hanako and Kiyomi ate in silence for a while. Hanako was always amazed that all of the restaurant's tables were occupied, but the waiters never seemed rushed. And as soon as a table of diners left, the dishes were cleared, the glass top wiped clean, and the table reset. There was never a line of people waiting at the restaurant, yet within a minute, another group would come through the doors, walk past the bank of saltwater aquariums, and sit down at the empty table. If only the Tempura House crowd was half as orderly, Kiyomi or Hanako would say every week.

Kiyomi mentioned the Tempura House's newest waitress; she was only twenty-one. "She has a tattoo on her ankle. Of a pretty rose. I love that tattoo. I may get one."

"*Iie.* No, you wouldn't."

"Does Hana have a tattoo?"

"I wouldn't be surprised. I think she's a pothead."

"What?" Kiyomi dropped her chopsticks. "Hana?"

They laughed when Hanako told her about the joints Tina was bringing to her.

"Have you tried it?" Kiyomi whispered.

Hanako shook her head. "I never smoked even a cigarette. How about you?"

"Not me either."

They dished up more shrimp, fish, and vegetables, and

ate as Kiyomi talked about the kitchen remodeling needed to meet new Health Department regulations. The restaurant would have to be closed for a few weeks.

As Kiyomi listed all the things she was going to do with her time off, Hanako recalled when she finally had told Hana about her diagnosis. She had started the conversation asking her what she knew about multiple sclerosis. The two words came out slowly, hard for her to pronounce. Hana had said that she didn't know much about it. Why?

Because I have it, Hanako said.

She remembered the sound of Hana inhaling sharply, then a long silence. Oh, Ma, Hana finally said so quietly that she could barely hear. Hana said that she'd get the next flight home. It's the middle of the school year, Hanako protested. She told her daughter that she didn't want her to come home then. There was really no reason. She just wanted to let her know.

A group of four people seated themselves at a table that had just been cleared and reset. Kiyomi said, "I'd love it if the Tempura House were half as orderly as this place."

"Me too," Hanako said. She ate a piece of delicate white fish that dissolved in her mouth. She put down her chopsticks. "Kiyomi-*san,* I have another problem."

Kiyomi was about to get a bite of rice. She looked taken aback by Hanako's abruptness.

"It's Hana. I think I made a big mistake."

"A mistake?"

Hanako folded her hands together, then she unfolded them and rested them on her lap. "You know her boyfriend practices *shodô.* When he moved here, I told him about a school in Berkeley, the Zenzen school."

"Zenzen? Nothing? That's a strange name for a school."

Hanako nodded, then went on: "Robert-*san* was excited when I told him about the school." The words were sticking in Hanako's chest, like a spicy shrimp that didn't make it all the way down. She let out a breath of air. "I knew the school's sensei. In Japan."

"In Japan?" Kiyomi asked. Her chopsticks remained poised over her bowl of rice.

Hanako nodded. She had never told anyone who Hana's father was, not even Kiyomi. And Kiyomi had politely never asked.

Kiyomi repeated, "In Japan? . . . You mean, he's Hana's father?"

Hanako nodded.

"And Hana doesn't know?"

Hanako shook her head.

"I always wondered who her father was," Kiyomi said. "But I thought he would be in Japan."

"He's here. He's always been here." Hanako had kept track of the sensei, heard about his school, though she had never contacted him.

"You followed him here, and he wouldn't have anything to do with you?"

Hanako shook her head. "The other way around."

"He followed you. . . . It must have been traumatic for you to come here pregnant, alone. Hana doesn't know any of this?"

"I never told her."

"But now she's met him, because he's Robert-*san*'s sensei. She doesn't know yet?"

"No."

"That's a problem, all right." Kiyomi leaned forward and quietly asked, "Are you sure he's Hana's father?"

"It could only be one other person, my ex-husband. But I know his blood type. I also know mine and Hana's. Her father is the sensei."

Kiyomi leaned back into the booth. "You don't want Hana to know that he's her father."

Ki ("tree") is a pictograph of a tree with sweeping branches. In drawing this character, make sure the "branches" look lively, as if moving in a light wind. Do not make the character too symmetrical, as it will appear artificial.

Mori ("woods") is literally "many trees," the top tree is slightly small, making it appear more distant. The feeling of the woods in its context (a place of life or darkness) should be reflected in the strokes.

Hanako didn't, but she didn't want to explain why either. There was too much pain to bring up. "She seems fine not knowing. She used to ask me, when she was younger, but not now."

"You're afraid this sensei's going to tell Hana that he's her father?"

"I don't know if he's aware that she's his daughter. But that may not matter. He's had a stroke and can't speak. That's why Hana became interested in him."

"Because she studies the brain. And language," Kiyomi said. "My husband's grandfather had that happen to him. I think I told you about him. Broke his heart. The grandfather's, I mean. He loved to talk, told lots of great stories. He came to San Francisco on a boat when he was sixteen." She paused. "I loved those stories."

"I'm sorry."

"If you don't mind my asking, why didn't you tell Hana about her father?"

"I couldn't. I'd have to explain." She reached for her teacup, then stopped, and folded her hands.

Kiyomi quickly said, "It's okay."

After a moment, Hanako said, "Look at this." She took out the piece of paper from her purse.

Kiyomi took the paper and studied it. "What is it? Looks like a kid practicing penmanship. I remember practicing for hours."

"The sensei made those marks. Hana tells me that he might be trying to write something. Trying to communicate, she said, but he can't put the strokes together right."

Kiyomi handed the paper back to Hanako. "Doesn't make any sense to me." She looked at Hanako. "Can you understand it?"

"No. I've tried." Using her chopsticks, she pointed to the one on the top right. "It could be the left part of 'water.' "

"I see what you mean," Kiyomi said as she traced over a few of them. "This could be part of 'tree' or 'forest.' "

"Or 'woods.' "

"Right. And this looks like part of 'flower.' " Kiyomi stared at Hanako. "Part of your name."

Hanako closed her eyes; the wrinkles at the corners of her eyes creased and deepened.

HANAKO LET HERSELF IN her building, walked past the elevator parts piled on the tarp, then started her slow climb up the five flights of stairs. As she reached the third floor landing, she felt the first twinges of a muscle spasm, then the hot pricks of phantom needles. She stopped on the landing, sitting on the bottom step of the next flight of stairs, and hoped that no one would see her. She took out the sensei's drawing that she had shown Kiyomi. She traced over the fine brushstrokes that had no meaning. She traced them again and again but no meaning came to her.

She stopped thinking about the sensei's brushstrokes. Stop thinking . . . how many times had the sensei told her that? But how can I concentrate if I stop thinking? she asked him. Good question, he said. Then he told her about hard concentration and soft concentration. Hard concentration is brittle; soft concentration is flexible, hard to break, like trees dancing in the wind.

She began to trace the sensei's brushstrokes once again. Like trees dancing in the wind.

Hayashi ("forest") is represented by only two trees. Be sure to make them appear mature and strong.

Hana ("flower") is a combination of the forms for "grass" or "plants" combined with "change," likely referring to "blossom." *Hana* is a good practice kanji as it has many radicals, and is easy to remember. It also represents much more than "flower." *Hana* refers implicitly to "cherry blossoms," the symbol of the bittersweet impermanence of life.

Instructor's Journal,
Zenzen School of
Japanese Calligraphy

Help me
empathize
in the end
abandon
each in their well

BERKELEY

"How's the sensei?" Tina asked Gozen as they walked into the front room of the Zenzen school.

Gozen had dark circles under his eyes. "He seems happy to be home. He can do most things okay, except some trouble walking."

"Has he made more drawings?"

Gozen gazed toward the sensei's studio. "That's all he does. I can hardly get him to stop and eat."

"I suppose that's good, that he's doing something."

Gozen sighed. "What's he supposed to do with his life? He can't teach *shodô* the way he is. Will he ever get better?"

"I can't say." Between readings for class, Tina had studied the chapter on aphasia in her neuroanatomy book. The chapter gave detailed descriptions of the neuropsychological basis for the condition, showing the complex neuronal pathways involved in communication. With extensive damage, the brain couldn't rewire itself.

While reading the chapter, she decided the sensei's case would be interesting to include in her presentation in Professor Alamo's class. Her contribution to the grand neural theory of consciousness, although she had no idea what that would be, or even how to get there. Something to do with language and consciousness. At least she had been assigned to the last presentation. That gave her twelve weeks to think about it.

The last presentation—did that mean she was the last one picked to be in the seminar?

Tina told Gozen he should go home, get some rest. He yawned, and said he hadn't slept well since the sensei had come home. He told Tina that the sensei needed little sleep since his stroke. Tina wondered if his stroke had disrupted his sleep patterns.

When Gozen left, Tina went to the sensei's studio. The sensei twisted awkwardly to face her and bow.

Tina quickly returned the bow. The gesture made her self-conscious. She knew that she didn't do it correctly—the angle wasn't right, her demeanor wasn't Japanese enough. The sensei returned to his calligraphy, his drawing. Tina sat on her heels, behind him and to the side.

On a fresh sheet of paper, he drew the same unreadable brushstrokes. She glanced through a pile of about ten that were on the floor near her. His work had become more abstract, yet more coherent, less like doodles. Perhaps it was because she was becoming familiar with them.

The sensei finished his drawing and showed it to her by moving to the side. It had an arc, almost a semicircle, and a dot above it. Like an eye? Tina nodded enthusiastically.

"Wonderful. *Sugoi*," she said, although she wasn't sure if that was the right use of the word.

The sensei suddenly got up and walked unsteadily but deliberately out of the studio. She didn't follow him, supposing that she would if he didn't return after a while. Perhaps he was finally going to sleep.

She looked through his abstract calligraphy for two or three minutes, when the sensei returned with a box. He squatted down, took the inkstone out of the box, and put it on the table. He picked up a stick of ink and rubbed the edge in the well of the inkstone. His motions were not clumsy, but not smooth either. He poured some water from the small pitcher and then rubbed the inkstick some more. The water and ink turned a deep black.

He picked up a brush and offered it to Tina.

"Me? I'm sorry, I never learned calligraphy. I hardly know any kanji." She tried to think of how to say all that in Japanese.

The sensei stared at the brush. Tina was about to take the brush when Mr. Robert called out from the front of the house. Tina apologized and got up.

"Tina?" Mr. Robert said when he saw her. "I thought . . . I thought Gozen would be here."

"He was exhausted. I told him I'd stay with the sensei."

"But you've got school, all those papers and books to read."

"I'm here partly because of school."

He took a step toward the studio as if to protect his sensei. "You mean, you're here to make him a research project."

"I wouldn't put it that way. I'm trying to help him."

"How?" He crossed his arms across his chest.

"I don't know for sure. Not yet."

He headed toward the studio. "I'm here now. I'll take care of him."

Tina watched him walk away. As if she'd seen him for the first time, his back looked too large, out of proportion to his slender frame, almost hulking. She turned away, picked up her backpack, and walked out of the house.

In your hands
I'll rest here

AFTER CLASS, Tina poked her head into Wijjie's office. His feet were propped up on his desk, a book in his lap. "How about I buy you dinner somewhere," Tina said.

"And take me away from studying?" He shut his book and stood up. "Deal, but you don't have to buy. How about my place. I make a great pasta."

"As long as I can buy a bottle of wine. Or two."

ON THE TABLE WAS the ziti pasta with veggies lightly sautéed in olive oil, freshly grated Parmigiano-Reggiano, and mixed salad greens with balsamic vinaigrette. Of the two bottles of wine Tina bought, the white was finished and the red was two glasses gone. Tina had kept up with Wijjie until her third glass, after which she slowed down.

"He's trying to communicate, I know," Tina said of Zenzen sensei. "His drawings, his sort-of calligraphy means something to him."

"How can you tell?" Wijjie said, taking a bite of his second serving of pasta.

Tina thought for a moment, her mind was swimming. "He acts like it's supposed to mean something. He works so intently on it. He's not just making random marks—I know that's an assumption on my part. But then he shows it to me, like he wants me to read it."

"That's the problem, though, isn't it? In these kinds of cases, we don't know exactly what the patient, or research subject, is thinking."

"True," Tina said, spearing a tomato wedge and mopping it in the dark red vinaigrette. "Say I'm making an hypothesis." She put the tomato in her mouth.

"What do you think he is trying to communicate?" Wijjie asked, then added, "As an hypothesis?"

"I have no idea, not yet." She took a sip of water, and looked at her pasta, trying to decide if she should have another bite. "But there's something there, it's almost as if he wants me to help him, or, I don't know, there's just something there."

"Something there?"

Tina took a last sip of wine. "Right, something there."

WIJJIE SERVED THEM chocolate biscotti and coffee from his espresso machine. "Don't tell me you made the biscotti, too?"

"Nope. I picked it up at the Rockridge Market."

"It's good."

They were sitting on the couch. Wijjie took a drink of

coffee. "The sensei is an interesting case. You should keep up with him. A good research subject will get you a long way in this business."

Tina stirred her espresso, dissolving the sugar. "Funny."

"Funny?"

"That's what Professor Porter said too. She's acting strangely about the sensei."

Wijjie shrugged. "Academic researchers are all strange. It's part of the process. Being such an expert in one narrow topic makes the brain lopsided, out of whack."

Tina laughed. "I see these big heads, one side of the brain huge, the other side atrophied to nothing. They have to keep pushing their heads back onto their shoulders because they keep falling to one side."

"You got it."

Tina settled back into the couch.

Wijjie did the same. They said nothing for a while, then Wijjie said, "Feeling good?"

Tina smiled and turned her head to face him. "Very."

Wijjie leaned toward her. She relaxed into his kiss. She kissed him back, tasting all the ziti and garlic and olive oil and wine and vinaigrette and espresso and chocolate, the tastes piling up on each other. His tongue, lightly probing, met hers.

The kiss lasted a long while. When Wijjie pulled back, Tina said, "That was nice."

"Nice . . . ?"

"I mean, very nice, wonderful. *Sugoi.*"

"Sue what?"

"Never mind."

Wijjie leaned toward her, kissing her. She put her hand on the back of his neck. He put his hand on the side of her neck, just under her ear, then let it slowly slide down to her breast.

She continued kissing him while he gently caressed, then she pulled away. Wijjie's eyes opened and focused on her.

"I should be going. Before we go any further."

"Oh?"

"I'm living with a guy."

"I know. But you're here right now."

Tina crossed her arms in front of her, then uncrossed them when it reminded her of Mr. Robert. "I know, but I'd have to go home sometime. I'd rather wait until I'm no longer living with him, if that is what's going to happen."

Wijjie rested his hand on her shoulder. "Fair enough."

Tina stood and picked up the coffee cups. "Come on, I'll help you clean up. I need to get home early for once. I'm feeling sleep-deprived."

Zenzen sensei dipped his brush into the inkstone, as he had many times before—so a feeling told him. He had no feeling for how much time had passed since he last used the inkstone. Time no longer held meaning: no minutes or hours or days or years. The feeling of time was emptiness, a void in his existence that could not be expressed.

The void was immense. The more he tried to understand it, to communicate it, the more he found that he couldn't, as if he were tied to invisible bindings. As if a force gripped him, held him down.

Then, suddenly, there had been the insight—it was the ink-stone. The inkstone would provide a connection, a path, that he must follow to fill the void. If he could only find a way to push aside the emptiness, all would be good, all would be complete.

A wave of dense, heavy emptiness submerged him.

Neatly tucked and tied
it won't contain my life

SAN FRANCISCO

Tina had been asleep only a few minutes when Kiyomi called. "Hana," Kiyomi said, "it's your mother."

"What's wrong?"

"We were walking home; I mean, I was walking your mother home. After work. We had to work late." Kiyomi caught her breath and said, "She stopped."

"Stopped?"

"Just stopped walking. She said she couldn't move her legs anymore. She sat down on the steps of that theater, you know, on Bush. I'm sorry. I'm sorry."

"It's okay, Aunt Kiyomi. Where is she now?"

"She's still there. I ran back to the Tempura House to call you, that's where I am. I wanted to call an ambulance, but she told me not to worry."

"I'll be right there."

Mr. Robert was standing next to Tina when she hung up. "What's up?"

Tina moved to the closet and slipped on her jeans and a bulky sweater. "It's Ma, she's had an attack and Kiyomi's worried about her."

"I'll go with you." He reached for his jeans.

"No, please. I'd rather go alone."

Mr. Robert glared at her, then, without a word, got back in their bed.

TINA RAN UP the stairs to her mother's apartment and opened the drawer where her mother told her she had hidden the marijuana. In the back of the drawer, she found the joints.

Tina ran down Bush to the Nob Hill Theater. On the steps leading up to the theater, her mother was sitting, Kiyomi standing next to her. Even in the dim light, Tina could see that her mother was pale.

"You didn't have to come, Ha-*chan*. I'm just catching my breath."

Kiyomi said, "More than that, she says her legs won't move."

Tina sat next to her mother. "Will you be okay?"

"It just takes a few minutes."

Tina looked up at Kiyomi and said, "It's okay, Aunt Kiyomi, I'll wait with her."

"Are you sure? I can wait."

"I'm sure. Thanks."

"All right. I'll be at home if you need me." She stepped over and patted Hanako on the shoulder.

Hanako gave her a weak smile. They watched Kiyomi walk back toward the Tempura House. "Do you want to try to walk?" Tina asked.

"Not yet," her mother said. "I'm sorry."

"What does it feel like?"

Hanako thought for a moment. "Like someone squeezing my legs."

Tina said, "You mean like when your legs fall asleep?"

"Yes, like that."

Tina took out the joint from her pocket along with a book of Tempura House matches. "Ma, do you want to try this?"

When she didn't say no, Tina put the joint in her mouth and struck a match. She lit the joint and took a couple of shallow puffs.

"Smelly," Hanako said.

Tina took the joint, pinched between her thumb and index finger, and held it near her mother's lips. Hanako hesitated, then leaned forward.

"Take a puff, hold it in your lungs as long as possible."

Hanako put her puckered lips on the joint as if she were kissing it rather than smoking. She took a tiny puff. She tried to inhale it, but most of the smoke had already escaped. She coughed a little.

"Try again," Tina said. A young couple dressed in black approached. "Cool," one of them said as they sniffed the smoke.

Hanako waited until they passed, then she opened her lips and put them around the end of the joint. She took a deep, inhaling breath, and she leaned back. She held her breath—like a child learning how to swim underwater. After a long moment, she let out the smoke with a cough, as if getting her breath back after drowning.

"Take another," Tina said.

Hanako, coughing, pushed Tina's arm away. Tina patted her mother on the back as she inhaled a deep breath.

Tina took a hit off the joint, just to keep it lighted. Her mother's coughing gradually slowed. Tina said, "You must have gotten a lot."

Hanako coughed.

When she stopped, Tina held the joint out to her. "Another?"

Hanako shook her head. "That's worse than the pain."

"Just one more." Tina handed her the joint.

Pinching it as if it were a bug, Hanako put the joint to her lips and inhaled deeply. She held it in, then expelled it in one big puff. Tina laughed.

They sat there for a while, watching the traffic whiz by. A few patrons walked out of the theater. Tina felt a mild buzz. Good stuff, Gillian.

"How are you feeling?" Tina asked.

"Tired. A little dizzy." Hanako stood up and said, "I'm going home. Are you coming?"

HALFWAY UP THE STAIRS to Hanako's apartment, Tina said, "You should be getting a reduction on your rent."

"The manager said the elevator would be finished soon."

In the apartment, Tina followed her mother into the kitchen where she started some water for tea. She always had to be cooking or making tea when there was anyone in the apartment.

Hanako got out the teapot, cups, and tin of green tea. Tina sat at the table and watched. She put the half-smoked joint onto the table. "I suppose you want me to throw the rest of this away."

Hanako glanced at the joint out of the corner of her eye, like a sleepy cat nonchalantly watching a moth before it swipes at it. Hanako swept her hand over the joint and it disappeared. She opened the drawer with her collection of chopsticks and put the joint inside and closed the drawer.

Tina said, "I can get you some more."

Hanako put a few pinches of green tea into the pot. "From your friend the doctor?"

"Not Wijjie. Another student."

"He's your new boyfriend?"

"Mother."

"Robert-*san*'s not happy about him."

"Mr. Robert shouldn't be talking to you about my personal life."

Hanako touched the side of the kettle. While she waited for the water to heat a few more degrees, Hanako said, "You should be nicer to Robert-*san*. Listen to what he says."

Tina's jaw clenched. She took out the folded paper that was in her pocket and changed the subject. "I brought some more of Zenzen sensei's drawings."

Hanako did not turn to look. She touched the kettle again, shut off the burner, and poured water into the pot, then a little into each cup. She waited a few seconds, then emptied out each cup.

Tina watched her mother, knowing that she had heard. Tina was tired. She put the drawings aside, and waited for the tea to steep—only ninety seconds, otherwise it gets bitter.

*What's worse
caring enough
to hate
or not caring
at all*

MR. ROBERT CAME into the kitchen where Tina was studying, her reader open on the table. Her nearly full cup of coffee had gone cold. When she noticed him standing at her side, she reached for her cup and took a sip. She grimaced and got up to put the cup in the microwave. She turned the timer to ninety seconds.

Mr. Robert said, "I'm stopping by your mother's today, before I start teaching. Need to tell me anything about her?"

"Like what?"

"I don't know. That's why I'm asking."

Tina said, "She's fine now. She had temporary paralysis, her legs. It went away."

"Good."

The microwave timer dinged. Tina retrieved her coffee.

Mr. Robert said, "You aren't going to see Zenzen sensei today, are you?"

"Yes, I am, why?"

Mr. Robert watched her drink a sip of coffee. "We appreciate your help, but you really don't have to do anything. We have enough students to help out. And you've got your classes, work. Not to mention the time you've had to spend with your mother."

"I'm okay."

"Really. I don't want you to have to worry about him."

"I'm okay," Tina repeated with impatience. "I've got my life under control. But I really need to study now." She turned a page in her reader and picked up her yellow highlighting pen.

TINA FINISHED THE ARTICLE, not remembering much of what she had read. She closed her reader, capped the marker, and took her coffee over to the tiny balcony of their condo that overlooked the courtyard. The small patch of grass looked artificially green, as if it had been painted.

She wasn't sure when it started to go wrong with Mr. Robert. They had their first real fight when Tina decided she needed to move back to San Francisco to be closer to her mother; Mr. Robert hadn't wanted to move. He was still a year away from finishing his master's degree. Tina said that he could stay in San Diego to finish, but he wanted to be together. Didn't she? he asked her. Of course, she said. He said, Well, let's just go. She said, What about your degree? He shrugged and said it wasn't as important as her mother. When she was accepted in the Ph.D. program at Cal, she said that he should see about transferring to a program there as well. Not interested, was all he said. Why not? she said. Just not.

But the problems—general disinterest, conversations that

died in the middle, a sex life that had waned ("In the mood?" "Nah." "Okay.")—had started before the fight. Mr. Robert was "into" his studies, he told her one night when she asked him if anything was wrong. He apologized and promised to take her out to the beach that weekend. Have a picnic somewhere. And they actually went, but Mr. Robert spent most of the afternoon staring out to the sea with an intensity that made it seem he was looking all the way to Japan.

Tina realized then it was disappointment that Mr. Robert was feeling. And she knew it was disappointment not only about his life, his slowing pace on his master's degree, his disappointment about being back in the States and returning to the bottom rung of the ladder (in Japan, as a teacher, he had been at the top—a sensei), but mostly his disappointment seemed directed toward Tina. She didn't know exactly what he wanted from her, but even if she did, whatever it was, he had already decided that she couldn't give it to him. Her offer of letting him stay in San Diego to finish his degree was his out, she thought, so she was surprised when he vehemently wanted them to stay together.

Back in the kitchen, Tina poured out the last few swallows of her coffee. The brown cold, bitter liquid swirled around the sink and flowed down the drain.

BERKELEY

Tina watched the sensei prepare the ink. His dexterity had improved perceptibly over the few days she had been watching him.

She and Gozen had just returned from taking him to the hospital, where his doctor gave him a checkup, and his physical therapist put him through a rehabilitation regimen. While

Gozen waited outside the hospital, Tina led the sensei inside and stayed with him until they finished.

Zenzen sensei picked up his brush and gazed at the blank paper for several moments—Tina wondered if he was having a problem, some cognitive dysfunction—then, in a blur, he quickly dipped the brush into the inkstone and splashed ink on the paper. He turned to Tina, then moved to the side, away from the worktable. Tina scooted on her knees across the *tatami* mats to see what he had drawn. The drawing looked less like any Japanese character or stroke she had seen him create. His work was a swooping line, almost like a wave. Drops of ink had splashed randomly on the paper.

The sensei noticed Tina and handed the brush to her. She took it, not sure what he wanted her to do. He adjusted the brush until her fingers were pointing down and the brush was vertical. Moving back, he made a quick movement with his hand, drawing the stroke in the air.

Tina traced over the sensei's drawing without touching the brush to the paper. She traced the stroke again. The sensei took away the paper and replaced it with a fresh sheet from the stack near the table. He put the paperweight on the top edge to hold the paper in place. Tina dipped the brush into the ink. She poised it above the paper; the brush felt light in her grasp, almost as if it weren't there. The ink flowed onto the paper as she copied the sensei's stroke.

Her face flushed hotly when she finished. Her drawing bore little resemblance to the sensei's. Tina had seen Mr. Robert's practice calligraphy that his instructor had graded by drawing red circles around errors. Tina's attempt would have been covered with red.

When she put the brush down, the sensei was gazing at her drawing. His expression was one of a strange, almost tearful, satisfaction.

When things become muddled
I see clearly
It's ambiguity that blinds me

Winter's Moon,
Dying

JANUARY 1977
KYOTO, JAPAN

The twenty-ninth Daizen sensei, Shimano, watched as Hanako drew the character for "winter." Her technique, after only a little more than a year of practice, was refined and elegant, her works rich with feeling. When she had completed the poetic phrase "Winter's moon, dying," she set her brush on the stand.

"Good," the sensei said.

"Thank you for saying so, but mine is so different from yours." Hanako compared her effort to his original work that she was copying.

"Different, yes, but still good."

"*Shodô* reveals a lot about a person, doesn't it?" Hanako pointed to her version of "moon" and said, "See? Mine lacks the movement of yours. As if the moon were stopped dead in the sky. And the strokes aren't as strong. Mine are wilting."

The sensei studied her calligraphy and decided that she was right. How could he not see what was so obvious when she pointed it out? To make the thought vanish, he asked, "What do your strokes say about you?"

Hanako leaned over her work, the movement revealed the side and nape of her neck. The sensei resisted touching her. When she sat back, her hair fell over her neck, hiding it again. "I'm not sure," she said. "Perhaps I'm not very strong. That I'm not progressing. What do you think?"

"I could only conjecture." He moved close to her for a better view of her work. She didn't move away and, in the space between them, the heat of their bodies mingled. "The lack of movement may indicate that you are too hesitant."

"That's right," Hanako said. "I do feel hesitant. I have to stop and consider my every thought or action."

Relieved that she took his comment so well, he said, "That would show in your calligraphy. The subconscious knows how to make a good brushstroke, but our conscious mind thinks it knows better."

She nodded. "It wants to be in control."

"Exactly."

"What about my wilting strokes? They are so weak, compared with yours."

The sensei studied her work again. "Now that I look at them, I wouldn't call them wilting, or weak."

Fuyu no getsu: "winter's moon."

The original meaning of the character *fuyu* ("winter") is not known, although the present character evolved from the phonetic use of a pictograph that meant "gather together" as in "compact." This interpretation may refer to ice compacting in the winter. The feeling is often imparted metaphorically in poetry to lost love, as the heart itself hardens and shrinks.

Getsu ("moon") evolved from a pictograph of a moon. The center stroke represents the moon's

"No?"

"I'd say they were honest. You see here," he said, pointing to "moon" and tracing the upturned tail of the second stroke, "your extension is much more in keeping with the poem."

Hanako tilted her head to look closely at the stroke. "I'm sorry, I don't understand. Mine dies away . . . oh, I see."

The sensei pointed to his calligraphy, tracing the end of the second stroke. "My extension is sharp, moving upward briskly. A classical correctness. But not at all in the mood of the poem."

"Mine is also correct?"

"Yes. What do you think about, what do you feel, as you draw the characters?"

Hanako thought for a moment, then said, "At first, I concentrate on my form. Posture, breathing, the flow of my *ki*. Then I visualize the character. Just before I start drawing, I try to stop thinking at all, just let the feeling of the stroke come through the brush."

"That's good," he said.

"Sometimes, though, in the middle of drawing it, I start to think about what I'm doing, and it all comes out wrong."

The sensei nodded. "That happens often." It had been happening more than he wanted to admit.

"That's a lot like life, though. Isn't it?" Hanako said.

"Is that what you have experienced?"

Hanako sat back on the *tatami,* relaxing from the rigid posture she maintained while drawing. She turned to face the sensei. "One can think too much, try too hard. It's a struggle, isn't it?"

"Part of defining yourself?"

"I can think about what I want to be, but I can't force myself into being what I'm not. No matter how desirable that might be."

The sensei nodded. "And the more you think about it, the harder you try, the more you become the undesirable self?"

"I am changing," she said softly, as if to herself. "Your teaching has started to change me."

If only he could tell her that she had started to change him, much more than he could possibly be changing her. "A good change, I hope."

With a tilt of her head, she thought for a long moment. "Sensei, may I use the inkstone? The Daizen Inkstone?"

"Of course." He got up and took out the inkstone from its velvet-lined box. After setting it on their worktable, he prepared a pool of ink in its well. Hanako took a clean sheet of rice paper from the stack near the table. She got into the proper position, took a deep breath, and exhaled slowly. She picked up the brush and adjusted it in her hand until she had the proper grip. She dipped the brush into the ink, and drew the characters for "deep," "self," and "discovery."

She set the brush down. "I didn't stop to think at all."

"Look." The sensei pointed to the character for "deep." "You captured it so well, the feeling of deep, as if it were enticing me into it."

"Do you think so?"

"And the others . . . as if you left part of yourself in them. Excellent. You should sign it."

"If you'll countersign it."

"Of course."

She took out her signature seal from her bag and dipped the seal into the pot of red seal ink. "Where?"

The sensei pointed to a spot on the left side of the paper, about a quarter of the way up from the bottom. Placing the seal in the correct place was as critical to a work as the quality of the calligraphy. But knowing where to place the seal was not easily taught, as each work demanded a different placement, to attain proper balance.

When she had sealed the work, he put red ink on his own seal, the seal of the twenty-ninth Daizen sensei that he had hand-carved soon after his inauguration. He placed his seal just below hers.

AS HE WATCHED her clean the Daizen Inkstone at the sink in the back of the studio, he moved close to her, until they were touching. Hanako leaned into him; she could feel the heat of his body. They dropped to the floor, she put the inkstone next to her and pulled him toward her.

"DON'T FORGET to take your calligraphy," the sensei said.

"I couldn't," she said. "You must keep it."

"You should take it."

"But I can't," she said, then hurried out of the studio to the taxi that was waiting for her.

BERKELEY

Tina picked up a brain scan from the stack that was now higher than when she started her duty. She was getting quicker at reading Howard's scrawled annotations and entering them in the database, but he could write faster. At this rate, she'd never catch up, at least until Howard graduated. Or died.

Finished with a scan, she took a deep breath and stretched. Except for the slight humming coming from the computer, the filing room was quiet. It reminded her—in both good ways and bad—of her closet bedroom. Good, because the room had the same cocoon feel; bad, because she was still stuck in a closet.

There was a knock on the door. She got up and opened

it. Looking tired, as if he were about to yawn, Wijjie said, "Working?"

She pointed to the stack of brain scans. "Entering data."

As Wijjie walked over to the scans, he looked around. "This is a depressing little room. How can you stand being shut up in here?"

He picked up the top scan on the stack and looked at it. "Slave labor is what you're up to," he said, holding the scan in front of her. "Can you read this writing?"

Tina twisted her head to read the notes: "Broca's area lesion, approximately one centimeter—"

"I'm impressed, but I can't believe you have to do this kind of crap. They could hire a data-entry person who'd finish it in a couple of days."

"Professor Porter said it would help me get up to speed on the research." Tina took the scan from Wijjie and put it back on the stack. "You look like you missed a couple of nights' sleep."

"Just one. Gillian dragged me out."

Tina forced a smile. "I bet she had to tie you up and throw you in her car."

"Practically," he said while he yawned. "Sorry."

"Where did you go?"

"The City. Not one, not two, but *three* clubs."

"You're too old for that."

"Tell me about it." Wijjie sat on a chair and stretched. "But I didn't look you up to get a bunch of grief."

Tina sat down. "How'd you find out where I was?"

"I stopped by your office. Howie was there, told me to check in here." Wijjie took another scan from the pile and glanced at it.

"Howie?"

Wijjie grinned. "Don't you call that Howard guy Howie?"

"I don't think he'd like it. Besides, he doesn't seem like the Howie type."

"But then you call all the professors 'professor.' Professor Porter, Professor Alamo. This is Berkeley, not Cambridge. They want to be chummy here, on a first-name basis with us grad students."

"I call Professor Porter 'Karyn,' at least when she reminds me. What do you call Professor Alamo?"

" 'Alonzo' to his face. 'Alamo' behind his back." He put the scan back on the stack and picked out another one. "I haven't gotten to the 'Al' stage with him."

Tina pointed to the scans. "Don't get those mixed up. Howie has them in a very specific order."

"See, 'Howie' has a certain ring to it."

"A sarcastic ring."

Wijjie shrugged, then rubbed the back of his neck and tilted it from side to side. "Anyway, the reason I found you was that I had a great idea about the calligraphy teacher you told me about. A very cool research study."

Tina felt a twinge of alarm, and she got up and shut the door.

"What was that for?" Wijjie said.

"Professor Porter would be mad if she knew I was talking to you about the sensei. I told you she's pressuring me into using him in her research."

"Classic signs of paranoia and delusions of grandeur." Wijjie scooted his chair closer to Tina and leaned toward her. For a moment, she thought he was going to kiss her.

"Here's what we do," he whispered. "We put the sensei in the H-Fifty-one-hundred and show him his drawings, one at a time. While he looks at the drawings, we take a series of fMRI scans of his brain."

"So we can see what areas are active in his brain? And if they vary from image to image?"

"I'm thinking we can get a correlation between different drawings and the activated areas. Say one drawing activates the right brain, near his temporal cortex region, then that drawing would likely have something to do with a past event, because that's where those kinds of memories tend to be stored. We might be able to further narrow it down to a more specific memory if another region is also activated, say the ventromedial nucleus, the appetite control center."

"Then the memory would be about food?"

"Can't say for sure, but you'd have a strong case for that conclusion."

"If we find strong correlations, then we could figure out what the sensei is trying to communicate, in a crude way."

"It might lead to something more refined, even broader than just interpreting his drawings."

"I like it." Tina smiled and stood up. "Let's check the lab schedule for tonight."

WHEN THEY FOUND that the schedule was open early that evening, Wijjie drove Tina to the Zenzen school. One of the students was taking care of the sensei, but Gozen had told him that Tina was helping with the sensei.

The three of them watched the sensei at work in his studio. He had finished several more drawings. Tina bowed to the sensei and after he returned the bow, she took the stack into the front room. The sensei didn't notice, or care, as he picked up his brush and started another.

"That's all he does now?" Wijjie asked Tina.

"Yes. All day, and most of the night."

"Classic signs of stroke-related obsessive behavior."

She and Wijjie went through the drawings and picked several to use in the experiment. They told the student that they would be back in about an hour to take the sensei for tests. The student didn't question them.

Back in Wijjie's office, they scanned the drawings into his computer, formatting them to be used in the image display of the H-5100. Then, in the lab, they loaded the files on the computer. As Wijjie manned the controls, Tina checked the display in the machine. "It's working."

THE SENSEI FOLLOWED Tina out of the school and into Wijjie's car. He seemed confused as they drove up to the loading zone of the institute, got out of the car, and walked down the stairs. When they entered the lab, Tina flipped the switch that lighted the sign just outside the door: "Experiment in progress, do not enter."

When he saw the MRI machine, he relaxed and climbed onto the platform bed.

Wijjie set the controls of the H-5100 while Tina adjusted the head restraint. The sensei calmly gazed up at the ceiling.

"Ready," Wijjie called out.

Tina said to the sensei, "Just focus here." She pointed to the image display screen. "Here's where the images will come up."

The sensei made no sign that he understood, but his eyes focused on the end of her finger. Two lines intersected in the middle of the screen. Tina backed out of the room, watching the sensei to make sure he didn't move his head. In the control room, she sat at the computer. "All right, I'm ready."

Wijjie said, "Three . . . two . . . one. Go."

Tina pushed a key and the image on the computer monitor changed from the target cross to the first image. After a two-second interval, the image disappeared and the cross target reappeared on the screen. Then another image appeared.

They repeated the procedure several times for about fifteen minutes until Wijjie said, "Okay, that's it."

He and Tina went into the scanning room and helped

the sensei out of the machine. He wobbled a little as Tina guided him to a chair. Tina sat next to him, but he didn't seem to notice she was there.

Reposed in respite
I feel regal
Benignly in control

TINA AND WIJJIE returned the sensei to the school, and he went immediately into his studio. Tina thanked the student for waiting. On the way back to the institute to download the scans of the sensei, Wijjie stopped at a liquor store. "Be right back," he said.

He returned with a chilled bottle of champagne. "Thought we should celebrate while we finish up."

"We can see what our brains look like on champagne."

Wijjie laughed. "While I was in there, I realized we forgot one thing in our experimental design."

"What's that?"

"A control group."

Tina tapped the dashboard and turned to Wijjie. "We need to do fMRI scans of someone other than the sensei. A comparison."

"Yep. Maybe we could both take a turn in the machine looking at them. That way we'd at least have two comparisons."

"You want to go first?"

WIJJIE WAS IN THE H-5100, his head in the restraint, the stimulus display screen set above his eyes. "I'm ready."

In the control room, Tina started the image display and the scanning. When finished, Wijjie and she exchanged places. He positioned her head in the restraint. "Comfy?"

"I could fall asleep."

"We wouldn't get much on your scan," Wijjie said as he walked back to the control room. "Focus on the target. The images will start in about thirty seconds."

The images began to appear one after the other, and as they did, she began to find patterns in them, some looked less like Japanese characters than others.

When all the images had been presented, Wijjie helped her out of the machine. They went back into the computer control room and printed a page of their scans.

"Here's your brain," Wijjie said, showing her one of the prints.

"Any similarities between yours and mine?"

"Not if you're lucky."

They spread the prints out on a layout table in two rows.

"Not much going on," Tina said. "What about the sensei's?"

Wijjie printed out a page of the sensei's scans and placed it next to the other two. "What do you think?"

"Hard to tell from just these."

"I'll start printing the rest out. How about that champagne while we wait?"

They toasted, touching paper cups of champagne together. "To our first experiment," Wijjie said.

"To your experiment," Tina said, then took a sip. "Very nice. Good choice."

"Yes, it is nice, isn't it? A day without champagne is . . . well, a bad day." Wijjie grinned and took a drink.

"You never seem to have a bad day," Tina said. "Champagne or not."

"Pathological ignorance, I suppose."

"I'd settle for a dose of that right now."

"Actually, I avoid all things that might be the least bit uncomfortable."

"You can't *always* avoid them. Surely you must have had a bad day once in your life."

Wijjie gave her a weak grin. "Had one really bad day."

"What? Tell me," Tina said.

"You can't tell anyone else."

"Of course not."

"And one other thing."

"What?"

"After I tell you what happened, I don't want to talk about it. Not a word."

Tina started to ask why, then she shrugged. "Not a word."

Wijjie took a big gulp of champagne, refilled their glasses, then started: "I was a resident in a hospital in a suburb of Denver. There was a children's hospital near where I was working, and I volunteered to work on a research project there. A study of kids with severe peanut allergy. The researchers were testing a new vaccine that reduced the severity of their allergic reactions. Perhaps, they hoped, reduced it enough to save lives; peanut allergy reactions can be fatal.

"The researchers had set up a control group of kids who didn't have peanut allergy. Half of that group got the vaccine, half got an injection of a peanut solution. The experimental group, the kids with the allergy, were also divided into two groups."

Tina said, "None of them got the peanut solution, right?"

"Right. One half got the vaccine, the other a placebo. My job was to administer the injections to some of the kids. Of course, it was a blind experiment." He paused for a sip.

"You didn't know which kids you got or what you were injecting them with?"

"Yes, that was the research protocol. This one night—I remember that I had worked a long day—I showed up at the children's hospital. I picked up the tray of injections from the researchers, just like usual. Each was marked with one of the kids' names, again as usual. I went to the rooms where the kids waited for their injections. One of the research assistants always accompanied me. They kept the records and made sure the kids got the injections with the names on them.

"Everything was going fine. I was tired, but the kids always got me going again. They acted so brave getting the shots in their thin little arms. This one boy, Jeremy, especially talked tough. 'I'm ready, let's do it,' he'd say. He was eleven, talked about going into middle school the next year.

"I gave him his injection, told him he'd have a good time in middle school, at least once he started growing to catch up with the girls. He said, 'Who cares about girls?' 'Good point,' I said.

"I went down to the next room, almost finished, glad to be. I just wanted to go home and crash. I hadn't been in the next room for a second, when one of the nurses at the hospital came in. She said Jeremy was having a problem.

"It was more than a problem. By the time I got back to him, he couldn't breathe. His airways were completely constricted; his pulse was fluttering. He just kept looking at me, with his eyes pleading for help as his face and throat swelled like a balloon. He had all the symptoms of anaphylactic shock. I assumed that he was having a severe reaction to whatever I had injected him with. He needed adrenaline right away. I yelled at the nurse to get me some epinephrine, and she was off to get it. But by the time she got back it was too late. I injected Jeremy, but it didn't help. By the time he died, his eyes had swollen shut."

Wijjie finished the champagne in his cup. Tina didn't know what she would have said, even if Wijjie would have let her say something. Then he looked up at her and said, "One of the researchers had mixed up the solutions. Put peanut solution in Jeremy's injection. Jeremy was in the experimental group. Highly allergic."

Tina said, "Wijjie—"

"Please," Wijjie said.

They sat in silence for a while.

She finally said, "So it's a conscious thing you do."

Wijjie rubbed his jaw. " 'Conscious thing'?"

"Avoiding pain."

"I suppose it's mostly subconscious. Like a big gorilla in the jungle. Can't see him but you know he's there. And you don't want to go where he might be."

WHEN THEY FINISHED the bottle of champagne, Wijjie leaned toward her and they kissed.

Wijjie leaned away and said, "Nice vintage. Seventy-seven? Seventy-eight?"

"Seventy-eight." Tina kissed him this time. "I have to make a confession."

Wijjie leaned back. "Uh-oh."

Sexual responses are largely controlled and directed by nuclei of the *hypothalamus*, although the male and female neuroanatomy (and responses) are very different. In males, the *medial preoptic nucleus* directs autonomic responses to the penis (increased blood flow = erection), and sends a signal to the cortex, giving rise to conscious sexual excitement. In females, the *ventromedial nucleus* largely directs sexual arousal. (Interestingly, the ventromedial nucleus is also involved in appetite for food; that might explain dual hunger–sexual response to cannabinoids. Question: Why do we know so much about the biochemical reasons for what we experience, but still know so little about consciousness? Why do I know so little about myself? I mean, I'm just a bunch of cells that act in regular, predetermined ways. How does "self" arise from chemical reactions? Why is so much still a mystery, so unpredictable?)

Neuroscience Notebook,
Christina Hana Suzuki

Tina smiled for a moment. "I've been thinking of something kind of kinky."

"Kinky?"

"Definitely kinky."

"Okay," Wijjie said, drawing out the word slowly. "How kinky?"

"Have you ever wondered what your brain looks like when you're having an orgasm?"

Wijjie glanced over to the H-5100. "That would be kinky. But—"

"It's not like we'd be having sex," Tina said before he could bring up what she had said the other night in his apartment.

"No?"

"We'd be doing it in the name of science."

Wijjie took her cup that she was gripping and put it down. "If it's in the name of science."

SAN FRANCISCO

After the walk home from the Tempura House, and the long trek up the stairs, Hanako took off her kimono and wrapped herself in a *yukata* robe. Sitting at the kitchen table, she spread out the sensei's drawings. With a chopstick that she held like a brush, she poised it over the drawing. She thought back to the sensei's lessons on the value of tracing the works of master calligraphers. The student could begin to feel the proper movement.

But she didn't know where to start tracing the sensei's drawing. Which of his strokes would come first?

There was no way to know how he would have drawn it. She tried a few variations, tracing it one way, then another, until a pang of regret came over her. The feeling was also of loss, of intense grief. She stopped tracing the character and closed her eyes. The sharpness of the feeling gradually receded until it was merely a shadow of emotion. She opened her eyes and started tracing it again.

Regret, definitely regret, flooded over her, catching her breath like a blast of winter wind. The chopstick fell from her grasp. She got up from the table and went into her bedroom. On top of her dresser was an old coffee mug filled with a dozen Tempura House pens. The bundle of pens had been there for years, yet now looked different to her, as if someone else had put them there and she was seeing them for the first time. Or as if someone had arranged them differently. And yet it reminded her of something familiar. The feeling made her shiver, and she plucked one of the pens from the bundle.

In the kitchen, she wrote the kanji for "regret" on the back of the first drawing.

Correct stroke order must be mastered so completely that the calligrapher is not consciously counting or planning the strokes while drawing a character. This effort would destroy the mind-body unification required of *shodō*.

Tracing the works of master calligraphers can help the beginner train the hand and mind in the movement for fine brush-strokes. One must not spend too much time doing these exercises, as calligraphers must develop their own minds.

Instructor's Journal, Zenzen School of Japanese Calligraphy

Cut open
and laid bare
cold air
and painful
but thickening skin
will suffocate

A Defining Moment

FEBRUARY 1977

KOBE, JAPAN

The walk home from the neighborhood grocery took twenty minutes, a pleasant stroll, when Hanako wasn't in a hurry. That morning, she gave herself plenty of time to plan that night's dinner, clean what needed to be cleaned of the house, and take her bath before walking down to the store.

By one in the afternoon, she had returned from the store, eaten a light lunch of leftovers, and prepared what she could for dinner—washing and chopping vegetables, thawing the fish. She would have an hour to practice calligraphy before leaving for her lesson. Her practice sessions were always focused, and always gave her a sense of satisfaction, even on the days when she could tell her calligraphy wasn't very good.

She kept her calligraphy supplies in a department store box that once held linen napkins, hidden in a closet full of mops, brooms, buckets, and the vacuum. She would dispose of her practice sheets with the newspapers for recycling.

When she returned from her lessons in Kyoto, she would finish preparing dinner. Then she would wait.

While she waited, her mind aimlessly bounced from thought to thought. No one had told her about the waiting. Her mother had told her about cooking and cleaning, about maintaining wifely demeanor, such as being properly demure when addressed, especially with a husband such as Tetsuo Suzuki. Waiting had never been discussed.

Sometimes she would read, while she waited, or listen to music. But she couldn't practice her calligraphy, not with her husband coming home at unpredictable times. She wouldn't have time to put away her supplies. Often, bored with reading or music, she would sit at the table, holding a chopstick like a brush and drawing phantom characters until time accelerated into nothingness.

"HELLO," HER HUSBAND CALLED out one evening as he came through the door.

The greeting was unusual. Tetsuo rarely said anything until after he had changed, taken a bath, and had a gulp or two of scotch or *sake*.

"Hello. A good day?" Hanako ventured.

"Yes. Excellent," he said.

"Good." She helped him out of his suit.

"A new hotel deal," he said. "In Hawaii. Maui."

"Maui. That's good."

"Five hundred luxury rooms, all with ocean views. Championship golf course. Four pools. Upscale shopping complex."

Hanako hung up his suit coat as he went on. "A deal with Osaka Travel Group to send all their honeymooners there. Package deals with vacationers. And"—he paused for a moment—"I'm letting your father and his bank handle the financing."

"He'll be pleased."

"Pleased?" Tetsuo laughed in his short, precise, sharp way. "This will make his career. This will make him president of the bank one day."

"Thank you," Hanako said. She bowed her head.

"I'll be leaving tomorrow for a few weeks, maybe longer, to close the deal. Hire architects and contractors."

"Of course," she said.

"Maybe when all my business is completed, you can join me there. For a few days of vacation."

"Of course."

TETSUO, STILL FLUSHED with the excitement of the deal, took Hanako to bed right after their dinner of Hokkaido crab. She didn't have a chance to wash the dishes. When he was on top of her, she began to trace kanji characters on his naked back. The patterns seemed to arouse him, and he repeated his performance with barely a break.

When at last he fell asleep, she got up and quietly washed the dishes. When she was finished, she sat in the dark.

KYOTO

Kando had just gotten off the phone with Gozen in Berkeley when Aragaki walked into his office. Kando said, "I just talked to our contact in California."

"Good."

"Unfortunately, not good."

Aragaki raised an eyebrow. "Oh?"

"He has informed me the situation has changed."

"He doesn't want to return the Daizen Inkstone?" Aragaki's voice raised in anger.

Kando waited a moment for Aragaki to cool down. "Precisely speaking, it's not his to return. The person in California initially contacted me when your predecessor apparently no longer had a use for the Daizen Inkstone. That situation has changed."

"Can't you be more specific?" Aragaki said, his anger still evident.

"The contact was not forthcoming."

"I do not want to give up on this. Not now." He took a deep breath. "What do you suggest that we do now? And I say 'we' because I want to hire you. To represent me in these negotiations."

The twenty-ninth Daizen sensei was Kando's original client in this case, and that would have made representing Aragaki against Shimano a conflict of interest. But that was so many years ago, Kando had fulfilled his obligations. "Obligation," Kando thought out loud.

"Excuse me?"

"I believe that if you go to California and meet with this person, without obligating him to anything, just to talk, you will be able to convince him that the best course of action will be to return the inkstone to the Daizen school."

Aragaki said, "You seem sure."

"I'm nearly certain," Kando said. "He seems a rather indecisive personality, and you should be able to sway him."

"Of course I'll go. Please set up the meeting," Aragaki said, then added, "I will hire you, as I mentioned."

Kando gave the sensei a slight nod in assent. "But I didn't finish. I also think I should go to California first, to find out about the 'situation' he referred to. That would help you decide the most strategic way to present your request."

Aragaki hesitated. Kando knew he was trying to decide if he could trust him. "That makes sense," Aragaki said, standing up and bowing formally. "Please help me write another chapter in the history of the Daizen Inkstone."

History of the Daizen Inkstone
Part 2

WINTER 1656—SUMMER 1658
EDO, JAPAN

Ihara's labor for the tea distributor went on; his pay never amounted to much, not enough to satisfy all his father's creditors. Every day after work, he escaped to the teahouse to practice *shodô*. The old woman—her name was Kurokawa—would serve him a bowl of tea and a bit of grilled fish before he practiced. After he finished, they would share a little *sake*.

He felt warm and full of energy while he was in the teahouse. His calligraphy came easily, as if the time away from practice had been better than ten thousand strokes a day. His calligraphy had changed too, perhaps from being away from home, perhaps from not being under the watchful eye of Daizen sensei. Maybe the sensei had been right when he told them that they must find their own way.

One evening, as he practiced, old Kurokawa entered the room. "Excuse me, someone is here to see you."

Ihara went to the front. There, he found Noguchi and his brother, Shinju. Ihara gave a curt nod to his younger brother and a glance at Noguchi, wondering how she knew where to find him. He had never mentioned his work at the teahouse.

"Please," old Kurokawa said to all of them, "let me serve you tea."

The two brothers and Noguchi sat on cushions around a low table while old Kurokawa went into the back room. Shinju looked around. "Not much of a teahouse. Not what I expected of Edo. We have better teahouses back home."

Ihara asked, "Why are you here, Brother?"

Shinju gave his older brother a long, hard stare. "It has been months, and you have not sent the proceeds of the sale of the business."

"Things have been difficult."

"I see," Shinju said, looking pointedly at Noguchi.

Noguchi said to Shinju, "He has been working hard."

Shinju clenched his jaw. "He has been working so hard, while we are practically destitute at home."

"Mother sent you?" Ihara asked.

"Mother did not want me to come. She said you would be doing the best you could. I had to come to see myself."

Ihara said nothing.

Shinju added, "And you did not even come home for Father's funeral."

Old Kurokawa came in with tea. Noguchi helped her serve while the two brothers said nothing.

The tea and snacks did not settle their nerves.

Shinju said, "I have had to go to work, Older Brother."

"That is a tragedy."

Shinju's expression flared in anger. "The tragedy is our mother having to scrape together a few coins for food, a few more coins for medicine for Grandmother."

"I am sorry." Ihara said, "I have not told Mother, but I will tell you that Father left many debts. In fact, he died at the hands of a creditor."

"What? I thought he died of his illness."

Noguchi said, "In a way, he did die of his illness."

Ihara resisted his urge to strike her, the woman who had sucked the life out of their father.

She went on, "It was the pain of owing so many people money, the pain of seeing his business go down, the business that his father had given to him, the family business. He could barely stand to be alive."

The brothers were looking down at their tea bowls.

"He tried to save the business, but he could see it was not going to work. He started drinking to soothe the pain. It was the illness brought on by drinking cheap alcohol that killed him, not the creditor's attack." She paused. "Your father was already dead."

THE TWO BROTHERS and Noguchi left the teahouse and went to the boarding inn. Shinju said, "Older Brother, this room is not so pleasant. Why do you stay here?"

Noguchi said, "Where else would we go?"

"I do not know, but I cannot stay here."

Ihara said, "We might be able to find a better place, but it will cost more money. I am trying to pay off the creditors, trying to get the business sold at a fair price."

"I am sorry to say so, Older Brother, but you do not know much about money, do you? In the first place, everyone is out for themselves, you have to think that way too. I will show you how to deal with these robbers. First, I need all of the money you have."

Thinking about it for a long moment, Ihara finally gave him all the coins that he had. Shinju took the money and walked back in the direction they had come until he stopped at a midscale inn that Ihara recalled had caught Shinju's eye when they walked past it earlier.

"Wait here," Shinju said.

Noguchi and Ihara waited outside, without saying a word. The wait was long, enough for Ihara to wonder if his younger brother left through the back door with his money. Finally, he did return. "We can have a room. Not the best accommodation, but three *tatami* mats larger than where we were. Enough room for the three of us. And they serve a morning and evening meal."

Ihara said, "We do not have enough money to pay for that large of a room and service."

"We will," Shinju said.

"How?"

"All you have to say is that our father died suddenly, leaving us his huge empire to assume, along with his vast fortune that will take a week or two to get unencumbered."

Noguchi said, "They believed you? They will let us stay on that promise?"

"I told them we would pay a little more than their usual rate to compensate for the delay."

Noguchi laughed. It was the first time Ihara had heard her laugh.

LATER THAT NIGHT, much later, when it was well toward dawn, after they had moved into the inn, had eaten their first meal there, and had lain on their futons to sleep, Ihara heard a rustling, then, from the direction of his brother's futon, a very quiet moan from Noguchi.

A WEEK CAME and went quickly. On the first full day together, Ihara had told his brother everything he knew about their family tea business. "I see," Shinju said, pointing to the ledger. "We can use the chain of distributors to our advantage. If we strengthen our relationship with one of them, the others should follow."

Ihara had to admit that his brother's plan made sense. "All right, Younger Brother, I see your point. You will handle these transactions?"

"Of course. I will try my best to regain the honor of our family."

"I will be happy if you do."

Ihara had barely seen his brother the rest of the week.

The first few days, he had felt as if a great burden had been lifted; toward the end of the week, he grew a little worried, especially as the innkeeper's brow furrowed every time he walked past him on the way to their room.

But he decided to trust his brother. When he was not working or practicing, he spent much time wandering about the city. Near the center of the city, one evening when he was taking a break from practicing, he came across a poster that announced a calligraphy contest that was going to take place in a few days at a shrine. Ihara memorized the details of the event, including the amount of the winner's prize, then went back to the teahouse.

"Do you think I should enter the contest?" he asked old Kurokawa.

"You would win."

"I need more practice."

"Why not stop working? You may spend all day here if you wish. I will give you food, clean your brushes, supply you with ink and paper."

Ihara bowed to her. "Thank you."

IHARA SPENT HIS DAYS and most of the nights at the teahouse, practicing as much as possible. He used his last few coins to give to old Kurokawa for new brushes. He rarely saw his brother or Noguchi, and took his meals at the teahouse. When the event came, Ihara felt ready and anxious at the same time. His calligraphy had changed much from the days he had been at the Daizen school, even much since he had come to Edo. But was it a change for the better?

The day of the event came and Ihara packed up brushes, inkstone, ink, and paper. Old Kurokawa bowed to him as he left, not saying a word. Ihara hurried across Edo, and arriving early at the shrine, Ihara signed in (the registrar was impressed with his previous school affiliation) and then set up on his designated spot. Trying to relax, he walked around the grounds of the shrine as spectators and other contestants arrived and set up. Most of the others seemed to know each other, as they chatted in friendly terms. Ihara could only watch them.

Finally, the beginning of the contest was announced. The sponsors of the contest and the judges were introduced, the rules explained. Five poems would be read, the contestants could pick three of them from which to produce their calligraphy before the sun set. The announcer signaled for the contest to begin.

Ihara copied the poems on a scrap of paper as they were read. They were from the Man'yoshu collection of ancient Japanese poems; most were love poems. Ihara picked his three and tried first to imagine in his mind how they should be laid out on the paper, and the kinds of strokes that would work best. His heart pounded when he knew what he would do. He said a silent prayer to the dead Daizen sensei, then began.

With sunset, the contest ended. Ihara put down his brush, and found that his arm and back ached from drawing for an entire afternoon. He selected his best effort for each of the poems, and placed them on top.

The contestants moved away, over to the gallery and crowd of spectators as the judges made their way around the entries. No one talked to Ihara, although he did catch a couple of the contestants looking at him out of the corner of their eyes.

The judges retreated to a far corner of the shrine and conferred. They took turns giving their opinions. There was a vote, followed by an animated discussion. There was another vote, after which the discussion was even more boisterous. The crowd began to murmur. After another round of discussion followed another round of votes. This time, the results were handed to the announcer.

The second- and third-place prizes were announced. The crowd gave murmurs of approval. When the first-place winner's name was announced, there was a loud explosion of surprised cries. Ihara finally realized they had called his name, and he could not move until the announcer gestured for him to come to accept his prize.

HE STOOD BY HIS WORK for a long time as the contestants, spectators, and judges congratulated him and asked him about his technique and association with Daizen. Several of them went out to eat and drink, the celebration went until late at night. He made a few agreements to give lessons before he was allowed to leave the celebration.

When he got back to the inn, light-headed and dizzy, the innkeeper yelled something he did not understand. The innkeeper yelled it over and over.

Ihara finally understood: he wanted money.

"Your brother and sister have disappeared. There is no money. There is no business. I want what you owe me now or I will call the authorities."

His hand trembling, probably from the drink as much as the innkeeper's threat, Ihara counted out his prize money; it was not enough to cover the bill. He opened his bag of calligraphy tools, offering the innkeeper his brushes. The innkeeper looked disgusted, but grabbed them. He pointed to the door and at the pile of Ihara's belongings that had been tossed on the ground.

IHARA SLEPT OUTSIDE the tearoom until morning, when old Kurokawa opened the screens to the morning sun.

Ihara stayed in the teahouse, humbly bowing when she offered her grandfather's calligraphy studio as a bedroom as well as a studio. He never heard from his brother or Noguchi, but did find out that all the Ihara tea company's assets had been sold.

Ihara wrote a long letter to his mother, explaining the situation without implicating his brother. He said he would continue to send her money, and hoped to restore the name of their family as soon as possible.

Ihara contacted those who had pressed him for calligraphy lessons, after making arrangements with old Kurokawa to hold them in the teahouse. He gave a lesson or two a day. The teahouse became busy too, as the students came before the lessons to have some tea and snacks and to meet with fellow enthusiasts, then stayed after for some *sake.*

Ihara received a letter from his mother, thanking him for sending money and that she was sorry to hear the business had not gone well for him. She told him she had sold their house and had moved in with a medicinal herb practitioner from a neighboring town. She hoped that he would find his way in Edo.

"I would like to give a formal name to my school," Ihara said to old Kurokawa one evening after the crowd had left.

"Yes, you should. The Ihara school sounds wonderful."

"The Kurokawa school is much better, if you give your permission. I will become an instructor in the Kurokawa School of Calligraphy."

"I would be honored," she said, then added, "Kurokawa sensei."

THE KUROKAWA SCHOOL became popularly known as the Teahouse School or the New School. Within two years, the school dominated the competitions in Edo. The teahouse overflowed with customers, soon becoming one of the hubs of *shodô.* The money that the school was earning allowed them to expand into the building next to the teashop. Old

Kurokawa wanted to repair the old teahouse, but the sensei wouldn't allow it. "It is perfect now," he said. "It fits the style of the school. In fact, I would like to fix the classroom building to match the teahouse."

Old Kurokawa laughed.

ONE WINTER DAY, after a light dusting of snow had fallen, old Kurokawa interrupted the sensei at practice. "Someone is here to see the sensei of the New School."

"Another student?"

"I do not believe so. I asked him to come back if he wanted lessons, but he said it was a more personal matter."

Kurokawa sensei put aside his brushes. He went out to the front of the teahouse. The man—dressed in samurai trappings—had his back to him and was studying a work of calligraphy.

"Hello?" Kurokawa sensei said.

The man turned; it was Sakata from the Daizen school.

"You?" Sakata said. "You are the sensei of the New School?"

"Welcome to the Kurokawa school, Sakata sensei."

The samurai sensei bristled at the mention of his family name. "I am Daizen now."

"Daizen sensei, then. The fifteenth Daizen sensei, to be precise."

Old Kurokawa served them tea. A few students wandered in but sat far away from the two.

Kurokawa sensei said, "You were right to take the sensei's inkstone."

The new Daizen sensei remained impassive, his mouth frozen into a lack of expression. Finally, he said, "You were wrong to let it go without a fight."

"A fight? I would have lost. I have no fighting skills."

"Yes, you would have lost that kind of fight. But I do not mean that kind of fight."

Kurokawa sensei sipped from his tea bowl.

Daizen sensei gazed at his tea bowl, turning it three times before taking a sip. "It is a mere coincidence that I am here. I was not searching you out. I had to come to Edo in service to our provincial governor, and heard of your school. So, you see, I merely came here to pay my respects."

"Your respect has been paid by visiting our humble school. Though as Daizen sensei, you are the one who should be paid the respect."

Daizen sensei thought for a moment, then said, "I am not one to waste time. I wanted to visit the school that has created a good reputation in such a short time."

Kurokawa sensei gave him a slight bow in thanks.

"But now that I am here, and you are who you are, I must confess that I have also harbored some resentment toward you."

"You are direct."

"I resent the fact that I took the Daizen Inkstone, and the school, in the manner that I did."

"You resent me for something you did?" Kurokawa sensei thought for a moment. "I believe I understand."

"Will you allow me to avenge your deed?"

Kurokawa sensei drank from his tea bowl. "What are you proposing?"

"What should have been proposed before."

Kurokawa sensei looked his former fellow student in the eyes. "A challenge?"

"Yes. A challenge."

"What would be the purpose?"

"To see who should be the rightful Daizen sensei."

"But you are Daizen sensei. I do not want to be Daizen sensei. I am happy being here."

Daizen sensei sipped from his tea bowl. "But if I do not deserve to be Daizen, then I should not be Daizen."

"Deserving or not, you are the Daizen sensei. You are making the school in your image now. I am doing the same with my school."

"You are making this difficult."

Kurokawa sensei pushed his tea bowl aside. "But the Daizen Inkstone is another matter."

"The inkstone?"

"A challenge trophy."

Daizen sensei thought for a moment, then pushed his tea bowl aside. "Accepted."

THE CHALLENGE BETWEEN the venerable Daizen School of Calligraphy and the Kurokawa New School took place at a Fukugawa shrine two months later. The rules were established and judges selected. The day of competition began just after sunrise with the younger students of the two schools competing against each other, to be followed by the middle ranks, then the higher ranks, and finally the two sensei competing for the inkstone.

The morning of the competition was bright with a yellow-white sun. Only a few calligraphy aficionados arrived to watch the younger ranks compete, but by the time the upper ranks were competing, the shrine was packed with spectators.

Kurokawa sensei waited until late morning to leave for the shrine. He did not want to be hovering around while his students competed, that would be too teacher-like, the students needed to stand on their own, not feel as if he were watching over their shoulder, ready to critique every move. But he was anxious for them and paced back and forth in the teahouse. He was more anxious for them than for his own competition.

Old Kurokawa watched him pace, knowing that she

could do nothing for him. She had tried to prepare him some tea or a meal, but he had politely refused. Finally, he said he would walk over to the shrine.

The summer sun heated his face; he wiped a bead of sweat with a cloth. Walking slowly to the shrine, he felt better, and composed a poem:

> Strolling to the shrine
> Sun as warm as a bath
> Thinking of nothing

On the grounds of the shrine, small groups of people were scattered about, some of them his students. They bowed to him when he walked up to them. They seemed worried that he was going to be late or not show up at all. One of the older students told him of their successes and difficulties. He told them all they had performed well. The older student took his package of brushes, ink, inkstone, and paper, and walked with him into the shrine. Following a few steps behind were the younger students.

The crowd in the shrine parted to let him inside. Just finishing the senior rank competition, the judges were announcing the winners. The second prize went to a senior student from the Kurokawa school, first prize to a Daizen student. Kurokawa sensei saw Daizen sensei seated in a corner of the shrine, his back rigid and his expression frozen in intensity, like a samurai about to do battle.

Kurokawa sensei took up a corner opposite his foe, and tried to relax as his senior student laid out his brushes and prepared his ink. The head judge, an official of the local *shodô* association, first went over to Daizen sensei and asked him if he was ready, to which he got a curt nod in return. The judge came over to Kurokawa sensei and bowed. The sensei said that he was ready.

The head judge returned to the other judges, spoke to them, then began to announce the final event of the competition. He gave a summary history of both schools, Kurokawa's was much shorter than Daizen's. He gave a brief biography of the two sensei, Kurokawa sensei's not as illustrious as Daizen's. After he explained the rules, the judge went over to Daizen sensei and took the box the sensei offered to him. The judge returned to the center of the room. He opened the box and held up the Daizen Inkstone.

"This is the Daizen Inkstone, the symbol of the most venerated calligraphy school in Japan, the oldest existing school, which will be the prize of this final event."

The crowd murmured in appreciation. Kurokawa sensei felt his stomach muscles catch and squeeze at the sight of the inkstone. So much had happened since he had last seen it. He glanced at Daizen sensei and saw that he had been watching him, and he flushed, not wanting the sensei to know that now he realized that he did care about the competition, that he did want to win the inkstone.

"Begin the competition," the head judge announced. The other four judges began by each reading a poem, the head judge reading his last. As Kurokawa sensei copied them in quick script on a scrap of paper, he realized they were difficult poems, with complex characters to execute. The poems would be more easily accomplished in Daizen sensei's classical style than his free-flowing style.

He picked two that were best suited to his style, and decided to delay choosing his last poem until he had finished the first two. He selected a brush and piece of paper. Visualizing how the poem should be laid out, he began, and immediately after the first stroke, knew that he had started wrong. He pushed that paper aside, placed another on his table, and calculated the best way to lay out the poem.

He almost started again, but a seed of doubt stopped him.

His old sensei's voice crept into his consciousness: "Always plan out the separate strokes in detail, individually, yet all of them as a whole." When he was a student, it had taken him months to understand what the sensei meant, and years to be able to execute it. Thinking of where the individual strokes belonged on the paper was difficult to do without thinking of them as parts of whole characters, and the whole characters as part of the poem.

His sensei's voice had not entered his mind, at least not so vividly, since he had been in Edo. What else would his sensei tell him? There were so many things: Focus on the tip of the brush, not the paper, not the ink. Think of the meaning of the poem, yet do not think of it. Ten thousand strokes for ten thousand days. Had he achieved that goal yet?

His brush remained unmoving. He could sense a steady flow of characters from his opponent. The crowd was watching Daizen sensei, perhaps too embarrassed to be watching him paralyzed with doubt. He could feel his students watching him, though. He was letting them down; they had performed so well for him, now he was doing nothing for them.

Kurokawa sensei tried to start on the other poem he had selected. He tried thinking of his own poem he had composed this morning, tried thinking of nothing. And still nothing would flow from his mind through his brush. He wanted to leave, to find a garden, a place in the mountains, perhaps, where there were no people, where he could let his mind wander freely, where he could do his calligraphy for himself, when he wanted to, and not do it when he did not.

Then he caught a glimpse of the Daizen Inkstone, the head judge had placed it in the center of the shrine, on a pedestal. There was something powerful in it, something he had felt over the years as a student of the old Daizen sensei, when he would rub an inkstick on the inkstone, and mix it with water in just the correct proportions. It was as if the inkstone had welcomed him to prepare the ink in its well. As if he were replenishing something in its very essence, as if the purple-gray rock had a soul.

Kurokawa sensei had imagined, as a young student, dipping his brush into the inkstone's well, his brush becoming alive with the magic that he had seen his sensei perform on paper, with brush and ink. Magic, that made his sensei's characters—each stroke—have a life.

Kurokawa sensei stood up. All of the spectators turned their eyes to him and watched as he walked over to the head judge. "I am sorry," he said. "I have a request."

"Yes?"

"I wish to use the Daizen Inkstone in the competition."

The head judge's brow wrinkled. "Why do you wish this? Daizen sensei agreed not to use the inkstone so that it would not seem an unfair advantage."

"I feel that I can perform at my best only if I use the Daizen Inkstone. Without using it, I shall have to forfeit this competition."

The head judge glanced nervously from the inkstone to the Daizen sensei, who looked up from his work.

The head judge said, "I will have to ask the owner of the inkstone." Kurokawa sensei bowed to the judge and returned to his place as the judge explained the situation to Daizen sensei. Their conversation was short, and Daizen sensei stood up, stepped over to the Daizen Inkstone, picked it up, and brought it to Kurokawa sensei.

"If you will stay and compete, you may use the Daizen Inkstone, of course."

"Thank you," said Kurokawa sensei, bowing low until his face nearly touched the floor of the shrine.

Kurokawa sensei's student helped him prepare the ink in the Daizen Inkstone, as he had done so many times when he was a student. When the inkwell was filled, Kurokawa sensei positioned his brush above the blackness. He slowly lowered the tip into the well, let the tip of the brush disappear into the liquid.

He slowly pulled up the brush, and found the paper, and let the ink flow across the paper. The ink sparkled with something alive, something that touched him deeply with a feeling he had never experienced before, something that he couldn't explain.

KUROKAWA SENSEI ACCEPTED the bow from Daizen sensei as he said, "Congratulations, sensei. I enjoyed the competition, even though I lost. If you agree, we should have another contest in three years, the same time period since we last parted ways."

"I would be honored," Kurokawa sensei said.

The fifteenth Daizen sensei left the shrine with his solemn students trailing behind.

Kurokawa sensei walked over to his corner, where his students were cleaning up. The spectators were milling about admiring the calligraphy, still buzzing with the unexpected victory of the New School. He donated two of his winning works to the shrine. The other he saved to give old Kurokawa for her teahouse.

BERKELEY

After the research group meeting, Tina and Professor Porter drove to the Zenzen school. Tina had reported during the meeting that she had no success in communicating with the sensei, nor had any family members come forward who could give permission for him to be in a study. She didn't say anything about her and Wijjie's experiment.

"Then I should see him myself," Professor Porter said. Before they left the institute, Tina called the school to see if it was a good time for the two of them to come over. Gozen answered and, after Tina explained, said it was fine with him if they visited.

Tina and Professor Porter parked in front of the school. "This is it? Not much of a school, is it?"

"It's a small school." Tina wished she had lied, told her that the sensei was back in the hospital. Or had returned to Japan.

Gozen opened the door to the school. Tina introduced them. "This is Dr. Porter. I told you about her on the phone. This is Gozen sensei, the senior instructor of the school."

Gozen and the professor exchanged greetings and a handshake, then they followed him into the main room of the house. Tina noticed Professor Porter gazing at the calligraphy on the walls, at the Japanese furnishings, and at the *tatami* mats where group lessons were held.

"Interesting, very interesting," Professor Porter said. "I've never been in a calligraphy school before. I've seen Oriental calligraphy before, of course."

Tina noticed the professor's voice sounded too loud. She hadn't realized before that she spoke in nearly hushed tones in the school.

"How is the sensei?" Tina asked Gozen as they sat in the main room.

"He hasn't stopped working for hours."

"Since he was released from the hospital," Tina said to Professor Porter, "he has been working nonstop on his drawings."

"Usually, after brain injury," Professor Porter said, as if she were giving a lecture, "there are changes in psychological behavior. Clinical depression, for obvious reasons, is prototypical. Obsession is one of the more prominent behavioral changes, likely due to a disconnect between rational thought, located largely in the prefrontal lobe, and the repetitive behaviors, located largely in the motor areas and brain stem."

Blinking rapidly, Gozen said, "Oh?"

"Is the sensei working now?" Professor Porter asked.

"Yes."

"I'd like to observe."

From the studio doorway, they watched the sensei at his low table, dipping his brush into the inkstone. The ink flowed onto the paper in the sensei's liquid strokes.

"His drawing has no meaning?" Professor Porter asked.

Tina peered at the paper. "It's hard to tell from here, but I don't think so." She looked at Gozen, who shook his head.

Professor Porter said, "Let's go look." She walked over to the sensei and held out her hand, "Hello, I am Dr. Karyn Porter."

The sensei finished his stroke without pausing, then looked at the professor. He put down his brush and bowed until he was prostrate. Professor Porter dropped her hand and nodded her head in a little bow.

The sensei straightened up and looked behind the professor to Tina. His expression became more animated, his mouth twitching as if he were trying to smile, or perhaps to speak. He pushed himself back into a sitting position and put a clean sheet of paper on the table. After staring at the paper for several moments, he dipped his brush into the inkstone. He quickly drew a few strokes onto the paper, then offered the drawing to Tina.

Professor Porter, closer to the sensei, reached out for the paper, but the sensei held it away from her grasp. Tina took a step toward him and took the drawing: it had three long strokes that formed a triangle. Two short, arcing strokes crossed the legs of the triangle.

"Interesting," Professor Porter said. "May I look at it?"

Tina handed it over to her. The professor studied it for a moment, then pointed to a stack of the sensei's drawings. "All of those have no meaning?"

Tina said, "They aren't kanji, Japanese characters, but they may have meaning to the sensei."

"They must have meaning to him," Professor Porter said. She bent at the waist, leaning near the sensei. "These are marvelous. We are very interested in them. Would you agree to be in our research study?"

When the sensei didn't answer, the professor turned to Tina and asked, "Could you ask him in Japanese?"

"My Japanese isn't that good." Tina turned to Gozen.

He nodded, kneeled next to the sensei, and repeated the question in Japanese. The sensei gave him a blank glance, then returned to his work.

"I'm sorry," Gozen said.

"Thanks for trying," Professor Porter said. "I understand there's no family who could speak for him? The research would be a benefit for him and others with his condition."

"He has never mentioned them," Gozen said with obvious reluctance. "He has never returned to Japan nor had visitors since I have known him. But I suppose he still has family in Japan."

"I could work on that," Tina said, deflecting the professor's attention from Gozen.

"Good," Professor Porter said. "But it will have to be done immediately. We can't let this golden moment pass."

*A smile
laced with fangs*

SAN FRANCISCO

Tina had fallen asleep studying on the floor of her home office. She woke up when Mr. Robert was washing his breakfast dishes.

"Good morning," she said.

"Good morning," Mr. Robert said, but he didn't look up at her. When Tina stepped next to him, he turned off the faucet and walked away.

Tina stood at the sink, watching the bubbles of soapy water, popping as their surface tension broke.

She walked back to the bedroom; he was looking in the closet. "Is something wrong?"

"I was going to ask you that question," he said, his voice muffled by the rack of hanging shirts, pants, and martial arts outfits. "You couldn't even make it to the bedroom last night." He had selected a shirt and began to put it on.

"Sorry, I fell asleep studying. Nothing personal."

Mr. Robert shrugged as he buttoned his shirt. He tucked it in his pants and zipped them up. "It doesn't matter because I give up."

"What?"

He turned toward her with his arms raised above his shoulders, his hands open as if in surrender. "Your new life, your new friends, win."

Win? The word irritated her. Win what?

Mr. Robert's voice poked its way into her thoughts. "Or, I should say, that Wijjie person wins."

Wijjie? Had Mr. Robert found out about the MRI lab? Surely he hadn't. Besides, the incident—the sex—had been playful, almost laughable. Certainly not erotic. Well maybe a little. Just getting into the right position—any position—on the platform was nearly impossible. Besides, someone had to be in the control room to actuate the scan.

Her orgasm had been a long wave of pleasure. Her brain scan at orgasm did not show the same patterns as had Wijjie's, his brain had at least 50 percent more activation. On her scans, only a few dots of brightness showed up.

"All I want," Mr. Robert said, "is my life back, so I can continue with my *shodô* practice."

"What?" Tina said. "I never took anything from your life."

"What about Zenzen sensei?"

"I haven't taken him from anyone. He's had a stroke. I'm trying to understand what his condition means for him, what might happen to him. If he will ever recover his ability to communicate."

Dorsomedial nucleus: a small grouping of neurons in the hypothalamus that triggers ejaculation.

Can there be subconscious pleasure, or any such feelings? An hypothesis: There must be feeling below the surface of consciousness. Such feelings would no doubt be necessary to help keep the body in equilibrium. When there's pain, there's pleasure too. Like the sympathetic and parasympathetic nervous systems, one increases a rate of function, the other decreases it.

Neuroscience Notebook, Christina Hana Suzuki

"You are taking him away. I just want that back. Nothing else."

"What are you talking about?" Tina's voice rose a notch. "I'm not taking him from anyone. I'm trying to help."

Mr. Robert's voice turned cool. "I'd prefer it if you would leave him alone. Please stay away from him."

"You don't understand. I haven't done anything with the sensei. I'm not doing anything to him."

Mr. Robert picked up his teaching materials from his desk and put them in a backpack. "Please just leave him alone." He tossed his pack onto his back and walked out of the condo.

TINA LET HERSELF into her mother's apartment, her hand shaking as she inserted the key. "Hello, Ma?"

"Ha-*chan*? In here."

Her mother was in the closets, peering into an open cardboard box that had once contained half a dozen gallon containers of Kikkoman soy sauce.

"What are you doing in here?"

"Just putting some things away." She dug in the box. "What are you doing today?"

"Going to school to study and work. I'm already getting behind in everything."

"Behind? Because of me?"

"No, Ma. Because I'm a slow reader."

Tina stayed in the doorway of the closet and watched her mother put old bills and receipts into the box. Tina wanted to tell her mother that she and Mr. Robert were through. She wanted to curl up on the single bed in her closet bedroom with the doors shut so that it would be utterly dark.

But she could only watch her mother close the box and put it in a corner of the closets.

Kando was getting ready to catch a train to the new Kansai airport—the one built on fill earth that was sinking three times faster than predicted into the muck at the bottom of the bay and was a metaphor for the Japanese economy—when Tetsuo Suzuki called. Kando felt a chill when he answered the phone and heard Suzuki's voice. Did he find out he was going to San Francisco to work on a case involving his ex-wife?

But Suzuki had another job for him.

"Sorry," Kando said. "I'll be out of town for a few days on another job."

"This can wait a few days," Suzuki said. "But not much more than that."

"I'll call you as soon as I get back."

"Good. Where are you going?"

Kando said, "You know how I keep all the work I do for you confidential? Then you'll forgive me if I can't tell you."

Suzuki chuckled. "Sure, if you say so."

INTERLUDE

Worth Nothing

JUNE 1977

KOBE, JAPAN

On his way home, Kando stopped at a tiny *nomiya* drinking stall that served *sake,* distilled *shôchû,* and small dishes of Kyoto-style delicacies: mostly tofu and lightly grilled fish. The owner of the *nomiya* was an old man whose face would turn the color of a pickled *umeboshi* plum whenever he got excited about something. Kando ordered a flask of chilled *sake* and let the owner select whatever dishes were best.

The day had been long and frustratingly unproductive. The kind that would need more than one flask of good *sake* to make him want to chalk it up to bad luck and start over in the morning. The three cases he was working on—a missing person, a possible embezzlement, and a background check—were nothing, really, but for some reason, all of his inquiries were stonewalled, as if the cases were of highest national security. People were becoming suspicious of everyone.

The day's failings had been his fault. He was distracted: the case of the sensei and Hanako Suzuki wouldn't leave his mind. He had wrapped up the case two weeks earlier: he had found where Hanako Suzuki lived and worked, written a report and invoice, and delivered it to the sad-eyed sensei. Finished.

A week after delivering his report, the sensei's disappearance became public (a stress-related suicide was consistently raised as the most likely explanation; there was no mention of the love affair). But the revelation that the Daizen Inkstone was also missing generated the most press. Why the inkstone, just a rock, would be so important was perplexing to Kando.

He did some poking around on his own; he had the time, but even if he had been busy, he would have dropped everything. Thinking about his curiosity, he supposed that he hoped the sensei hadn't committed suicide as a result of his investigation. He speculated, to near certainty, that the sensei had gone to San Francisco. Still, he wanted to be sure.

Investigating the source of the rumors, he poked around the sensei's neighborhood, but didn't find out anything. He made a few inquiries in Shimano's hometown, but no one had seen the sensei there. Next he learned about the Daizen school. The school's finances were in excellent shape according to a contact in the banking industry. The sensei had not taken any of the school's money with him.

The senior instructor, Aragaki, would most likely be elected the new Daizen sensei, according to those who knew the school. Because Aragaki was ten years older than Shimano, he would probably have been bitter about being overlooked at the time Shimano had been ranked above him. It seemed unlikely to Kando that Aragaki would have had anything to do with his predecessor's disappearance.

One especially intriguing bit of information Kando uncovered was that the school owned an isolated mountain retreat. The next day, the investigator took the train to Jûzu-mura. Kando found the ride pleasantly relaxing, a nice break from the daily routine. He settled in and gazed out the window until he dozed off lightly. When he had to change trains, he bought a *bento* boxed lunch that actually tasted good, not stale.

When the train arrived at Jûzu-mura in the early evening, he was glad to get off and stretch his legs. The mountain air was crisp and clean, spiced with a light scent of pine and the last of the snow that buried the village in the winter. Kando walked from one end of the village to the next, taking all of ten minutes. He checked into the inn, and had a refreshing soak in the outdoor bath that overlooked the river flowing through town. The weighty hardness of city life, to which he thought he was immune, dissolved in the hot water.

After eating dinner in the inn, he walked to the local pub he had seen on his first jaunt through the village. There, with a couple of locals—older men for whom he bought two rounds of drinks—he found out the name of the caretaker of the retreat. They also told him that they had seen the sensei there several months ago, but not recently. One of them mentioned, almost casually, that the last time the sensei visited, he had been with one of his students. A woman.

In the morning, Kando tracked down the caretaker, who confirmed the story he had heard in the pub. The old man, who walked with a brisk pace despite his considerably bowed and creaky legs, showed him the retreat after Kando claimed he was the school's insurance investigator following up on the disappearance of the sensei. The old man shrugged as if he cared nothing for the world outside the village.

If Kando lived in the village, decided the investigator, he would not care for the outside world either.

The caretaker opened the retreat for Kando, then rambled off after showing him how to lock up. Kando did his investigative routine, poking in the nooks and crannies of the cozy home. There was no evidence of anyone staying there recently, although if there had been, the caretaker would have already cleaned up. Kando could imagine the sensei and Hanako staying there, and could feel the languid sexuality that the mountain air could easily engender.

As he walked back to the village, he couldn't stop wondering about the sensei and his student: two people who had it all—one at the top of his art, the other in the upper strata of society. They had tossed away what they had for something that in the end was worth nothing.

SAN FRANCISCO

Kando slept all but two hours of the flight from Tokyo to San Francisco. He went through immigration, then customs. He got a cab to the Miyako Hotel, in Japantown. The ride took twenty-five minutes. At the hotel, he took a quick shower, dressed, then got out and stretched his legs.

Japantown was small, only about four or five square blocks. It was dominated by a shopping mall, a theater, and a bowling alley. He had imagined it would be much bigger.

He checked his map and caught a bus toward downtown. The neighborhood he passed through during the short, ten-minute ride consisted mostly of four- to five-story buildings that had retail stores on the bottom floor and apartments above. There were a few Victorian houses—painted in shades of gray, and trimmed in bright colors.

Kando got off the bus at Union Square, where the tourist crowd was thick. He looked around the square, at the big-name stores: Tiffany's, Disney, Macy's, Nike. He checked his map and located the address of the Tempura House. It was just up the block from where he was standing, on the street where the cable car was running. He had two or three hours to kill before he should go there. He wanted to wait until the dinner crowd would have thinned out.

Feeling like a silly tourist, he ran to the middle of the street and grabbed the cable car to Fisherman's Wharf.

BERKELEY

Tina was walking out of the institute when she ran into Gillian. "What's up?" Gillian said.

"The usual. Studying. Working. How about you?"

"Me too. Where are you off to?"

"I'm meeting Wijjie for a coffee."

"What are you two up to?" Gillian asked. "Another experiment? I heard about your last one."

Tina blushed. "He didn't."

"He showed me his orgasm scan. The whole thing lit up! I loved it."

"It was a spur of the moment thing. It had been a long day, and we had some champagne . . ."

"Jeez, Tina. Don't apologize. What a great idea!" Gillian gave her a quick hug. "I've got to take off myself. Let's get together soon."

IN THE HALF NOTE COFFEE HOUSE, Tina ordered a latte and sat at one of the tables. She waved at Wijjie when he walked in.

"I'll get a coffee. Be right back." He dropped his backpack on the floor next to hers. She watched him pay for his mug of coffee.

Wijjie took a sip of his coffee when he sat down. "I needed that." Looking at her, he said, "Are you okay? You don't look too happy."

"I just ran into Gillian."

"Oops. I shouldn't have showed her those scans."

Tina shrugged it off.

"You aren't mad at me, are you? I couldn't help myself."

"Forget about it. I was embarrassed at first, but it's just Gillian."

Wijjie nodded gratefully. He pulled a folder from his backpack. "Here are the copies of the sensei's scans." Tina scooted her chair around the table.

Wijjie put two of the scans side by side with a printout of one of the sensei's drawings. "There are some definite patterns, even with this small sample." He pointed to the drawing. "See, both of these scans were taken with image number five."

Tina could see the similar active areas in both scans, not perfectly so, but definitely similar. "Which areas are these?" she asked Wijjie.

"Well, I wouldn't say I'm an expert, but this area here"— he used his finger to trace a circle above one of the scans— "this could be the amygdala."

"Emotion?"

"Right. And this area, of course, at the back is the visual cortex."

Tina nodded. "That makes sense, he's looking at the image."

"Yep." He pointed to another spot of color. "This is a motor area. Not sure which, but I believe it would be his right hand."

"A motor area? But he wasn't moving when we scanned him."

"Exactly, he might have been experiencing the movement he made when drawing it." Wijjie took a gulp of coffee. "But the prefrontal area is of most interest." He pointed to a region on the scan.

Tina looked at the scan. "There's no activity."

"That's right. Usually, there's some in this area, where we experience most of our conscious awareness. It suggests that his experience with the drawings is pure movement and emotion."

Tina sat back in her chair, her hand wrapped around the warm latte glass mug.

WIJJIE BOUGHT THEM another round of coffee. When he brought the mugs to the table, Tina said, "To tell you the truth, I didn't think we'd find anything with our little experiment."

"Why?"

"He had such severe damage, for one thing. And the drawings seem so meaningless. Like a kid's drawings."

"I know. I'm excited. I think we might have something here." Wijjie gestured to the pile of scans. "I could approach Alamo about it. I think he'd be very interested."

"Professor Alamo? He'd probably just laugh at us."

"No, he definitely didn't laugh."

"Didn't?"

"Sorry, I couldn't resist just feeling him out a little. Get some direction." Wijjie smiled weakly. "In fact, I suggested that you might make a good addition to our research group, especially since you'd be bringing along an excellent research subject."

"What about Professor Porter? She'd kill me. She wants the sensei too."

"Porter isn't going anywhere."

"Going anywhere? As in . . . ?"

"As in superstardom in the scientific world. Alamo has a shot at the Nobel prize."

"He does?" Tina said, staring at Wijjie. "You're serious?"

"Serious."

"But I just started with Professor Porter."

"The best time to switch."

Tina took a long drink of coffee. "I don't know, it seems too disloyal."

Wijjie patted her arm. "Just promise me you'll think about it."

"Okay."

SAN FRANCISCO

Tina stopped at the Powell Street station on her BART ride home in the early evening. She walked through the crowd, past Union Square and the homeless sleeping on the benches until the police rousted them out, past the customers coming in and out of the Borders bookstore, past the Double Rainbow ice cream shop.

The Tempura House—its atmosphere thick with the odor of tempura oil and fried batter—was busy. Kiyomi saw

Tina when she came in and came over to her. A strand of her hair had gotten loose and hung over her eye, making her blink.

"Busy?" Tina asked.

"Very. There's your mother." Kiyomi pointed across the restaurant.

Hanako smiled at Tina as she carried a platter of sushi to a table.

Kiyomi asked Tina, "Did you want something to eat?"

"I was just stopping to see how she's doing. But I am hungry, how about vegetable tempura?"

"No shrimp?"

"Um, just one."

"You can take that table in the back," Kiyomi said, hurrying off.

Tina sat at the table and watched her mother and the waitresses rushing back and forth. The customers always smiled when Hanako was at their table, they always seemed satisfied.

After her mother stopped to quickly say hello, Tina took out her reader to read a research article for Professor Alamo's class. She comprehended little of the article on nonrepresentational memory, something about how the brain doesn't store hard-coded symbols that are recalled perfectly.

When the last customer—a Japanese man with graying hair and a slightly slouched posture—paid and left, Hanako sat down at Tina's table. She sagged against the chair. Tina almost told her mother that she shouldn't be working so hard, that she shouldn't tire herself out, that she might consider cutting back her hours.

Kiyomi brought a pot of tea and three cups to their table. They sipped the tea in silence, Kiyomi and Hanako occasionally looking around as if they might have forgotten some customers.

OUT OF THE CORNER of his eye, Kando had watched Hanako take the order at the table next to him. He recognized her from the twenty-three-year-old photograph he had used on the original case. Other than a few gray hairs, some tiny wrinkles at the corners of her eyes, she looked younger than her age. He wished he could say the same about himself.

He was surprised that she was still working at the same restaurant. Not much had changed in her life. But she was a cheerful and efficient waitress; she had found her place in life.

His waitress was a young Japanese-looking girl, with a tattoo of a rose proudly displayed above her ankle. He tried his few words of English, and was relieved when she spoke Japanese. He ordered a beer and sushi to start.

When a young woman with a backpack—he assumed she was a college student—came into the restaurant and sat at a table not too far from him, he knew that Hanako's life had changed in one respect. She had a daughter.

Kando watched the young woman and Hanako while he ate. The daughter was studying while she slowly ate. Hanako would stop by when she had a moment. Seeing them together, Kando was sure they were mother and daughter. The daughter had her mother's striking features. She also had the sensei's height and angular body.

When he finished his dinner, he paid and walked out of the restaurant. He found a shadow in the entryway of a clothing store across the street. About twenty minutes passed before the two walked out of the restaurant. He started walking in the same direction on his side of the street. He hoped they didn't get into a car.

When they turned onto Bush Street, he hurried across the street. He stayed back about half a block, as there were few people on the sidewalk. After three blocks, they turned into an apartment building with the same address as the one he found in 1977.

TINA AND HANAKO WALKED PAST the broken elevator. A sign had been posted: "Sorry for the continued inconvenience. Parts back-ordered."

As they climbed the stairs, Hanako had to take a short break at each floor. Tina said, "Maybe they'd give you an apartment on the first floor until they get the elevator fixed."

"No vacancies," Hanako said, then started up the last flight of stairs.

In the apartment, Tina said, "Can I get you anything?"

"*Iie, sumimasen.* I'm fine." She went into her bedroom, while Tina looked into the closet-bedroom. She wanted to ask her mother if she could stay the night, but that would mean telling her about Mr. Robert.

Tina went into the living room, and sat on the floor next to her backpack. Her mother came in, changed from her work kimono to a simple housedress. She sat down on the sofa and said, "So, you and Robert-*san*? Problem?"

"He talked to you."

Hanako nodded and waited.

"I don't want to talk about it." She didn't know what she would say. On the BART ride to the City, it came to her that the reason she no longer loved him was because she wasn't Japanese enough for him. She looked Japanese, but she didn't speak or read Japanese as well as he did, she didn't know flower arranging, she didn't act Japanese.

Hanako leaned back on the sofa. "Isn't that why you visited this morning? And stopped by the restaurant tonight?"

"Can't I see how my mother is doing?"

Hanako adjusted a pillow under her legs. "You have moved out?"

"I think so. I don't know."

Hanako rubbed her legs. "You can stay here."

"Thanks," Tina said. She unzipped her backpack and

took out a file folder. "I have some more of these." She handed Hanako another stack of the sensei's drawings.

Hanako took the drawings and began to leaf through them. "They look different than the others."

"I thought so too. More like abstract art."

"May I keep them for a while?"

"Sure. Let me know if you can figure them out."

Looking at the drawing on the top of the stack, Hanako said, "I didn't think you were going to see the sensei anymore."

The words sounded familiar. "Is that what Mr. Robert told you? He told me to do the same thing. 'Stop seeing the sensei.' "

"I'm not telling you what to do, Ha-*chan*."

"Mr. Robert said something to you about the sensei?"

"We were talking," Hanako said.

"What is it about the sensei?" Tina asked. "How do you know the sensei, anyway? You told Mr. Robert about him."

"I heard about his school."

"Do you know anything about him? His family? We need a family member to give permission for Professor Porter to work with him as a research subject." Tina stopped. Her mother's face was pale and pinched in pain. "Ma?"

Hanako got up from the sofa—though her slow, awkward movement made it seem as if she were falling. On her feet, she ran out of the living room. Tina got up from the floor and followed her down the hallway. Hanako had gone out the door of the apartment; it was still open. Tina hurried after her.

She heard a sharp cry—it was definitely her mother's voice—and then a thump from the stairwell. Then silence. She ran to the top of the stairwell and looked down. Hanako lay crumpled on the landing. Tina ran down the stairs, and dropped at her mother's side.

"Are you hurt?"

Hanako's eyes were tightly closed as she moaned and reached for her leg.

Tina touched the leg, Hanako winced. Her ankle was already starting to swell. "What happened?" Tina asked her.

"My legs. I couldn't move them. I just fell."

"Anything else hurt? Your head? your neck?"

Hanako shook her head as she grimaced.

"Don't move. I'll call an ambulance."

"*Iie.* It's just my ankle."

"You may have broken it."

Hanako looked at her ankle. "I just want to go back upstairs."

"Can you walk?"

Hanako tried to push herself up, and get her leg under her. She winced, and sat back down.

"I can't carry you. I'll get one of the neighbors to try to help us up the stairs."

"*Iie,* not the neighbors. Call Kiyomi," Hanako said, through clenched teeth.

"She can't help you."

"Have her husband come over. He can carry me up."

"Ma, it's late, why don't I call an ambulance."

I believe in certain things
they're revealed
just often enough
to remind me

KIYOMI AND HER HUSBAND helped move Hanako back upstairs and onto her bed. They elevated her swollen and purple ankle and packed it in ice. Tina thanked them for helping
and, when they offered to stay longer or to take her to the
emergency room, she said they would be okay.

In the bedroom, Tina asked Hanako if she needed some
aspirin.

Hanako shook her head.

Tina watched her mother sitting against the pillows. "I
know. I'll call Wijjie."

"You shouldn't bother him."

"He won't mind."

Tina went out to her backpack. She got Wijjie's number
from her notebook, and dialed the number. "It's me. Sorry
to call so late."

"Tina?"

"My mother fell down the stairs in her apartment building and hurt her ankle."

"You want me to come over?"

"I know it's an imposition."

"No problem. Is she staying off it?"

"Yes. We've got it on ice and elevated."

"Good."

When she hung up from Wijjie, she called her own number. The answering machine picked up. Tina left a message: "I'm staying at Mother's." That was it, she didn't have anything else to say.

HANAKO SAID, for the third time since Wijjie had arrived, "I'm sorry to make you come all the way here."

"It's no problem, Hanako. Just let me know if it hurts."

Hanako winced but didn't say anything when she touched her ankle.

Tina said, "You're supposed to tell him if it hurts, Ma."

Wijjie said, "I don't think it's broken, but it's hard to tell because of the swelling. She should have an X ray."

"Or an MRI?" Tina said.

"Sure, that would work too. It's a lot more expensive."

"Unless we do it ourselves," Tina said.

Wijjie smiled. "We do have experience with the H-Fifty-one-hundred."

Tina asked her mother, "Are you up for a drive to Berkeley?"

"Berkeley?"

"You need to know if your ankle is broken. We can go to Berkeley or to the hospital."

Hanako nodded.

Tina said, "How are we going to get her down five flights of stairs? The damn elevator."

"Guess we'll have to carry her."

THREE HOURS LATER, Wijjie deposited Hanako on her bed. Tina said, "Thanks for carrying her up."

"No problem," he said, though he was breathing heavily. "How are you feeling, Hanako?"

"Fine. Sorry, I made you go to so much trouble. *Arigatô gozaimasu.*"

"No trouble," Wijjie said. "I'm glad it's not broken."

Standing by the bed, Tina said, "It's not broken, Ma, but it's in pretty bad shape. You'll have to stay off it for several days. Right, Wijjie?"

He put a pillow under the ankle. "That's right. The fall stretched and twisted everything in there. I'll come by and check on you tomorrow." He looked at his watch. "I mean, later today."

"Sorry," Tina said. "It's late."

Wijjie and Tina went into the sitting room. He sat on the sofa, Tina on the floor. "How come you always sit on the floor?"

"It's more comfortable. You have to force your body to fit the couch."

"If you say so."

"You think her ankle will heal okay?"

"Should. If she takes care of it. She should get some physical therapy when the swelling goes down."

"Will her MS slow the healing?"

Wijjie thought for a moment. "I don't know about that. I'll have to check." He turned and looked out the window. "Nice view."

"The nice views are up a few more blocks."

Wijjie gazed out the window some more. "Still, it's the City. I better leave before it's morning."

"You can stay as long as you like." Tina wrapped her arm around one of his legs. "Thanks again."

Wijjie slid off the sofa and down next to her. "You're welcome." He put his arm around her shoulders and drew her to him. Tina relaxed into the kiss.

After the long kiss, Tina said, "I'll see if she's asleep."

Tina walked into the hallway and peeked in. Her mother's breathing was deep and regular. Tina quietly closed the door and went back to Wijjie.

HE LEFT JUST BEFORE DAWN. Tina curled up on the bed in the closet. She drifted in and out of sleep until she heard a loud thump from the direction of her mother's bedroom. Tina got up, slipped her jeans on, and opened the bedroom door. "Ma?"

It is instructive for the beginning *shodô* student to consider the roots of kanji. The philology of kanji begins more than three thousand years ago in China with literal drawings of worldly objects. They are the kind of crude sketches that people with no artistic training still make today when trying to explain some physical object. These line drawings evolved into the abstract character seen today. For example, the original pictogram for the sun was a simple circle with a dot or dash inside, which gradually became squared off so that now it looks more like a box.

Her mother was sitting on the bed, her good leg on the floor. The chair in the room had fallen over. It looked as if she had tried to use it to support herself and it had fallen over.

"What happened?"

"I have to use the *benjo*," she said, using the Japanese colloquial word for bathroom.

"I would have been glad to help."

"I tried calling you."

"I didn't hear. Sorry, I must have been asleep." Tina helped her into the bathroom, then went into the kitchen. She started some water boiling and searched for some breakfast. She found bread, raspberry jam, and orange-pineapple juice in small cans.

When Hanako called out that she was finished, Tina helped her out of the bathroom. Hanako insisted that she sit in the kitchen with her daughter, saying that she couldn't stand another minute in bed. Tina put a couple of chairs facing each other. She helped her sit in one, then she went into the bedroom and returned with a pillow to put under the ankle.

"Tea?"

"I can do it," Hanako said.

"Just stay there. I'll make it. And I'll try to do it right," Tina said. "Are you hungry?"

Hanako said, "A little."

"Toast and juice okay?"

"Whatever you're having."

Tina got out two plates and took out two more slices of bread. Tina watched the kettle, ready to catch it before it got too hot. "Ma?"

"Yes?"

"Why did you run from the apartment?"

Hanako didn't say anything for a long while. "*Gomen, neh*? I don't know."

While Hana was in the shower, Hanako took out the sensei's drawings. They changed every time she looked at them, bringing different times, different places, into her mind. Some of them reminded her of the primitive pictograms that had a raw, visceral feel to them. The feel of a human thousands of years ago scratching a few marks in bones or tortoise shells, telling a story they hoped would outlast their short lives.

And so the concrete became representational, and the representation became the abstract symbol that has lost its true meaning. It is up to the calligrapher to return the concrete and deep meaning to the abstract symbol.

The *taku* radical is one of the *eiji happô*. Similar in appearance to *ryô*, it is drawn with steady pressure, unlike *ryô*, which is drawn with a gradual reduction in pressure. The beginning of the stroke is important, a firm yet light touch, as one should approach life in most aspects.

Instructor's Journal, Zenzen School of Japanese Calligraphy

INTERLUDE

Becoming Nothing

MARCH 1977
KOBE, JAPAN

Tetsuo had been gone nearly a week, working on his hotel deal in Maui, when Hanako was finally convinced that he really was gone. At least for two months. She didn't have to rush through her practice to clean and put away her calligraphy supplies. She didn't have to hurry home from her lesson to finish preparing dinner. And the greatest burden had been lifted: she did not have to wait.

In the quiet of the well-insulated model home, she could hear the whisper of the brush as it glided across the coarsely smooth rice paper. If she concentrated, she could hear the ink flowing onto the paper, could hear it start to dry. In the quiet, she could hear her thoughts: about calligraphy, about the sensei, about his inkstone, the Fourth Treasure.

In the quiet, she could also feel herself slipping. She had felt it before, when she left home to attend school in Kyoto. She knew what the feeling meant, and feared it. The more she practiced *shodô,* the more she slipped. The more she slipped, the more she was seduced by the power of it.

Relax the grip of your mind, Daizen sensei told her, let your subconscious do the work. It has the most power, but it's not merely the part of the iceberg that is submerged. The subconscious is the *water,* he said, a great ocean where consciousness floats and drifts, eventually melting away, becoming nothing.

SAN FRANCISCO

Kando was in his hotel room, waiting for Aragaki to arrive. The day after he had seen Hanako, he had taken the BART train to Berkeley and found the Zenzen School of Japanese Calligraphy. When he knocked on the door, a mid-thirtyish Japanese man answered.

"Gozen sensei?" Kando said.

"Yes?"

"I am Kando."

The name didn't register with Gozen for a moment, then

his jaw twitched, making him stammer as he said, "The investigator from Kyoto?"

Kando said he was indeed the investigator from Kyoto. He and Gozen went inside, where the *shodô* instructor showed him to the main room of the school. Kando declined tea and got to the point. "I'm here to arrange a meeting with you and the Daizen sensei."

"A meeting?" Gozen said.

"As soon as possible, of course. Would the day after tomorrow be satisfactory?"

He took a breath. "Yes."

"Good." Kando looked around the school. "Is Shimano here?"

Gozen started to say something. He clamped his mouth shut.

"Don't worry. I'm not going to do anything. I just want to make sure it's worth having Daizen sensei travel all the way from Kyoto." Kando got up. He stood still, giving Gozen a stare.

"Yes, he's here," Gozen said. He got up and showed the investigator to the studio. They watched from the doorway for a minute, then walked back into the main room. Kando sat down and said, "Tell me what happened."

WHEN KANDO RETURNED from Berkeley, he called Aragaki to tell him the meeting was set. Gozen would meet him at the airport.

"SENSEI?" GOZEN ASKED the man who had peeled off from the rest of the passengers departing from customs.

"Gozen?" Aragaki said.

Gozen sensei bowed deeply from the waist until his upper body was parallel with the floor. "It is an honor to meet you, sensei."

Gozen straightened up and took Aragaki's bag. They walked through the airport without a word. Gozen tried to think of small talk, as Americans did so well: "How was the flight?" "Have you been to San Francisco before?" "I've admired your calligraphy for years." But the thirtieth Daizen sensei didn't seem like the type who would enjoy small talk.

Outside, Aragaki took a deep breath of the warm air as he followed Gozen into the parking structure. Gozen pointed to his car, certainly not worthy of transporting a dignitary such as the Daizen sensei, but Gozen couldn't afford to rent a limo. He had already stretched his budget getting the sensei a hotel room for three nights in San Francisco at two hundred dollars a night.

They drove in silence on the crowded Highway 101 up from the airport into the City; Gozen's hands were moist as they gripped the steering wheel. When the skyline of the City appeared as they crested a hill, Aragaki said, "Wonderful." Gozen relaxed a little.

They stopped at the Miyako Hotel in Japantown; Gozen had taken the long way around, so they could see the Golden Gate Bridge ("Wonderful," Daizen sensei had said again). Gozen brought Aragaki's bag into the lobby, where they checked in and picked up the key to the room. A bellhop took the bag and rode up in the elevator with them. At the door to Aragaki's room, Gozen bowed and said he would meet him in the lobby after he had a chance to freshen up.

THE PHONE RANG in Kando's room: it was Aragaki.

"What should I do next?" the sensei asked.

"What are your impressions of Gozen?"

"He's nervous, but sincere."

"I think you can handle him from here. But if you need any help, call me."

GOZEN WAITED ALMOST AN HOUR before the Daizen sensei appeared in the lobby. Gozen bowed again and asked if the sensei's room was adequate. Aragaki responded with a nod.

The two sat in a quiet corner of the hotel lobby.

"Thank you for contacting Kando about the Daizen Inkstone," Aragaki said, his longest utterance since he had arrived.

"It was nothing."

"It was more than nothing. I must ask you directly, what do you want for returning the inkstone to the Daizen school?"

Gozen looked momentarily confused. "Want? . . . I want nothing, sensei."

"Kando said you have changed your mind about returning it?"

Gozen could feel the temperature of his face rise a few degrees. "Yes, the situation has changed."

"Kando also relayed that information. I understand the sensei had a stroke."

"A severe stroke. He can no longer speak, and does not seem to understand when spoken to."

"Tell me more about his abstract drawings. They are not calligraphy?"

"No. He can hold a brush and use it, but what he draws makes no sense. Some of the brushstrokes look like kanji radicals, but together they are not kanji."

"Too bad. Too bad," Aragaki said, shaking his head. "What do these drawings look like?"

"They are difficult to describe. You must see for yourself."

"Yes, that would be good. Should we go now?"

Gozen sucked in a deep breath. "Yes, sensei."

His heart pounding and his face flushing red, Aragaki peered into Zenzen sensei's studio. He didn't recognize his rival at first—the sensei's hair had gone completely white, his once rigidly perfect posture had been replaced with an awkward slump to one side. Aragaki quietly stepped inside and up to the table where Zenzen sensei was diligently working. When he saw the Daizen Inkstone, Aragaki inhaled sharply.

Zenzen sensei turned toward the sound. He gazed blankly at Aragaki, then turned back to his brush and paper.

TINA GOT OFF the BART train at the downtown Berkeley station and followed the crowd up the escalator. She had left Kiyomi with her mother for a few hours while she went to class. Outside in the hot air—unseasonably in the nineties—a crowd of homeless teens was half heartedly panhandling with two panting puppies, their water bowls improvised from Big Gulp cups. Three gray-haired women were holding protest signs: "University of California—Nuclear Bomb Makers." A tall white man was passing out leaflets. A short black man was selling baked goods to benefit the Church of Islam.

Tina walked away from the university, toward the sensei's school. The walk felt good—she only got a few hours' sleep taking care of her mother and had arrived groggy after dozing on the BART ride. When she got to the Zenzen school, Gozen sensei's car was parked in front. She knocked on the door, then opened it. "Hello?"

Gozen came from the sensei's studio. "Hello."

Tina said, "How is the sensei?"

"He's fine. I mean the same." Gozen looked over his shoulder and back. "I'm here with another *shodô* sensei. From Japan, another calligraphy school."

"I just wanted to tell you that I may have to cut back my time with the sensei. My mother had an accident."

Gozen said, "I'm sorry. You need to help her, of course."

"I can still help with the sensei. Just not as much."

Gozen nodded. "Of course."

Tina waited, then said, "Is it okay if I see him? He might have more of his calligraphy for me."

Gozen hesitated. "I suppose it will be okay." He walked down the hall, Tina following him.

Inside the studio, Gozen introduced her to Aragaki, who was watching Zenzen sensei drawing his abstract images. "Her friend Robert-*san* is a student at our school."

Aragaki bowed low, then straightened up.

Tina bowed. *"Hajimemashite. Dôzo yoroshiku."* Pleased to meet you.

"You speak Japanese?" Aragaki said in slow but otherwise good English.

"No, only very little. *Gomen nasai.*"

Aragaki waved off her apology as if shooing away a fly. "Gozen said you were helping with the sensei. You are a doctor? Excuse me, but you are so young."

"I'm a student at the University of California. I'm studying neuroscience."

Aragaki looked at Gozen, who translated the last word into Japanese. Aragaki nodded. "Excellent. What can you tell me about the sensei's condition? Please understand that I do not have much knowledge of medical and scientific things."

"The stroke damaged the language centers of his brain. The doctors do not know how much exactly. We know he can't speak, as his speech production areas are nearly destroyed. We do not know if he can understand what we say to him, though he seems to be able to hear, but the area of his brain that helps him understand speech is also damaged.

He can still use his *shodô* brush, but he can no longer write in the way he could before the stroke. We don't know what his drawings mean. If anything."

Aragaki had been intently listening. "Thank you. I could understand most. Will you be able to return his communication?"

"No, sorry. I'm only trying to understand more about his condition. Maybe understand what he is communicating with his drawings."

Aragaki nodded. "As you said, if anything."

AFTER TINA PICKED UP the stack of the sensei's drawings and left, Aragaki said, "Remarkable."

Gozen gave him a questioning look.

"You don't see it?"

"I'm sorry. See what?"

"The resemblance? No?"

Gozen had a blank look.

"Never mind."

*The first thing
I need to do*

TINA STOOD with Wijjie and Gillian outside the conference room where Professor Alamo's class had just ended. Tina said, "Nice presentation, Wijjie."

"Thanks, but I don't think Alamo liked it. He kept raising an eyebrow."

"I saw that," Gillian said. "I wanted to punch him."

"Maybe you were saying something provocative," Tina said.

"Thanks, but I don't think so," Wijjie said. "Speaking of Alamo, do you mind talking with him?"

"Actually, I was going to head home to take care of my mom. Aunt Kiyomi's there waiting for me. What does he want to talk with me about?"

"He's really interested in the research we did with the calligraphy teacher."

"Wijjie . . ." Tina started to complain.

"Aren't you two the serious scientists," Gillian said. "I'm off to do something fun."

"Just for a couple of minutes," Wijjie said to Tina when Gillian was gone. "I promise."

WHEN THEY WALKED into Professor Alamo's office on the third floor of the institute, he swung around in his swivel chair and waved at Wijjie to shut the door. When it was closed, he gestured for Tina and Wijjie to sit in the chairs. Tina wished she had gone home.

Alamo crossed his legs and put his hands on his knee. "William tells me you've encountered an interesting case. A Japanese calligraphy teacher with agraphia."

"Yes. He's a friend's sensei." She had thought about saying "ex-boyfriend," but didn't like the word.

"William told me a little about the sensei, and that you've been able to get some very interesting scans of him viewing his drawings."

"I think they're interesting. But of course I'm just learning about all this."

"Yes, that's where we can help. We"—Professor Alamo

nodded toward Wijjie—"would be very happy to become research partners in this effort. In fact, I'd be willing to fund the venture, as well as your complete education here. I do have a few grants that I can tap."

"Thanks for the offer," Tina said slowly.

Professor Alamo raised his hand. "I understand that Porter is your advisor and has funding for this year, but, between you and me, her future funding is a little tenuous. She may find herself with a gap of a year or two. Of course, funding is not the most important thing. It's the kind of research one is doing, the quality, the relevance. 'Big Science' as I call it. Now Porter does fine work, valuable, don't get me wrong, but what we're doing"—he again glanced at Wijjie—"is Big Science. The kind that gets you big grants, big book deals, big appointments at big universities. Big awards."

Tina took a breath, started to speak, but Alamo added, "Big Science requires the best in researchers, the best equipment, the best in everything."

He uncrossed his legs and leaned forward until his forearms rested on his thighs. "But even with all that, sometimes it takes a lucky break. The calligraphy teacher might be such a break. With his help, and yours, we could take an important step in the understanding of how the brain and body make subjective experience."

Tina gave a little nod in understanding. "Maybe I'm naive, but it seems that there would be a lot of cases similar to the sensei's."

"That's precisely the problem," Alamo said. "Brain damage suffered is different for each afflicted person. It's the amount of brain damage, that is, the severity and location that matter. Judging from the scans from the sensei that William has shown me, we may have the right combination. A winner, so to speak."

Tina turned to Wijjie. He was staring at the floor in front of him.

Alamo went on: "Of course, you would share in the research, the publications, the credit. I will have it no other way. I know this is a lot of pressure for a first-year doctoral student. On the other hand, it's a good time to switch over, before you get too involved in Porter's work. It's also critical for us to get to work on the sensei with sophisticated tests, his brain is changing, rewiring, as we speak."

Wijjie spoke up, "Alonzo, maybe she could think about it? She needs to get home."

Professor Alamo nodded. "Yes, sorry, I heard about your mother."

"Thanks. A little time to think about it would be helpful."

"Of course. Let's chat again soon. As you know, time is of the essence in cases like the sensei's. Any questions you think of, I will be happy to answer."

Tina and Wijjie stood up.

"By the way, Christina," Professor Alamo said, "you're doing very well in the class."

"Thanks. That's good to know."

SAN FRANCISCO

Back in her mother's apartment—her apartment too, until she figured out where to live—Tina watched the lights of the City disappear as the dawn lightened the sky. The night before she had gone to sleep only an hour after she had eaten dinner with her mother. Tina had cooked a simple meal— rice, grilled tofu, and a salad. Her mother ate only a little; she said it was too hot to eat—it had reached 98 degrees that day—and went back to bed. Tina tried to read some of her homework, but fell asleep after reading only a paragraph.

When the first arc of the sun cleared the horizon, Tina got up from the sofa and went into the kitchen. She found a small jar of instant coffee. It would do for now, but she'd have to squeeze in a shopping trip if she was going to stay here much longer.

Tina made coffee and toast, and sat at the kitchen table reading an article for Professor Alamo's class. But she couldn't focus on the words, it seemed as if she was going backward in her education, losing the concepts and knowledge like a clock running backward loses time. She wished Wijjie hadn't told Professor Alamo about the sensei; it had only complicated things.

She tried to focus on the article.

Her mother woke up when Tina had read a few pages. She helped her into the bathroom. She winced in pain when her bad ankle touched the doorframe.

"Oops," Tina said.

When she was finished, Tina helped her into the kitchen. "Aunt Kiyomi's coming over early today. I have to go to school, do a bunch of things. Do you need anything at the store? I'm going to stop on the way home."

"*Iie, sumimasen.* I'm sorry you have to do so much for me."

"It's okay, Ma." Tina started the water boiling for her mother's tea. "And you might as well know, Mr. Robert and I broke up. You don't mind if I live here for a while? Until I can find another place."

Hanako frowned. "Are you going to be okay?"

"I haven't had much time to think about it."

TINA OPENED THE DOOR to the condo. "Hello?" she called out.

"We're in here," Mr. Robert said from the living room.

Tina put her backpack in her office and walked into the living room. Mr. Robert, Aragaki, and Gozen were standing up. On the coffee table was a pot of tea and three cups.

Aragaki said, "Good to see you again."

Gozen gave her a quick glance.

They all sat down, except for Mr. Robert, who went to get her a cup.

Aragaki said, "We're sorry to intrude on your home."

"You're not intruding," Tina said. All she wanted to do was get her things and go. She thought Mr. Robert would have been gone already.

Aragaki said, "We came to talk to you, so it's good you have returned."

"Actually, I wasn't going to stay too long. Just pick up a few things."

"I understand," Aragaki said. "I'm here because of an event that happened several years ago, more than twenty. I thought the situation was resolved, but it has recently come to light again." Aragaki paused, then, with a slight smile, said, "I would like to ask you, Suzuki-*san,* how long you have known Zenzen sensei?"

"Only a short while. Since the end of last month." She pointed toward Mr. Robert, who had returned with another teacup. "He introduced me, after the sensei's stroke."

Aragaki nodded. "That's what I understand. But your mother knew of him, isn't that right?"

"She told Mr. Robert about the calligraphy school."

Again Aragaki nodded. "Your mother must have talked to you about him before? Mr. Smith tells me that your mother spoke very highly of him."

Tina said, "I never heard my mother talk about Zenzen sensei."

"I see," Aragaki said. "And nothing about the Daizen Inkstone?"

"The what?"

"The Daizen Inkstone," Aragaki repeated. "Zenzen sensei was once the head of the Daizen School of Calligraphy in Japan."

"No. I've never heard her mention that."

"I see. *Domo arigatô.*" Aragaki stood up. "We should not keep you."

IN THE BEDROOM, Tina was trying to decide what clothes to bring back to her mother's when Mr. Robert came in.

"You don't have to move out," he said.

"I do."

"I mean, I'll move out."

"Thanks for the offer. I need to take care of my mother, anyway." Tina grabbed a pair of jeans and shirts and put them in her backpack.

Mr. Robert said, "How is she?"

"She's not too happy. Being cooped up all day."

"I can imagine."

Tina put a few pairs of socks in her bag. "What were all those questions? They were kind of personal."

"He was probably just curious."

"What's the inkstone thing?"

"I don't know about that."

"Does this have to do with telling me to stay away from the sensei?"

"I told you what that was about."

"Staying out of your life?" She zipped her backpack. "No problem."

Tina dropped off her clothes at her mother's and then hurried back to the BART station. She caught the train and settled into a seat. When she got to Berkeley, she finished the article she had started earlier, and felt she understood about three-quarters of it, a noticeable improvement in her reading speed and comprehension.

At the Half Note, she got a latte to go, and headed to the institute. The sun was still hot, and everyone was wearing shorts and skimpy tops.

At the institute, Howard was working on his computer in their office. Tina put her latte and backpack on her desk. "Sorry I haven't been around so much. I know I'm behind with the work."

"No problem. I put some more annotated scans in the data room." He checked his watch. "Speaking of which, I've got to get down to the lab."

Tina watched him grab his backpack and walk out of the office. She took out her reader, deciding to read another article and finish her coffee before starting on data entry.

TINA WAS JUST FINISHING READING another article when the phone rang in their office. "Tina," Professor Porter said when she answered, "could you come into my office?"

Tina put down the article and walked down the hall and up the stairs to Professor Porter's office. She was behind her desk and gestured for Tina to sit.

The professor looked at her for a long time. "I must say that I'm disappointed."

A lump grew in Tina's throat. "I'm sorry, I don't understand what you'd be disappointed about."

"I understand you are already thinking of changing to a different professor."

Tina gulped, swallowing the lump. "I don't know what you heard. I did have a meeting with Professor Alamo."

"It was about the calligraphy teacher, wasn't it, Tina?" Professor Porter clasped her hands together. "I don't know how you can be so cavalier at this stage of your graduate education."

"I'm sorry if it looks that way. He called me into his office. Yes, it was about the sensei. I was talking about him with one of Professor Alamo's students."

"You see what can happen?"

Tina nodded. "I didn't think what I said would go any further than that. Not to Professor Alamo."

"You're not thinking of leaving us?"

"No, not at all."

Professor Porter drummed her fingers on the desk. "All right. I'm glad we cleared that up."

IN THE ZENZEN SCHOOL, Aragaki had just gotten off the phone with Kando at the Miyako Hotel. The investigator confirmed that the woman Shimano sensei had followed to San Francisco was indeed named Suzuki. Hanako Suzuki. The investigator was not able to confirm that Hanako had a daughter fathered by the sensei or not.

"So many connections," Aragaki said to Gozen. "Shimano, Suzuki, her daughter, the daughter's friend, you. And all of these people, all these circumstances, brought together by the Daizen Inkstone."

SAN FRANCISCO

Hanako and Kiyomi had the television tuned to a soap opera with the sound on low. Kiyomi yawned when a commercial came on for disposable diapers. "Are you sure you don't want me to fix anything to eat before I leave?"

"No, thank you. Hana will be home soon."

"Okay," Kiyomi said. "You know, I missed going out last night. I love our Tuesday-night dinners. You know we've only missed a few nights in, what is it, twenty-three years?"

"Only a few," Hanako agreed. "Two Tuesdays a year when you go on your Hawaii vacation."

"I love my Hawaii vacation, but every Tuesday when we're there, I think of how I wish I was at the China Seas, eating spicy rock shrimp and steamed white fish."

"When you were gone one year, I went to the China Seas with one of the other waitresses. I felt like I was cheating on you."

Kiyomi laughed. "Next Tuesday I'll go there and get take-out. We'll have our dinner here."

"Next Tuesday I'll be walking there with you."

Kiyomi grinned. "Okay."

They watched the soap opera for a while. During the next commercial, Hanako said, "Will you go to Berkeley, to the Zenzen school, and find out about the sensei? I can't find out from Robert-*san*."

"Of course," Kiyomi said.

"The sensei is making these strange calligraphy drawings." She asked Kiyomi to get the stack of drawings from her bedroom. Together, they went through them.

"They are strange," Kiyomi said. "But beautiful."

TINA ARRIVED HOME in the late afternoon, dropped her backpack on the kitchen table and went into the sitting room. Her mother was on the sofa and Kiyomi in the easy chair, both asleep with the TV on so low she could barely hear it. The windows were open and the hot dry air spilled in. Tina tiptoed out.

So the pain I feel in my viscera—my chest, my stomach, my guts—as a result of Mr. Robert and the end of us, about Wijjie and what seems good sometimes and so wrong other times, about my mother and all that pains her and what I can't do for her or she won't do for herself, about the sensei and that I can't understand what he wants so desperately to communicate, about taking a giant step back to live again in a closet, is merely type-C fibers telling my neocortex what my body is experiencing: the dull ache of some neurochemical sent via descending pathways in response to everything. And the more I feel what my body registers as pain, the stronger it becomes. That is the chronic pain pathway.

Neuroscience Notebook,
Christina Hana Suzuki

Back in the kitchen, she started a kettle of water, and opened her neuroanatomy textbook. In the class, they were tracing the pathways of pain—acute pain and chronic pain. Tina tried to recall the differences without looking at her book: acute pain is fast, short-lived, sharp, and transmitted via type-Aδ nerve fibers; chronic pain is prolonged, burning, dull, and transmitted via type-C nerve fibers. Pain, whether acute or chronic, Tina wrote in her notebook, is a complex process of conscious awareness and emotional response to the pain. Therefore, pain itself is not an emotion, but merely the information that sensory ascending nerves transmit to the cortex.

BERKELEY

It was late the next afternoon when Tina knocked on the door of the Zenzen school. After waiting a few seconds, she tried the door—it was unlocked and she went inside. "Hello," she called out.

One of the school's students came running to the front from the back of the house.

"Hi," he said. "You're Tina?"

"Yes."

"Gozen sensei said you'd be coming over. You weren't scheduled to come for a few more hours."

"Right. But I wasn't doing much anyway. I can take over if you'd like."

"Cool. I've got tons of crap to do." He zoomed out the door.

Tina went into the sensei's work area, where he was working at his table. He didn't notice her, his focus intent on the rice paper and brush. His posture seemed to have become more slumped, as if he had aged. Maybe he was just tired: there was no telling how long he had been working, but the stack of drawings he had completed reached the bottom of his worktable.

Tina watched him work for a while, as he applied ink to brush and then to paper. She wondered what to do next, what would help her understand the sensei and his drawings. Wijjie's brain scan idea had been an interesting study, but it didn't seem likely that she could use the results to interpret the drawings.

She went into the kitchen to make some tea. There was a tea kettle on the stove. She poured water into it from the faucet, and turned on the burner. She opened a couple of the cabinets before she found the tea. She dropped a few pinches into the teapot. In another cabinet, she found a pair of teacups. The sensei might want a cup, she thought.

After a couple of minutes, she touched the kettle, as her mother did. It was just short of boiling. She poured the water into the teapot, and emptied the rest into the sink. When she turned, she saw the sensei watching her. He was holding his small pot that held the water he used to mix his ink.

His eyes were moist—Tina thought it might be a problem due to his stroke. She'd read that damage to certain parasympathetic nerves can cause the tear ducts to continually overflow. Then she noticed he was looking at her hands. She glanced down at them, but didn't see anything out of the ordinary.

The sensei started walking backward, oddly, as if something were pulling him, unseen, from the back. Tina followed him. He backed into his studio and was seated at his table, blank paper in hand, when Tina looked in. He placed the paper on his table and picked up the brush, as he had probably done millions of times, thousands just in the past few days.

He quickly drew a shape, then another, as Tina slowly

walked around to his back and watched. He drew several more, then poised his brush over the paper, as if deciding whether to put more onto the paper.

He put the brush down, and picked up the paper and held it out to her. She took it. There were several of his "characters" done even more abstractly than previously. They were different, too, than the others she had just studied. They were more complete than the others, more unified. They were placed—in relation to each other—not in the standard rows and columns, but as in a painting, as if they were elements in a landscape. Or perhaps a still life.

One of the images, Tina thought, could have been a teahouse. Or a teapot. She was just making tea, perhaps it looked that way because of that. One of the other figures was flat, perhaps of an inkstone, but, again, it could have been almost anything.

"Hello?" a voice from the front of the house called out. Tina stepped out of the studio and looked in that direction.

Gozen and Aragaki were walking into the school. Gozen gave her a nervous glance, then looked away, but Aragaki seemed pleased to see her. "How fortunate that you are here. How is the sensei?"

"He seems to be fine. I was just about to have a cup of tea, would you like one?" Tina asked.

"Thank you," Aragaki said. Tina looked at Gozen who gave her a quick nod.

Tina went back to the kitchen and found some more cups. She brought the teapot and cups to the front room. As she passed the studio, she looked in and saw that the sensei was back at work.

She served them tea in the front room; Aragaki took a sip and complimented her on the tea. Gozen sipped noisily from his teacup.

Aragaki said, "Has the sensei made more of his drawings?"

"Several," Tina said.

"Are they the same kind as before?"

"Yes," Tina said. She was thinking of telling him about the one he had drawn that looked like a teapot when there was a knock at the door. Gozen got up and opened it. Wijjie and Professor Alamo were standing there.

Professor Alamo said, "Yes, we're—" Wijjie tapped him on the shoulder and pointed to Tina. She got up and went to the door.

"Tina," Wijjie said. "Sorry, but I thought Professor Alamo should see the sensei for himself."

Professor Alamo said, "I forced William to bring me here. The more I hear about the sensei, the more curious I am about his condition. We tried to contact you, but you weren't in your office. And you must not have checked your e-mail lately."

"I've been a little busy, with my mother," Tina said.

After an awkward silence, Tina stepped back and let them in. She introduced them to Gozen and Aragaki, then she went to the kitchen to get two more teacups.

Wijjie followed her. "I'm sorry, Tina," he said in the kitchen.

"Sure, Wijjie. I understand. He forced you."

"He kind of did. But I didn't think it would hurt to show him the sensei. Besides, maybe after he meets him, he might leave the sensei and you alone."

"How do you figure that?"

"Maybe he'll decide the sensei wouldn't make a good research subject."

They went back into the front room just as Gozen was opening the door again. Professor Porter was there with Howard.

"Tina," Professor Porter said, seeing her walk up to the door.

Gozen moved back and the two stepped into the house. Still holding the teacups, Tina introduced them to Aragaki and Gozen.

When she was finished, Professor Alamo said, "Karyn."

"Alonzo," Professor Porter said. "What are you doing here?"

"Obviously the same thing as you."

Professor Porter said, "I find your presence here inexplicable. Tina is my student."

Alamo said, "I was consulted in the matter."

As they jostled for space in the main room, there was another knock on the door. Tina opened it and stared at Aunt Kiyomi.

"Is something wrong with Ma?" Tina said.

"No, Tina. She's fine. I'm . . . just checking . . . seeing if everything's okay."

"Everything?"

"The sensei." Kiyomi explained how Hanako had shown her the sensei's drawings. "I love them," she said. "Your mother was wondering how the sensei was doing, since Mr. Robert wasn't coming around anymore."

"You know, I guess."

"You can talk to me anytime."

"Thanks, Aunt Kiyomi. I will," Tina said. She showed her into the school and introduced her to the others.

IN THE MAIN ROOM of the Zenzen school, all of the visitors had finally settled in the chairs, drinking tea and awkwardly looking at each other. Tina picked up an empty teapot and walked back to the kitchen. She put it in the kitchen, then slipped to the back of the house and found a door that led to the outside.

She went back to the studio and dropped to the floor next to the sensei. She said, "We need to leave."

The sensei's hand, gripping the brush in his way of not-gripping, was poised above the paper. Tina took his brush and put it down on the holder. She picked up the inkstone, poured out the excess ink into a waste bucket, and put the inkstone in its box. She put the box, a handful of brushes, and three inksticks into her backpack. She also picked up the stack of his latest drawings, and put them into a nearly full package of paper.

That finished, she stood up and touched the sensei lightly on the shoulder. He rose and followed her to the back door.

I'll drink
and not worry
too much
where it came from
or how
or why

SAN FRANCISCO

The train descends into the dark. Around curves with a screech.
The train stops. Then goes.

Moving through the forest of feelings—all of them nameless, yet
all of them connected with shapes—of faces (hers), of places (a

mountain retreat), of things (a cup of tea in a restaurant near a train station, the touch of a hand on a tea kettle). The feeling of knowing, yet having still more to discover. The feeling of suddenness that takes forever to reveal.

The feeling of her is a forest that expands forever, at least as far as he can know. And yet the forest compresses as well, distills feelings into their essence. In those moments, the images flow through the brush, onto paper, through the darkness and too-bright light, through the morass of feelings without words.

When the forest again expands—he has no control over the shifts—the feelings of immense joy, and loss, evaporate the ability and desire to use the brush. Not like a weight pressing on his arm but the opposite: an oppressive lightness, a lethargy, as if an army could be defeated without a fight, brought to their knees with just a single, airy thought.

Then light. She leads him out of the train, touching him lightly on the arm. Not guiding him so much as connecting with him. A connection that reached through the infinite depths.

At that moment, when she dipped a brush into the inkstone, the infinite forest had expanded beyond its limitless boundaries.

*Is it possible
to stop
get off
to live*

TINA PULLED ON the BART ticket to remove it from the turnstile and stepped through the gate when it opened. She reached across the gate and put another ticket into the slot. When it registered and opened the gate, she tugged on the sensei's sleeve. He walked through the opening and the gate closed with a mechanical "whoosh."

Up the escalator, along the crowded sidewalks of Powell Street, up Bush Street to her mother's apartment, he never left her side. They walked as one, as if their movements were controlled by a single cerebellum, their motor nerves inner-vated by a single impulse from the motor area of the cortex. Tina wondered if that was how conjoined twins felt when they shared parts of their bodies. As if two conjoined sisters shared an arm and hand. If the hand touched a hot stove, the reflex nerve fibers would automatically pull it back from the heat, because reflex fibers do not need to go through the brain to work—no conscious effort needed. Both of their brains would register the sharp pain of the heat through sep-arate acute pain pathways. And each would feel the dull ache of the burn.

So many people, so many buildings. The feeling of overwhelming pressure—too much, too many, too tall. They stop outside one of the buildings. The feeling of familiarity and emptiness. Then of lost hope, of a shattered life. Inside the building, the familiarity is gone, replaced by possibility, of imagined space. A space filled with her.

Side by side
with those
I'll never understand

"KIYOMI?" HANAKO CALLED out when the door to the apartment opened. "Is that you?"

Hanako was in the bedroom with several of the sensei's
drawings spread out on her bed. She had written notes on
them.

"It's me," Tina said, as she led the sensei quickly past her
mother's bedroom door and into the sitting room. She ush-
ered him to the sofa and he sat down. He gazed around the
room, then out the windows. Tina walked back to the bedroom and poked her head inside.

"How are you feeling?" Tina asked.

"*Genki.*"

"What are you doing with the drawings?"

"Trying to read them. Isn't that what you wanted me to
do?"

"Sure. If you want," Tina said. "I'm going to set something up in my old room; you don't mind if I move some of the boxes around in there, do you?"

"Your old room?"

"You know, the closets."

"Okay."

"Thanks. I'll be back to talk to you in a few minutes. Can I get you anything?"

Her mother shook her head slowly. Tina closed the door behind her.

She went into the closets and turned on the lights. She took off the boxes on top of her bed and lined them against the wall. She piled the other boxes on top of them, so that there was space to move. She took one of the boxes, one that was about the size of the sensei's worktable in his studio, and placed it in the open space in the middle of the room.

Back in the sitting room, the sensei was still gazing around in his unfocused way from the chairs to the sofa, to the table with its small vase of flowers, to the bookshelf holding books and knickknacks, to the poster of San Francisco viewed through the Golden Gate Bridge.

Tina picked up her backpack and went back to the closets. She kneeled on the floor and set up the sensei's inkstone, inksticks, brushes, and holders. She put the pile of unused paper next to the table. She went into the kitchen and filled up a small, old teapot with cold water, then brought it back into the closet room and placed it on the floor.

She went back to the sitting room and tugged lightly on the sensei's sleeve. He followed her into the closet room. When he saw the work space that Tina had set up, he bowed reverently to it, then dropped to his knees and placed a piece of paper on the makeshift table.

Tina watched as he prepared his ink, then left him alone, closing the doors to the closets. She went into her mother's

bedroom and sat on the floor near the bed. "I saw Aunt Kiyomi today. She was at Zenzen sensei's studio."

Hanako didn't say anything.

"She was a little vague on what she was doing there.
Something about seeing how the sensei was doing."

"I asked her to go."

"Why? What's going on?"

Hanako started to say something, then shook her head.
She settled back into her pillow.

Tina knew that her mother wasn't going to talk. She
could clam up for months if she didn't want to talk about
something. "Ma," Tina said, "I better tell you that I brought
a guest home."

"A guest?"

"I brought the sensei here, Zenzen sensei. I put him up
in my old bedroom. I'm sorry I didn't ask before I did, but
it was just so crazy at his place. All those people wanting
something from him. I just grabbed him and brought him
here. Don't worry, I'll take care of him. I'll take care of you
both."

Hanako's hands clasped the sides of her face as if her head
were about to fly off her body.

Just one
small corner
is fine
safe and
quiet

第四章

the inkstone metaphor   PART THREE

Kneeling on the floor near the sensei, Tina watched him draw his abstract calligraphy. He had yet to relax, and seemed agitated, as he had been since leaving the school. His drawings were different, too: more free-form, the brushstrokes thicker, wilder. He seemed to wield his brush as if in desperation.

He turned to look at her, or at least in her direction, and handed her the brush. She hesitated, then took it from him. He placed a clean sheet of paper on the table and moved to the side, giving her room to work. Shifting her legs under her, she took a deep breath and settled back on her heels.

The sensei held up the drawing he had just completed; Tina assumed he wanted her to copy it. She dipped the brush tip into the inkstone; the ink glistened on the brush hairs when she poised it above the paper. As she tried to reproduce his drawing—it could have been a river, or a cloud, or practically anything—she could feel the brush wavering. She inspected her attempt: the brushstrokes were weak and varied randomly in width.

Tina handed the brush back to him and moved away from the table. His face fell in disappointment, she felt, but he took the brush and started drawing on another sheet of paper. Tina got up, watched him for a while, then left him in the closets. She went to her mother's bedroom door and knocked before she opened it. Hanako was lying on the bed, appearing to be asleep until she opened her eyes.

"I have to go to school. Kiyomi should be here any minute. Do you need anything?"

"No. Can't you wait until Kiyomi comes?"

"I need to catch BART. You'll be okay."

Hanako gave her a little nod.

When Tina closed the door and was walking down the hallway, she heard the bedroom door lock.

*We're imperfect so
wonders are amazing
disappointments despairing*

The feelings came furiously, without pause, piling on top of one another. The strongest was an enormous wall of time that had to be scaled. The others, smaller, were like shards of pottery that had to be put together. There were shards of happiness, moments of comfort, of sensual pleasures, of ecstasy. And there were shards of pain, longer and deeper, more dangerous, than the ones of happiness. Yet they too had to be part of the whole.

*Is there not some
sort of protection
from all this*

HANAKO REACHED DOWN to the stack of the sensei's drawings and took the top one. She traced the drawing, her finger following the sinewy path, until she thought she understood. Until the brushstroke had meaning. She wrote down her interpretation and began to trace the next drawing.

*The art of decision
changed more
than my mind*

The Poem of Five Years

MARCH 1977
KOBE, JAPAN

The Daizen sensei had called Hanako earlier in the day: his
wife's father had passed away and her lessons would have to

be canceled for at least a week. She said she was sorry to hear the news. Thank you, he said, and the call ended.

The quiet of her home closed in on her, like night in a forest. She opened a fresh inkstick, the paper covering making a crinkling sound, and she carefully made her ink. Selecting a brush, she propped it on the ceramic holder. Then she placed a fresh sheet of rag paper, the kind she used for practice, on the table.

Since Tetsuo had been in Hawaii, she had been working on a poem, one that she hoped would be her first large work of calligraphy—like the old triptych screen she had seen at the Kyoto Traditional Arts Museum. The calligraphy poem by the first sensei of the Kurokawa School of Calligraphy told the story of a woman whose parents were paralyzed in a mountain landslide when she was twelve years old. She took care of them for the rest of their lives—and they lived for many long, bitter decades. The girl had sacrificed her own happiness for her parents and, in the end, her own sanity. When her parents finally died, she had no idea who she was, or what she was supposed to do with her life. One winter day, she wandered away from her home and was never seen again.

Hanako's poem was going to be about five years of her life, *the* five years. They had started the year she entered Kyoto Women's Junior College, when she moved out of her home to live in the school dormitory. Her three roommates were friends from Tokyo. Hanako tried to be social, but they didn't pay much attention to her. Not that they intentionally snubbed her; they had so much in common that a newcomer could never catch up. They had already established the things they liked to do with their free time: shopping, going to movies, eating sweets.

Between classes, with her free time, she would go to museums. She used her spending money to buy yearly passes for a handful of the local museums, the Traditional Arts Museum one of them. She especially liked the exhibits that told a story—about heroism in battle, about illicit lovers. And especially those like the story of the girl who took care of her parents.

After a month, she began to spend more than just her free time at the museums. School was hardly worthwhile: the classes too easy at first, then boring; she missed more than she attended. Her roommates had become invisible. People on the street were ghosts. It was as if all she could see were the exhibits.

One day her father arrived at school; he was waiting for her with the school's dean of students. When Hanako showed up, after a quiet afternoon at the Nishijin Textile Museum, she was eased into the family car, her roommates watching, and taken home.

For the first several days—actually, she didn't know long it was, the days may have been weeks—Hanako stayed in her bedroom. Her parents gave up trying to coax her out. They tried anger, then silence, even stopped serving meals to her for a day. Eventually, they called Dr. Sumita, a psychologist.

He sat with her for an hour that first visit. He didn't say anything; she didn't either. The next day was the same, and the next, for a week. On the first day of the second week, he started talking—about the weather, about what his wife cooked for dinner the night before, about a hike he once took in the Japan Alps—and didn't stop talking for the hour. Hanako couldn't have gotten in a word if she had tried. On the fifth day of that week, the psychologist started his soliloquy, but this time, at the half hour mark, he stopped. The silence in Hanako's room became so intense, she clapped her hands over her ears.

Then, from the inside pocket of his jacket, he pulled out a brochure for a museum in Osaka. He spent a full five minutes reading it aloud, turning the pages deliberately, tantalizing her. When he was finished, he handed it to her. She stared greedily at the glossy photographs advertising the exhibit of *sumi-e* ink paintings. Then she smiled.

That afternoon, Dr. Sumita took her to the museum. He watched her as she studied the exhibits, reading every word of the explanatory signs. When they had seen it all, they sat in the museum café and shared a pot of the best green tea. He asked which of the paintings she found most interesting. She didn't say anything for a long moment, then a flood of words burst from her: she listed her favorites, told him the story behind the paintings, about the artists, everything she had absorbed that long afternoon.

Once a week, for nearly a year, Dr. Sumita and Hanako visited a museum. Afterward, they sipped tea while discussing the exhibit. She did most of the talking, he merely offered an occasional question. The rest of each week, Hanako was busy. Her mother had set up several classes for her to attend: tea ceremony, flower arranging, the proper way to wear a kimono and tie an obi. All of the wifely arts. At the end of the year, Dr. Sumita no longer visited her, their museum excursions were replaced with French-cooking classes.

At the end of three years, Hanako began to go on arranged dates with carefully selected potential marriage partners. It was clear to her that the first group of young men were only for practice; the real tests came later. And the ultimate prize, in her parents' eyes, was Tetsuo Suzuki. At the end of four years, she was engaged to him, and at the end of the fifth, ensconced in her model home.

She had passed the tests. All of them.

But her poem wouldn't be just about those specific events. She wanted it to echo her feelings during that time: the mysteries of pain and comfort in the stories she'd found in the museums. And she wanted to express the fragmentation, the dissolving, that nearly overwhelmed her while she sacrificed herself for her parents' satisfaction.

BERKELEY

Tina knocked on the door to Professor Porter's office. She wanted to explain why she kidnapped the sensei, hoping to salvage her life at the institute. She would assure Professor Porter that it would never happen again, that she would try to make it up somehow. There was a good chance that the apology would be futile; her career at the institute, only a few weeks old, was irrevocably damaged. No other professor—certainly not Alamo—would take her on after defying two prestigious faculty members.

When there was no answer, Tina walked to her own office. Howard was working on his computer. He stopped clacking on his keyboard when Tina entered.

She said, "I'm sorry about ducking out on everyone yesterday. I thought it was the best thing to do for the sensei. Too many people, too much going on at once, if you know what I mean."

"No problem," Howard said.

"You haven't seen Professor Porter, have you?"

"Not today." He went back to working on his computer.

TINA FOUND WIJJIE in his office. He looked up from his book. "Tina, I'm sorry about yesterday, about bringing Alamo along." Wijjie held an imaginary gun to his head.

Tina sat down in one of the chairs. "What kind of trouble am I in?"

"Trouble?"

"I must be in some kind of trouble. I defied my advisor, and another professor in the program."

Wijjie twisted in his chair and put his book on his desk. "I think it'll all blow over."

"That's one hypothesis. The alternative is that I'm dead here."

"Come on, Tina. Don't think that."

Tina shrugged. "Well, I better let you get back to studying."

"Dinner later?"

"Can't. Got to take care of Ma."

"How is she?"

"Hard to say. She doesn't talk much. I think she's depressed. Not getting to work and all."

"Makes sense," Wijjie said. "It must be rough on her. And the stress must be aggravating her MS."

"I'm sure it is."

"But she seems to be handling everything pretty well."

"I don't know about that." Tina got up to leave. "Thanks, Wijjie. I feel better."

"Any time."

SAN FRANCISCO

Hanako leaned across her bed and unlocked the door. Kiyomi came in. "Hanako, what's wrong? Why is your door locked?"

Hanako sat back on her pillows, her ankle throbbing with the sudden rush of blood from the effort.

Kiyomi sat on the edge of the bed. "Are you okay?"

Hanako moaned. "The sensei's here."

"Here?"

"In Hana's old bedroom." Hanako nodded. "She brought him here."

"It's my fault. Tina saw me at the school. I had to tell her you wanted me to check on the sensei."

"No, it's not—" Hanako reached for her legs when a wave of spasms gripped them.

"Hanako?"

Hanako winced and pointed toward the kitchen. "In the chopstick drawer."

Kiyomi hurried out of the bedroom. The pain of the spasms was worse than ever.

"You mean this?" Kiyomi asked, shutting the door. She showed Hanako a marijuana joint and a book of Tempura House matches.

Hanako nodded. Kiyomi handed Hanako the joint. She put it to her lips. Kiyomi struck the match and it flamed up. Hanako took a deep puff when the flame touched the joint. She inhaled a lungful, then coughed as she exhaled.

Kiyomi said, "I've never tried it."

Hanako handed her the joint. Kiyomi took a puff. She exhaled quickly, then gave it back to Hanako. She took another puff, managing to hold in the smoke without coughing.

She handed it back to Kiyomi, who took another dainty puff, then held it out for Hanako. She shook her head, then let out the smoke slowly.

Kiyomi said, "Two puffs is enough?"

Hanako nodded.

Kiyomi extinguished the rest of the joint by pushing the lighted end against the closed matchbook. "I feel light-headed." She sat on the edge of the bed.

"Me, too," Hanako said.

After a couple of minutes, her legs started to relax, the spasms faded.

"Feeling better?" Kiyomi asked.

"Hai. Domo."

"Good," Kiyomi said. "You know the new waitress?"

"What about her?"

"She's doing a good job."

"Good."

"Real friendly with the customers."

"That's nice."

"Not as friendly as you," Kiyomi added quickly. After another long silence, Kiyomi said, "You have to tell Tina. She'll understand. Then she'll get him out of here."

"I know that, but there's so much . . . ," Hanako said, her voice softening with each word.

BERKELEY

Using the library's Internet connection, Tina searched for the Daizen school. Several pages came up, most in Japanese. One English-language Web site on Japanese *shodô* provided a sketch of the historical details of "one of the most important" schools in Japan. The page gave a timeline with the names of the school's chief instructors and dates they served. It also gave a brief account of the origins of the Daizen-Kurokawa competition and listed the winners.

The thirtieth and current Daizen sensei, Aragaki, had been Daizen sensei since 1977. His record in Daizen-Kurokawa competitions was five wins and two losses. Tina scrolled up the page. The most wins others had achieved were four, except for one who had six, in the late 1800s.

Shimano, the twenty-ninth Daizen sensei, had served from July 1975 to June 1977, wins—0, losses—0. A note beside this entry read: "The twenty-ninth Daizen sensei, Kiichi

Shimano, left the school before participating in a single Daizen-Kurokawa competition. The Daizen Inkstone also went missing at this time. Refer to the historical account for more information about the Daizen Inkstone."

She located the *History of the Daizen Inkstone* in the Asian studies section of the main campus library. She couldn't understand much of the Japanese. She found no other books listed in the library's database on the Daizen Inkstone or the Daizen School of Calligraphy.

In her notebook for Alamo's class, Tina wrote down the main dates and historical events, and noted the URLs of the sites. She checked out the *History of the Daizen Inkstone* before leaving the library.

History of the Daizen Inkstone
Part 3

SPRING 1657
EDO, JAPAN

Kurokawa sensei awoke one morning feeling tired. A year after his victory, the Kurokawa school was flourishing with more students than he could handle. The energy from the competition with the Daizen school had kept him going for many months, like a wind at his back. But now teaching so many students had become tiring, and his daily ten thousand practice strokes had become tedious.

That morning, he asked old Kurokawa, "Would you allow me to go on a short journey? I feel I must renew my spirit."

Old Kurokawa nodded. "I have felt that you have become tired."

"But I do not like to leave my students."

"A tired teacher is not a good teacher."

That was true enough.

"Where will you go?" she asked as she picked up his
empty dishes.

"I would like to go see the place where the Daizen Inkstone was discovered."

KUROKAWA SENSEI STEPPED UP to the entrance of the rustic
mountain inn, his feet sore and his legs cramped from the
long hike off the main road. The innkeeper, an old man,
greeted him at the door and helped him with his bag. He
showed him to a room that was built over the river that ran
through the tiny village of Jûzu-mura.

Since winning the competition, Kurokawa sensei had
grown curious about the Daizen Inkstone, about its power.
He had decided to write a history of the inkstone during his
sabbatical.

After settling into his room, he went for a long soak in
the inn's bath, then had a leisurely meal before he fell asleep.
He woke the next morning refreshed, as if he had been away
from the school for a year instead of a few days. He ate his
morning meal, the food as fresh and delicious as anything he
had eaten. After, he took out the Daizen Inkstone from his
travel bag, and prepared the ink. Using a small writing brush
and sheaves of the highest quality paper, he began:

> The Daizen Inkstone began its life as a mountain that was
> the center of an inland province, near the village of Jûzu-
> mura. The inkstone did not start as the entire mountain,
> of course, but one tiny piece of that mountain. At some
> point in its most ancient history, the mountain began to

disintegrate, as all objects do, as all people do. A sliver of the mountain dislodged and became free from the crushing weight of its parent.

It fell down, losing chips as it collided with jagged out-croppings of the mountain. When it settled at the foot of the mountain, it did nothing for a long time. It lay there, contemplating its free life.

Gradually, the stone was pushed by water rushing off the mountain to the river that flows through the village of Jûzu-mura, although all this happened before the village was a village. Not sure if it would like being in a river, the stone tried to stop itself, but it did not have that kind of power. Its powers were other kinds, those that it did not know of yet.

Eventually, the stone slid into the river. The feeling of the water was so strange, so powerful. Exerting a different power than the static power of the mountain, the river was all motion, never-ending flow. The force of the flowing water didn't chip off pieces of the rock, as falling down the mountain had, but slowly, ever so slowly, wore away the rough edges of the stone.

Many, many years later, after the stone had smoothed and mellowed, a wandering poet and calligrapher came to the river, and stayed in Jûzu-mura for a while. The poet had been wandering about the area, not sure why, except that he was looking for inspiration for his art. He had grown stale, he felt, and needed to see new sights, feel new emotions. The poet—Jinmai—sat by the river, the sunlight reflecting off the water like flashes of fire.

Suddenly a dark cloud floated by and blocked out the sun. Jinmai could see into the water and noticed the rec-tangular stone wedged between two boulders. It looked imprisoned, as if it wanted to be released to continue a journey downstream. Not unlike Jinmai himself.

The poet scooted down to the river and fished it out. "If you do not mind, I think you would make an outstanding inkstone."

The stone, of course, had nothing to say.

Kurokawa sensei put down his brush and glanced outside. The warm, late spring air wafted under his nose, beckoning him to take a break from his writing. Enjoying the mountain environment was, after all, one of the other reasons he had come to the village: to relax, revitalize his spirit, and get away from the hectic capital city. He did not have to finish the history in one day.

The sensei put away his writing and cleaned the brushes and the inkstone. The innkeeper directed him to a trail that led through the forest along the river. "There are many beautiful sights, sensei," the old man said, almost sadly, as if he could no longer experience them himself, but only vicariously through his guests. Kurokawa sensei thanked him and accepted the offer of mountain potato cakes for an afternoon meal.

The path took him along the river, and followed it so closely he often felt a drop of water spray. When he came to a small tributary, he followed it for a while. A mere trickle of water flowed in the streambed. When he was far enough from the noisy river, he could hear the trickle as it flowed over a rock and dropped into a small pond formed by other rocks, making a pleasant plopping sound.

Kurokawa sensei squatted on his heels and listened to the sound. It soothed him, delighted him, and he smiled.

"There are more of them," a woman said, her voice as soft as the stream's. Kurokawa sensei turned around. The woman, younger than he was by several years, was dressed in a simple kimono, bound loosely as if for a mountain hike. She said, "All along this stream there are water music spots such as this, sensei."

"Water music spots? I would like to hear them."

"Will you walk with me?"

"Yes."

She walked slowly, carefully placing her simple straw foot coverings on the mossy rocks, her ankles flashing in the sunlight.

"How did you know who I am?"

She did not say anything for a few steps, "It is a small village. I am sorry to be so forward."

"No. It is a small village, of course."

"We have all heard about you. We know a little bit about the world, despite being so isolated."

The woman stopped at another place where the stream flowed over rocks. They both squatted near it and listened. The trickle split in two, though unequally, with the larger portion flowing more heavily and steadily—its sound was deeper—while the lesser portion trickled lightly. The two sounds combined like musical instruments playing in harmony.

The woman said, "It does not always sound so well. Some days it is not in tune. Today is a special day."

"The water music sounds different every day?"

She laughed softly. "Oh, yes. The world is different every day, is it not?"

They stayed there for a long while, listening. "Would you like to hear some more?"

"Yes."

They found three more, each sounding different than the last; they stopped at the last one to share his lunch. "Do you often come to hear the water music?" Kurokawa sensei asked.

"As often as I can."

"I am glad I found them. I am glad that you were here to show me the others."

She bowed a little, showing him the nape of her neck. When she looked up, their eyes met, briefly, before she got up and said, "I should leave now. Most people come here to be alone."

The sensei did not want to be alone, but she was already away, walking much more quickly and nimbly than she had on the way up.

KUROKAWA SENSEI WROTE each morning, putting down the history his sensei had told him. He wrote the history as stories, as if he were there through the generations, through the wars and social upheavals, through the personal triumphs and tragedies experienced around the inkstone. He would have admitted that he embellished the facts, at least those events told to him by his sensei. The more he wrote, the more he embellished, to the point of becoming one with each sensei's story and how it revolved around the Daizen Inkstone.

Each day, after writing, he would pick up something to eat, then walk along the path, always following the small stream to listen to the water music spots. They did indeed change sound daily. And each day he would find her, the water music woman, at one or the other of the spots. They would listen quietly, for a while, then, wordlessly still, play each other as living musical instruments. And it was, as is the world, different every day.

EVENTUALLY, Kurokawa sensei reached the end of the history of the inkstone, the end being his own tale. It was the hardest to write. His story was too real, he was too close to it. Or perhaps he did not want the story to end, never to listen to the water music with the woman.

He would have given the Daizen Inkstone away to have stayed in Jûzu-mura, but he knew he had to return to the

"Music"—*ongaku*—is a combination of two characters, *on*, meaning "sound," and *gaku*, meaning "music" as well as "pleasure." *On* is derived from the characters for "mouth" and "tongue." *Gaku* is an obscure reference to "threads on an oak tree," possibly referring to silkworms and the pleasure of finding them (as in to sing out in joy?). The strokes for these characters must sing out for joy, as when discovering a true love, one that comes unbidden yet cannot be denied no matter how hard one tries to push it away.

"Place"—*tokoro*—comes
from the characters for
"door" (used phonetically)
and "ax" or "chop." It is
not clear why the sound
of something being
chopped represents
"place." Perhaps the
unique sounds of each
place are used to identify
it. Sounds are indeed part
of a place as much as its
sights and smells. These
strokes must be solid, as
"place" represents some-
thing solid in our memo-
ries, some place our
emotions can cling to,
as a wall holds up art.

"Joy"—*yorokubu*—is
derived from "mouth,"

Kurokawa school. He had so many responsibilities now, so
many students, a whole tradition that would die if he never
returned.

On the day that he finished the *History of the Daizen Inkstone,* he asked the innkeeper about the water music woman,
casually, saying that he had run across her one day and she
had shown him another path to take. He said that he wanted
to thank her, and give her a small present, as he was giving
all the residents of Jûzu-mura who had made his stay so
pleasant.

"You mean Yamano-*san.* She is always wandering about
the hills when she is not taking care of her parents, because
of the accident."

"What happened?"

"A tragic story, her parents were severely injured in a
rockslide. They can no longer walk. She is the only one who
can take care of them."

"That is tragic."

The sensei returned to his room. He did one final work
of calligraphy: the characters for "water," "music," "place,"
and "joy." The characters flowed from his brush as never before, with a delicate power, as if from someone else.

He finished packing up his belongings and gave the
innkeeper a calligraphy work that he had done in thanks. He
also asked the innkeeper to give the Yamano woman his final
calligraphy work. The innkeeper said he would be happy to.
Kurokawa sensei thanked the innkeeper, then hurried down
the mountain slope, away from Jûzu-mura, afraid if he lingered, he might never leave.

Tina opened the door to the closet bedroom. The sensei was still working at his drawings. On the floor, next to the makeshift table, the pile of completed drawings had grown. Tina stepped quietly over to it and took the stack with her.

She closed the door and put the stack on the kitchen table. Then she walked to her mother's bedroom. Rapping gently before trying the knob, she said, "Ma?" The door was locked.

Kiyomi opened the door. Tina smelled the lingering odor of marijuana. She looked inside. Hanako was lying on the bed, her ankle propped up on the pillow.

Kiyomi said, "Her legs were—what do you call it?—cramping."

Tina noticed the stub of a joint. "Aunt Kiyomi?"

"Just curious," Kiyomi said. "You know. I need to go to work. I'm already late."

Tina walked out of the bedroom with her. "How is she?" Tina asked her.

"She's okay now."

"Did she talk about the sensei?"

Kiyomi nodded. "She's not happy about it."

"I didn't think she would be. I hope he won't be here for long."

"Sorry, I should go."

"Thanks for coming over, Aunt Kiyomi. I really appreciate it."

"LET ME LOOK at your ankle," Tina said to her mother. She pulled back the towel that protected it from the ice bag. The swelling had lessened, but it had turned awful shades of blues, blacks, and greens. "I better have Wijjie come look at

and "plant," and "food vessel," as in cooked vegetables, all of which mean "eat," and, in turn, "pleasure." It's strange that eating, and taste, became the sense used to represent pleasure. Why not sight? Why not represent pleasure by the sight of a fully blossomed cherry tree? Or the touch of a lover?

Instructor's Journal,
Zenzen School of
Japanese Calligraphy

it." She rearranged the towel and ice bag. "You had some MS pain today?"

"Yes. But it went away."

Tina, suddenly tired, could have gone to sleep if she closed her eyes. "Can I make you some dinner?"

"I'm a little hungry."

Tina nodded and got up. Before opening the door, she said, "I'm sorry about bringing the sensei here. I didn't realize it was going to be such a problem. Don't get stressed out by him. I'll figure out something soon."

AFTER DOING THE DISHES, Tina sat at the kitchen table, studying the sensei's latest drawings. They were more abstract than the previous ones—wilder departures from the traditional calligraphy she had seen Mr. Robert draw. She laid the drawings out in rows, arranging them into groups: ones with single drawings, and ones with several. There were no other discerning patterns that she could determine.

She wondered why the sensei would leave Japan with the Daizen Inkstone. If it was so valuable, so rich in history, that act was very drastic. The *History of the Daizen Inkstone* might provide a clue, if she could get it translated.

She moved the sensei's drawings again, this time into groups that had elements that were more angular or more curved, but there seemed to be no way she would ever understand what they meant. Not if she had the rest of her life to study them, not if she could take continual fMRI scans of his brain activity. Without him being able to tell anyone what his drawings meant, then how could anyone ever understand them? They had no obvious connection to reality.

Understanding the drawings was as difficult as measuring another person's conscious experience: without having that person verbalize what he or she was experiencing, it seemed impossible. You could measure the object or substance that was being experienced, like the amount of light reflecting off a building, or the levels of sodium in soup. And you could measure the brain activity as the person looked at the building or tasted the soup. But what that experience was like, if not verbalized, could not be measured. We could only imagine what the experience would be like by comparing it to our own.

Tina stacked the drawings in a pile, then noticed kanji on the back of one. She hadn't noticed any kanji on them before. Her mother must have written it. Tina closely inspected the two kanji characters, but she didn't recognize them.

In the sitting room, she found the kanji dictionary and the Japanese-English dictionary and took them into the kitchen. She counted the number of strokes that made up each kanji, and ran her finger down the list of kanji with that number of strokes until she matched them: *kôkai*. She looked up the word in the Japanese-English dictionary: "regret" or "remorse."

WHEN TINA HAD GONE to sleep in the sitting room, Hanako moved her legs off the bed, putting her weight on her uninjured ankle. With a hand on the bed, then on the dresser, she balanced herself and moved slowly to the door. Carefully, quietly, opening the door to her bedroom, she looked down the hallway.

Using the wall for support, she hop-walked to the closet bedroom. The door nearest her was open an inch; light streamed through the opening. She peered inside. The sensei had his back to her. She wouldn't have recognized him if she didn't know it was him: he was slumped awkwardly over the table as he worked with his brush; his hair so white, long, unkempt. Like one of the homeless people near Union Square.

She pushed herself away, and then down the hallway to

the kitchen. On the table was the stack of the sensei's latest drawings. Hanako lowered herself onto a chair, and began to trace his brushstrokes.

I know him
I like him
I love him
for years
still he
melts my
heart

The Well

MARCH 1977
KYOTO, JAPAN

In the hour before the first lesson after his father-in-law's funeral, the Daizen sensei tried to prepare for Hanako's return to his studio. His many responsibilities during the week of the funeral had been debilitating: making the arrangements, greeting mourners, coming up with a suitable speech for the service. He had to do more than was typical because his wife's mother was so distraught—the death had been unexpected, his father-in-law had seemingly recovered completely from the surgery he had many months earlier. Yuriko spent most of the week consoling her.

The sensei was having trouble deciding what to do for Hanako's lesson, the week off only part of the problem. For one thing, his wife had been making odd, offhand statements: how much he had become wrapped up in his work, how the students must appreciate getting so much individual attention. Exactly what she was referring to, he wasn't at all sure, though a shudder went through him when he realized the comments applied to Hanako and him. Perhaps he was being paranoid; they may have meant nothing.

Also, he was unmotivated, not only about teaching, but also about his own calligraphy, in particular, preparing for the first Daizen-Kurokawa competition of his era. It was still several months away, but to stand a chance, he had to start practicing seriously. The week away from Hanako had made it harder to concentrate.

His life was unraveling.

He spent a lot of time thinking about her; he was looking forward to seeing her again. He had decided not to plan much of a lesson. They could start off casually, seeing how each other had survived the week. A friendly conversation that would get them back into the flow.

By the time Hanako arrived for her lesson, he had become more tense. He did prepare a quick lesson—a block of six characters for her to practice—just in case they found they didn't have much to say. Hanako bowed low to him when she entered the studio, her face in solemn respect for his loss. He bowed low in acceptance.

The calligrapher who goes beyond mere proficiency must find a well of emotions from which to draw. The calligrapher who tries to accomplish great feats without such a well will end up with proficient works but superficial calligraphy. That calligrapher's art will lack spirituality, lack depth, lack any true meaning.

Instructor's Journal, Zenzen School of Japanese Calligraphy

When they were settled into the studio, the sensei started off by asking how she had been.

"Very well. I have missed my lessons."

"I have missed them too."

"But it gave me time to think," she said.

"What about?"

Hanako took out a small notebook from her bag of calligraphy supplies. "It's only a start," she said, handing it to him.

The sensei opened the notebook and began to read her poem. As he did, his emptiness began to fill, as if he were drawing from her deep well of emotions.

SAN FRANCISCO

"Thanks so much for helping with Ma, Aunt Kiyomi," Tina said.

"You don't have to thank me all the time. I don't mind."

"But I'm sure you have better things to do. Especially with Ma not able to work."

"We're doing fine," Kiyomi said.

"Are you sure? Who is filling in for her at the Tempura House?"

"No one, right now. We're trying to cover with the regular staff. It does get a little hectic."

"How about me? I could take her evening shifts."

Kiyomi smiled. "That's nice of you."

"Really, I'd be glad to help."

"Who would take care of your mother?" Kiyomi asked, then added, "And the sensei."

Tina thought of Granny and suggested her. "How is she these days?"

"She gets around pretty well. I'll ask her. But what about school?"

"I've got plenty of time to study. To tell you the truth, I think Ma is worried about money. Even though I'm pretty sure she's got a lot saved, I hardly touched any of my college money."

"You really think she's worried about money?"

"With all these health problems, I don't know. She won't go to the doctor."

"Doctors are expensive. I don't think she has much health insurance."

Tina nodded. "I didn't think so."

Kiyomi gazed in the bedroom. "She was never sick more than a couple of days since I've known her."

"I know."

"Now all of this." Kiyomi turned toward Tina and smiled brightly. "If you want to come work at the Tempura House, you can."

Tina grinned at Kiyomi's sudden enthusiasm.

BERKELEY

The copies of the sensei's fMRI scans were scattered across Alamo's desk. He had made several notes about each, and attached the slips of paper with plastic paper clips. His notes pointed out all of the areas that were active and, more interestingly, those that weren't. In each image, there was evidence of the large area in the left temporal lobe that had been devastated by the sensei's burst middle cerebral artery. That the sensei could function at all was amazing. He must have received quick medical attention—that kind of stroke could have easily killed him.

Alamo had seen other cases of brain-damaged patients who had portions of their frontal cortex severed from their emotion pathways. These patients tended to be highly erratic. The sensei showed strong evidence of that as well. It was amazing that he was so docile; normally, such patients were given to severe mood swings, not unlike an infant. Their behaviors, and likely their thoughts, were dictated by either pure emotion or pure reason. Evidence increasingly showed our emotions allow us to make choices *by feel* rather than strict logic.

Porter would disagree—language, she claimed, is the key driver of most cognition. Through language, we develop concepts, metaphors, and other symbolic ways of dealing with the world, which in turn drive how we experience the world. She had explained her theory to him after they ran into each other at the calligraphy school.

When they discovered Suzuki had left with the sensei, it had been he who called a truce with Porter. Not only because he was on shaky ground—Suzuki was her student, after all—but because he saw a way that they might collaborate, both benefiting from research with the sensei. He asked her to go with him for coffee. That casual meeting might be recounted in a future history of great moments in neuroscience, perhaps named the "Berkeley Java Summit" or something catchy like that. He had saved the napkin on which they had sketched out neural pathways and a collaborative research agenda.

Alamo was about to file the sensei's scans when he noticed on the top scan a small spot, a little bulge, like a tiny worm. Under his desk lamp, he studied it more closely. It could be an anomaly in the scan—the images that Cruz and Suzuki had made of the sensei weren't the highest quality. Alamo wasn't a clinician but thought it might be something serious. Someone should take a closer look at the spot.

He brought the file along with him to class. Arriving in the Hebb Conference Room, precisely fifteen seconds before class start time, he placed his notes on the table. All the students were there except Suzuki.

As he was noting that fact, she came into the room and sat down. "Let's begin," he said.

TINA HAD HAD TO RUN from the BART station to the institute; the train was running late due to an earlier "police action," according to the announcement from the train driver. She had missed the earlier train because of her talk with Aunt Kiyomi.

Class ended without her saying a word. She hadn't intended on saying nothing, she didn't have the energy to jump into the discussion. As the class got deeper and deeper into the three hours, she felt her mind crawling inside itself, like an animal burrowing to hibernate. At the end of class, Tina walked out with Gillian. Wijjie was talking with Professor Alamo.

"How's it going, Tina?" Gillian asked.

"I've had better times. My mother severely sprained her ankle and can't get out of bed. She can't work, so that's made her depressed, which likely makes her MS worse. I broke up with my boyfriend. And I haven't had time to study."

Gillian shook her head, her dreadlocks bouncing with the movement. "Makes me glad my mother won't have anything to do with me, and that I don't have a boyfriend. Not that I wouldn't turn one down."

"How are you doing?"

"Not bad, I'm already way behind too. But only because I'm lazy."

"There's too much reading."

"It's physically impossible to read all of it, let alone digest any of it."

Tina nodded, then quietly asked Gillian if she had any pot on her, for her mother. Gillian gave her a soft chuckle and fished in her bag. She pulled out her small cigarette case and handed it to Tina. "Take what you need."

Tina picked out a couple of the joints. "I'll be happy to pay you for them."

"My contribution to your mother's health."

Tina thanked Gillian, who then said she was going to the library. "For some hard-core studying."

Tina walked up to her office. When she tried to open the door with her key, it wouldn't open. She checked the room number, then tried again; the key was not even turning.

Surely, she thought, they hadn't changed the locks on her. She knocked on the door. Howard opened the door, his face was flushed.

"Look, I'm really sorry," he said.

"What?" Tina asked.

"They've moved your office down the hall."

"What?"

"Well, Karyn moved you down there. I'm really sorry. I tried to talk her out of it. But she'd kind of freaked out. I don't know, that situation with the calligraphy teacher."

Tina stood at the doorway, not knowing what to say.

"I've got the key for your office," Howard said. He went back into the office, and returned with a key. He handed it to Tina, who took it and held it on her open palm as if weighing it.

"Room two-twenty-three, down the hall, take a right. Sorry. We already moved your stuff down there. There wasn't much."

Tina stared at the key.

HER NEW OFFICE WAS A LONG, narrow space, with a dinged-up worktable for a desk. There was a single narrow window;

she opened it to see if she could get rid of the musty smell. After she put up her things—her few books and notebooks, and miscellaneous office supplies—she called the number of Gozen sensei. At least there was a phone and a computer in the office.

When Gozen answered, she asked if she could meet with him at the Zenzen school. "I'd like to talk with you about the sensei."

"Okay."

"Is the other sensei with you?"

"Daizen sensei is in San Francisco."

"Good. I'd like to talk with you alone. In fifteen minutes?"

He paused, then said he'd be there.

"HOW IS THE SENSEI?" Gozen asked.

"He's fine, still working nonstop on his drawings."

"Who is taking care of him?"

"Right now, Kiyomi is. You remember her."

Gozen nodded. "When will you bring back the sensei?"

"When things settle down." Tina hadn't decided what she was going to do with him. "I thought I'd bring a few of the sensei's things to him. We left in kind of a hurry. Could you help me?"

While they gathered a few things from the bathroom, his toothbrush, his razor, hair brush, Tina asked him, "I'd like to study calligraphy, *shodô*. Would you teach me?"

"You want me to teach you?" Gozen was looking at her in surprise.

"You're an instructor, aren't you?"

"I am an instructor of the Zenzen school. But Zenzen sensei would have to approve it."

"But he can't right now, can he?"

"No, not now."

"What happens to the Zenzen school if the sensei can no longer perform as sensei?"

"Typically, the senior instructor takes over."

"Is that you?"

Gozen's brow furrowed and he sucked in his lower lip. "Yes, that's true, but . . ."

"Giving me lessons might be your first official act."

"I don't know. The sensei is still the sensei. I have to think about it."

In the sensei's bedroom, where they went to get some of his clothes, Tina stopped just inside the door. The simplicity of the room, with only a dresser and a futon rolled up next to a floor lamp, made it look as if he were just passing through, rather than having lived in the house for more than twenty years. As the sensei opened the dresser, she noticed the calligraphy scroll on the wall. When she stepped up closer to it, Gozen said, "Here are his clothes, what do you want to bring him?"

Tina turned away from the scroll. She helped Gozen pick out some clothes and put them in her backpack. Gozen closed up the dresser drawers and they went into the studio, where he picked up a few things—a box of inksticks, the sensei's carved signature block, a pot of red ink—and he handed them to Tina. "He would probably want these." Tina accepted them and put them in her backpack.

On their way back to the front of the house, Tina asked Gozen, "I'm interested in a book I just found, the *History of the Daizen Inkstone*."

"Yes. I've heard of it," he said casually. "Why?"

"I need someone who can help me translate it."

"Sorry, I'm not good at translating Japanese to English. The other way around I can do okay."

"I think you'd be perfect. You know about calligraphy, you know about the Daizen school."

Gozen pleaded that someone else would do a better job.

After Tina left, Gozen drove to the Miyako Hotel. In the lobby, he met Aragaki sensei and Mr. Robert. They went to a small restaurant in Japantown, next to an Asian antiques store. When they had settled in and had ordered Sapporo lagers, Gozen gave his report about his meeting with Tina. He told them how she was becoming very interested in the Daizen Inkstone, even asking him to translate the *History of the Daizen Inkstone* for her.

"I told her she should have learned Japanese," Mr. Robert said, speaking the language impeccably.

Aragaki made a clucking sound. "As I feared. We need to make our move sooner, rather than later."

"Our move?" Gozen said.

"The more Tina Suzuki knows, the more likely she will keep the inkstone for herself," Aragaki said. "Kando is going to come up with a plan." He picked up a bottle of Sapporo and filled the others' glasses.

Early Evening

JULY 1977
KYOTO, JAPAN

It was early evening on a hot, sultry day. Kando wanted nothing more than to get into a cool bath, drink a beer, and eat a dinner of cold *soba* noodles. He was filing away the day's activities reports when the door to his office burst open. He turned around and recognized Tetsuo Suzuki immediately, having seen his picture many times. Kando didn't recognize the two thugs with him, but he knew their type, and why they were there.

"I'm Tetsuo Suzuki. But I'm sure you know that."

"Yes, I do," Kando said. He was surprised his voice didn't crack when he responded.

"Smart guy," Suzuki said to his thugs. They didn't respond, only kept their eyes on Kando.

Suzuki started to wander around the office, gazing at the couple of cheaply framed photographs of flowers that Kando inherited from a previous tenant. Suzuki stopped at Kando's investigative license. "You're a real private investigator."

Kando didn't say anything.

Speaking to the framed license, Suzuki said, "Since you're a real private investigator, then you should know why I'm here."

"Yes, I do," Kando said.

Turning to face him, Suzuki said, "Then tell me."

"That seems unnecessary."

Suzuki's eyes grew narrow. "Tell me."

Taking a deep, slow breath, Kando said, "I have been making some investigations that have perhaps tread upon your life."

"No 'perhaps.' "

Kando nodded. "No 'perhaps.' And you don't like it. I can certainly understand that. Tell me what you want."

Suzuki grinned. He had very straight, white teeth. "That's efficient of you. Get it over with. All right, first I want to see all your information about my wife."

"I'd rather not," Kando said. "But if I refuse, your friends will probably give me a good roughing up, then ransack my office and find the files anyway."

Suzuki nodded once. "As I said, smart guy."

Kando shrugged and turned to his filing cabinet. He pulled out the reports and gave them to Suzuki. He sat in a chair and quickly leafed through them.

"Very professional," Suzuki said, standing up. "I'll take these with me."

"Of course," Kando said. "I assume I get my roughing up now anyway."

"If that's what you want."

"Not really."

"Tell you what. I'll put off that roughing up, as you call it, forever, if you do something for me."

"What's that?"

"When I have a job that requires your expertise, I will call you, and you will do that job without hesitation. Of course, I will pay you; I'm not asking for free services. But if you ever refuse a job, your probation is ended."

SAN FRANCISCO

Wearing a kimono was never one of Tina's favorite things. As a little girl, she had to wear one in a school play, what it was she couldn't remember. Aunt Kiyomi had helped

Hanako and her pick one out at the child's kimono shop in Japantown. The obi was the worst part of it all, cinched so tightly she could hardly breathe. It was hard to walk in the outfit—she had to shuffle, barely picking up her feet and hardly bending her legs. Not to mention the beautiful, but impractical, slippers and one-toed socks that she had to wear.

Wearing a kimono at the Tempura House, Tina shuffled between the tables to a table in her station. "Sorry to keep you waiting, are you ready to order?"

The four were probably a family from Japan, a father and mother, and a son and daughter-in-law. The parents were perhaps celebrating their thirtieth anniversary with a trip to America. They were probably hoping their son was about to announce that he and his wife were finally going to have a baby.

Tina was glad when the daughter-in-law spoke very good English. After taking their order—they must have been hungry from their sight-seeing, ordering tempura all around and a big sushi boat with a few side pieces of sushi as well—Tina shuffled back to the kitchen to turn in their order.

"How's it going?" Kiyomi asked, holding a sheaf of menus.

"I'm sorry I'm so slow."

"You're not slow at all."

Tina slipped the tempura order onto the cook's counter and the sushi order back through a window out to the sushi bar. Kiyomi said, "Thanks for filling in. I know you're busy."

"You didn't tell Ma I'm doing this, did you?"

"I wasn't supposed to?"

"That's okay."

Tina loaded a tray with four bowls of *wakame* seaweed miso soup garnished with slivers of green onion, and four small bowls of iceberg lettuce salad with curly shavings of carrots and daikon, and topped with a ginger dressing. How many times had her mother loaded up the trays with soup and salad? As Tina shuffled carefully out of the kitchen, she made a quick calculation: twenty-three years, fifty-two weeks, six nights a week, maybe forty tables a night—about a third of a million trays of miso soup and salad. The number made Tina stagger, almost trip.

The number was astounding, it was crushing. The tray got heavier with each step just thinking about it. She made it to the table, where she steadied the tray and served the soups and salads for the family who had no idea of the number of trays her mother had carried between kitchen and table.

THE YOUNG WAITRESS with the tattoo served Kando again. She brought him a beer and a dish of *edamame*—boiled soybeans in their pods. She recognized him and asked if he was having a good stay. He said he was.

He wasn't surprised to see that Hanako wasn't working that night; he had heard from Tina's boyfriend that she had sprained her ankle. But he was surprised to see the daughter working. He hadn't heard that she worked at the restaurant.

He had decided to have dinner again at the Tempura House to find out anything more about Hanako: how long she was going to be out from work, if she would be out of her apartment for any long stretch of time, and how long they were going to keep Shimano.

His waitress didn't know much when he asked her casually about Hanako. She pointed out Tina. "She's her daughter. I can have her come over."

"Thanks, but she's too busy. It was nothing important."

AT THE END OF THE NIGHT—it had been a busy one—Tina sat at the table with Aunt Kiyomi. Tina's legs were numb and ached at the same time. She loosened her obi, but that made it feel as if the kimono were about to fall off. After nibbling a bit on the food cooked for the help (she wasn't hungry at all after watching all those people gorge themselves), she went into the office, where she changed back into her jeans and sweater and sneakers. Nothing had ever felt so comfortable.

Adding up her tips, she had made a hundred and ten dollars, more than twenty dollars an hour. Her mother made pretty good money, not a fortune, but good money nonetheless. But to do it again the next night, and the night after that, Tina moaned. She didn't think she could do it a second night in a row, but when Kiyomi asked if she could, she said yes.

Before making her way home, she stopped at Double Rainbow Ice Cream, just before they closed at eleven, and got a dip of lemon chiffon ice cream in a sugar cone. It was what she always got after eating at the Tempura House when she was growing up. On the way home, she wondered how her mother felt every night going home, traipsing up Bush Street so she could sleep, then get up to do it again the next day.

Licking the ice cream cone all around the rim before it melted, Tina walked up to the apartment building, wishing she could be sleeping in her old closet bedroom, instead of on the sofa.

Hands

JULY 1977

SAN FRANCISCO, CALIFORNIA

Hanako took the rickety elevator to the fifth floor, walked past the wide staircase that was at one time elegant, its banisters now chipped and dull with no finish. She unlocked her apartment door and went inside, leaving her shoes just inside the door. The bathroom was just to her left, the kitchen straight ahead. To the right was a hallway that led to the bedroom and two huge walk-in closets. The sitting room with bay windows was at the end of the hallway.

She took off her coat, hung it up in one of the closets, and went into the sitting room. Next to one of the picture windows, she sat on the tired sofa that came with the furnished apartment, and curled her legs under her. Rubbing one foot, then the next, she watched the lights in the city being devoured by the fog that rolled in.

When her feet had stopped aching, Hanako counted out the money from her accumulated tips, her paycheck, and what she had left from the money Tetsuo had given her. She wanted to be sure she would have enough to take care of the baby when it was born, and especially during the weeks she would have to take off from work.

As Hanako put away her savings, the buzzer from the downstairs door rang. Perhaps Kiyomi was stopping by. She had a couple of times, just to chat. Hanako pushed the button to open the door to the building, leaving the door to her apartment open. She hurried around the apartment, checking to see if she needed to pick up anything and put it away.

Satisfied, she hurried back down the hallway. When she

turned toward the door, she stopped. Standing just outside the door was Daizen sensei.

She wanted to run but there was nowhere to go.

"I'm sorry not to have called, or sent you a letter before I arrived," he said.

"How did you find me?"

He opened his mouth, a mouth that had become sad, then closed it. He shook his head. "That's not important."

"Please don't."

"Don't?"

"Please." Hanako found her legs able to move and she took a step back, then she ran forward to the door. "Please, leave me alone. I'm sorry." She reached out. The sensei thought she was reaching out to him, but she was reaching out for the door. Her hands passed by his outstretched hand, the hand that had taught her how to hold the brush, and she took hold of the knob and pushed the door shut.

SAN FRANCISCO

There was a knock on Hanako's bedroom door. "Yes?"

"It's me," Tina said.

Hanako leaned over and unlocked the door. Tina came in with a breakfast tray and set it down on the dresser. "Good morning," Tina said.

"Ohayo," Hanako said.

Tina unfolded the legs of the lap tray and set it up on the bed. She put her mother's breakfast on the tray. "How was Granny last night?"

"Not much help. All she did was watch TV."

"At least she was here if you needed anything." Tina poured tea into her cup.

"She can't hear a thing. She has to turn up the TV so loud."

"I'm sure she could hear you."

Hanako thanked her for the tea and breakfast. "You don't have to work at the Tempura House for me."

"I don't mind."

"But you should be studying."

"I've been studying." Tina finished setting out the food: toast and an egg, and a bowl of mixed fruit. "Where should I put the tip money?"

Hanako gestured to the dresser. "Bottom."

Tina opened the bottom drawer and found a small, fire-proof money box.

"The key is on a chain, under the drawer above."

Tina found it and put the money inside. "Shouldn't this go in the bank?"

"When it's full, I go to the bank."

"Okay," Tina said.

Hanako leaned forward and took a sip of tea. "I just want it back the way it was."

"I know, Ma. I know."

Hanako set the teacup down. She picked at the egg and nibbled a corner of the toast. She washed it down with another sip of tea, then leaned back onto her stack of pillows and closed her eyes.

TINA WASHED THE DISHES before she checked on the sensei. Earlier, before she had served her mother, he had eaten breakfast quickly, not as if he were hungry, but as if he were in a hurry. He was back at work on his drawings. Opening her backpack, Tina took out the things she had gotten at his studio, placing the calligraphy things near his work area, and stacking the clothes near his—her old—bed, though there were no signs that he was sleeping at all.

Sitting on the floor, she watched him work for a while, studying his movements, trying to see if there was any correlation between his facial expressions and what he was drawing. Mostly his expression was blank, as if lost in a deep place.

When he finished a page, he reached for the seal that Tina had returned to him. He wet its surface with the red ink and stamped his drawing. The movements seemed automatic; likely he had done it as many times or more than her mother had carried trays of miso soup.

The sensei held up the drawing, as if deciding where to hang it. Tina thought back to the sole framed work she had seen in his bedroom in his house. It had two stamps, one was the sensei's elaborate stamp, and the other was smaller, less complex, a simple signature stamp—like a *hanko*. And now that she thought about it, there was something that she recognized in the smaller one. Tina knew the kanji characters for Suzuki; the smaller stamp might have been those characters. But the stamp had been somewhat stylized, and she had only gotten a glimpse of it.

Tina tried to study at the kitchen table, but her mind wouldn't focus on the article. She rubbed her forehead, then her calves, which still ached from her waitress stint.

Just as she was going back to the beginning of the article, the door buzzer rang. She got up and, holding the article, went over to the buzzer and pushed the button. It was a little early for Kiyomi to come over.

Tina waited by the door reading the abstract of the article again until she could see Mr. Robert walking up the stairs. He was carrying a plastic grocery bag that he handed to her. "Mail. And some other stuff."

"Thanks," she said, taking the bag.

They stood at the door to the apartment, Tina leaning against the doorframe, Mr. Robert with his perfect posture developed from years of training. Tina finally said, "Would you like to see Ma?"

"Sure. And the sensei?"

"I suppose."

Tina went into the apartment, clutching the bag. Mr. Robert knocked on the door to Hanako's bedroom.

"*Konnichiwa,* Robert-*san,*" her mother said.

Tina went back into the kitchen and started again on the article.

BY THE TIME MR. ROBERT finished his visit, Tina managed to get through the article and grasp most of it, though many of the details were fuzzy. "Thanks," Mr. Robert said, standing in the doorway to the kitchen.

"Sure."

In a whisper, he said, "She seems depressed."

"She is."

"She'll be better when she's up and around again," Mr. Robert said. "The sensei seems the same. All he does is draw?"

Tina nodded.

"When are you going to let him go home?"

"I'm not holding him prisoner here."

"But he can't tell you if he wants to go home."

Changing the subject, she said, "I was wondering if you could look at something for me." Tina took out the photo-copied book from her backpack. "It's the *History of the Daizen Inkstone.*"

He took it from her and studied the first page.

"I was wondering if you could translate it, just the main ideas, really, not the whole thing."

He carefully turned the copy's pages, stopping now and then with a puzzled look on his face. "It will be hard, this is old Japanese."

"You don't have to do it."

"Oh, no, I want to," he said with enthusiasm. "It really shouldn't take too long to get the main ideas for you." He skimmed a few more pages and, as he did, Tina realized they would never get back together. Not after what she had said to him, not after he realized it must have been the truth.

AFTER MR. ROBERT LEFT, Tina checked her mail—there was nothing worth his trip there. She read a chapter in Professor Porter's book on language. Tina closed up her book and went into the closet bedroom. The sensei acknowledged her presence with a brief change of focus of his eyes before returning to his drawing. She would have to get him some more paper soon, she noticed as she sat on the floor next to him.

IN THE BEDROOM, fighting the gripping pain that came in waves, Hanako's mind wanted to leave her body, to fly away. Tears streamed from her eyes—in sadness at the thought, in pain, in longing.

When I get hurt
I have to reconcile
for a scar

Hanako and Tetsuo

APRIL 1977

KOBE, JAPAN

Hanako opened the windows and began her new routine with a light breakfast and cup of tea before beginning to work on her long poem. At the suggestion of the Daizen sensei, she had divided it into parts, which consisted of sections of several characters. She practiced one section a day, the practice sheets spread throughout the house.

She worked until noon, had her light lunch, then went to her lesson, bringing the best work of the morning with her. The sensei was very enthusiastic, at first she wasn't sure he would be. She knew that her project was ambitious for a beginner.

The sensei worked closely with her, his suggestions on content and execution always well taken. He excitedly offered his points, as if it were his project, perhaps somewhat too much so. His face would change subtly as he read her poem, as if deep in thought.

She returned from her lesson to find Tetsuo unexpectedly home from Hawaii. He was sitting in one of the chairs in their living room, her practice sheets strewn across the floor at his feet.

"Hello, Wife," he said. His voice penetrated her with its coldness.

"Welcome home," she said, trying to sound casual. "I didn't know you would be here, I would have cleaned all this up."

He picked up a sheet of her calligraphy. "What is this?"

"I've taken up *shodô*."

"You're a real natural talent."

"Thank you." She kneeled on the floor and began picking up the sheets. "How is the hotel coming along?"

Tetsuo picked up another sheet and looked at it. "It was going very well, until I got a call."

"A call? A telephone call?"

He began to tear the sheet; Hanako flinched. "Yes, a telephone call. From someone who told me you were having an affair with your *shodô* sensei." The sheet ripped in half. He picked up another and started to tear it. " '*Shodô*?' I said. 'My wife's not taking *shodô*.' "

Hanako could say nothing as he tore another sheet, then another.

" 'My wife's not taking *shodô* lessons,' I said," Tetsuo repeated. "But you are taking *shodô* lessons." Rip. "And you are having an affair."

Hanako trembled.

"I know all about you and your sensei," Tetsuo said as he got up. He went into the kitchen, where her calligraphy supplies were out on the table. She got to her feet and followed him.

He picked up one of her brushes and snapped it in half. "This is what I'm going to do to your sensei's brushes." He picked up her inkstone and brought it down forcefully on the edge of the table. It cracked in two. "And this—"

Hanako gasped. Tetsuo dropped the inkstone halves onto the floor. They clattered on the wood flooring.

She dropped to her knees, fumbling for the broken inkstone. She tried to put the pieces together, but couldn't fit them. She tried again and again, but they wouldn't fit. "No," she pleaded. "Don't do that. I'll do anything." She looked up at Tetsuo, his stern expression full of disgust.

"If you ever see him again, I'll do that and more."

Hanako nodded.

"I want you to leave this house. You will leave the country so I never have to see you again."

She nodded again.

Tetsuo grabbed her hand and pulled her up. "Before you leave, we are going to pay a visit to your parents so you can tell them what you've done."

AT THE IIDA HOME, Hanako was kneeling in front of her parents, who were sitting on the *tatami* floor. Tetsuo was sitting to the side, his back rigid and his arms across his chest. Hanako's head hung low.

"Look at your parents," Tetsuo ordered her.

She tilted her head up, just enough so she could see her parents' faces. Her father's jaw was clenched tight, his eyes bulging. Her mother was staring in horror at her daughter, her face red. Hanako shut her eyes.

"Tell them," Tetsuo barked.

Hanako couldn't speak, her entire being seized by a cold paralysis.

BERKELEY

After neuroanatomy class, in which they had traced the cuneocerebellar tract from the cerebellum to various muscles, Tina stopped in Wijjie's office. He was working on his computer.

"Tina," he said. "How's your mother doing?"

"It doesn't seem like her ankle is getting better. I'm trying to get her to a doctor, but she won't go."

"She should," Wijjie said. "Do you want me to stop by?"

"If I can't get her to go." Tina sat in a chair and held her backpack on her lap. "The worst thing, though, is her mood."

"Depression?"

"I think so."

"It's understandable, she's been active all her life, now to have her illness, and then her ankle. A tough change."

"I know."

"I'll talk to her."

"Thanks."

Wijjie gave her a shake of his head: "I heard something about you getting kicked out of your office. What happened? Porter punishing you?"

Tina didn't know why; she thought she had smoothed things over. Maybe she was being sent a message. "I guess."

Wijjie got up and stretched. He told her that the offer from Alamo was still open. If she was interested.

"Thanks. Not right now."

Wijjie sat on his desk. "There could be changes around here. Alamo has been spending a lot of time with Porter. Ever since we were all together at the calligraphy school."

"What?"

Wijjie shook his head. "I can't believe it either."

"WHAT DO YOU WANT to know about *shodô*?" Gozen asked. Tina was meeting him for her first lesson. They were in the main room of the house, sitting across from each other at one of the tables.

"How about the basic philosophy first."

"We usually give an introductory lesson, is that what you would like?"

"Yes."

Gozen thought for a moment, then said, "First, *shodô* requires a rigorous approach."

"More than a creative approach?"

"Creativity is important, but rigor must be there. It depends on what kind of *shodô* you want to practice. It depends on what you mean by creativity. Even in the most traditional *shodô*, the best work exhibits a certain personality that can be described as creative."

"In what sense?"

Gozen looked pained. "Well, that's difficult to put into words. There are some guiding principles that must be adhered to—such as balance, weight—but using those principles in unique ways will be found in the best *shodô*."

"Would the sensei's drawings be considered creative *shodô*?"

Gozen put his hand on his cheek and let it slide down until only his fingertips were resting on his chin. "No."

"What kinds of changes should I expect to have to make in my life to become a good *shodô* practitioner?" she asked.

"Changes? Well, of course, to become good, one must practice intensely, every day. Ten thousand strokes for ten thousand days, is what they say."

A hundred million, Tina calculated. Over about thirty years.

NEAR THE END OF HER LESSON, Gozen was showing her a copy of the school's instructor's journal when one of the school's students came to the door. While Gozen talked with him, Tina went to the back of the school. In the sensei's bedroom, she looked at the signature seal on the work of calligraphy. With a pen and piece of paper, she copied the design.

The *taku* radical is the last of the *eiji happô*. It has the same-sounding name as the seventh radical, but is entirely different. This *taku* is used in many kanji, though it is one of the more difficult radicals to perfect. The direction of the brush changes slightly at the end of the stroke. The pressure is also increased as the brush is moved from the upper left to the lower right. The end of the stroke is thicker than the start, but must be in proportion.

Instructor's Journal,
Zenzen School of
Japanese Calligraphy

What
who
have I
become

SAN FRANCISCO

Before she went to work at the Tempura House, Tina stopped at home. Kiyomi had left for work. Granny was there, watching TV. She smiled at Tina, and Tina smiled back.

In one of her mother's boxes she had moved out of the bedroom closet to make room for the sensei, Tina dug through the stacks of old receipts, school reports, and other odds and ends. Near the bottom, she found the small cloth bag that contained a wooden Japanese signature seal—a *hanko*—and a small inkpad. When she was in grade school, she used to play with it, stamping the seal on her hand or her schoolwork.

Tina found the piece of paper on which she had copied the design. She opened the inkpad—it was still moist with ink. She pushed the *hanko* onto the pad, then onto the piece of paper. She didn't know how many signature seals would look alike, but these two seemed identical.

A Gaze

APRIL 1977
KYOTO, JAPAN

The Daizen sensei was looking at the calligraphy that Hanako had completed and they had sealed. He had hung the work in his studio, replacing a work of his own that seemed so lifeless compared to hers.

When Hanako was late for the lesson, he immediately thought something had happened, as she had never been late before. Perhaps she was delayed in traffic. Maybe the trains were running late. As the time grew later, he imagined worse things: an accident, an illness.

When she didn't show up the next day either, he dialed her phone number, his heart pounding. After twenty rings, he hung up. He thought about driving to her home, but did not know where she lived, except that her home was in Kobe. He paced about the studio, imagining that she was seriously ill or, hysterically, that her husband found out about their affair and had murdered her.

That afternoon, he couldn't pick up a brush, couldn't focus on the students that came for their lessons, couldn't think of anything else but the empty pit in his gut, and his

The *enso* is a painted circle—not kanji—that represents the concept of infinity in Zen. Drawing the *enso* requires a high degree of mind-body unification, because it is drawn blind. That is, the calligrapher's hand blocks a complete view of the circle as it is drawn.

Begin the *enso* with a lot of pressure on the brush and gradually reduce it as the circle is completed. The stroke must not end abruptly, indeed, the calligrapher's *ki* should continue in the circular motion, even when the *enso* has been completed.

Instructor's Journal, Zenzen School of Japanese Calligraphy

heart that beat sluggishly as if the life were draining from him. When the lessons were over for the day, the sensei dropped to the floor, onto his knees, in front of her calligraphy.

Yuriko came into the studio, her gaze cool, unquestioning. And then he knew. He knew that his wife was the reason that Hanako would no longer be taking lessons.

SAN FRANCISCO

Tina's second stint as a Tempura House server was not as busy. During a lull, she had time to help Aunt Kiyomi fold napkins.

"How is your second night?" Kiyomi asked.

"A little slow."

Kiyomi laughed. "Ready for action?"

"I didn't have time to think last night. Everything just happened."

"That's when it's best. I love busy nights." Her hands moved again, folding the napkins quickly and efficiently.

"I have a question, Aunt Kiyomi. Did my mother used to be one of the sensei's students? I found some calligraphy in the sensei's studio. It looks like it was sealed by my mother."

Kiyomi's hands stopped in the middle of creasing a fold. "I think she did mention that she studied calligraphy. But you should ask her."

KANDO JOINED ARAGAKI, Gozen, and Mr. Robert in the Miyako Hotel lounge. They ordered a round of drinks.

Kando's first question was: "Are you sure it's the Daizen Inkstone?"

Aragaki looked at Gozen, then said, "Yes, I believe so. I saw it."

"When was the last time you saw the Daizen Inkstone?"

"I see your point," Aragaki said.

"You need to be one hundred percent sure before you go to all the trouble of retrieving it."

Gozen said, "How do we do that?"

"Do you have a picture? A description?"

Mr. Robert spoke up: "I have a description and drawing of it, from a book."

"The *History of the Daizen Inkstone*?" Gozen said.

"Yes," Mr. Robert said.

"It's a simple inside job, then," Kando said, nodding toward Mr. Robert. "He has access to the apartment and the means to verify."

"I understand," Aragaki said. "And if it is the Daizen Inkstone, then he may as well bring it out with him."

"That's for you three to decide," Kando said. "I can't tell you what to do."

They sipped their drinks for a while before Kando looked from Gozen to Mr. Robert. "I need to ask you two a question. What's in it for you to have the Daizen Inkstone returned to Japan?"

Gozen glanced at Aragaki, who said, "I can answer that. In exchange for their help, I have offered them the rank of senior instructors at the Daizen school."

AN HOUR-LONG RUSH started at the Tempura House just after eight. When she was delivering the last *mochi* ice cream to a table, Tina noticed Mr. Robert at the front of the restaurant.

"Come to have dinner?"

"No, thanks. I have the translation you want."

"You finished it?"

"The main gist of it anyway. I worked on it all day." He

waved at Kiyomi, who was in the back of the restaurant talking with one of the other waitresses. "I had some help. One of the other teachers at the school who's from Japan knows a lot about classical Japanese writing. I made a bunch of notes. I could read them to you, explain what the book is about."

"Okay, let me ask Aunt Kiyomi if I can get off."

"I can wait," he said.

"I'll get you some beer or tea."

"Tea will be fine."

Tina finished up her tables, then sat with him. "It's a bit difficult," Mr. Robert said, "to explain a lot of what happened in the book. A lot of words have no direct translation into modern Japanese. Most Japanese wouldn't understand them."

"Like reading Chaucer in the original?"

Mr. Robert cocked his head. "Yeah, I guess."

Tina poured herself some tea. Referring to his notes, written in his precise handwriting, Mr. Robert described the main points of the book, the beginnings of the Daizen school coinciding with the first sensei's discovery of the rock and how it was shaped into the Daizen Inkstone.

"The second half of the book," Mr. Robert said after a sip of tea, "largely describes the founding of the Kurokawa school, an offshoot of the Daizen school, and how the inkstone became the prize in the Daizen-Kurokawa competition. Interestingly, the second half is also sort of a love story."

"A love story?"

He flipped through his notes. "While the Kurokawa sensei was in the mountains, staying in the village of Jûzu-mura, he describes walking in the mountains along a stream. He met a woman who was also walking along the stream. She showed him where to listen to the sounds that the stream made as it flowed over rocks, like natural water sculptures."

"Like in Japanese gardens."

"He fell in love with her, but she couldn't leave—a family problem—and he couldn't stay."

They sat in silence, sipping tea. The tea in her cup had gone cold.

"That's pretty much it," Mr. Robert said.

"Thanks, that was great."

Mr. Robert turned the pages until he came to the drawing of the Daizen Inkstone. He turned the page so it faced Tina. "This is the Daizen Inkstone. Is it the one that the sensei is using?"

"Yes."

"Are you sure? Maybe I should come over and check."

Tina got up. "All right."

THE APARTMENT WAS QUIET. Kiyomi's husband had already picked up Granny to take her home. Tina stopped and checked the sensei first; he was working on his drawings. Mr. Robert stepped into the closets while Tina went to check on her mother. Hanako was propped up on her bed. A stack of the sensei's drawings beside her.

"Granny get you everything you needed?"

"During commercials."

"Good, at least she's helping, huh? Can I get you anything?"

"*Iie, sumimasen.* How was the Tempura House?"

"It started out slow, then picked up." Tina kneeled down and opened the drawer with the money box. Tina fished for the key on the chain. "I was doing a little research on *shodô* and found out the sensei—Zenzen sensei—is actually the twenty-ninth head sensei of the Daizen School of Calligraphy in Japan."

There was a growing stack of bills and a mound of change in the money box; another couple of nights and she would have to make a deposit. "He's using a very famous inkstone called the Daizen Inkstone. It's hundreds of years old." Tina turned to face her mother. Hanako turned away from Tina's gaze.

Tina closed the money box and sat on the bed. "You already knew this, didn't you? Because you were his student?"

"How did you find out?" Hanako asked quietly.

"I saw a work of calligraphy with your seal on it, at the sensei's studio."

"Mine?"

"Yes, it was your seal, I'm sure. I couldn't read the kanji, but they looked very beautiful."

Hanako nodded slowly. "I was his student in Japan."

"Why didn't you tell me you studied *shodō*?"

Hanako sighed. "It was only for a short time."

"You must have done very well at it. Why only a short time?"

"*Doshite?* . . . Why? . . . I moved here. So no more lessons."

"But then the sensei came to California," Tina said. "Why?"

"*Wakarimasen.*" I don't know. "Ask him."

"You know he can't talk," Tina said, exasperated, then picked up one of the sensei's drawings. "But you can understand these, can't you?"

Hanako pushed herself up so she was sitting straight, as if ready to crawl off the bed and limp away. "I don't know. I only think I know."

"What do you think?"

"He's . . . ," she started. *Wakarimasen.*

Tina turned over the drawing she held; she couldn't read the kanji. "What's this say?"

Hanako looked at it. "In English," she said so quietly that Tina could barely hear, "it means 'What, who, have I become.'"

Tina thought about the words and looked at the drawing.

The words her mother put to the drawing were not interpreting it, they expressed what her mother felt, but couldn't say.

TINA LOOKED IN on the sensei and Mr. Robert. He was kneeling by the sensei, watching him work. She whispered to Mr. Robert, "I'm going to sleep. You can let yourself out."

"Okay. Thanks."

"Thanks again for translating the book."

"Sure. Good night."

"Good night."

HANAKO TOOK THE LATEST of the sensei's drawings and placed them across her bed. The patterns were not becoming any clearer, but at least she had a feeling about their meaning. Her feelings were telling a story of loss, pain, regret, and misunderstanding. She couldn't have explained why she felt that; she may have been imagining it all. After looking at his strange brushstrokes for so long, perhaps she had convinced herself she could understand them. Maybe she wanted the drawings to say that to her. Maybe it was what she had wanted to say to the sensei.

I wish I hope
I plead I pray
no one listens
to me
but me

WHEN THE APARTMENT had been quiet for several minutes, Mr. Robert took another inkstone from his bag. Kneeling next to the sensei, he waited until the sensei had loaded his brush with ink and began another drawing. He switched inkstones and poured the ink from the Daizen Inkstone into the other. He stood up and backed away. In the harsh light of the closet, he compared the Daizen Inkstone with the drawing. It looked identical.

Mr. Robert clutched the inkstone tightly and ran out of the apartment.

*I don't like you
and I don't like you
and me*

SWINGING HER LEGS off the bed, Hanako tried putting weight on her sprained ankle; a shot of pain went up her leg, but not as bad as it had been. She hopped once, twice, over to the dresser. Walking gingerly, she walked to her door and quietly unlocked it. She opened the door slowly; it made no sound. She took a step into the hallway then, bracing herself against the door, took a step toward the closets.

Just inside, the sensei lay crumpled on the floor.

Hanako kneeled next to him and put her hands on his shoulder. She turned him slightly, so that she could see his face. She searched for hope, for forgiveness, for understanding, for any of the emotions she had once seen in herself but had buried so deep they had withered and died.

Utter darkness. As dark as sumi *in an inkstone that is deeper than an ocean. The darkness was peaceful, quiet. Only thoughts existed, but only for a moment before they were gone, like sparks flying into a night sky. But in that split second all was clear: it was the inkstone, not him, that she feared. The inkstone's power had helped her find who she was, helped her find a true self. But it wasn't a self she had wanted to discover . . .*

Floating on the dark, free. The thoughts disconnected, untethered. Everything said.

Here I sit and speak and sparkle others sit and stare

Last Encounter

JULY 1977

SAN FRANCISCO, CALIFORNIA

He saw her a few weeks later, coming out of the restaurant, only this time she was walking toward him. She saw him, too. He couldn't run; it would seem as if he were following her.

She said, "I see you're still in California, sensei."

"I'm teaching in Berkeley. At the East Bay Center for Japanese Arts."

"Berkeley . . . I haven't been there yet. What about the Daizen school?"

"I gave it up to come here."

"You should go back."

"I can't now. What about you? Will you return to Japan?"

A cable car clanged past them. When it was gone, she said, "I have to stay."

"Perhaps we should meet. Have you been practicing *shodô*?"

"No. Not once."

"Would you like a lesson again sometime?"

She shook her head. "No."

"But I have the inkstone. The Daizen Inkstone."

She glanced up at him, her face and body stiffening. Without another word, she hurried past him.

The doctor talked with Hanako and Tina in the waiting room. "He had a massive hemorrhagic stroke. We have him breathing, but his higher level brain functions have ceased."

Tina looked at her mother—she was sitting rigidly still in the plastic chair. Tina asked, "Where was the stroke?"

The doctor said, "We don't have it pinpointed, but in the right hemisphere."

"He had a previous stroke over a month ago," Tina said.

"I thought so, there was evidence of that."

"In the left temporal lobe, some prefrontal. He couldn't speak or write, I doubt if he understood, either. Agraphia and aphasia." Tina's voice was detached, as if reading from a dry textbook.

"Medical student?" the doctor asked.

"Grad student. Neuroscience."

"UCSF?"

"Cal."

He nodded.

Tina asked him, "Would it have made a difference if he had gotten here sooner? There was a problem in the building with the elevator. The paramedics had to climb up and down five flights of stairs."

"Bet they loved that. But I doubt it made a difference."

"Was the stroke related to his previous one?" Tina asked.

"Hard to say. Strokes often come in a series."

"It might have happened at any time?"

"Yes. At any time. Why?"

"Just curious."

The doctor glanced at his clipboard, then said, "I'm sorry to be blunt, but he's not going to recover. We need to know what to do about taking extraordinary measures. I assume you're next of kin?"

Hanako glanced at Tina.

Tina looked at her mother as she said, "I'm his daughter."
Hanako nodded.

Making a note, the doctor said, "Okay. Come with me,
you'll have some paperwork to fill out." Then he said to
Hanako, "That ankle looks nasty. While you're here, why
don't you let someone have a look at it."

Hanako started to say something, then nodded.

AFTER THE BRIEF FUNERAL SERVICE at the Japantown Buddhist
Temple, they gathered at the China Seas restaurant: Hanako
and Tina, Aunt Kiyomi and Uncle Shinichi, cousins James
and Annie, Granny, and a few others from the Tempura
House. Wijjie and Gillian were there too. They were in a
banquet room off the main dining room, and had ordered a
set menu, except for the addition of Aunt Kiyomi and
Hanako's favorites: spicy rock shrimp, steamed white fish
with light garlic sauce, and seasonal vegetables.

"Have some shrimp," Aunt Kiyomi said to Tina. "Your
mother and I have eaten spicy rock shrimp almost every
week since she came to the Tempura House."

"Then I'd love some," Tina said, calculating they had
eaten about twelve hundred dishes of spicy rock shrimp.

Kiyomi spooned out a portion for her, then some for
Hanako, who was sitting on the other side of her. Hanako
was sitting in her chair diagonally so that her ankle, sporting
a soft cast, would be comfortable. A pair of crutches was
leaning against the wall behind her.

Taking a bite, Tina said, "This is delicious shrimp."

Aunt Kiyomi said to Hanako, "She thinks it's delicious."

Hanako said, "It is delicious, isn't it?"

Tina was hungry. She hadn't eaten much lately, and what
she had eaten, she couldn't remember. Over the past days,

What makes something
delicious? The taste, olfac-
tory, tactile, visual, and
aural nervous systems
coming together to pro-
duce a neurally generated,
subjective experience.
Each person's conscious-
ness of a specific "deli-
cious" experience is
unique, yet has some
commonalities across all
people.

By itself, the Daizen Inkstone has no meaning ex-
cept when used in the

she had to set up the funeral service, schedule the cremation, and contact the sensei's relatives—his mother and a brother were the only ones left. The Japanese consul had helped Tina contact them; he had acted as a go-between, setting up the calls, talking to them first. Tina's newly discovered uncle and grandmother didn't want to talk to her. They merely relayed through the consul that they desired the sensei's remains be sent to Japan for burial in the family plot.

To them, Tina had no meaning.

Tina hadn't noticed the Daizen Inkstone had been switched for a day. She asked her mother if she had taken it. She said, *Iie.* No. Then Mr. Robert was the only person who could have switched them, Tina told her.

The next day, Mr. Robert had called when he heard the sensei had died. He gave his condolences and told her that he was moving to Kyoto to study and teach at the Daizen school. "That's great for you," she said, then asked him about the inkstone. He tried to explain, but Tina said she didn't care about his reasons. She asked her mother if she wanted to talk to him. She said, *"Iie."*

That first bite of spicy rock shrimp awakened her dormant hunger. She devoured the shrimp, the white fish, the crisp steamed veggies, and the other dishes. After eating, they mingled around the banquet room, talking and laughing, as they had at family get-togethers.

Wijjie was in a deep conversation with Tina's "cousin" Annie. Gillian was listening to "cousin" James, and looked bored. Tina joined them and asked James how he was doing.

"Got laid off. Venture capital dried up."

"That sucks."

James gave her a grin. "I've got another job already. Twice as much salary. I'm not taking stock options this time."

"Good for you."

process of conveying meaning, of communicating conscious and subconscious experience. The inkstone holds the ink that clings to the brush that is deposited on the paper. The objects and processes are place-holders for meaning. Conscious experiences depend on place-holders, like spicy rock shrimp, that not only contain proteins, oils, spices that the sensory nerves react to, but also hold meaning. Like the meaning accumulated through twelve hundred dinners.

The Daizen Inkstone has accumulated centuries of meaning. The inkstone itself, as a rock, has no meaning but for this accumulation of use, of being coveted, of being prized. And so it is with conscious experience; it is accumulated meaning.

Neuroscience Notebook, Christina Hana Suzuki

"Thanks," James said. "Annie and I were thinking of going to Japan next summer for two weeks or so. Want to come along?"

Tina started to say she needed to stay close to her mother. "I'd like to go."

"Cool."

Tina asked Gillian if she could talk to her, and they found a quiet corner in the room. "When we first met, you said you had switched to neuroscience from IGB, right?"

"Yep."

"Could you tell me how you did that?"

"It's a little tricky. First, you've got to know someone who will take you on in the other program. Why?"

"I'm thinking of switching to another program."

"No way. To what?"

"Cellular biology. Maybe research on multiple sclerosis."

"You'll make great discoveries that will help your mother," Gillian said. "I'll be happy to help you switch."

"Thanks," Tina said.

"Next, you'll be getting a tattoo."

Tina grinned. "I've been meaning to talk to you about that too."

IN THE MIYAKO HOTEL LOBBY, Aragaki and Kando waited for Gozen to arrive to take Aragaki to the airport. After the sensei died, Gozen had decided to stay in California to run the Zenzen School of Japanese Calligraphy. Tina, who was going to inherit the house, had asked him to stay. He agreed, but only if she would take lessons. She said she would.

Kando told Aragaki that he was going to spend a few more days in San Francisco to "see the sights."

A hotel employee walked up to them. "Excuse me, sir," he said to Aragaki. "You have a phone call. From your airline."

Aragaki got up.

"I'll watch your bag," Kando said.

Aragaki followed the hotel employee to the phone. The phone call Kando had arranged from "airline reservations" was exactly on time. Aragaki would be away for two or three minutes.

When the sensei was out of sight, Kando dipped into Aragaki's carry-on bag and took out the box that contained the Daizen Inkstone. He put the box into his own bag, the one he carried with him when sight-seeing. From his bag, he took out a box identical to the one that held the Daizen Inkstone and put it into Aragaki's bag.

THE BANQUET AT THE CHINA SEAS was winding down when the stoic waiter brought a box to Hanako.

"For you," he said.

Hanako took the box from him. "It's heavy," she said, as a spasm gripped her legs.

TINA AND HANAKO took the renovated elevator to the fifth floor. "Nice, huh?" Tina said.

"Sugoi," Hanako said.

When it came to a smooth stop, they opened the door and walked into their apartment. Hanako was getting good with her crutches.

As her mother went to the kitchen to start tea, Tina said, "I'm going for a drink with James and Annie, and Wijjie and Gillian. You'll be okay?"

"I'll be okay. Thank you for setting up the funeral and everything else."

"I'm sorry about the sensei."

Hanako bowed her head. "I'm sorry about your father."

Tina rubbed her mother's back. "Why did you leave Japan? Why didn't you get back together with him?"

She could feel her mother tense. "I can't explain. Not in words. Someday, maybe."

"That's okay, Ma."

THAT NIGHT, in the closets, Hanako picked up the Daizen Inkstone, one of the sensei's brushes, a stack of paper, and an inkstick. Using one crutch, she hobbled carefully into the kitchen with the four treasures.

She arranged the paper, the inkstone, and the brush on the kitchen table. She dribbled a little water in the inkstone, then rubbed the inkstick back and forth, watching as it slowly dissolved. When the *sumi* was just the right shade of black, she stared into it, as if trying to see through it.

A flurry of spasms gripped her legs. She thought about taking some of her medicine, or smoking the marijuana that Hana's friend Gillian had given her. Instead, she let the pain course through her body, through her mind. The more she gazed into the inkstone, the sharper and deeper the pain cut. But it was no longer just physical pain; the inkstone represented the pressing burden of shame that her affair had brought her, the crushing disappointment that caused her parents to loath her.

She had found herself, her emotional self, her irrational self, through the inkstone. What she found wasn't intrinsically bad. She found that she could *feel*: that she could love, that she could experience life on her own terms, not on her husband's or her parents'. The inkstone had also given her Hana. It had brought her to San Francisco, where she could exist on her own terms. It had given her Tuesday night dinners at the China Seas with Kiyomi.

The inkstone had been a door opening to the place within her that was peaceful, so comforting. The place where she could descend below herself, into the ocean where her consciousness floated. A place where she longed to be, but if she went too far, she could never come back.

No, what happened wasn't the inkstone's fault; it could only bring out what was already within her. It wasn't the sensei's fault either. He had given all of himself to her, given up everything that mattered. She wished he were still alive, so she could tell him that it wasn't him. That she had loved him, but the pain she felt when she saw him was too much for her to bear.

She had wanted to tell Hana all this, but knew the words wouldn't come. Maybe there were no words.

Holding the brush unwaveringly with all of her *ki,* the surge of power, of fullness, of being, that she had experienced when she first used the Daizen Inkstone welled up from her subconscious. As she dipped the brush into the inkstone, the pain, all of it, began to wash away.

So be it
not so I want it
but be
with it

ACKNOWLEDGMENTS

The author is grateful to the readers of early drafts who offered many valuable suggestions: Marilyn Colter, Tracy Ekstrand, Teresa Funke, Jean Hanson, Kathy Hayes, Luana Heikes, Paul Miller, Karla Oceanak, and Linda Shimoda. Without the insight and enthusiasm of Sean McDonald, I would still be struggling to shape the story and characters.

The following references were invaluable in writing about the art and science found in this book; any errors of factual details are due to my misinterpretation.

CALLIGRAPHY AND JAPANESE CHARACTERS

Davey, H. E. *Brush Meditation, A Japanese Way to Mind and Body Harmony.* Stone Bridge Press, 1999.

Earnshaw, Christopher J. *Sho: Japanese Calligraphy.* Charles E. Tuttle Publishing Company, 1988.

Henshall, Kenneth G. *A Guide to Remembering Japanese Characters.* Charles E. Tuttle Publishing Company, 1988.

Japan Foundation Japanese Language Institute. *Basic Japanese-English Dictionary.* Bojinsha Company, 1986; Oxford University Press, 1989.

Yamaguchi, Momoo, and Setsuko Kojima, eds. *A Cultural Dictionary of Japan.* Japan Times, 1979.

Neuroscience

Burt, Alvin. *Textbook of Neuroanatomy.* W. B. Saunders Company, 1993.

Carter, Rita. *Mapping the Mind.* University of California Press, 1998.

Damasio, Antonio. *The Feeling of What Happens: Body and Emotion in the Making of Consciousness.* Harcourt Brace and Company, 1999.

Diamond, Marian, Arnold Scheibel, and Lawrence Elson. *The Human Brain Coloring Book.* HarperPerennial, 1985.

Greenfield, Susan, ed. *The Human Mind Explained.* Henry Holt and Company, 1996.

Moonen, C. T. W., and P. A. Bandettini, eds. *Functional MRI.* Springer, 1999.

National Institutes of Health. *Mind Over Matter: The Brain's Response to Drugs.* 1997.

Veggeberg, Scott. *Medication of the Mind.* Henry Holt and Company, 1996.

The artist thanks Hugh Davey, director of the Sennin Foundation, who patiently taught her how to wield a *shodô* brush, not knowing that she would stretch the boundaries of that wonderful art.